ENCHANT ME NOT

Alexandre broke away but did not breech the distance. "This isn't right."

"Why isn't it? Did you not want to kiss me?"

"I did. But your position—Margot, I am your employer."

"An excuse made up by a man afraid of his own emotions."

He opened his mouth to speak but let his lips fall together in silence. And then, "You deem to know much about me, Margot."

"I'm learning," she countered with a step forward. Their bodies touched at the waist, at the arms, the thighs, and hips. He teetered but did not step backward. "Why can't I learn *this* part of you?" She touched his lips.

"Mademoiselle, I should warn you, impropriety lingers—"

"On these lips?" She stood on tiptoe and closed her eyes, pursing her lips but inches from his face. "Perhaps you should silence my words before impropriety has a chance to leap out."

Determined not to open her eyes, Margot felt a slow triumph as Alexandre seemed to relax, his arms settling and his rigid stance smoothing into a pose that brought his breath across her lips. *Please,* she begged silently. *You can trust me.*

Gentle pressure eased along her mouth. Not his lips. The firm press of his finger skimmed the plump center of her upper lip. Margot shuddered. She wondered what color he viewed her lips to be. Or perhaps they were a distinct shape or succulence? Didn't matter, he could study her body parts for as long as he liked.

<u>BOOK YOUR PLACE ON OUR WEBSITE</u>
<u>AND MAKE THE</u>
<u>READING CONNECTION!</u>

We've created a customized website just for our very special readers, where you can get the inside scoop on everything that's going on with Zebra, Pinnacle and Kensington books.

When you come online, you'll have the exciting opportunity to:

- View covers of upcoming books

- Read sample chapters

- Learn about our future publishing schedule (listed by publication month *and author*)

- Find out when your favorite authors will be visiting a city near you

- Search for and order backlist books from our online catalog

- Check out author bios and background information

- Send e-mail to your favorite authors

- Meet the Kensington staff online

- Join us in weekly chats with authors, readers and other guests

- Get writing guidelines

- AND MUCH MORE!

**Visit our website at
http://www.zebrabooks.com**

ENCHANT ME NOT

Michele Hauf

ZEBRA BOOKS
Kensington Publishing Corp.
http://www.zebrabooks.com

ZEBRA BOOKS are published by

Kensington Publishing Corp.
850 Third Avenue
New York, NY 10022

All Kensington titles, imprints and distributed lines are available at special quantity discounts for bulk purchases for sales promotion, premiums, fund raising, educational or institutional use.

Special book excerpts or customized printings can also be created to fit specific needs. For details, write or phone the office of the Kensington Special Sales Manager: Kensington Publishing Corp., 850 Third Avenue, New York, NY, 10022. Attn. Special Sales Department, Phone: 1-800-221-2647.

Zebra and the Z logo Reg. U.S. Pat. & TM Off.

First Printing: February, 2001
10 9 8 7 6 5 4 3 2 1

Printed in the United States of America

For my mom, Gloria Svedahl,
for everything you've done
and will do,
much love

Synesthesia—a sensation produced in one modality when a stimulus is applied to another modality, as when the hearing of a certain sound induces the visualization of a certain color.

—*Random House Webster's College Dictionary*

Only ten people in a million are . . . born to a world where one sensation *involuntarily* conjures up another. Sometimes, all five clash together, along with a feeling of movement. That makes for six separate sensations that can mesh. . . . It is easier to approach the synesthete's world if we let go of judgments and preconceived notions about how things are supposed to be.

—Richard E. Cytowic, M.D.,
The Man Who Tasted Shapes

One

*In which the Princess of Practically Everything
meets the King of Oranges. Er . . . sort of.*

Versailles, 1664

The base of Alexandre Saint-Sylvestre's teacup touched the crisp circle of porcelain plate at the exact moment the brown click of his door lock turned. "And so it begins."

Madame Trouvelot, his daughters' nursemaid, was currently en route to Paris to spend her final days with her family. She'd taken ill weeks before, something frightful for the odd contortions she'd suddenly slipped into or oaths that would spout from her mouth.

Stephen duMonde, a new friend Alexandre had gained since moving to Versailles, had mentioned his discovery of a willing candidate for nursemaid, and had—rather reluctantly—agreed to see her to that morning's interview.

Reluctant indifference could not begin to describe the pair of rag dolls standing in the entrance to Alexandre's bedchamber.

Stephen's hair had not seen a comb, nor had his two days' growth of beard been touched by a razor. Though he smiled at Alexandre, it was perhaps because of the position of Stephen's right hand, slung over the young woman's shoulder and firmly cupping her breast. Not a sexual grasp, Alexandre observed, more a supportive clutch to keep the sleepy-eyed woman steady. She yawned, revealing a mouth of well-cared-for teeth. Her light brown hair was bundled atop her head in a make-shift style and secured with a paste jewel comb jabbed at an odd angle above her left ear. Her gown was presentable—to an extent. Alexandre squinted to study her more closely. The bodice hooks were off by one or two, making the left side much lower than the right, and exposing a rosy cusp of nipple.

"Monsieur," she offered with a yawn and curtsy, though that action was halted by Stephen before she could drowse off and collapse at his feet.

Alexandre looked to Stephen, who immediately defended in a wave of perceptible red triangles, "What did you expect, setting the interview so damned early? The blessed sun has yet to rise!"

Stephen's voice possessed a lusty sharpness that never ceased to amuse Alexandre for its conflicting attributes. He liked the color as well; rather a rosy red, friendly. Even the points were soft, dulled.

"Five A.M. is the only time of day I have to spare for personal concerns, Stephen. Le Nôtre sets foot on the grounds at dawn, and I must be at his side. I work an inordinately long day. The least you could do, if you're so eager to help me, is see that she is properly dressed!"

The truth of the matter suddenly struck Alexandre. Of course Stephen had helped dress the woman, because she had most likely just tumbled from the man's bed.

"Monsieur, I look forward to working for you. I do so adore children—though I hope they do not rise as early as their . . . their"—a long yawn stretched the woman's voluptuous mouth—"their father."

Soft, squeezy cream, her voice. Not altogether displeasing in color, though not entirely desirable either.

Resigned that while his choices were few he must make the best of the situation, Alexandre gestured to the rag doll she sit in the chair behind his desk. Stephen succeeded in depositing her upon the hard walnut chair that rarely served its master, then wandered to Alexandre's bed, where he collapsed with little display.

The woman's head wobbled dangerously close to her shoulder. Steeling himself against reaching out and holding her bobbling visage upright, Alexandre spoke clearly and loudly. "My children generally rise around eight A.M. Will that be a problem, Mademoiselle, er—"

"Eight!"

Even a three-hour reprieve seemed to startle the woman. But only long enough to widen her eyes, produce another yawn, and sling her head back across the chair. A snore seemed imminent.

Alexandre glanced to his bed, where Stephen's shoeless toes were but the only part visible of the man's lanky frame. A wide hole stretched across the heel of his hose.

"Bother. This isn't going to work. Perhaps I should hire a surgeon for Trouvelot and bid her return."

He needed to sit, to focus his thoughts on a solution. He had only the chair and bed in his crowded bedchamber, both of which were serving duty. Settling to the floor by his work desk, Alexandre closed his eyes. His life had been irrevocably changed upon the death of his wife just four months earlier. And while he'd never enjoyed the whole idea of marriage and all that had accompanied that institution of shared lives, he was feeling rather abandoned right now. At odds.

"I never realized how much I would miss you, Sophie. For the children's sake. Was I so blind to the effort you put forth these few short years of our marriage?"

Yes, his thoughts answered. *You chased her away with indifference.*

But he had known no other way. Versed in love and the arts of passion he was not. He simply hadn't the time to concern himself with such frivolities.

"I promise I'll not rest until I find the proper care for our Lisette and Janette," he said now to the memory of his wife's ever-pouting visage. "Someone who is loving, as you were, and quick to spoil. Yet eager to listen when there is a problem. Much as our own relationship had never blossomed, you did have that, Sophie, you were a wonderful mother."

"Mmm, Monsieur."

Slender fingers snaked through Alexandre's hair, and an illicit moan purred from behind him. He jerked away and studied the rag doll's face. Sleeping. Or, rather, dreaming, if the smile wriggling her plump mouth was any indication.

"I'm afraid you're not quite the sort I require, Mademoiselle. No offense meant, you must understand," he whispered.

He rose and went to his bed to lift the crocheted quilt from under Stephen's hand. Laying it carefully over the nameless woman's figure, Alexandre then sidestepped a stack of towered clay planting pots and snuck out of his bedchamber.

He and his twin girls lived in a nest of apartments tucked within the Orangerie, which was located beneath the southern terrace of King Louis XIV's hunting lodge-cum-château-cum-palace. It was a small, dark, ill-ventilated corner of the grounds that had eventually drove Sophie to Paris.

You should have gone with her. Things would be so different.

Alexandre's boots crunched upon the crushed-stone path that wound around the new orange trees he nurtured in the Orangerie before they would be assigned to take up guard in the château. His left thigh pulsed with a subtle ache. The year-old injury made him limp. There were some days, often during the chill winter months, that troubled his gimp leg to no end. Fortunately, the summer months provided a reprieve, though not complete relief.

Many hundreds of construction workers and groundsmen were beginning to spill across the lawn like a colony of ardent ants. Courtiers were another matter entirely. Curtains were drawn and shades pulled down to the sash in order to block out the rising sun's vile interruption to sleep. Indeed, Alexandre should not have expected a coherent applicant. Of course, if she were to care for his girls, she must be bright and pleasant when they rose.

Most certainly not a possibility in this case.

Himself, he could not imagine rising after the sun had brightened the sky. Why, half the day was frittered away in bed when one could be out of doors, breathing in nature and tending his work.

Life was predictable, prosperous, and, well . . . a bit different now without Sophie's icy, round whines echoing inside his head. But it was a difference he was slowly adapting to, as he adapted to everything else.

In a few hours Alexandre would sneak away from the gardens, greet and dress his daughters, and watch them break their fast while he watered the seedlings set in rows just inside the walls of the Orangerie. It had become a challenge, this juggling of duties to the king and to his own family with Trouvelot's increasing illness, and now her absence. But he hadn't a choice.

There would always be work, as his girls would always require care. As for himself, well, he hadn't time to worry of his own needs. He felt sure he must have them—needs. It was just that life had become too complicated to discover them, and it showed no sign of slowing its pace.

Alexandre stood back and looked across the expanse of gardens—or what would in years to come be a great and grand garden to surpass all gardens before and ever after. He smiled at his master's grandiose description of the future grounds. The man was a wizard with dirt and seed and naked branch. If André Le Nôtre foresaw such splendor, then it would be so. Alexandre had only to envision the gardens of Vaux, his former employer, to know grand elegance shaped in yew and grass and stone was possible. Pity Vaux's owner, Nicolas Fouquet, had squandered his upstanding by extorting from the king's coffers. The man now sat rotting in a seaside prison, his home, Vaux-le-Vicomte, ransacked by the king's command to outfit the growing château and the grounds of Versailles.

But splendor and grandiosity would never grace this vast stretch of dust and dirt and swampland unless Alexandre, too, set to work. The previous morning Le Nôtre had announced he was headed for Italy for a fortnight to study the workings of mechanical water fountains. The Francini brothers had extended an invitation after hearing of Le Nôtre's plans for Versailles.

With a grand swoop of his Venetian-dewdrop-laced wrist, Le Nôtre had put Alexandre in charge of the dozens of men under his tutelage—Joffroi and Pierceforest were excellent foremen, had been supervising their charges for well over a year now—and bid him adieu.

Alexandre pushed up his sleeves and secured them with a black ribbon attached just above each elbow. A few moments of silence before the cacophony of the day fell upon him. Inhaling a deep breath, he drew in the utter freedom of sensations that when in Paris had pounded his brain constantly.

But here, ah, here in the distant wilderness of the village Versailles, his senses had become more relaxed, not so troubled. Peace and space granted him a certain calmness of sensory perception. No longer was he pummeled by the vicious distraction of a noisy crowd and the blinding shapes and colors attributed to the rotting stench coating the streets of Paris. Not that Versailles was devoid of sound and strong odors, mind you, but it was spread out across a greater distance and wasn't held together in a threatening muck by so many bustling bodies.

Alexandre smoothed a hand along a glossy leaf dangling from an orange tree, cherishing the smooth texture as one would the feel of a child's hand clasped in his own. Though he'd not nurtured them since seedlings, these were his children. Le Nôtre had granted him adoptive charge since moving to Versailles, and they had flourished under his attentions.

Much as Sophie had not.

Alexandre kicked the crushed-stone walk with his boot toe, tensing his fists at the thought of his wife. Ill-winded thoughts that always blew upon him with great precision. Hell, he knew he'd not given his wife the attention she had needed. But could indifference lead to death?

You know you had everything to do with her death. If she had never left, she would have never come back. And if she would have never returned, the accident would have never happened.

A flash of pale pink quavered in Alexandre's peripheral sight. Too sweet a vision for his dark thoughts. He tried to ignore the ripples of motion off in the distance, but movement near the pond so early in the morning was a rarity.

"What on earth?"

A clatter from behind alerted him. Pierceforest had come for the spade Alexandre had said he could borrow. He gestured inside the inner Orangerie hall, then returned his interest to the row of trees paralleling the Swiss pond that capped the south side of the grounds. The morning sun did not penetrate the heavy froth of leaves that tented the column of elm, but the shadows did not hide the brilliant pink skirts. An odd symphony of abbreviated feminine gasps blended with the snorts of a rooting animal. The sounds were a bit too distant to form definite color or shape in Alexandre's vision.

"Pierceforest, is that a pig? On a leash? Dragging that woman?"

Pierceforest eyed the elm grove with a cock of his head and a half-open mouth. A chuckle shot through his lips that startled Alexandre with its piercing green points. "Oh, that's just Curiosity."

"Curiosity? The woman's name is Curiosity?"

"No, the pig, man. I think the woman's name might be Magrot or Mugwort. Something crotchety like that."

"Sounds like an old hag's name."

"Indeed. I see her every which and when in the kitchen. She's a different case, always sneaking about, doing odd things. I've heard rumors she's a witch. That she reads the stars for portents and brews herbs and dead animal parts to cure people what ails them. Perhaps the pig is her familiar?" Pierceforest gripped the spade and started toward one of a set of a hundred steps that paralleled the Orangerie. "Stay away from that one, Monsieur. She'll put a spell on you."

Pierceforest left Alexandre staring into the slash of construction-raped forest. "A witch? Riding a pig named Curiosity?" Alexandre smoothed a callused finger under his chin. "How very . . . curious."

Margot set a basket of smelly black lumps on the long, pristine pine table holding court down the center of the kitchen. She then slumped into the rush-seated wicker chair near the hearth and took to prying the dirt out from under her fingernails.

Cook did not immediately see her as she crossed the unevenly cobbled floor with a kettle of water, but she did spy the basket. "Oh! So many truffles! The king will be beside himself with joy."

"I shouldn't expect anything less for the pains I go through to obtain those ugly lumps of culinary gold."

Cook turned to Margot and, when it appeared the woman was ready to smile, the curve slipped from beneath her button nose and she sputtered into a contorted expression of dismay, horror, and then downright repulsion. "Child, you look as though you've been dragged behind an ox set on plowing an entire countryside of fields!"

"I feel that way too." Margot blew a renegade strand of hair from her face, only to have it spring back to its position straight down the middle of her nose. "But you must admit the results are more than worth the trouble. I've twice as many truffles as before. And the king did rave the last time. According to the duchess, he gobbled them all up himself."

"Well now, I expect he'll throw a fête in your honor for this basket of jewels." The soft-voiced elderly woman plucked at the mud-encrusted lumps of fungus, lifting a few of the largest to her nose to inhale. Bliss coated her reverent words. "Like fine wine."

"Rather disgusting if you ask me. How anyone"— Margot blew at the corkscrew of blond hair jutting down her nose. No luck—"can even bear to eat those things is beyond my comprehension."

"I wager you've never tasted them."

"Wouldn't be able to get the smelly thing close enough to my mouth before my nose forced me to retreat. 'Course, what should I expect? Versailles is a virtual smorgasbord of offensive smells and tastes and sights. *Mon Dieu,* but I believe the builders broke through the king's privy wall last eve for the wave of noxious fumes that floats like a cloud above our heads. Do you think a person could take ill from smells? I should wonder."

Margot slipped into her wondering pose, legs crossed, elbow propped on one knee, and chin cupped in her palm.

"It is rather distasteful. One would expect the country air to far exceed the stench of Paris." Cook hefted up the kettle and hung it on the iron hook under the hearth. "I'm blessed for my position here in the kitchen. It's a rare day that the king's privy can overtake my parsley roast."

"Mmm." Margot drew in a deep breath, tasting the luscious flavors of Cook's culinary creations on her tongue. Forget wondering about the ill effect of smell upon one's health, it was certain Cook needed someone to test her wares before serving them to the king. "And your sweet cakes and brandy pears, they're the most heavenly of earthly delights."

She felt the light touch of Cook's fingers on her nose as the woman smoothed the rogue curl from her face. Since Margot had arrived at Versailles a month before, Cook had taken a motherly position in her heart. Much as Margot did not like the conditions of her stay here, she could easily overlook that horrid bargain when she knew *Maman* and her seven siblings would eat well for years to come.

She'd received word in June that the duchess Ducette would be passing through Caen, where Margot lived, and would escort her to Versailles as a lady's maid until the Baron de Verzy could arrive in September to meet her. Though Margot had yet to rise from emptying the duchess's chamber pot to one of the giggling handmaids that chose her clothing and dressed her, Margot was quite pleased to have the opportunity to travel from her small reed-thatched cottage to the grandness of the king's blossoming palace. Most certainly a short stay here would provide the opportunity to learn about the world beyond the farm life she knew.

But thus far, grand was proving to be privy stench and building dust and clatter and muddy gardens.

"It'll shape up," the duchess frequently lamented. "Just carry a clove-spiked orange and do invest in a fine veil, dear. And by all means, desist with your odd ways before the baron arrives!"

Her odd ways. Hmmph. Everywhere Margot walked, whispers of witchcraft reached her ears. The mere fact that she viewed the world differently than the marionettes that walked and talked only at the king's touch of their strings was enough for her. She was not a witch. Let them think what they like. All the beribboned courtiers did was think unoriginal thoughts passed from one ear to the next.

Did no one ever wonder anymore? Why, the world was filled with wonders that just needed someone to wonder about.

Margot studied the dirt pressed deep into the whorls of her fingertips. She smoothed them over the front of her gown—fine pink silk that her mother had pleaded her to reserve for September, but her plain woolen skirt was currently soaking in boiled soapwort, and she'd yet to unpack the crimson plush, which was much finer than this silk.

Upon closer inspection of the various dirt specks and grass stains, Margot found something clear and sticky streaming down the center of the bodice. "Hmm, now, I wonder what this is?"

"It's a crime what you've done to that dress," Cook muttered from the hearth, where savory smells perfumed the air. "A girl shouldn't ought to be rolling about in the dirt in silk and lace. It's easy enough to soak your woolens for a day or two, but fine fabric won't take to such vigorous methods. How do you intend to get that clean?"

Margot sighed and teased a length of lace at her elbow with a flick of her finger. "I shall scrub and soak—"

"You cannot scrub silk!"

"Yes, well . . ." She dismissed the dilemma with a shrug and a sigh. Her everyday shoes were wet as well. She lifted a silk-slippered toe, knowing the smooth-bottomed shoes were the very reason the pig had been able to pull her through the trees as if a mere acorn tethered to the back of a giant rat.

"Where is Curiosity?"

"I've left her in the stables. She becomes rather exhausted after a morning of truffle sniffing."

Margot recoiled as her wondering brought her to a realization of what substance clung to her bodice. But of course. Pig, er—humors. Rather vile and thick. All together . . . well . . . interesting. 'Twas unfortunate she'd not yet discovered a microscope here at the château. It certainly would prove an aid to her wonders.

"I cannot understand why you don't gift Curiosity to the king for a fine supper and find yourself a smaller pig. That beast will surely trample you one of these days."

"It is not in my control what happens to a pig when it smells a truffle. Curiosity ruts like a wild beast for the ugly chunk of fungus. 'Tis a battle every time to get to the smelly morsel before she inhales it. I figure I lost a good dozen today alone."

"That's what I mean by you finding yourself a smaller pig, Margot. Look at yourself!" If a cringe could have screamed, Cook's sudden jerk at the sight of the slime coating Margot's bodice would have echoed throughout the grounds of Versailles. "Now, listen, child, how do you ever expect to please your gentleman's eye with such ways?"

Margot bristled, fitting her hands at her hips and lifting her chin. "My ways are exactly the way I have always been and always will be. If a man does not find me pleasing because of *my ways,* then I believe that should be his concern and not mine." Then she added under her breath, "Especially if he is a toad."

"Oh, Margot, you've much to learn about life."

"Exactly my intention during my stay here at the château. As *Maman* said on the day I left, I must discover who I am before I become someone I am not. 'Tis necessary, she said. If not, I may spend a future regretting what I could have done, could have known. I must make the best of these few months. I will learn exactly who Margot deVerona is before that name is taken from me and replaced by another."

"Oh! You're so dramatic about things, Margot."

"Just being practical."

"Practical is securing home and making it comfortable for your husband and children."

"Yes, and by all means *male* children," Margot repeated the words added to the contract she'd reviewed before traveling to Versailles. The Baron de Verzy had added a few stipulations to the original document.

Ah, but the glimmer in *Maman's* eyes when she'd revealed the baron had been willing to pay the dowry in return for Margot's hand had spoken volumes. Margot's father, one of many superfluous wheelwrights living in Caen, had passed three years earlier. And left alone to raise eight children, well, it was a difficult task for *Maman.*

Margot envisioned the weary gloss that resided in her mother's pale hazel eyes. Genuine smiles were rare, save the surprising laughter that would accompany the song of one of her children or the sudden eruption of merry giggles that always greeted the nights when *Maman* would bathe her children.

So the marriage contract would be fulfilled. With the condition that a request of Margot's own was included.

For part of knowing herself, who she was, and what she wanted included an education in the entomological sciences. Or perhaps the astrological sciences. Whatever she decided, Paris's Sorbonne University was now within her grasp, thanks to her forthcoming marriage. At last, an education would be hers. Just a few more months . . .

Cook's voice interrupted Margot's thoughts. "So what is it you need to discover about yourself?"

"Hmm? Oh, well, certainly I should like to decide which vocation would serve my interests best, the stars or the insects. I do so enjoy gazing at the unreachable glitter in the sky—but then, the insects that skitter at my toes are just as fascinating, and within reach. I guess I won't really know until I discover it!"

The cook's gut-shaking laughter filled the aromatic kitchen. "I see, and such discovery includes being towed behind a pig?"

"Of course! I want to do it all, Cook. I may own claim to practically nothing, but I am rich in aspirations." Margot spread her arms wide to joyously encompass her intangible desires. "I want to travel and learn and never stop wondering. I want to chase a storm and find its beginning. I want to stand in the spot where the rain begins so my left shoulder is wet and my right shoulder is dry. I want to swim underwater with the fishes and follow their paths to Atlantis. I want to study insects and butterflies to learn why it is that flowers are their sanctuary. I want to do everything out of the ordinary, Cook. I want to know what it is that pleases me and in turn what repulses me."

"If you ask me, you've already laid claim to practically everything."

"Yes, practically everything, that is what I desire to do."

"You've some fascinating dreams, child."

"They are not dreams," Margot reiterated with a punch

through the air. "They are aspirations. Desires yet unfulfilled. And I shall touch them, each and every one."

"I've no doubt you will," Cook said as she stirred the chunky meat and vegetables swirling inside the iron pot. "You are a dreamer, Margot. I admire that about you. Vex all those who think you a witch. I know better. And you know I live vicariously through your dreams. Don't ever stop that wondering you do. Promise me."

"I promise."

But enough with the sitting about and speaking of aspirations. Margot jumped to her feet. Things didn't happen unless one made them happen. And nothing happens when one is sitting in a chair. "I'm off. I've a trip to the duchess's chamber pot, then I believe I'll search out the royal library. I hear tell a new shipment of books has arrived from Paris."

"Oh!" Cook shot up from the kettle, a spittle of stew dripping from the wooden spoon. "Then you haven't heard? Of course not, you've been out all day."

"Heard what?"

"Oh, dear, I completely forgot to tell you. The duchess was exiled this morning. King Louis heard about her comment regarding his average taste in women. You know how the gossip travels around here."

Margot's shoulders slumped. "I knew that comment would never rest peacefully."

"She was ordered to leave with but the dress on her body and but two handmaids."

"Oh." And being a mere chamber-pot attendant, Margot knew where that left her. "Bother." She settled onto the wicker chair, forgetting her inner call to adventure. "Now what shall I do?"

"Well, if you ask me, this sounds a boon to your enterprising adventures. You must remain at the château until the baron comes for you."

"True. But the duchess has abandoned me. Where

shall I sleep? What shall I do that regards a position so I may remain at the château?"

Cook toggled a truffle under her finger, then gave Margot the glad eye as she tossed the chunk of dirty fungus in the air. She caught and displayed it between two fingers before her smiling face.

Reading the woman's unspoken thoughts, Margot dashed to the table. "Do you really think?"

"I don't see why not. The king would hate to see his royal truffle snuffler—er, sniffer . . . hmm, what exactly do you call yourself?"

"Curiosity is the sniffer. I'm the one who wrestles with two hundred pounds of sweaty pig flesh and flying mud to procure a lump of smelly fungus."

"Er, right." Cook shuffled her hands over Margot's shoulders, reassuring with a firm squeeze. "Let me see to that. You'll be going nowhere as long as there are truffles underfoot."

Margot sighed heavily. "There are not enough trees in this stinking valley to produce the black gold. It is fortune and luck that I was able to snuffle up the few morsels I found today. And true truffle season does not begin until after I am gone."

"Well, after that you'll just have to invent another title for yourself," Cook rallied with a spoon raised in the air. "Who knows, maybe the king will need a storm chaser? It might do to know where the rain begins when it comes to planning fêtes."

"Oh, yes!" Margot clapped her hands and then flung a generous hug around Cook's shoulders.

"You'd best go claim your things before the guard has the duchess's rooms completely cleared out."

"Yes, oh—" She paused mid-dash for the door. "But where shall I sleep?"

"You may share my room. It's nothing fancy, but another warm body beneath the blankets is against all argument."

"You're so good to me, Cook, thank you. Such heaven it will be sleeping wrapped in the aroma of your cooking."

Spinning to the iron-banded door, Margot gracefully curtsied with a lift of her grass- and dirt-smeared skirts, then spun out into the hallway . . . into the arms of a dark-haired man with equally messy hair and dirty fingers.

Set on a narrow, sun-browned face, his dark eyes twinkled curiously beneath thick black brows. His mouth, a grim line, wriggled at the corner, as if fighting a smile.

"Pardon." Margot slipped a finger through the patch of goo that had rubbed off on the stranger's shirtsleeve. "It's merely pig snot—er, humors. It should wash out with a good scrubbing. If not, I'm quite sure it will dry clear. *Bonjour!*"

Alexandre smoothed a finger through the glob on his sleeve as he watched the woman with a voice of wavy pink lines skip down the hallway. Rubbing the slimy concoction between his fingers, he muttered, "More and more curious."

TWO

Soused butterflies and giggling kittens

"How do you do it in this wretched heat, Monsieur?"

Seated at the edge of the Orangerie's outer broderies, Alexandre looked up from his notepaper to the young woman seated across the makeshift trestle table he'd composed for interviews during his afternoon meal break. What he could see of her face beneath the wide-brimmed straw hat and red velvet mask and high lace fichu pulled up around her neck were a pair of eyes and the tip of a nose. An extremely pale nose. A match to the pale circles that were her voice. He couldn't quite place a color to the transparent spheres that rolled in his vision, perhaps similar to the color of a sun-starved seedling trapped under a log.

He hadn't a clue what she had asked. "What?"

"You do know the sun works horrors on a person's skin? Why, just last week Cecile Clicquot was laid up for days after spending ten minutes beneath the noon sun. It turned her nose bright red and then the very flesh began to peel from her face! Dear, this is horrendous." She tugged at the fichu, but it would not budge without then revealing her pale bosom. "I'm not sure I can continue the interview if you insist we sit out in the open.

And that dust!" She flipped a gloved hand toward the northern terrace, where the grounds were being razed and cleared for two circular pools.

"But you do understand, Mademoiselle Duhême, that the girls will need daily outdoor activity?"

"You can't be serious? What good is the out-of-doors to a child? They'll develop a nasty condition from the moist, and their skin will slough off from the sun, and the cool wind will bring a pox that will have them sniffling and sneezing and dripping all sorts of foul substances from every orifice!"

Yes, well, wasn't this interview going well?

Alexandre scribbled a few words about Mademoiselle Duhême next to her name on his list. Hmm, could one consider it a list when it was so short? He had but two more names, written down by Stephen's hand.

"I do thank you for . . . braving the elements this afternoon, Mademoiselle Duhême. I must speak to a few other applicants, you understand, but I promise you'll hear from me before the day is up if I'm in need of your services."

And hell would see to freezing over.

"Of course." She stood and offered a gloved hand, which he assumed he must kiss. "You'd best seek me out before the sun has set" rolled past his eyes in those droll, sun-starved balls. "I like to become horizontal by then to combat the dizzying effects of being vertical for eight hours a day."

"And you do require the girls at mass daily, Monsieur Saint-Sylvestre?"

"Daily? As in . . . every single day?"

"Godliness is a trait that must be ingrained in their tiny bodies at an early age. They will say matins and vespers daily as well."

Alexandre gripped the wine bottle and lifted, but it sprung easily upward. Empty. He'd downed the entire lot listening to Mademoiselle Duhême whine about the hazards of the outdoors. What would he now use to dispel the anxiety Mademoiselle Giroux caused? And those sharp, piercing jags of green. All his life he'd been able to judge a person entirely by his reaction to their voice. The colors either appealed to him, produced endurable indifference, or they irritated—which generally meant avoid at all costs.

Daily vespers and matins? And scrubbing floors to show their humility? His girls were but four! Mademoiselle Giroux would have them in nun's robes before their fifth birthdays.

"How are you for the sun, Mademoiselle?"

"The sun?"

"Do you tolerate it? The children do need their afternoon walk, and they like to skip and play."

"Play is for the idle." The woman's mouth pinched into a severe line. Alexandre closed his eyes to block out the green stabs of color. "I assure you I shall have your daughters on a routine immediately. Letters and Latin, and sewing and the feminine graces. You need not fear for their souls, Monsieur. I'll see that they are saved."

Saved?

"Er . . . next?" Alexandre muttered as he drew a careful black line through Mademoiselle Giroux's name.

This one was beyond tolerance, thought Margot.

Mademoiselle Bernier wore carmine lip rouge and the same on her cheeks. Her raven hair was done in curls and paste jewels, and her bodice was in danger of exposing more than just her charms. Since sitting across from Monsieur Saint-Sylvestre and spreading her skirts as wide as her sly grin, she had dodged every question he had posed regarding her love of children and nursing skills. Instead, she worked her green eyes like a tiger enticing a newborn rat onto its tongue.

Monsieur Saint-Sylvestre was naively blind to such efforts.

Interesting man.

Margot adjusted her position on the back of the lion statue that overlooked the Orangerie. Behind her, a feisty cherub played a switch across the lion's hindquarters in anticipation of a grand ride. She'd initially been attracted to the edge of the south terrace by the giggle of children. The twins had come skittering out of the shadowed inner rooms of the Orangerie with dinner in hand and had placed it before their father. The dark-haired child tucked a linen in her father's shirt and kissed his cheek, while the tight-curled blond had taken to braiding the long, loose hair that sprayed down the center of his back like an Arabian stallion's elegant tail. She did a fair job at it too, using four separate ribbons knotted up and down the length of the braid to secure the creation.

'Twas almost as if the girls were his caregivers, seeing their father properly fed and groomed and loved. The scene touched Margot in her heart. How many times had she done the very same thing for *Maman*—gathering her long, gray hair into a neat chignon and securing it with a sharp-tipped willow stick—while she nursed an infant or tended the evening's rabbit stew?

But one question kept poking at Margot's thoughts as she watched the interviews below. What had happened to this sweet little trio that saw their father frowning more often than smiling?

And the girls—the blond one appeared a bit older, more poised than was expected of a scatter-dash, giggling four-year-old. Though, the dark one did make up for the two of them as she spun about with her rag doll, her white skirts flicking the box hedges with sharp hisses.

White satin and ribbons. Most certainly their father's choice.

A wistful remembrance of Maximillian's first step— right into a fresh rain puddle—birthed in Margot's head. She did miss her family, a sweet coo wisping over a baby's lips, even the challenging shouts of her younger brothers as each tried to outdo the other in wood cutting or swordplay.

The family below appeared, for all purposes, happy and close. But their roles were oddly altered. Or maybe it wasn't odd at all. Margot caught her chin in palm and began to wonder. Where was their mother? And why did she not care for her children?

A swish of feminine skirts redirected Alexandre's attention, from Mademoiselle Bernier toward the pond. Another prospective interviewee? No, he'd seen only the three names on Stephen's list.

Hmm . . . He voided out Mademoiselle Bernier's seductive melon tones and focused on the pink vision wandering in the distance. Hadn't he seen those same skirts the previous day? This time, from what he could see, they were not chasing a truffle-seeking sow. Instead, they fell to the ground over near the swampy land that surrounded the pond. No motion followed save the flutter of orange . . . hmm . . . some sort of bird. No, much smaller. Ah, butterflies. Alexandre wasn't sure why, but the insects were attracted to that grove of odd trees that had been imported from a distant land.

But here! There was a woman inside those pink skirts. She might be hurt to lay there without making a sound.

"Monsieur?"

Someone had addressed him. "Huh? Ah, yes!"

"Are you quite well, Monsieur?" Mademoiselle Bernier asked. "You seem distracted. Perhaps we could continue the interview in my chambers?"

He stood, disregarding the feminine fingers that grasped for his hand, and stepped onto the crushed-stone pathway. Now that he noticed, but fifty yards from the woman Lisette spun in fairy-princess circles, her arms extended to embrace the sky. A few strides away from her sister, Janette had taken to eating grass.

Hmm, well, a little grass never hurt anyone.

"If you've not the inclination to give me your attention—" Behind him, Mademoiselle Bernier huffed and marched away, her skirts violet swishes of anger.

Leaving his silent minions of leaf and blossom, Alexandre sprinted across the granite walk and out of the Orangerie. As he ascended the low slope of groomed grounds that led to and circled the pond, he slowed, finding the woman who'd smeared pig drool over his shirt was moving.

Oddly.

Flat on her back she lay, her skirts splayed in dirty wrinkles around her legs. No shoes dressed the soiled row of wiggling toes. An open notebook lay carelessly at her side. All about her, golden-winged butterflies hovered . . . then dropped. The delicate creatures seemed to be expiring right over her.

Alexandre crept closer. An odd smell accompanied the leather-leafed trees that the king had relegated to the swamp exactly because of that astringent odor. Vibrant and square, the scent filled Alexandre's head and danced over his vision in a transparent symphony of sharp geometrics. This was only the third or fourth time he'd been near these trees, and the smell, so new and unique, always fascinated. He reached out and smoothed his fingers along the corners of the smell, very tangible corners, that he could clearly see—

"Monsieur?"

Startled from his fascination, Alexandre saw the woman's concern narrow her brows toward her nose. He snapped his hand to his chest and curled his fingers into a loose fist. *Caught, you foolish man!*

"Are you very well, Monsieur?"

"Well? Er, um . . . But I've come to ask the very same of you. I thought you had fallen, injured yourself." *Yes, change the subject.* She'd forget his strange actions, as most others did when he let down his guard and exposed a part of himself he should not.

"But what is this? Might I inquire as to what you are doing lying on the ground covered in insects?"

"Why, I'm casting spells," she said, as she slowly pushed to sit upright, taking care not to crush any of the fragile butterflies.

An admonishing finger raised before him. The teasing look glittering in the woman's blue eyes stopped Alexandre from spouting a retort. "Casting spells?"

"That is what you thought, isn't it?" Her eyes glittered a jewel-encrusted indigo. Hard, crisp, and lucid. She clasped her hands casually in her lap. Another butterfly dropped to her wrist, which she cupped in her palms before giving Alexandre a teasing glance. "I'm enchanting the butterflies, Monsieur."

. . . *enchanting the butterflies* . . . As she spoke, her shimmying words began to seduce.

"You see the command I have over them?"

. . . *command I have* . . . Pearly-pink waves rippled with every dancing lilt of tone. Spikes of brighter pink interjected the soft, hushed gasps. Delicious. Though he could not taste the sound, only see it.

With grand display she drew her hands before her, blew into her palms, opened them, and the butterfly took to wing. "So I must be a witch, eh?"

"You don't sound convinced of it." Alexandre knelt on

one knee by her skirts and toyed with the lace-edged wing of a grounded butterfly. It twitched, then relaxed, content to sit in repose near a human without worry.

Perhaps she *had* bewitched them?

"Surely you have heard the rumors. Though I wouldn't subscribe to the prattlings of the court *précieux* . . ."

. . . *you have heard the rumors* . . . Without thinking, Alexandre reached out and touched the tops of the pink waves that danced before his eyes. *Tap, tap, tap.* So soft and tangible the design. He could actually slide his finger over the cusp of each wave and around the cool convex back of her voice-shape. He had always seen a person's voice in color and shape—oftentimes the shapes were tangible so that he could touch them—but never before had a voice so entranced him.

"Monsieur?"

"Hmm?"

"What did you just do?"

"What? Er . . ." Retreating quickly from his actions, Alexandre stuffed his fist under his opposite arm. "Whatever do you mean, Mademoiselle?"

"You just . . . tapped the air between us. Tap, tap, just like that."

"I did?"

She crossed her arms and threw a side glance at him. "You would have me believe you did not when I am sitting but an arm's reach from you?"

"No, course not." Fool! Twice now he had let his guard down before this woman. And that was a bad thing. Most disagreeable. "Um . . . it was a fly. I was shooing it away."

She retained her stiff pose; not a bit of belief in her eyes. Ah, but he had become an expert at changing the subject of conversation. Reaching for one of the butterflies that ornamented her curly tresses, he drew it close for inspection. Small brown spots dotted the upper wings.

The gold-orange scales segued to butter yellow near its plump brown body.

"*Nymphalidae,*" he said as he decided on the genus fluttering and falling like fat snowflakes around them.

"You're an entomologist?"

"Er, no," he said, a little surprised at her question. Most women at court hadn't even a grasp on the term beyond knowing it had something to do with the less desirable creatures that tormented their powdered wigs. "Botany is my field, but I do have occasion to pick up the genus names here and there from various botanical texts."

"Nymphalidae," she said. "I shall have to remember that. Certainly I must write it down!" She grabbed her notebook and began to scribble. "How do you spell that?"

"Isn't so important as just knowing it is simply a butterfly."

"Oh, it is important to me."

Intrigued, Alexandre touched a branch of leaves that lay on the ground. The delicately winged insects coated the smooth bark. He carefully spelled the word for his surprisingly eager student.

"And do you know what that smell is?" she wondered aloud, the point of her pen tapping her pursed lips. "I'm familiar with it, I'm sure, but I can't quite place it. These trees, they're quite unique."

"Eucalyptus," Alexandre offered, and then at her prompt spelled that as well. "They were sent to the king as a gift from an Arabian prince. But Louis does not care for the aroma, so the swamp it is for these majestic trees."

"A most powerful elixir." She lifted another butterfly on her palm and repeated the blowing ritual, which set the creature off on a woozy journey into the sky. "The tree has made them drunk. You see how they wallow in the overindulgence of spirit?" She lifted another. "They fall to the ground and cool off. Then they need a little boost to take wing. A breath of warmth."

Fascinated by her explanation of drunken butterflies, Alexandre scooped a soused fellow onto his palm and tried resuscitation.

"Not so hard." She touched his palm and pulled his hands toward her to study his patient. The heat of her breath warmed Alexandre's fingers, though he had no notion to flight. Rather, he wanted to stay put, right there in the woman's presence. Close to her breath. To her pink voice.

"Grasp it by the abdomen, gently, or you'll harm their wings."

He felt a giant with the world in his hand. A very fragile, delicate world. He could feel the skitter of legs and antennae against his palm, hear the woman's voice in his mind, and see her speech superimposed over all. One more breath, this time her lips touched his flesh. Startled but wise enough not to show it, Alexandre drew in his own breath. She touched him so casually. So unconditionally.

Margot slowly parted his hands, allowing his captive freedom.

"Amazing," he said as he watched the butterfly's flight up into the pale white sky. He clasped his hands around hers. "You're not a witch, you're a butterfly tavernkeeper. You souse them and then you set them free." He laughed, but the motion of such utter frivolity made him realize he was holding her hand. "Forgive me." He dropped her hand and stood. What the hell was he doing?

"Careful." She scrambled to grab his leg.

Alexandre tottered but held his position. "Mademoiselle, do you mind?"

"You'll step on them."

"Oh." He carefully adjusted his stance. "So it is the scent that attracts them? Interesting, very interesting."

Yes, yes, do change the subject again.

He should return to his work. From here he could see the girls spinning in circles near the Orangerie entrance. They needed supervision. Idle conversation served no good but to make idle hands.

But there was nothing whatsoever idle about this woman who could command the lace-winged insects with a kiss of life. "And what finds you sousing innocent butterflies when you might be . . . er, chasing pigs?"

"Curiosity doesn't rise until well after the king's lever, and we all know how long that tarries on."

Until well after the breakfast hour, Alexandre knew from Stephen's reports. No wonder His Majesty's humors tended to clog his insides, as rumor would report. The king lay horizontal more than he was vertical. Not good for any man's body.

"Besides, truffles are quite scarce here in the valley," she said on a sigh, and then added, "I'm Margot de-Verona."

"Forgive my manners, I am Alexandre Saint-Sylvestre. I work under Le Nôtre in the gardens."

"Yes, I've noticed." She pointed to his arm. "That'll wash out easily enough."

He clutched the crust of pig drool that had dried on his sleeve. Trouvelot had generally seen to the laundering. Himself, he wasn't sure how things got clean, just that when he laid soiled clothing aside, it usually appeared folded and smelling of lavender a few days later. "I thank you. Er, not for the mess, but for the washing instructions. So, you are the royal Procurer of Truffles? Indeed, there are not many mature trees surrounding the château for which to find the fungus. What will you do after the truffles are gone? Have you a lady you attend as well?"

"The duchess Ducette."

"But I thought—"

"Yesterday afternoon. I'm here on my own recognizance until the king either discovers I'm of no service to anyone or Cook kicks me out of her bed."

"Cook? You're in her . . . bed?" Interesting woman, indeed.

"She's sharing her room with me until I can procure a proper position here at Versailles. At least until autumn comes—"

"You're looking for work?"

"Yes." She sighed. A carefree, delightful melon sigh, subtler in color than the pink tones of her voice. "I like to keep busy, you see. I shouldn't think the king would be all too pleased to know he's a freeloader around."

"And where is your family?"

"*Maman* and my seven siblings live just east of Caen."

"Seven?"

"Oh, yes, there's Marcel, Maria, and Michel. Muriel, Marc, and Maude. And Maximillian, he's the baby, precious little thing."

"And you are Margot," he observed with a grin. "Your mother likes the letter M, I see."

"She's always said it's the most majestic of all the letters."

Indeed, the gilded ivory letter was majestic in Alexandre's mind. So much more appealing than say, a rusted green B or the plain brown S.

"I miss them," she continued with a thoughtful lift of her chin. "But I know they are getting along well without me. I'm the oldest of eight. But the boys are quite handy and they look after themselves extremely well."

So she had experience with children. Hmm . . .

"It's such a delight to be away from the demands of caring for one's siblings. This month at the château has been a joy. I couldn't begin to conceive of returning to the position of caregiver when I've only just discovered such freedom."

Oh.

"So you are the gardener?"

She might have made an excellent nursemaid with her experience, but not if she was finally away and free, as she had said.

"The gardens? Yes, well, as I've said, I am Monsieur Le Nôtre's second hand. I'm in charge for the next few weeks while he's away watching fountain machinations in Italy."

"What a delightful excursion, watching fountains spew water."

He might not have put it in quite such favorable words. "I suppose one can find a bit of delight in the monotonous cascading of water."

"You don't seemed convinced of such delights."

"Oh, no, of course I am. Versailles demands nothing but the finest and most advanced machinery. And with the water problem we have here, we'll need all the help we can get."

"It's an amazing wonder, the entire grounds." She crossed her legs at the ankle and cupped her chin in her hand, contemplative.

"Not quite as wonderful as the intoxication of winged insects." Alexandre carefully lifted one of the somnambulant butterflies in his palm and blew. With a few restorative puffs of warmth the fragile creature fluttered its wings and took to air. Wonderful, indeed.

"The girls get along well by themselves?"

He quirked a brow at her question. Curious how that one curl desired to find its way down the center of her forehead no matter how many times she tried to bat it away.

"Yes, as long as I am close and within seeing distance." He turned and gestured to his daughters, still safely in sight. "Their nursemaid is gone to her family in Paris, I believe to spend her last days. And with their mother passed on, there's no one to take the girls outdoors when I'm busy working until dark."

"I'm so sorry to hear about their mother. Was it recent?"

"A few months."

"Oh. How horrible for you, a young father with a tremendous workload left to supervise two girls. And the nursemaid gone. You should seek an assistant."

"Yes, I've been interviewing candidates. Whatever Stephen duMonde can rustle up from his bed."

She paused from her resuscitation of a butterfly. Alexandre waved away his comment. "Forgive me, I do not normally offer such ribald conversation." He glanced up to the umbrella of leathered leaves. "Must be the eucalyptus. If I'm not careful, I may be the next creature to fall into your lap—er—" *Oh, really?* "Do forgive me, Mademoiselle. I did not mean—"

Now what god of mischief had put those words in his mouth?

"I shall catch you if you fall," she offered in a promising tone, pink and sweet, and temptingly enticing.

Alexandre felt his lower jaw relax. Those soft blond ringlets bounced almost of their own volition. A half dozen butterflies nested in the shimmering curls, decorating her coif with more elegance than any gemstone could ever achieve.

But how to get out of this particularly delicate conversation? What the hell was wrong with him anyway? He did not indulge in conversation with women. Ever. Sophie would never approve—

Hmm, that excuse could no longer be exercised, eh?

"I should return to the girls. I wish you luck in securing a position here at the château. One that does not require looking after children, as it may seem. It would be a pity to lose someone like you."

"Really?"

When she tilted her head, myriad curls sparkled in the high-noon light, and one long ringlet slipped over her forehead. She blew at it, only to have it land in the exact same spot right between her eyes.

Enchanting.

"Really." Alexandre felt a rush of confidence surge through his veins. He rather liked this woman. Pig snot and all.

He turned and walked away, a little conscious of his limp as he did so. Why, he couldn't really be sure. Certainly he did not care what that woman thought of him. Did he? No. He hadn't time to consider women and relationships.

"Papa, that was a very silly lady!" Janette rumbled up to him. "Was she dead?"

Both girls plunged into his arms, and Alexandre cuddled them close. "No, she was catching butterflies." He blew sprigs of grass from Lisette's hair. "But do you know she speaks in waves of pink satin?"

"Oh, Papa," Lisette cooed, and snuggled against his gut.

"And I touched them," he said, recalling his brazen actions. How to explain that he saw people's voices in colors and shapes without her thinking him mad, as many others did? Well, it was simply unthinkable.

"Do me, Papa," Janette pleaded. "Tell me the color I am."

"Very well. You, Janette, are round bouncing balls of aqua. I could watch your voice for hours without ever growing tired. And you!" He hugged Lisette's squiggling form. "Are amber lines that flow with barely a ripple. Steady and strong, my Lisette. Now, what of me, girls?"

The two scrambled out of his arms and huddled before

him for a private whisper. When they broke, their giggles sparkled in a myriad of textures and colors before him.

"So?" he wondered with arms spread.

Lisette stepped forward. "You, Papa, are dirty!"

Twin giggles induced Alexandre's own laughter. Threading his fingers through the crown of Lisette's soft hair, he remembered the morning had begun with intentions of finding a nursemaid.

He searched out the retreating flash of pink skirts. She had gained the top of the hundred steps and now strode purposefully toward the château. Margot deVerona wasn't a woman concerned with the dangers of the sun, nor did she seem a religious zealot. And she'd yet to bat a catty lash at him. Words and bugs and healthy exercise outside. She was perfectly agreeable to him.

But he wouldn't dream of asking her to take on two children when she'd made it perfectly clear she was enjoying her freedom away from siblings. Unfortunate. She was the one thing Alexandre needed most.

In more ways than he cared to imagine.

After sneaking into Cook's chamber and slipping on her gray woolen, Margot vowed she'd pound the dirt out of the pink silk with her fists before she'd allow Cook to see its condition.

Later. Respite beckoned.

It was difficult to escape the clang of iron hammers and shouts of workmen, for every outer corner of the château was being retouched, reconditioned, torn down, and rebuilt. But the cacophony was muffled here within the small solitude of the king's library. He used it rarely, and so Margot had found it easy enough to gain access.

An original Moylanard timepiece sat before her on an elegantly curved rosewood table, its steel cogs and wheels clicking effortlessly behind the thin glass. Something she might never have had a chance to see in her entire lifetime had opportunity not led her to the château.

No, no. She wouldn't really consider her being at the king's château opportunity, more like fate. A dreadful fate.

Catching her chin in a cupped palm, Margot peered through the wavy glass set into the diamond-shaped windowpanes. Verdant greens and olives and apple-bright shades colored the leaves on the surrounding trees and shrubbery. But not for much longer. Fall would soon consider France. And with autumn, so would come the baron.

And then her life would change so drastically, she still could not determine whether to gauge it as good or horrid.

But why waste time fretting over a future that could not be changed?

With the sun's reach receding from the grounds, she adjusted the position of her candle to guide its warm light across the pages of an insectary she'd discovered sandwiched between heavy volumes on a dusty shelf. A waft of delicious roast meat drifted down the marble-tiled hallway and snuck through the door she'd left partially cracked.

Following the fragrance was the dull *click-chunk* of heels. Not court heels, she surmised from the lack of irritating clicks made by the silk-heeled frivolities most fops wore. Rather . . . a workman's boots. Each step, slightly off pace, for the obvious limp.

Hmm . . . She'd noticed the gardener had walked with a limp. That being the least of things she'd noticed about him. Kind eyes. Long, glossy hair. And a wriggling mouth that fought a smile. But why the struggle against mirth, she did not know. Certainly he must be in mourning for his wife. And just so very busy with his duties and the girls to tend.

She smiled as her attention was aimed at the floor near the door. First sight was as suspected, a pair of mud-crusted boots. "Monsieur Saint-Sylvestre." Margot raised her gaze to meet his rather confused expression.

"Mademoiselle deVerona." He nodded politely and approached, his limp obvious but not seeming to pain him. His eyes averted to catch a glimpse of the text lying before her. "You . . . read?"

Her grin segued into a chuckle. "Yes, Monsieur. Contrary to popular belief, my species does, on occasion, read."

"Your species? Ah, yes . . . woman. And here I thought them good only for beauty and charm. And the occasional casting of spells."

His mouth remained in that straight grim line, but a certain mirth glittered in the depth of his obsidian eyes. So dark, yet not at all cold. Margot decided she could spend a ridiculous amount of time gazing into his eyes. There was where the true root of his emotion grew. Scandalously ridiculous.

"I should have expected as much after your careful recording of entomological terms this morning. Quite out of the ordinary, you are, Mademoiselle."

"Huh?" Startled out of her scandalous behavior, she adjusted her thoughts to the conversation. "Out of the ordinary? Oh, indeed, I would never consider myself ordinary."

"Most certainly not."

"Though I should counter you with the same remark."

"Me? Dear no." He crossed his arms over his chest. The black ribbons securing his loosely rolled sleeves above his elbows skimmed his sun-browned arms. "I am a rather dull man once you get to know me. Nothing extraordinary at all."

She doubted it but didn't know him well enough to challenge that statement. Yet.

"What brings you to the library, Monsieur? Mud and all."

He turned and grimaced at his trail of mud, then smoothed a hand over his long, braided hair and thrust his other hand to encompass the room. "Actually I'm in search of my daughters. We were engaged in a game of seek and find when I seemed to have . . . well, misplaced them."

"Dear! You don't seem overmuch concerned. You should organize a search party—"

"No, no I believe they are quite close. Up until a few moments ago I was following their giggles. I feel sure I shall find them in the kitchen just down the hall. They rather favor Cook's blueberry tarts."

"As long as you are sure? I could assist you."

"No, really, I shouldn't worry, Mademoiselle de-Verona. Actually, I might select a book before continuing on my search. The girls have requested a story. Though I wonder should the king's library have children's tales?"

"But you needn't a book to grow a tale of knights and princesses."

He quirked a brow. A dark, elegant brow that did not so much overrule his gaze as it merely enhanced. "I'm afraid my imagination does not include knights and princesses."

"No dragons?"

"Afraid not. Their mother was the principal storyteller, but since she is gone . . ."

"You said it was only a few months ago that she passed?"

"Four months."

"You must have loved her immensely."

"Well . . ."

Odd how he seemed to linger on that word, as if not sure to go on or perhaps turn and race from the room. Margot had the intuition he wished to run.

"It might be harder on the children than me. The relationship between my wife and me . . . It was different from most. A friendship of sorts, if you will."

"Oh." For a man who looked like he wished to run, Margot was quite captivated by his honesty. She reached to touch the back of his hand. "But you did love her?"

"Perhaps that question presses the bounds of polite conversation."

"Certainly I do beg your forgiveness." Scandalous indeed. Here she was, prying so deeply into this man's life. And they had known each other for all of a quarter of an hour.

"Mademoiselle . . . you are holding my hand."

Margot looked at her fingers relaxed upon his palm, a palm shaded with the French soil. "Indeed I am Monsieur."

He did not make to pull away, so she leaned over her book and studied the deep lines that etched in telling arches and jets across his palm and up and down his fingers. The flesh held evidence of all the gardens of Versailles. Dirt seeped within the fine lines and into the pores; his thumb and fingertips were stained a deep green from the leaves of roses and the linden trees. A spot of deep crimson had to be the tears of a crushed petal.

"These are the hands of a hard worker," she said. "They bear evidence of a man who is proud of his labor, a man who digs and prunes, nurtures living things and tiny seedlings into exquisite and fragrant works of art, all for the enjoyment of others."

He pulled away, squinted at his fingertips, then frowned. "All that from the palm of my hand? I thought you said you weren't a witch."

"Merely observant," she stated with a smile, hoping that expression would spread to his own face. But the grim line remained, and he now rubbed his palms together as if to wash away all they'd discussed thus far.

He was like a new insect discovered in the wild. The desire to crack open her notebook and begin making notes and sketches made her fingers tingle for activity. But he'd drawn the line in their conversation. Much as she desired to learn more about this man, she mustn't step over it.

"Mmm, that delicious smell just keeps getting stronger and stronger. I do so look forward to this evening's meal. What do you suppose it is?"

"Roasted meat." Alexandre turned and drew in the aroma wafting through the doorway. "Perhaps game or pork. Definitely pork, judging from the triangles."

Margot jerked her attention from the savory aroma. "Triangles?"

Caught in a pose of sensory enjoyment, nose to the air and eyes closed, Alexandre suddenly pulled out of it. "Did I say that?"

She nodded.

"You heard me incorrectly. I meant . . . truffles."

"I distinctly heard *triangles*. I've never known pork to be pointy—"

"So be it. Triangles." He splayed his hands before him in defeat and took a limping step toward the door. "Beware the points when you dine this eve." With that he left the library, hands thrust on either hip, the tails of his shirt tugged from the back of his dirt-smeared breeches.

"I will!" Margot called.

He turned at the door before exiting. "You will?"

"Be careful," she offered with a sheepish shrug. "Of the points."

He raised a finger to retort, then, seeming to accept her playful response, nodded and offered her what might have been a smile. His lips remained straight, but there was definitely a smile glittering in his eyes. "I should ask you a question, Mademoiselle, if you do not mind?"

"Go on."

"I'm in desperate need of a nursemaid for the twins since my wife's passing. Their current governess took ill and is no longer with us. Now, I know you had mentioned your great joy in being away from your family, but I must ask, I shall never forgive myself if I do not. Have you an interest in watching two girls?"

"Oh." Margot looked down at her book, the lines of text insignificant against the question Alexandre had just asked. Much as she adored children and felt comfortable around them and had even been missing her own family, the idea of committing to their daily care when she had no plans to remain at the château beyond the coming autumn . . .

"Mademoiselle?"

"Monsieur, I do appreciate the offer . . ."

He reacted to her reluctance with a curt straightening of his relaxed pose. "I understand, no need to say anything more."

"They do seem to be sweet and well-mannered girls."

"You needn't justify, Mademoiselle. I can see in your expression you're not sure how to say no. So I shall say it for you. As I've said, I had to ask. It seems there are not quite as many qualified women here at the palace as Stephen duMonde would lead me to believe."

Forcing herself to smile, Margot nodded and waited until Alexandre left. He closed the door behind him, and Margot caught her forehead in her palm with a dull smack.

"That was most cruel of you, Margot. Can't you see the man is desperate? His wife has passed and he has two rambunctious little girls on his hands as well as a very demanding position. You might have at least offered to assist with the children until a proper nursemaid can be found."

She sat back, reflecting on her insensate reaction to the man's desperate request.

Perhaps she should not have been so hasty in her refusal. A position as nursemaid would be just what she needed to discover more about the captivating Monsieur Saint-Sylvestre. A man who with every meeting intrigued her more and more.

Three

Pointed pork can prove most distasteful.

Led by the gorgeous aroma of roast pork, Margot skipped down the three stone steps that flowed into the kitchen. *Beware of the points,* she thought with a smile. Whatever that might mean.

"What is that heavenly smell? My mouth waters at thought of eating." She plucked an onion from the long table and began to peel the papery coat from its back.

"You haven't been outside to take a peek?" Cook offered in a rather lugubrious tone.

"My path is set for the courtyard." Margot released the onion of its tight jacket. Setting it on the table, she skirted the wide, dill-spiked pickle keg. "First I wanted to compliment the chef on perfuming the entire château. Would you like me to test the main course? See if it's roasted long enough?"

"Margot."

She stopped in her tracks as Cook laid a hand over hers. Deeply carved lines weighed down the woman's heavy jowls, making it seem an impossibility to produce a smile. For the first time since she'd arrived at Versailles, Margot felt a leery chill creep up her spine. "Cook?"

"You haven't heard?"

"Heard what? I've been in the library most of the afternoon, trying *not* to hear anything. Though I find it utterly impossible in this racket." Thoroughly itching with a curious dread, Margot sat on the stool at Cook's side and implored her to speak.

"The king choked on a bad truffle last eve."

"Oh—" The horror of the situation struck Margot with an invisible blow to the gut. *"Mon Dieu,* does the king know where to find me?"

"He's already taken matters into hand."

"But—but I don't understand. It was I who found the truffles. Are you not telling me something, Cook? Am I to be shipped off like the duchess? Or worse!" She didn't want to imagine what might become of her had the king died instead of merely choked.

"He's already administered punishment for the guilty party."

Margot held Cook's gaze until she could read the answer in the old woman's teary eyes. She glanced over Cook's shoulder, past the scatter of copper kettles and braid of summer garlic skimming the wall and out the window, where fragrant smoke rose from the roasting spit. She could barely make herself speak the name. "Cur-curiosity?"

"I'm afraid so, child."

She'd had that pig for three years. Much as she dreaded her weekly truffle hunt and struggles with the two-hundred-dred-pound sow, she'd come to adore the way Curiosity wiggled her dirt-freckled snout after she'd successfully rooted up a truffle and gobbled it herself.

Cook's warm fingers smoothed over Margot's wrist for a gentle squeeze. "I know you loved her, but she was getting far too large for you to control. I've already seen to claiming one of the newborn piglets in the stable in your name."

"That's awfully kind of you," Margot said, though she

wasn't really thinking as she formed the words. The scent that had enticed her all day now only sickened. Points, indeed. Sharp, stabbing points aimed right for her heart. "Perhaps I won't be attending table this evening."

"I understand. You must look to the bright side though."

"There is one?"

"The king didn't inquire of the pig's master."

Indeed, that was a boon. But what would become of her now? As feared, she'd lost yet another position. Could she remain inconspicuous until the baron arrived?

Margot stood and moved with lackluster energy toward the door. In less than two days' time she'd lost two court positions. "What shall I do?" she muttered, catching her palm against the bare stone wall as she toed the bottom step. "I shall be sent home. The baron specifically requested I remain at court and learn the finer graces."

Margot caught Cook's incredulous glance, the quick slide of her eyes. The woman knew exactly how much time Margot had been devoting to the finer graces.

"Well, I am in a palace—a soon-to-be-palace—that's got to count for something."

"I didn't say a thing."

"You were thinking it." Margot flopped unceremoniously in her favorite chair. She couldn't bother with her renegade hair today; instead, she closed her eyes behind the curls that so enjoyed tormenting her.

"You know I'd rather study the entomological sciences or master the constellations than become a courtier. I want to become an educated woman, Cook, not a frilly, lace-flouncing *précieuse*. My mother wanted me to go off and discover myself. 'Discover who you are, Margot, before you become what you are not.' "

"Wise words. But is that what the baron wants?"

"What that toad wants is not important. But he is paying for my education, so surely he will be pleased to find I'm not wasting all my time prancing about with the latest gossip tripping from my tongue."

"Perhaps I can implore the king to allow me another hand in the kitchen?"

Margot brightened at Cook's offer, then dampened. "You've already Beatrice and Pierceforest."

Cook snorted. "Pierceforest helps only when his duties to Le Nôtre do not keep him. And Beatrice shows only when she's bored with her lover's latest antics."

"All the same, I mustn't depend on your kindness to see me out of this situation. You've done so much for me already."

"Fine lot of good that did. 'Twas my hand that laid the culprit on the king's plate."

True. At this very moment they were both extremely lucky to be conversing instead of sulking in chains and the shadow of the gibbets.

Margot forced an encouraging smile onto her lips. "I am very thankful the king did not find guilt on your part. As for me, I had better lie low. Perhaps there is a chamber pot I can empty or an animal stall that needs mucking out?"

"There must be something you can do. You're a smart girl. Beautiful and kind, and you can even read. Why, you're already educated, Margot." Cook thrust her knife through the peeled onion. "You could do any number of things that the court *précieux* cannot even begin to imagine."

"I do rather have a knack for flipping the chamber pot 'just so,' so its contents do not splatter my skirt." She wilted against the wicker and pressed a palm to her aching temple. "Why does that not impress me at all? For it shall only serve me a future of emptying my husband's chamber pot. I must find something else to do. I fear that before a position is available it is quickly snatched up by those closer in the know."

"You must seek something that interests you . . . and then . . . study it! Study it so fiercely, those not in the know will believe it is your occupation."

"Practically everything interests me."

"Any particular thing that seems to pop right out at you?"

Alexandre Saint-Sylvestre?

Margot's spine straightened like a whip pulled taut. Well, the name *did* just pop right out at her.

Now, there was a man who certainly warranted further study. Tall and dark and . . . and wounded. She wondered how he had gotten that limp. Maybe he had once served the king in a foot troop? The man might be a war hero! How very romantic. Most definitely he required more intense study. But the gardener might think it rather odd if he noticed her lingering about, peeking through orange trees or slinking along the stairs bracketing the Orangerie. Although . . .

"Margot?"

Should she reconsider Monsieur Saint-Sylvestre's offer? Certainly he would welcome the help. Though it wasn't a position she could fill for very long. Perhaps she shouldn't reveal she would be leaving soon. She could simply tell him she would look after the girls until a proper nursemaid could be hired. No sense in complicating the situation.

"I believe I may know of a position that will ensure my stay here at the château."

"See how easy that was? What position?"

"There's a man; he works in the gardens; he's in need of a nursemaid for his twin daughters."

"That fine Monsieur Saint-Sylvestre, eh?"

"You know him?"

"His daughters come visiting every such and so. They favor my blueberry tarts. I don't know the man, but I've seen him around. My curiosity was piqued when his wife was still alive. Now, there was a piece of work. No people on this earth more opposite than those two, I wager. There was quite a scandal surrounding her death."

"Really?"

"Yes, and I'm not one for repeating it, God rest her soul." Cook snatched a waiting carrot and began vigorously chopping. "You'll have to learn it elsewhere if it really matters. Which it shouldn't."

"A scandal." Margot found she couldn't imagine what that might entail. "That poor man. He really does need someone to help him through such a trying time."

Steel slicing through carrot flesh ceased. Cook cast Margot the curious eye. "Sounds like you're interested in more than just chasing toddlers. You think that's wise with the baron arriving in but a month?"

"Cook! I said nothing of the sort." Though, now that she thought of it, the notion of her and Alexandre Saint-Sylvestre . . . together . . . "I should wonder."

"You'd best leave it to a mere wonder, child. Nothing good can come of tilting at windmills."

"Windmills?"

"Child." Cook laid her knife on the table. "Are you daft? You're to marry the Baron de Verzy, and yet you don't blink an eye to the notion of pursuing another man?"

Margot shrugged and lowered her gaze. "I would never do such a thing." She could feel more than see Cook's doubtful expression. "I won't. I promise!"

"It's not me you've to be making promises to. Far as I can tell, you've already made the one. And don't you be forgetting it, Margot deVerona."

"I won't." She glanced outside, where fragrant smoke only made the lump in her gut quiver. "Don't hold supper for me, I'll just have a glass of wine out on the terrace."

* * *

Eight A.M. brought a morning storm. Well, it was more a dribble than anything worth classifying as rain. Just enough to make work in the dirt a slippery mess. Stretching his aching back muscles out with a flex of his fists over his head, Alexandre straightened and arced. A long yawn cracked the dried mud on his cheeks. The rest of the work crew had paused to break their fast with wine and bread and a cursory glance over the plans.

Alexandre stabbed his spade into the soft ground and started toward his rooms to bid a good day to the twins. Sophie had conditioned him to such a schedule, insisting that the girls see their father at least once a day, else they might never recognize him should they pass on the grounds while playing.

Sophie had always tended to exaggerate to make a point. Much as she would often exaggerate his tendency toward silence around her, his cool reserve. He wasn't all that cool. It was more the deep shyness that he'd clung to as a means of protection from the accusing eyes of the world. An insistent mask to shake.

Hell, he must admit it had been difficult to know how to act around a wife he'd never desired. Most people in general. Alexandre had conditioned himself to guard his actions and emotions since he was very little. Mustn't have anyone think him an idiot for the way he spoke of sights and sounds and tastes. If they even knew that he could see a person's voice dancing before him, that he could reach out and touch it as if a tangible object—the gossip! The accusations! So instead, he'd learned to turn a blind shoulder to the attitudes and opinions of others.

Unfortunately, over the years, it had developed into a cold shoulder. Often without realizing it, he directed that coldness toward the ones he loved. Such as Sophie. He hadn't meant to, it was just difficult to pull himself out of the persona that shrouded his soul.

The girls were his one connection to life through the

years, so unconditional was their love. With them he could be himself. Though the time shared with them over the past four years had been precious little.

Ah! He wasn't a cold man. Very loving, in fact. And to really be honest—very much in need of love. But how to break through the armor and begin to seek such desires beyond that of the love his children gave him?

Did he want to love again? Or, rather, did he crave the new and unique thrill of *first* love, for Sophie had not been such.

"Nonsense," he muttered as his boots crunched over the crushed-stone pathway.

The interior of the Orangerie remained blessedly cool during the summer months, thanks to the thick stone walls and packed dirt floor. Knowing the twins rose around eight, Alexandre hoped to catch them still in their bed, perhaps stretching out their arms and rubbing the sleep from their eyes. He'd warned them last night they might wake alone, but not to fear, Papa would be in to greet them.

As he pushed open the door and peeked inside the hazy morning-lit room, the sight was nothing less than astounding. Both girls were dressed, their hair combed and festooned with ribbons, and their faces were clean and smiling. Janette sat on the narrow tester bed that both girls shared—immaculately made—tossing Ruby, her rag doll, up and down, while Lisette sat on the plain gray skirts of Margot deVerona.

What was that woman doing here? She had so adamantly refused the position just yesterday.

Alexandre hung back by the chamber door, the twins still unaware of his presence, and observed Margot as she pulled her fingers through Lisette's long hair, designing a circle of braids from ear to ear. The two had matching crowns of curls, soft and glistening in the morning sun.

"You're much nicer than old Crabcakes," Janette sang as Ruby took a dive and landed on her head near the foot of the bed. "Promise you'll take care of us forever?"

"Yes, forever!" Lisette agreed with a clap of her hands.

Alexandre pressed a finger to his lip. Forever would be nice. But far too much to ask of a woman who hadn't shown much interest in the position in the first place.

Wrestling with the pink satin ribbon she was weaving into Lisette's braid, Margot's raised brows told Alexandre she was in dire need of rescue.

"Mademoiselle deVerona, it is a pleasure to find you—well, what do I find you doing this fine morn? Come to greet my children?"

"Good morning, Monsieur Saint-Sylvestre," she managed to say with tongue stuck out the corner of her mouth, while she twisted and flexed to arrange the braid just so on Lisette's squiggling figure.

"Papa!" Janette sprang from the bed and landed in Alexandre's arms. Ruby clonked him on the head with her toes. "She's so lovely. Thank you, thank you, for finding us a new, not-sick nursemaid."

"I'm not sure—"

"Certainly I am not sick," Margot offered with a secret smile to her tone. "But, girls, I've agreed to help your father watch you only until a suitable nursemaid can be found. I will not be at the château for the forever you both require."

Alexandre looked up from Janette's squiggles and sloppy kisses. Margot's wink pleaded for him to accept her offer as such. "Of course. Mademoiselle deVerona is most kind to offer her services, but she is a very busy woman, children. But trust that I will find a most kind and qualified nursemaid for the two of you."

"But, Papa, she makes my hair dance around my head." Lisette twirled into Alexandre's arms, pushing

Janette away, and locked her hands behind his neck. "Don't you think me a princess this morning?"

"You're a princess every day, Lisette." He kissed her forehead and drew his lips down her nose to kiss the tip, which always made her giggle.

"What of me?" Janette pleaded, Ruby clutched in her tiny fist.

"You are twin princesses," he said, lifting one girl in each of his arms. They were still quite light. Another year's growth, though, and he would be grunting to lift one of them.

"You don't mind?" Margot adjusted the bee-embroidered lace around Lisette's collar. "That I assigned myself the position? I couldn't imagine when you might find the time to appoint someone yourself, you seem to be so busy in the gardens."

"Not at all, Mademoiselle. I would have never asked in the first place had I not wished you for the position. It is unfortunate that it is only temporary, but I'm sure I do understand."

Margot seemed ready to speak, to perhaps explain her need for electing only temporary work, but then she simply nodded, tossing her long curls over her shoulder, and received Lisette in her arms.

"The girls told me they generally do their letters in the morning, with a long break for play in the afternoon," she said with comical emphasis on the word *long*.

"Yes, Lisette is quite good with her letters, as Janette is a marvel with numbers. I'm sure the three of you will get along well."

The sight of Lisette's comfortable attachment to Margot did strange things to Alexandre's heart. First it wrenched the organ into a twist, then it released that tight hold and caressed it as gently as one would touch the petal of a morning glory jeweled with dew. An altogether vexing feeling, if he must qualify it. Was he jealous of this woman's easy connection to his daughters?

No. It was more a fascination. Much as he had been fascinated every moment he'd spent talking to Margot de Verona.

"Papa, you go back to the gardens," Janette sang. "Margot will be our mama today."

But then again . . .

What would Sophie think of such a statement, blithely made by a child's happy face? Alexandre and Margot exchanged tense looks. With the situation so new, now was no time to get into heavy explanations of life and death and the fact that Sophie was . . . well, gone forever.

Perhaps he worried over nothing.

"If you wish, I break for an afternoon meal around two?"

"And when do you come in for the evening?"

"Right before evening table."

He noticed the fall of Margot's smile. A very long day. For both him and this generous woman who offered her free time to watch two children she had no attachment to whatsoever.

"Though I do expect the rain to pick up again. The clouds don't seem to want to move away. Can't work when it's raining."

"You feel it?"

Alexandre most certainly did feel the searing connection that reached out to grasp his heart and squeeze when standing so close to this fascinating woman. "Yes, I do."

"I think it'll touch down around noon again," she said with a glance toward the window.

"Touch down?" Touch? Alexandre let his gaze roam. It landed on the soft rise of Margot's bosom, perfectly framed by the soft gray bodice. "Touch?"

"Yes, the rain."

"The rain? Oh, yes!" All this time she had been talking about the weather and he had—strangely—been thinking about touching her.

Now, where had that thought come from? He was a newly widowed man. Women did not interest him. He'd been burned badly enough during his previous relationship to know to avoid the female species. This woman was merely an employee. He could not allow himself to have such thoughts about her. It simply could not happen.

"Have you broken your fast?"

"Fast?" No, slow was how he wished things to proceed. So slow that he would have time to jump ship before it was too late.

"Monsieur, you don't seem to be paying attention."

"Huh? What did you say, Mademoiselle?"

Lisette huffed. "She said, did you eat yet, Papa?"

"Yes, this morning at five. I rise very early and greet Cook as the bread is pulled hot from the stone."

"Mmm." Margot twisted at the waist, inadvertently entertaining Lisette, as her eyes closed. "I love the smell of fresh-baked bread. All yeast and warmth—"

"And speckled rounds of convex disks." Alexandre joined in the delicious revelry of hot morning bread. He always felt the sensation of those round disks skimming his tongue with the scent of hot bread. When he looked at Margot, she stared with peculiar wonder at him.

Hmm, what had he said—damn!

"You have a rather unusual way of putting things, do you know that, Monsieur?"

Janette skipped between the two and spouted, "Papa has an applic—affric— Oh! What is it, Papa?"

Time to leave. Alexandre ruffled Janette's dark curls. "Nothing whatsoever, little one. I see it's time I must return to the gardens. Good day, children. And you, Mademoiselle—"

"Please, Monsieur, you must call me Margot. If we are to be working together, in a manner, I insist."

"Margot." He tried the name, finding its sound like sweet brown vanilla dripping over his tongue. But he mustn't tell her that. "Very well, but only if you'll see to calling me Alexandre."

"I would be quite pleased. Don't worry, Alexandre, the twins will be fine with me."

"I haven't even thought to worry, Margot." He bowed and left the giggles of his daughters as Margot swung Lisette around the room.

Outside, in the halls of the Orangerie, Alexandre picked up his shovel and tapped the rusted blade against the marble wall to shake off chunks of dried mud. The girls' nursery window was but five long strides away. Still, their giggles bubbled.

"Affliction!" he heard Janette pronounce triumphantly.

Ah, hell. What would this woman come to think of him?

And did he really care?

By rights he should not.

He started toward the circle of potted boxwood he had plans to prune but turned and zoomed in on the twins' chamber window as he did. Squeals of delight skittered through the air in Lisette's steady amber lines. Margot could make the girls very happy for the interim.

For that reason, he did care what she thought of him.

Four

Stay away from that one;
she'll put a spell on you.

"It is impossible, Monsieur Saint-Sylvestre!"

Alexandre raised his fist and expanded his lungs to shout a reply to Joffroi's staunch refusal to unearth the massive conglomeration of tree roots buried between the pond and the north terrace, but his conscience would not allow him to be so forceful. Instead, he merely waved the man's red-faced complaints off with a weary hand and grabbed up the spade himself. "Move aside. I'll do it myself and prove to you the possibility of the task. Everyone watch!" he shouted, hoping this little demonstration would have to be made only once, but knowing as well that it would have to be performed over and over again until all the lackwits staring at him opened their brains to a new task.

He jabbed his spade into the ground with a subconscious oath against Trouvelot for becoming ill and leaving him with his hands full. And to Sophie for doing much the same.

And then he recalled his early morning rescue. Thank God for Margot de Verona.

Now, if only his work could run as smoothly as his private life had become.

Cook had been right. One *can* pursue their dreams while holding down an occupation. Lisette and Janette took to the idea of an afternoon walk along the outskirts of the grounds with great enthusiasm. While Lisette sat ever so still, palm opened flat with a chunk of green melon in wait of the butterfly that bobbed gracefully overhead, Janette found that counting flower petals was much more enjoyable than counting flat white circles drawn on her lesson slate.

Standing at the peak of a moderate rise in the land, arms akimbo, Margot closed her eyes and let her head sway back across her shoulders. The sun warmed like fire across her cheeks, bringing them to a heady flush. The same heat spread like a lover's hand across her exposed décolletage.

She wondered now about the rest of that lover. Her options had increased to two: a toad and a gardener. Which to wonder about?

Well, there wasn't even a thought. Most preferably Margot should like to feel the gardener's hands playing across her breasts, his hot breath driving up her neck, his long hair tickling her cheek as he tilted his head to kiss her. Hands that could cradle a seedling with utmost gentility would caress her flesh with such a tenderness as to make her sob happy tears. Yet those same hands could hold her safe and protected with a power that had served to create the growing magnificence here at the château.

What a delight to snuggle up against Alexandre's lithe figure, measuring his muscles with the softness of her own body. To return his frenzied kisses until she had memorized his flavor, the pace of his heartbeat. To return his touches . . .

The moment of her fantasy was too brief. Dark clouds rolled like billows of hoof-stirred road dust across the graying sky.

"Isn't it magical just before the storm, girls?" Margot let her knees bend, and she collapsed onto the grass beside Lisette, who chastened her for scaring the butterfly. "The air becomes crisp and cool and so clean. You can almost grasp it and hold it in your hand, shake it around a bit and toss it back to the sky."

"I don't think it works."

Margot lifted her head to spy Janette, who'd taken to grasping the air and tossing it out.

"Tell more," Lisette said, now munching on the melon, having given up on the renegade butterfly.

"Close your eyes and smell," Margot said, as she did as much. "The fragrance of the earth and flowers and trees becomes heady and full. And the colors! Look. Open your eyes, Lisette. Isn't the sky the most interesting green right before the rain?"

"Papa calls the rain minty and blue." Janette plopped in the grass on the other side of Margot.

Margot pushed up to her elbows and studied Janette's serious little puckered face. "Your father has a unique way of putting things. What were you saying about him earlier? I don't recall."

"Mama says it is his applic"—Janette twisted her tongue and pressed her lips—"afric—oh! Lisette, what does Mama call it when Papa starts talking funny?"

"Affliction," Lisette slurped between bites of melon. "I miss Mama."

Affliction? Margot could not begin to imagine what sort of ailment Alexandre Saint-Sylvestre suffered that would make him such an interesting man to listen to. There was only the limp that she noticed. A war wound surely. But an affliction? Most four-year-olds wouldn't have a grasp on such an advanced word. But Lisette said the word perfectly and without question.

"What sort of affliction?"

"I miss her too," Janette said on a heavy sigh. She laid her chin on Margot's whalebone-caged stomach and toyed with the grass tips flicking up on either side of her waist. "When will Mama come back, Margot?"

"Oh," Margot said.

First day on the job and already she was being called to do the heavyweight assignment of explaining death. It really wasn't her place; this was a family matter.

Lisette now joined Janette's patient waiting. Both girls stared at Margot with eyes as wide and dark as their father's. And not a bit shy as Alexandre's gaze so often was.

"Hasn't your papa told you anything about your mother, girls?"

"Papa said Mama was called to heaven to do a very important secret mission."

"Yes, that only she can do," Lisette added. "But she can't be gone forever. I miss Mama's kisses. She used to kiss me always. Right here and here and here." Lisette stretched her hand to the crown of her head. "And here."

"And here!" Janette lifted her foot and touched her plump ankle.

"And where else?" Margot said with forced eagerness. Best to keep the girls on this track than the direction they were headed. "Here?" She touched the tip of Lisette's nose

"Oh, yes! Just like Papa does, 'cept he lets it slide."

"I like Papa's sliders," Janette giggled.

"A slider, eh?" Margot recalled Alexandre's kiss to Janette's forehead and his tickling trail down to the tip of her nose. The notion of Monsieur Saint-Sylvestre kissing her was a rather beguiling thought. Hmm, she wouldn't mind one of those sliders herself.

She had kissed a man only that one time. Not really a *man,* 'twas Jacques, her cousin. A quick kiss, one that both had wished to try for experimentation's sake. For surely a person must know how to kiss before they met their true love. It had lasted all of a second, and Margot knew Jacques's lips hadn't even touched hers. It had been the going through the motions that had satisfied both that one innocent adventure would serve them well in their futures.

She should wish to never kiss a toad, for Margot knew the fairy tale was just that. Baron or not, her future toad-to-be, would remain warty and distasteful.

But perhaps a gardener?

"Tell us a story, Margot. Please," Lisette singsonged, and Janette joined in with chanting *pleases.*

"That sounds delightful! Perhaps I can make one up."

"Really?" Janette's brown eyes widened in wonder. "How do you make a story?"

"Oh, girls, you don't know how to make a story? Why, it takes imagination."

"Ohhh," the girls cooed in fascination.

Margot patted the grass on either side of her and the girls took direction, nesting their crossed legs under the plain skirts she had chosen for them this morning. Their white dresses now soaked in the soapwort along with Margot's pink silk.

"Imagination, mixed with a hero, a heroine . . . hmm, let's see. . . . Oh, there must be true love and perhaps a villain."

"True love?" Lisette rolled her eyes and shook her curls.

Janette giggled and hugged Ruby to her chest. "What's a hero?"

"Generally"—Margot lay back in the dew-sprinkled

grass—"it's the man who falls in love with the heroine. The heroine being the lady in the story. So I shall start with her, because she will play the most important part, at least in this story. Let's see now, who shall our heroine be? She must be beautiful, kind, smart, and ever so ladylike."

"A princess?" Lisette offered sweetly.

"Fabulous! A princess she shall be."

Thoroughly pleased with the direction of the afternoon, Margot began to spin a story for the eager-eared girls. She scanned her memory for stories whispered to her siblings on cold winter nights in front of the fire. None had ever featured princesses, for her brothers most often requested goblins and fire-breathing dragons. So she'd have to make do.

"Once upon a time, for certainly all stories must begin with once upon a time, there was a princess who really wasn't a princess, but she went to live at a palace, so she decided once she was there that she must be a princess—"

"No one can decide to be a princess," Lisette interrupted.

"Why not?" Janette pouted.

Dismissing her sister's ignorant plea, Lisette wondered sternly at Margot, "What sort of princess just decides she'll be a princess?"

The sort that wasn't sure how to tell a story about a princess when she had no firsthand knowledge on the subject. Also the sort that didn't really care to match a challenge from a precocious four-year-old.

"You must keep quiet or I won't finish."

A disgust-laced sigh drifted from Lisette's tiny body. But she complied, lying back in the grass and stating most boredly, "Go on."

Perhaps it *was* time for a nap. The rain was soon to come. Just a few more lines of the story.

"Now, this princess lived a carefree life. She spent her days plucking flowers and her nights watching stars."

"Princess of what?" Janette implored.

"Yes," Lisette agreed. "If we must accept that she is allowed to decide she will be a princess, than she must be princess of something."

"Oh? Oh. Well . . ." Of course that was true. Precocious little busybody. Margot ruffled Lisette's crown of ringlets and tapped her melon-sticky nose. "Why not Princess of . . . Practically Everything? How does that sound? Our princess rules over the butterflies and the grass and the rain and the mud and the—"

"The mud?" Janette squeaked.

"There is nothing wrong with a little mud," Margot assured. "So we have our Princess of Practically Everything, who lives in a grand and elegant palace. Of course, I should say that the palace is in a perpetual state of redesign, as are the gardens. Much like a caterpillar curls into a cocoon and then becomes a butterfly."

"The palace has wings?" Lisette said on a dreamy gasp.

"Yes, wings," Margot said, falling into Lisette's dreams. "Wings of fine silk and diamond glitter that spread wide to admit the princess into the palace. She's a very happy princess. Basically. Well, certainly she is for the two little kittens that skip about her silk slippers all day."

"Two kittens?" Janette jumped up and thrust her arms above her in declaration to the darkening sky. "That's us, Margot!"

"Of course they may resemble a certain pair of girls I know. One is black." She flittered her fingers through Janette's dark locks. "And the other is white."

Lisette lifted her chin as she recognized the white kitten to perhaps be herself.

"And they both had long, curly hair that bounced when they scampered about."

"Long hair!" Both girls giggled. "Isn't that rather silly?"

"Oh, dear, no. Wouldn't you like to have a curly-haired kitten to cuddle next to you while you sleep?"

"Oh, yes!"

"Continue," Lisette pleaded.

"Well, the Princess of Practically Everything and the two kittens became very close, and played together every day behind the sparkling wings of the palace doors. The three of them were very happy, and it seemed nothing could ever blacken their spirits. But the princess did feel a sort of emptiness within. She needed something. But she wasn't quite sure what."

"Oh!" A cool splat of rain bombed Margot's cheek. And then another. "End of the story for today. Hurry, girls, we must find the beginning. Run with me!"

Heavy drops bombarded the field. All around, for as far as Margot could see, the rains fell. Where the sky opened into crystal blue it seemed leagues and leagues away. So difficult to reach on foot. Frustrated, Margot punched the air and spun beneath the shower as she declared to the sky, "I shall never find the beginning."

"But I like the middle!" Janette cheered as she danced circles around Margot.

Lisette lifted her skirt and held it out as if to catch a skirtful of rain. "Let's count them, Margot!"

"Hmm?" Margot reluctantly pulled herself from her search of the countryside. Perhaps she was destined never to find the beginning. It had to start somewhere. It was entirely nonsensical to believe the entire world was being rained on all at once. Or was it? What a delightful wonder. Perhaps there was no beginning!

"I count fifty-twenty million," Janette declared proudly.

"No, two-forty-forty," Lisette countered.

Feeling a cool shiver trace her spine, Margot realized that the sky was only becoming blacker. This rain was destined to become a storm.

"Girls, we should return to the Orangerie." Not that she worried they would become ill, no, she simply didn't favor the idea of washing another set of mud-splattered dresses. "Come along."

They giggled and slipped and danced their way toward the entrance to the Orangerie. Margot lifted her head and opened her mouth to catch fat splatters of rain as she walked. It tasted sweet. Sweet as Cook's pastries.

She must remember to thank Monsieur Saint-Sylvestre for his offer, for without this position she would be rumbling toward Caen, her few belongings tucked beneath her legs in a stuffy carriage that would most likely become stuck in the muddy high roads, only to await the baron at home with seven demanding siblings stumbling over her skirts.

Aware that Janette and Lisette trailed hither and thither behind her, their own heads tilted back with mouths wide open to catch the raindrops, Margot lifted her arms and spun in a circle. It felt good to be alive and on her own. And as reluctant as she had been to take on the position of watching two children, the girls had actually lifted her spirits far beyond the usual giddiness, and she knew her days would be filled with wonder and excitement—save a few runny noses and temper tantrums.

If she had to fix a description to her life at this very moment in time, it would be happy.

One final spin twirled her thoughts into a dizzy array. Suddenly Margot's body collided with an immovable object. "Oh!"

The immovable object gripped her upper arms and actually seethed. "Might I ask your reason for exposing my girls to the elements, Mademoiselle deVerona?"

"Alexandre—"

His gaze could not have been more angry or black. "But one day I leave my children to your care and already you've seen to expose them to sickness."

"But they won't—" She ceased argument as Lisette scurried up to her father with a squeal and a hug. The rain poured upon Margot's head, relentless. The storm had picked up, like the sudden and surprising anger she saw in Alexandre's eyes. "The rain will not cause them sickness, Monsieur."

Lisette clinging to his neck like a drowned kitten—a happy drowned kitten—Alexandre received Janette under his other arm. "We shall see about that when they are bedridden and wheezing. As of this moment, consider your position terminated, Mademoiselle de Verona. I will not tolerate such a lackadaisical approach to child care. I had expected so much more from you."

A protest burning on her tongue, Margot reached to help Janette up into her father's other arm. The rain-soaked family turned and began a hasty jog into the Orangerie, Janette screaming, her arms extended to Margot, and Lisette beating against her father's shoulder. "We love her, Papa," their unison cries echoed to Margot.

Streams of rain poured down her forehead and nose, camouflaging the tears that began to spill from her eyes. Terminated? Over a silly walk in the rain? Did the man not realize that a child did not become sick from a simple jaunt in the rain? Margot knew that well enough from raising seven siblings. Rainstorms were times to rejoice and dance and splash in the mud puddles. Never once had any of her brothers or sisters taken ill from such a thing.

She should march right up to him and declare her position. She was right, he was wrong. And she was an excellent nursemaid.

But the idea of raising her voice to a man who had

recently lost his wife and was faced with so many difficulties stayed her under the heavy downpour.

"What will I do now?"

Once again Margot had no position at Versailles. And nowhere to go but home.

It was a struggle to get the twins to finally stop their tears and settle into their beds. While Janette wailed over her loss of the lovely Margot, Lisette sat on the edge of her bed, glaring at Alexandre as he held her nightgown before her, imploring her with a weak shrug to please get dressed. Neither wanted a nap; both needed one.

A determined little imp, almost a half hour later Lisette finally drifted to sleep, arms crossed tightly over her chest, sitting upright. Alexandre laid her next to Janette and tucked the two in. He laid his palm over both girls' foreheads as he'd seen Sophie do on many occasions. Not inordinately warm. Their hair was still damp, so that might be keeping the two cool. He would have to return on the quarter hour to check for fever.

Alexandre tiptoed to the door that joined his bedchamber to the twins' room and carefully pulled it shut. He lit a candle held firmly in its pewter base by hardened wax globs from previous lightings.

Maybe he had overreacted?

"I did not overreact," he placated his conscience as he sat on the edge of his bed, the ropes creaking with his weight. "What was the woman thinking to have my children out in a storm?"

He smoothed at the tension that tightened his forehead and closed his eyes. Margot had seemed the perfect choice for the girls. Young and intelligent, with a hint of whimsy that was needed to entertain four-year-olds. And having raised seven children almost by herself, she was certainly qualified.

So what had gone wrong this afternoon?

"Now I must begin again to find another nursemaid," he said on an exhausted sigh.

He was tired and peckish. The day had already been a long one, what with his struggles to uproot that nasty oak stump. And with little help from anyone else. The window glass wavered with streams of water. The afternoon could be best spent studying in the library, but more than ever he just craved a moment to lay back and rest. And forget it all.

'Twas well after nightfall when a rhythmic creak- and thud-repetition woke Margot from her sleep. The storm had been brief but fierce enough to dampen her spirits, so Margot had remained in the kitchen, helping Cook the rest of the day. Cautious not to wake Cook, she slipped an extra wool blanket from the end of the bed around her shoulders and puttered barefoot from the bed-chamber in search of the noise.

The marble floor was cool under her toes, the balmy night air gently hugging as she tiptoed out onto the stone terrace that crowned the Orangerie. The creaking sound seemed to come from the ground beyond the farthest of the hundred stairs.

The scent of orange blossoms carried up from the trees below. Margot thought the flowers would make the most exquisite perfume. Perhaps the oil could be extracted from the flowers to make her own personal scent?

Another thud. This time Margot could make out the heave of a man's breath. A black velvet sky held but a few sparkles of starlight here and there. It was really quite dark for one to be out so late.

Creak, and the hollow *thud.* She hastened to the edge of the terrace and looked down over the stone balustrade. The glow of a torchère lit the pounded dirt ground where once grass had flourished before the reconstruction project had started. Encapsulated within the torch glow stood Alexandre, his hair pasted to his neck with sweat, and thin gauze shirtsleeves clinging to his arms. He wielded an ax. Rhythmic swings cleaved the metal wedge of blade into an upended log. *Crack* and *split* and *thud*. The split logs were tossed with ease to the ground, and another lifted for separation.

He was not aware she watched, for his back was to her, his concentration most certainly intense. The pace of his labor worked like a song in Margot's thoughts as she knelt down and settled her chin upon the stone border that kept courtiers from spilling over the edge. Unmindful of the wool blanket that now slid from her shoulders and puddled upon her thighs, she drew in a deep breath.

Fresh-cut wood. Astringent and new. After today's downpour this wood would surely have to sit for days to dry out before it could be used as firewood. What a strange hour to be working, she suddenly mused. It was well past midnight. "I wonder."

Cupping her hands under her chin, Margot drew her eyes away from the flash of the ax blade to the tense muscles that strained and moved beneath the form-fitting shirt. A slender man Monsieur Saint-Sylvestre, but most certainly carefully built. Constructed of muscle and sinew, his arms reminded her of a workhorse's legs as the beast would strain against the cart. A wide back flexed many more muscles and narrowed to an elegant waist.

His hair had dispersed from Lisette's tidy braid and clung to his shoulders and the side of his face in wet streams, liquid and glossy like a writer's ink flowing across the page.

Margot reached to brush away a curl from her forehead. Her finger trailed down her face and landed her lower lip. She closed her lips over her finger, as if to keep her hand from jutting out to reach for a glossy strand of Alexandre's hair. What it must feel like, all moist with the liquid beads of labor. 'Twould cling to her hand as it clung to his body. If only she could glance a finger along his cheek, smooth away the web of strands, and trace the hard lines of his face.

She was right when she had guessed that his smiles were rare. The hard set of his jaw would not allow it. Had such a rigid pose come recently because of the loss of his wife? Or had it always been there?

So much to wonder about this man. Margot's breast fluttered at the notion of learning more about him. An exotic aura cleaved to his person. Two sweet girls clinging to his legs and a fierce work ethic. Pointed pork and strange tapping of the air when she spoke. To judge outside appearances, one would pass over the man as just another laborer trying to make his way. But from her perspective, Margot sensed something so much more from this man, whose heaving swings did not cease. He was troubled, certainly. But the core of Alexandre Saint-Sylvestre glowed like red embers. Embers that had been doused and needed a breath of new air to light.

Dare she prod the embers?

Best to leave him to himself. At least for now. He had been disgusted over her mishap that afternoon. Though she quite expected that both Lisette and Janette would wake bright and shiny tomorrow morning without taking ill from the weather. Certainly much cleaner for the rain bath they'd taken.

Leaving the grump to his work, Margot felt compelled to stroll. The night was perfectly tempered with a breeze and a glint of starshine. In the distance the Swiss pond lay a black gloss upon the land with a few speckles of silver darting the quilted surface.

The first of the hundred steps caught her bare feet, and Margot found herself counting by twos as she descended. As she landed the final step, the distant pulse of Alexandre's labor receded and now the gorgeous flood of neroli swarmed through Margot's senses.

Plucking a crepe-thin white blossom from a tree whose curved ball of foliage stood but a foot above her own head, Margot pressed the flower to her nose. Ambrosia. She glanced down the row of orange trees that led up to the Orangerie, and to the side where two more militant rows stood silent sentinels awaiting Monsieur Saint-Sylvestre's command. There were many dozens. Surely no one would miss a skirtful of blossoms.

The last of the day's cut was finally chopped and piled. Alexandre set his ax against the stacked wood and with a flip of his head sent his hair over his shoulders. He wiped the perspiration from his brow, but it did no more than disperse the wet. He was soaked from crown to toe. As usual when he took to attacking his emotions.

Whenever anger beat at his nerves, always the chopping of wood lured him. 'Twas a soul-steeping act, the process of swinging and heaving and chopping, mindless and invigorating, and oftentimes enlightening.

The world and all its evils fell away when he raised the ax and swung it for hours. Sensory confusion blended into the thud of the wood hitting the ground. He noticed nothing, felt nothing beyond the knowing that things would work out, would be all right when finally he finished.

The girls had been right. He'd overreacted that afternoon, most likely due to his trials with the workers earlier. If the twins could not bear a good rain shower, he was mud.

Alexandre looked over his arms and legs and sniffed. Not exactly mud, more like sweat.

Time to loosen the tight rope he'd bound around his

morals. He'd been reintroduced to fatherhood and the responsibilities that came with it. And now he'd pushed that control to its limit. A little slack never hurt anyone. Indeed, it might feel good to remand some of the control and learn to relax.

To even think of relaxation . . .

A refreshing shower in the Orangerie pleaded. Thanks to a pipe he'd rigged up to flow from the pond to the inner halls of the Orangerie, he could wash away the day and sleep like a dead man.

And not a thought on that bewitching Margot de-Verona.

Instead of using her skirts, Margot laid her wool blanket on the ground and tossed a small pile of blossoms on it. Perhaps if she asked nicely and offered to scrub the kitchen floor, Cook would allow her a small crockery of oil in which to steep the orange blossoms. She would gift Cook with the exquisite scent and use some herself if the experiment succeeded.

Pleased with her booty, Margot gathered up the blanket and skirted the final orange tree, which brought her into the deep cool shadows of the Orangerie. She thought to look in on the twins, press an ear to their door, just to assure herself they were sleeping peacefully, but the splatter of water alerted her. It echoed from down the empty hallway that Margot knew was used to store the orange trees in the winter months.

Moonlight strained through the tall, curve-topped windows set intermittently down the hall. Thick stone dividers jutted out from the main outer wall, partitioning each of the large, grandly paned windows in closets. Water splashed in syncopated intervals. Couldn't be a leak. Certainly there must be an interior water system, perhaps piped from the Swiss pond for watering the trees. Had someone left it untended?

Margot turned back to the entrance, fear clutching her heart for a few heavy breaths, but then curiosity whipped that fleeing rabbit back into place. How foolish that she should be afraid. It was merely as she thought. Someone had left the water running. Alexandre might appreciate her seeing to it before the hall became flooded. Though she could not imagine the man would have forgotten such. Although . . . with his temper high today, anything was possible.

Wool clutched to her stomach, the scent of the flowers muffled, she stepped forward and peered around the stone divider.

For as little moonlight there was, she certainly had no difficulty making out the curves and lines of naked male flesh. My, but he was . . . well, hmm . . .

Margot chewed on her lower lip as she stretched her neck out farther. Streams of water flowed over broad-muscled shoulders and arms and down a back carved of strength and grace. Every movement of his arms to span out his hair and catch the water flexed the lines of his back. Silver arcs of moonlight worked over each movement as if a symphony.

Allowing her gaze to fall with the droplets, Margot bit her lip as the sun-bronzed flesh of his upper body suddenly stopped and became creamy white at about the place she would expect his breeches to rise. And there, graceful and smooth, just the slightest muscle flexing with his movement were perfectly lovely—

The sudden turn of his body pulled Margot from her ogling. She shot upright and dodged back two steps. Clinging like a snail to a rock, she pressed her body to the wall. From the corner of her eye she spied the white blossoms dotting the ground before the makeshift water-fall.

"Who's there?" Alexandre's voice called.

She squeezed her eyes tight.

As if that will make you invisible?

"Mademoiselle deVerona?"

He knew! God's body, what would she do now? There was simply no way to explain her reason for looking over his naked body in the middle of the night. No way at all!

"Margot?"

Oh, my.

"Yes?" she managed to say, and decided to thrust out one hand and do a little wave instead of peeking back around the corner. Certainly he would not mistake her for anyone else. "Forgive me! I was, er . . ." Just drooling over the sight of his backside, lingering on the flex of his buttocks as he stepped forward and back. "Picking flowers!"

"I see that," he called.

She heard the click of metal, or, rather, metal fitting into metal, and the water suddenly ceased.

"You've dropped something," he called.

"Indeed." Now what would she do? Did he think she might wish to retrieve those paltry flower blossoms while he stood there watching? Naked?

Oh, my. She certainly was a curious woman, but this time her curiosity had gone and pulled a nasty trick on her. "I had no idea anyone would be down here this late at night. I thought the water supply merely left running and thought to close it off for you. I certainly did not expect that I should find a nak—oh." She pressed a hand to her mouth and felt her stomach flip. *Don't even say the word naked. For then he will know you saw him. All of him.*

A bare toe glanced out of the stall and nudged the flowers now floating in a growing puddle. "You had better retrieve them and be gone. I'm liable to freeze if I stand here much longer like this."

"Of course."

Bending and easing her way down to the flowers, Margot kept her back to the stall. But when she knew she knelt right before the man, all she could think as she scrambled the flowers up into her skirts was that he was so tall and lean and . . . What did his front side look like? And how could she even think such a thing?

"Haven't you a robe?"

"Never had the need for one with my door just down the hall. My midnight showers are usually taken in peace, Mademoiselle."

"I'm so embarrassed. If I had known. Well, certainly I could not have known." She gathered her skirts to a bundle and made her way, half crouching, over to the wall again, where she could stand and release a breath in the darkness. "I shall be off, then."

"Before you go . . ."

"Yes?"

"I know this is rather awkward for all," his voice echoed in the stone-partitioned closet. A few water droplets *splinked* in the puddles at his feet.

"I shall not breathe one word of this encounter to anyone," she blurted out.

"That is not my concern."

Really?

"I've had a change of heart regarding your watching the girls," came the calm, deep voice from around the corner. "I was horribly mistaken to have spoken to you in such a tone earlier. Of course the girls show no sign of taking ill. It was a misdirected anger. The day has been long and trying. If you could see to forgive me, Mademoiselle deVerona—"

"Done!" she hastened, then started the opposite way. One more moment spent talking to a naked man, and she just might feel compelled to take another peek. "I shall see to the girls in the morning!"

As the swish of her skirts made haste from the Orangerie, Alexandre pressed his forehead to the wall and finally grinned that wide, irrepressible grin that had been aching for release since he'd seen the flash of Margot's skirts days before.

So she'd been spying on him, eh? The thought should have angered him, should have embarrassed even, but for some reason he could only smile.

Ah! It had been a long time since a smile had so easily overtaken his face.

And this one he felt in his heart as well.

Five

*Have you ever been so close to something,
yet still a star's journey away?*

Morning could not come quickly enough. Margot slipped into the plainest skirt she owned, the brown wool one that had a tear along the hem. Perfect for nature walks and afternoons spent frolicking with the twins. A matching bodice took extra effort to lace up and tie, for all the soaking had shrunk the fabric. Rather a generous bouquet of bosom burst from the neckline, but she could not place the lace fichu her mother had sent along with her things so did not give it another thought. She combed through her hair, touched the crock of oil that now brewed the orange blossoms, then made for the Orangerie.

Avoiding Alexandre would be an impossibility. So as she skipped down the hundred steps, Margot planned the quickest, least embarrassing encounter as possible. Nothing more than a good morning, keeping her eyes focused on her destination. Simple enough.

She spied his lanky frame bent over a pile of hedge clippings as she descended the final step. Thank the heavens he was fully clothed. His hair—for Lisette had yet to rise—was unbound and fell over the side of his face, blocking his view of her arrival. If she just walked quickly, and pumped her arms for speed—

"Good morning, Mademoiselle deVerona."

Margot paused—the door to the Orangerie within arm's reach—and spun around. He stood and offered a nod with his greeting. Those stunning dark eyes of his caught the sunlight and flashed back at her all the warmth in the world. Kind eyes, grim mouth. Yet there was a hint of a curve at the corner of his mouth. Completely stupefying, his calm actions. As if she'd never glimpsed his naked body.

"Margot?"

"Huh? Oh! Indeed. Good morning, Monsieur Saint-Sylvestre. I'm off to see to the girls, then."

She turned and walked right into the wall.

Margot pushed away and stepped to the side, positioning herself before the entrance. She turned and—oh, what could one say to that? Shrugging, she skittered into the shade of the Orangerie, where the delicious smile on Alexandre's lips was lost to her sight.

There was not black enough ink in the world to reproduce the color of his hair. Nor was there the right proportion of white space on her drawing paper to form those glistening stars in his eyes. Stars of kindness, of loss, or an indelible understanding.

Margot glanced her pen above the circle she had formed into a right eye, and created an eyebrow. Long, thick, but emotive with each subtle raise of his lids. Her anatomical drawings usually were quite lifelike. She'd drawn her mother and each of her siblings, plus a handful of travelers and guests who had passed through her life over the years. But this was the first drawing that did not instantly take form in a brief sketch of head, body, and clothing, to be later detailed. No, this one had started with wispy dark hair, a high, proud forehead, and now the kind eyes. But a mere pair of eyes did not a face make.

She swished a few long, flowing strokes across the page. Rain-splashed hair, glossy black and liquid, streaming down a muscled back, and just topping those firm white—

"I'm bored!"

"Me too."

Startled out of her forbidden fantasies, Margot set her notebook aside and glanced to Lisette and Janette, who both sat at their school desk, chins caught in palms and writing paper sprawled with black squiggles.

"I know how to write my letters," Lisette whined. "I want to do something different."

"Ruby wants to play," Janette said, with a lift to her tone and a glance across the room to where Margot had consigned the rag doll to the top of the armoire. Just until their lessons were complete, of course.

"Ruby is proving a most patient pupil," Margot said as she approached the girls and looked over their handiwork. "Besides, I've allotted half an hour to writing, and you've been at it but a quarter of an hour. You are right though, you've both mastered your letters. And look at the lovely swish in your *S* there, Lisette."

Lisette bristled proudly.

"My esses swish," Janette defended.

"Yes, I see that they do," Margot agreed. "They can also do backward dips."

Lisette sighed. "Isn't there something more we can do besides copying letters?"

Oh, to recall her own childhood lessons spent sitting before the hearth fire, her tongue firmly gripped between her lips and her fingers turning blacker than her writing paper. She'd been so eager to draw in information and learn new skills.

"There is something more." Remembering a suggestion once made by her mother, Margot knelt between the girls and took Lisette's pen in hand. "Now that you've mastered your letters with your right hand, you must then master them with the left."

"The left?" Janette could not hide her disbelief.

"Of course," Margot said as she wrote her name in neat, elegant strokes using her left hand. A grand flourish to the T always swept under her entire name. "If you do not exercise both sides of your body equally, you will become unbalanced. I always use both hands to do everything. I believe we shall eat with our left hands today as well. It's called being ambidextrous, and it's quite a marvel to try."

"Let me." Janette gripped the quill and Margot allowed it to slip from her fingers.

Tongue dusting the air, Lisette had already fitted the quill to her uncooperative left fingers and dipped it in the ink. Her first attempt was more a blob than an $A,$ but Margot encouraged them with promises for an extra long nature walk if they could at least copy out the alphabet once.

"What did you call this?"

"Ammi—ambree—" Janette tried.

"Ambidextrous. It keeps a body in balance."

"So you're never out of balance, Margot?" Janette mumbled, her concentration fixed on the paper before her. The quill shrieked across the page, she held it so tensely.

Margot touched Janette's hand, coaxing her to loosen her grip. "I try not to be."

"Papa is out of balance. He walks crooked."

"Has that to do with his affliction you girls mentioned earlier?" Margot thumbed the bedpost, not wanting to appear too interested. Though she was. "Why does your father limp?"

"Mama did it to him."

"Your mother?"

"Janette!" Lisette thonked her sister on the head with her fist. "We're not supposed to tell that. Mama said."

"But Mama's not here anymore," Janette said, rubbing her noggin.

Their mother had given Alexandre that limp? Why, it was too horrid to even imagine. Surely they were mistaken. It must be a war injury, a hero's badge of honor.

Much as she should not press four-year-old children for information, Margot couldn't help—no! She mustn't. "Your letters, girls."

Lisette released a heavy sigh and put pen to paper but eventually said, "She did it with a pitchfork."

"What?"

"We saw," Janette said with a nod of her head, "when we lived at the criminal's castle."

"That was Vaux," Lisette corrected her sister with a dip of her quill in the ink.

Vaux-le-Vicomte. Margot knew that the king's former financier, Nicolas Fouquet, had been jailed for embezzling funds from the crown's coffers the previous year.

"Mama didn't like Papa kissing another woman, so she poked him in the leg with a pitchfork." Lisette gave another that-was-that sigh and settled back to her lesson.

Thoroughly stunned at such a revelation, but seeing that both girls had obviously said all they would say, Margot settled backward, but missed the windowsill she had been sitting in and landed with a plop on the floor.

Lisette and Janette looked up but did not say a word. Instead, they looked one to the other, widened their eyes, giggled, then turned back to their lessons.

After spending the late morning out-of-doors with the twins, Margot was quite thrilled to find their energy levels had needed restoring. She had used that time to sketch a little more in her notebook. Both girls had woken with voracious appetites, and so a trip to the kitchen was a most agreeable idea.

"Delicious," Janette sputtered through a blueberry tart, her lips and cheeks and even the tip of her nose colored candy-sweet.

Lisette merely shook her crop of ringlets, agreeing completely but not allotting one moment's breath to that of speech when utmost concentration must be employed toward the tart cupped in her hand.

"She's rather like her father," Margot said, as she leaned against the hearth stones, crossing her arms over her chest. "Quiet and set on her task. I wonder if Janette is much like her mother?"

Cook knelt before the fire, stirring the evening's stew and sprinkling freshly chopped basil into the rich broth. "I should pray not."

Margot knelt next to Cook, eyeing the girls quickly to see they were too involved with their tarts to overhear the conversation. "Why would you say such a thing?"

"Madame Saint-Sylvestre was a most disagreeable sort," Cook whispered conspiratorially.

"I've certainly come to learn that."

"Have you now? Well, it was no surprise to me that the girls' father chose to spend his days away from his wife. Rather a snip. Nothing could ever please the woman."

Nor keep her from inflicting bodily harm on her husband. Causing permanent injury to her husband with a pitchfork? What Margot wouldn't give to learn the reason behind that tidbit. She slumped against the smooth stones. Alexandre was so gentle. She couldn't see him marrying a difficult woman. "Was she very pretty?"

"A gem among mere stones." Cook tapped her spoon on the edge of the kettle and gave a glance toward the girls. Ravenous little kittens too involved in tarts to give a care. "But she knew it too. Always holding her nose higher than the clouds and flipping those tight blond curls over her shoulder. Why, when I did see her with her husband, she was often chiding him or complaining about something that wasn't right."

Or poking him with sharp instruments.

" 'Twas a blessed day, indeed, when she took her death."

"Oh, Cook."

"Now, don't get me wrong, Margot. 'Tis surely unfortunate for the girls to be without a mother, but as for that man, your gardener . . ."

"How did she die?"

"I mustn't say. It's a sore spot with Monsieur Saint-Sylvestre, I know that much. I shouldn't expect he'd wish me to gossip on about his life."

"How very sad that such a kind man should be left with two little girls and a tremendous workload. The poor man. He's such a fascinating person beneath the silent facade, I just know it. It's like I can feel the vibrations of his soul when I'm near him, Cook. Oh, but what to do to uncover his real beauty?"

"It seems a certain young maiden is forgetting her own future. Isn't there a baron somewhere with plans to fetch you up and make you his wife?"

Margot sighed. "A mere toad when compared to the fine prince who tends the king's gardens."

"You'd best leave well enough alone, Margot. For your sake, and for Monsieur Saint-Sylvestre's. The man's troubled. He's"—she searched for a word—"different."

"I know. He's a very odd way of seeing things."

Janette's head shot up. "You mean Papa's 'pliction?"

"Affliction," Lisette corrected Janette sternly. In comparison, Lisette's face was pristine to Janette's disaster of violet and pastry.

"Yes, yes," Cook said. "I often heard the departed mistress mention his affliction. Sounded something horrid, it did."

"He's no more afflicted than you or I." Margot paced the floor behind the girls, hands on her hips. She swung a hand through the air in display. "Look at the man. He's lovely. He has a strong work value and virile strength. Sure, there is his limp—" She'd initially thought him a war hero, wounded in battle while risking his life for the king. Being stabbed by his wife wasn't quite as romantic. But it made him no less endearing. "But the rest of him—" And hadn't she seen quite a bit of the rest of him? "What could possibly be wrong with him?"

"It's nothing wrong," Lisette explained as she scraped her finger along the edges of the juice-stained tart pan. "Papa calls it his gift."

"His gift." Margot fell into the delicious beam of Lisette's smile as she voided out the idea of afflicted body parts and began to entertain the idea of a gifted man. But how so? It had something to do with his sight. Perhaps. Or his perception. She couldn't be sure. Twice he had seemed to fall off guard and expose himself to her. If only she could catch him again. Just being himself.

Don't you mean you'd like to see him exposed again? All naked glory?

Fighting her lascivious conscience, Margot turned to the girls. "What exactly does that mean, Lisette? Can you explain your father's gift to me? Does it have something to do with him seeing things and making contortions in the air when a person is speaking to him?"

"What's a contortion?" Janette slipped out between blueberry bites.

"It's something to do with money and being bad. Like Monsieur Fouquet," Lisette explained, then tilted a miffed expression up toward Margot. "My father is a very kind man. He doesn't have much money, but we make do."

"Oh, dear, I didn't mean extortion. A contortion is well . . . let's get back to your father's gift."

"Mama says we're not supposed to discuss it around other people."

Janette caught her violet chin in an equally brilliant palm and sighed. "I miss Mama. Can we ask God to send her home now?"

Margot glanced across the room, where Cook cast her a pitiful shake of her head. Time for activity. Something to keep the girls' minds from their mother. And her own thoughts from the idea of knowing their father so much more.

Six

A kiss beneath the stars . . .

Much as he enjoyed working under God's ceiling, the insects that had come to inspect the construction around the château were relentless in pursuit of a man's blood. Alexandre slapped a palm over the sting on his shoulder. The irrigation pipes had arrived for the main lake Le Nôtre had planned to alley down the center of the west gardens. It would eventually become the central walk in the Grand Trianon, but the finished project was years from completion. He worked morning until late afternoon, helping Joffroi and the rest of the crew haul the heavy clay pipes from the carts to the clearing in the valley. He'd forgotten to stop for a meal and now felt ready to collapse upon the boot-pounded ground.

He pressed a palm to the trunk of an oak—one of very few that were original and had not been uprooted for the master plan. The shade offered little respite. More than an hour before, the water bucket had run dry and Pierceforest had yet to return with fresh. It had been a long summer, and even with August beginning to paint the tips of the leaves a soft color, the heat had not caught on to the change of seasons.

Unfortunately he'd joined Le Nôtre as a student at the

end of his tenure to Fouquet. The gardens of Vaux were nearing completion when Alexandre stepped in to assist with the final trimming of miniature box hedges and planting a few raised parterres of flowers. This experience of starting with flat dirt and creating a masterpiece out of water and shrubs and flowers and crushed rocks—well, it was nothing less than astounding, if not a bit humbling.

A botanist he was by nature, not a construction worker. But Alexandre understood that in order to create beauty, one must get dirty and stretch a few muscles.

The deep points of his fellow workers' conversation echoed behind him, but a touch of rippling pink entered on a wave, rimmed with amber lines and aqua spheres. Alexandre spun around to find his girls giggling behind cupped palms, and behind them, with a mischievous grin on her sprite-kissed face, stood Margot.

"We brought food!" Janette proudly declared as she held a basket high. The girls plunged to the ground and began laying out a blue cloth.

Margot lifted a dark bottle of wine and offered him a nod. "You didn't show for your meal, so I assumed you'd be starving about now."

"Bless your perception," he said, and gestured they sit on the ground near the girls. "I was just wondering how long it would take the food fairies to arrive."

Both girls giggled and kissed their father before jumping up and dashing to a nearby pile of straw that had been stacked to feed the work oxen. "I shall braid your hair after I've played, Papa!" Lisette called, as she mounted the glistening mound of straw.

Alexandre waved them off and shrugged his fingers through the scatter of darkness falling from his head to the grass. "Lisette is always so concerned for my appearance. She likes to select my clothes if I've a meeting with the king. Not that I've much to choose from."

"She's a regular little wife," Margot said with a smile. "She'll make a fine match someday."

"She likes to take care of her papa." Alexandre studied the assortment of food in Margot's basket. A plump chicken leg, half a loaf of Cook's delicious rye bread, and a wedge of cheese. A feast for a king, if not a starving man. He accepted the wine bottle Margot held out, gripped the cork with his teeth, and jerked it free. "No goblets?"

"It is a picnic for one," she offered. "The girls and I had to test Cook's tarts to ensure eatability, so we're quite stuffed. Drink up."

Wine had never tasted quite so good. Perfect lines of satin running down his throat, followed by a hearty chunk of fowl. He snickered at Janette's attempts to straddle the large stack of rain-soaked hay. Lisette rocked the roll as if simulating a pony or carriage ride. "Trouvelot never seemed to stir up so many smiles in my girls. They are very happy with you."

"I'm happy with them," Margot offered. She sat beside him, stretching her arms out behind her to study the high sun, offering her face to the warmth. " 'Twas a good thing our arrangement was not ended before it began."

"Yes, it is." He offered her the wine bottle and she took it, swigging back a hearty swallow. " 'Tis also fortunate my pale limbs did not send you packing last night."

"Oh, forgive me. I can never apologize enough."

She blushed like a ripe peach that would coax a hungry traveler to the tree. Alexandre traced his lower lip with his tongue, sure of the taste as if he'd bitten into the juicy flesh himself. "It is forgotten."

"But it is not, you just brought it up."

"So I did. Then you must forgive me. Did your orange blossoms survive their disaster?"

"I hope you don't mind, I'm steeping them in oil to draw out the perfume."

"If you can extract the neroli from the blossoms, I'll be quite impressed. Many a king would pay a fortune for such an exquisite perfume. Why do you imagine I often find myself in the gardens at midnight?"

"The perfume must be overwhelming in the cool darkness," Margot said. Her eyelids fluttered shut, and she tilted her head back to worship the sun.

"Indeed. I can touch the columns of light and run—" Hell, dropped his guard again. "Forgive me, Mademoiselle. I digress, to . . . something entirely off subject."

He took a hearty swig of the wine, cursing himself for allowing that slip. Usually he was in much better control. Usually? Always he had control.

Why was it Margot's company always seemed to keep him teetering just off guard? And made him react in ways he'd never normally consider. Like a simple smile at her seeing him naked.

If he didn't know better, he might think Margot deVerona had gotten under his exterior of coldness that Sophie had so despised. But that was impossible, he'd honed his armor for years. It was simply a fluke that he had let down his guard.

A fluke three times over.

You never once regarded Sophie so intently. Had she ever worshiped the sun on a bright afternoon in the manner of this woman? Had you ever cared?

No. He must not allow himself to get trapped in the past. Margot deserved his full attention. Albeit, he needn't get all cow-eyed over her.

"I'd like to speak to you later this evening about seeing to finding the girls a permanent nursemaid," Margot said. "They're quite precocious. Perhaps you should look for a woman who is educated beyond mere child care? I realize they are but four, but Lisette is so good with her numbers and letters and Janette has quite a fantastical mind."

"Numbers and letters will bring a woman quite far; I see great things for my Lisette. But where will Janette's daydreams and fantasy get her?"

"To the king's palace," Margot said proudly.

Understanding her meaning, Alexandre nodded. How this woman had landed at Versailles, amid the stiff-corseted ladies of court who'd only in mind to compare fabric styles and the latest gossip, was truly amazing. What lady would even think to sit down upon the moist ground, much less venture out immediately after the rain? Nothing seemed to irritate Margot. In fact, she seemed to revel in the discovery of, hmm . . . practically everything.

"Tell me just how you did arrive at this dirty little château deep within the village of Versailles?"

"You think me unfit for a position at court?"

"Not at all. Just so out of your habitat. Compared to the court ladies, I find you to be a radiant peacock amid a chittering nest of mudhens. It is quite remarkable, your achievement. But I should imagine you would be more comfortable journeying the deserts of Egypt in search of the tombs of centuries-past kings, or perhaps slashing through the jungles of the Amazon on trek for a rare butterfly in need of sousing."

"I can only wonder what such ventures might prove," she said with a sigh, and caught her chin in her palms.

A dreamy smile curled upon her petite visage as she drifted before Alexandre's very eyes to the places he had just spoken. To possess such passions, such dreams, seemed an unfathomable reality to Alexandre. Nonsensical and completely illogical for sure. But fantasy flourished and blossomed in the heart of Margot deVerona and made her the enchanting woman she had become.

He watched as her long fingers tapped a slow beat

against her cheek. The motion seemed blatantly erotic in a way that surprised him. That fine, narrow finger, moving ever so worry-free against the high bone of her cheek. *Tap, tap, tap* . . . against his hard exterior of indifference.

A blond ringlet fell to the center of her forehead, startling her out of her sweet reverie.

"Ah! I journey so easily at times. Forgive me—"

"Absolutely not," he said, and followed with another slug of wine. Anything to douse the fiery roil that had stirred up in his loins. "Perhaps someday you'll let me in on your journeys?"

"They are not tangible places, just thoughts, imaginations. Silly stuff, really."

He chuckled and picked up the chicken bone to clean away the remaining meat. But his thoughts could not escape enchantment. This woman was not silly, she was whimsical and sprite. But never silly.

So very different from Sophie.

"So tell me, Alexandre, how does the chicken taste?"

He sensed a deeper meaning in the deep maroon tone of that question but couldn't be sure. Chawing off a last string of still-warm meat, he savored the delicious juices, then offered, "Like chicken.

"Oh."

Seeming dissatisfied with that answer, she stood and called, "Tonight, then?"

"I count the minutes."

"I'll see you then."

She skipped off, leaving Alexandre questioning his foray into poetical speech. *I count the minutes?* And delivered in such a whimsical tone.

Hell, what was this woman doing to him? Should he have paid more regard to Pierceforest's casual warning? Had Margot deVerona cast a spell of bewitchery upon him?

* * *

Both girls fell immediately into smiling dreams. Surprising, considering their long naps. But Margot hadn't time to wonder on the complexities of the childhood mind; she had some stargazing to do.

Armed with her grandmother's valise—stocked with her father's telescope and a book she found in the library, *The Constellarium*—she headed for the dirt mound at the opposite end of the Swiss pond to study the sky.

"Mademoiselle deVerona!"

Without stopping her rapid pace, Margot turned and spied Alexandre spilling up on her heels. As usual he wore the uniform of his trade—tan breeches and plain linen shirt. Simple suede boots, unrolled to his thighs, and his unruly mass of hair constantly at battle with the feeble ribbons Lisette used in an attempt to contain. Simple beauty, quietly devastating to her heart. "Ah, Alexandre, won't you join me?"

"But I thought you had wanted to speak to me about the girls?"

"Yes!" Dear, she had forgotten. But what a perfect evening to be out-of-doors. The sky was clear and bright, the air balmy and rich with the scent of scythed grass and freshly moved dirt. The meeting would be held. In her office. "Do join me then. I'm headed for the stars."

The twosome tramped over the uneven grounds that Alexandre explained would soon boast allees of linden and elm and great broderies of fine hedges and chipped granite walks. It would be resplendent, he stated. Fit only for a king.

Margot stopped at the base of the dirt mound, finding it was about two men taller than her. Much higher than she'd assumed it would be when she had spied it standing at the edge of the south terrace.

"You're not going to climb up there?" Alexandre observed with distaste.

"I need an elevated observation deck to see the stars properly."

"So you're going to read the stars and cast astrological charms?"

She shoved the astronomy book into his hands and placed the lit candlestick atop that. "Do you really believe me a witch?"

"I've already said I do not. Though I fancy that might explain your inquisitive mind and predilection for mud. And you do have a concoction of oil and flower blossoms brewing in your room."

"Ah, yes, a potion to beguile unwary men." She tucked the valise under her arm and started upward.

"But your skirts, they'll get soiled," he called behind her.

"That's what wash tubs are for."

"Ah, yes, fool of me to even suggest—"

"I'm winning!"

Margot chuckled as the soil sifted through her fingers. Purchase was slow but invigorating. When she peaked the hilltop she sat with legs crossed inside her skirts and waited for Alexandre to appear with her book and candlestick. "Success!" she declared, as his head bobbed above the dirt and he appeared noticeably exhausted.

He tossed her the book and wedged the candlestick in the dirt near her feet, then collapsed on the soil near her. "Your success comes only because your opponent has labored the entire day under the hot sun and should, by rights, be lying in bed at this very moment. If I had known our meeting would require physical labor, I might have protested."

"But look at the results." Margot stretched her hand

before her, taking in the glistening sky. A perfect evening dotted with sparks of light.

"Indeed," he said as he observed, as if suddenly noticing the delights the sky could offer. But his notice lasted all of three seconds. "Now, about a nursemaid for the girls."

"I know they are rather young," Margot said, as she paged through her book beneath the flickering candle glow. "But you might begin the search for a proper teacher so that in a year, when their schooling should begin, you will not be caught unawares."

"As I was so desperate to replace Trouvelot?"

"Exactly."

"I seem to have done quite well in that selection. Lack of time or not.

"I thank you. But seriously, I can start inquiring if you wish."

"Then I shall leave the task to you, since you are quite capable. And having raised a brood yourself, I'm sure you've done this before."

"Oh, never. My family could not afford a private tutor. I taught my siblings, along with *Maman* and Papa. It wasn't the most eloquent of educations, but sometimes I believe common sense to be far more important than memorizing lists and dates and exactitudes of life. Don't you?"

"You ask that of a man who has trained himself with books and lists and dates and exactitudes of life."

"Well then, I expect you've much you can teach your daughters yourself."

"As can you. But don't you think it rather a shame to begin a child's education too early, pressing figures and notions and all sorts of textbook information on them when they should be skipping about without a care in the world?"

"Your views on child rearing surprise me."

"You think me too lackadaisical?"

"On the contrary, I think you very compassionate to the innocence of youth." But for his own work ethics, she might have expected his views on education to be more stern. How refreshing. Everything she learned about this man only intrigued her more. "You're right, it would be a crime to force the girls into a rigid education too early."

"I should think a bit of education weaved in with song and play would be just the right mix until they are a bit older."

"You've no objections to my finding them a nursemaid that will teach them astrology and read them Descartes?"

"I should be delighted. As long as she's a song at the ready and perhaps a story or two."

His confidence in her skills filled Margot's being with a warm glow. Winning this man's approval was surprisingly heady. With him seated at her side, the night promised to be a good one.

He propped his elbows on his knees and pressed two fingers to his jaw. "Though I do have to wonder about this reverse-handed thing."

"Oh?"

"Yes, today Janette insisted I eat my bread with my right hand, for I normally use my left, else I should become unbalanced and topple from my chair."

"Dear, no."

"Exactly what *are* you teaching my girls, Margot?"

"It is simply an exercise in ambidexterity."

"You don't think my girls have enough to concern themselves with just writing with their favored hands?"

"I shall desist with that exercise if you require it."

"No, no reason to get so defensive. I suppose I should condition myself to expect the unique from a woman such as yourself."

"Meaning?"

"I simply mean you're not of the straight and narrow. Rather delightful, I must say. It'll be difficult to find your replacement. . . ." His voice trailed off, and he made to look at the stars.

Margot couldn't help but blush at his offhand comment, delivered without a thought. Delightful, eh? But still, he could not look directly at her when the conversation turned to personal things. And what she wouldn't give to be held again by his dark gaze, to be surrounded by the deep kindness that he could cast with a blink and a subtle nod of his head.

"So they can continue to write with their left hands?"

"As long as no one witnesses them. You know what they say about people who write with their left hands."

"They are of the devil."

"Indeed."

She dared to touch the back of his hand, resting casually on his knees. "Yet, you just now confessed to writing with your left."

"I do."

"And you are most certainly not of the devil," she said on a breathy tone.

A wry arc tickled the corner of Alexandre's mouth, and Margot suddenly realized what she had spoken. And *how* she had said it. She snapped her fingers away from his hand. Brazen flirt! But it did put a warm glow inside her belly. She liked this comfortable conversation with a man. But now to win back his gaze. "You're not, are you?"

He quirked a brow and cast her a sideways glance. "Of the devil? Did you see a tail the other night?"

The glow in her stomach surged up to heat her cheeks as images of his pale, muscled buttocks birthed in her head. Margot felt sure Alexandre could read her thoughts on her forehead as if a screen displaying them for all to see. She looked to her book, not sure what to say.

"Devil got your tongue?"

She smiled at his teasing comment. "It is the cat that holds my tongue, and I will thank you to leave that incident in the past, as it should remain."

"Forgive me. As I've said before, I'm not usually so forthright around women. It surprises me as well. There is just something about you that loosens my tongue."

"Perhaps you feel as comfortable around me as I you."

"You don't normally feel comfort in conversation?"

"Not with a handsome man!"

"Ah." He blushed, and with a nudge of a smile curling the corners of his mouth, he looked to the sky again.

Margot would take that small smile as triumph for the moment. To be captured by his gaze would come soon enough. She hoped.

"Well, you are," she offered. "Very handsome." With a sigh she sought to change the direction of their conversation. This sort of talk would certainly get them both in trouble. Not that she wouldn't mind a little trouble with this intriguing man . . . "Have you family? Brothers and sisters?"

"I've Mignonne, my sister, and Armand and Adrian."

"Are they here at Versailles as well?"

"All are off on their own. None of the three had a formal education, and . . . bother."

"And?"

He pressed a spread hand to his forehead, then waved his fingers through the air dismissively. "I didn't see a discussion of family histories coming."

"If you'd rather not."

His sigh strafed along Margot's heart. It wasn't a reluctant gesture on his part, perhaps more . . . leery.

"If you must know, my brothers worked the high roads as jewel thieves for a good part of their lives and almost succeeded in enticing my sister into their criminal adventures."

"How fascinating!"

He toyed with the string of wax that ran down the side of the candle. "Running from the guard is neither fascinating nor moral. I thank the Lord both brothers have gone to the good. Adrian lives at the family château south of Montrichard, and Armand is currently a much-respected member of the king's guard. He's recently married and has a son. Stephan, precious thing."

"And your sister?"

"She gave birth to girl last year and is again with child. The queen will not allow her to serve as her bodyguard in such a state—much to Min's protests—so she spends her days at Saint Cyr's."

"She teaches?"

"Yes, fencing and self-defense."

"What a fascinating family you have, Alexandre. And you, how did you happen onto botany?"

He rolled to his stomach and studied her book as she had found a page and spread it flat on her lap. "I've always been interested in nature and how things work. How does a seed become a flower? How, after a plant dies down in the winter, can it come to be renewed, season after season?"

"So you are a wonderer too?"

"A wonderer? Yes, I suppose so." A genuine grin blessed his countenance, almost ticklish in its surprise of its master. "Flowers have always drawn my attention with their wild shapes and sounds—"

"I've never heard a flower make a sound!"

"Did I say *sound*?" He squint his eyelids shut, as if in pain. Or regret for the words just spoken. "I meant . . . color. Yes. That's it."

No, it's not, Margot thought. He really did say sound. And it gnawed at her to find out exactly what he meant by that. Indeed, this man's perception of the world was quite different from her own or that of others.

"I imagine if a flower could make a sound it would be dulcet and true," she offered. "Much like their vivid colors."

"Perhaps." She'd lost him, avoiding the subject with his indifferent tone and a gaze that strayed to the stars. She had come to notice that he did that often. Most especially when the girls brought up the topic of his affliction. Or was it his gift?

A drift of Alexandre's long hair blew across Margot's shoulder. His dark hair and eyes made her wonder if he possessed a bit of Spanish blood. Surely his dark skin tone was not from the sun alone. Combine that with his ineffable perceptions, and he was an exotic breed. But how to classify his genus?

"The night makes it difficult to discuss the gems of the day and their colors," he said. "What constellation do you seek?"

Drawn back to her telescope, Margot lifted the brass cylinder to one eye and closed the other. "Pegasus. This book states it should be visible this month in the northern sky."

"Ah, but you needn't a telescope." She allowed him to take the metal scope from her hands and followed his pointing finger. "See there, between the peak of the pine and the curve of that distant hill? The brightest star there is Enif, I believe, the beginning of your Pegasus."

Framed within the black arabesques of the landmarks Alexandre had described sparkled the bright star Enif. "I do." Margot followed the star to the right and referred to her book to check for the next star. "Oh, it's perfect. Just as the drawing in this book."

"My mother used to love stargazing," he said, his voice far, far away from the quiet chirps of the crickets and faint smell of the swamp.

"The stars offer much to love." Margot touched his hand.

Alexandre reacted quickly, lifting her fingers into his palm and drawing them to his lips. As if to kiss. But . . . not. He paused, suddenly seeming to realize what he was doing.

"If you wish it," she whispered, her heart beating rapidly, expectantly. "Then, you must." Then with a defiant tone to her voice, Margot murmured, "Or I will."

He seemed to toss that idea around for a moment as he studied her eyes—he was really looking into her eyes deeply, for the first time since they had met. Success! And how delicious it felt, swimming in the depths of his gaze. But the moment was brief. Soon Alexandre focused all attention on her hand. He turned it over, exposing the meat of her palm to the warm night air and the drifting sweep of his hair across her fingers. Just as she had done for him days before in his room. As if studying one of his plants to determine its plans for growth, he perused the lines of her palm, drawing the pad of his finger over her flesh.

"My mother could read a man's life in the lines of his palm."

Margot closed her eyes, funneling the sensation of touch directly from her hand. From hand to heart, no other distraction such as sight. *Draw a map,* she thought, *direct me to your heart. I so want to learn the way there.*

The touch of his lips to her palm did not startle, only released a flood of anticipation in her veins to flow like thick syrup through a valley. This kiss was sweet like forbidden pastries. Oh, but if only it were on her lips . . .

"What do I taste like?" she whispered, her eyes still closed.

"Flesh." His voice grew husky and soft as he murmured against her palm. "Salt and woman."

Margot's shoulders slumped, the kiss shattered by cool

air and distance. Why not pink ripples or points? The thrill of the moment quickly dissipated. "Oh."

"You are . . . disappointed?"

"Yes. Well, no. Well . . . yes. It is only, your girls . . ."

Do it now, Margot. You must ask him, else you will never discover the workings of his exotic breed.

"The girls tell me of your affliction. And after a few of your comments regarding the way you hear and see things, I just thought, maybe . . ."

"My affliction, eh?" He stood and brushed the dirt from his breeches. With a rake of his fingers through his hair, he shoved the dark tresses over his shoulder. "I shall have to speak to the twins about spreading rumors of their father to strangers."

"I am hardly a stranger." Margot gathered up her book and stuffed her telescope into the valise, as it seemed he was set on leaving. And quickly.

Fists pumping at his hips, Alexandre descended the dirt mound in a billow of choking dust. Struggling against her skirts and her cumbersome load, Margot gave up halfway and slumped into an indent of the officious dirt.

When he reached the ground, he said with a stab of his finger through the air, "It is not my affliction! Nor am I cursed or bedeviled, as some might believe. It is simply the way I am. And if you do not like it, Mademoiselle—"

"I like it very much!" she called, stopping him in the midst of an air-jabbing tantrum. "I like the way you see the world, Alexandre."

Now silent, Alexandre studied Margot. She tried to force her expression into a pleasing smile while fighting the dust that threatened to choke her silly.

Cursed or bedeviled? What sort of nonsense was he speaking? And what exactly was this affliction that was not his affliction and simply the way he was?

"You see nothing, Margot," he finally said, slipping a

tired hand back through his hair and bundling it into a tight queue behind his neck. "And I see too much. I would accompany you to the château, but I've grown beyond tired and fear I would not be the best company for the remainder of the evening. Shall I send a lackey out?"

"No, I'm perfectly capable. Forgive me if I've offended you, Alexandre. I just . . . just wanted to know you. I've seen you through your girls' eyes."

"Yes, well, those are the eyes of two very young—"

"They've known you longer than I have. And from what I've gleaned from their image of you, I like what I see."

He gave an uncertain nod. "Oh," he said, and turned to walk away.

Margot watched him. His pace was rapid, his gate swinging. The limp in his left leg lended an interesting beat to his movement. But how splendid all the same.

His figure segued with the shadows that surrounded the Orangerie. Margot remained, wedged halfway down the hill, until she felt sure the light that momentarily flashed in the heart of the Orangerie was his. Just long enough to study the room, she surmised, then immediately collapse on his bed. Tired, confused, but hopefully intrigued by the woman whose hand he had just held.

And had kissed.

Margot spread her palm and held the candle close to her hand. There, in the center, just below the crease her mother had christened her heart line, was where he had kissed her. She folded her hand, watching the lines etch deep into her flesh.

Flesh and salt and woman.

She wondered now how Alexandre Saint-Sylvestre tasted.

Seven

*Aren't you glad the final choice
wasn't the King of Mud?*

The devil, that she had been thinking such things about Monsieur Saint-Sylvestre last night! How does he taste? Absolute foolishness. Completely insane. Beyond madness. Scandalously . . . intriguing.

"Watch me, Margot!"

Margot, startled out of her vexing thoughts, watched as Janette slid down a plump pile of hay stacked in the cool shadows of the royal stable. The king and his entourage had left at daybreak for the hunt. What an excellent chance to explore the stables with but a few horses left and all the stablehands running behind their master's mounts.

Giggles of delight and challenges to climb higher filled the musty space. Yesterday's rain had settled into the cracks and crevices with plans to grow into a verdant brew of nature. Margot skimmed her fingers along a time-smoothed wooden stall, following the slender thread of a spider's netting. The master of the web nowhere in sight, she wandered back into her thoughts.

She was not foolish, nor was she insane. Just . . . charmed. Charmed by a man. A kind and gentle man who had no intentions toward her person and did not bully women around with money or power as a certain baron she knew did.

And it was so exciting. Nervous energy hummed through Margot's body at the thought of spending time alone with Alexandre. While at the same time, she feared Cook's warning. She mustn't entertain thoughts of being more than just an employee to Alexandre.

Must she?

No. Certainly not. She was already spoken for. To even imagine developing feelings for a man she could never be more than just a friend to! But to know that her future held a loveless marriage . . . The rest of her life would be spent in the home of a man she thought a bully and a toad. Though the baron had agreed to pay for her schooling, he might never grant her the kindness she had seen in Alexandre's eyes.

And beyond the kindness surged a powerful charge of temptation.

What would be the harm in enjoying the short time she had with Alexandre and his children? Surely she must live life to its fullest, enjoy the freedom she had before being whisked away by the baron to a black life of boredom and dulled emotion? As her mother had said, she must discover who she is before she becomes someone she is not. Maybe Alexandre could help her to see inside to her own desires?

"Margot, we must have more of our story!"

Janette's energetic body plunged against Margot's skirts and upset the two of them into the stack of hay. Golden shards rained over their heads, and only Lisette could rescue the two of them from becoming buried.

"Tell us more about the Princess of Practically Everything and her kittens," Lisette pleaded. "We must know about the hero."

"Yes, the hero," Janette joined in.

Ah, the hero. At the moment there was certainly a perplexing choice. A man who would heartlessly whisk the princess away from happiness and joy, or a man who approached the princess with kindness and a sense of friendship. The heartless man would give the princess the one thing she wanted more than anything, an education. What could the kind man offer?

"I believe," Margot said as she gathered the girls under each arm, "the hero must be a great and generous man. Handsome, yet compassionate. Wise, yet youthful. Intelligent, yet whimsical."

"A prince?" Janette wondered. "Or maybe a king?"

"Oh, yes!" Lisette clapped. "But king of what?"

"Well, I'm not really sure. We already have a king of France and England and . . . hmm . . ." Margot paused to allow the girls to think this problem through themselves. She took great joy in watching their minds hum when left to sort problems themselves. Just as her own mother had encouraged her to think for herself and always, always question.

"King of the horses," Janette said with a grand gesture down the empty stalls.

"No, that's too smelly," Lisette reproved. The curly-topped doll crossed her arms over her chest and set her brows to a furrow as she stirred her brain for a solution. "Hay? No, too scratchy. Trees? No, too terribly boring."

Margot glanced outside to the vast stretch of excavated grounds that would blossom over the years to a formal garden. Hard work. Suitable to keep a man from becoming too emotional, too involved in the pursuit of his own happiness.

Did Alexandre seek happiness? Surely he possessed it in a degree of his own satisfaction. All people found happiness in assorted ways.

Lisette stood and followed Margot's vision across the

grounds, then spun around with a grand declaration. "We must call him the King of Oranges, just like Papa!"

"Oh, yes!" Janette leapt up to dance about with her sister, and the two completely forgot their story as they spun into the courtyard, chanting about sweet oranges and crowns fashioned of orange baubles.

Margot pushed up from her nest and went to stand beneath the half-shadowed arch of the stable doorway. "The King of Oranges," she mused. "And the Princess of Practically Everything?" A smile spread across her face and she hugged herself with crossed arms. "Indeed."

'Twas easy enough to locate the girls as the sun began to set on the silvery line of the Swiss pond. Alexandre could hear their giggles echo through the sky, even above the din of workers digging a trench through the soon-to-be north parterre. Twin circular pools were planned, with the Grotto of Thetis to cap off the northern point. It would be grand with the triple mind-power of Le Nôtre, Le Brun, and Le Vau behind it.

That it had been Nicolas Fouquet's folly that would eventually elevate Versailles to the grandest palace ever surely must haunt the misdirected financier from his prison in Pignerol. Two years earlier, Alexandre's brother, Armand, had helped to bring down the financier who had been extorting funds from the king's coffers in order to feed his own lust for grand architecture. Armand had secured a position in the king's guards through that brave act and had earned himself a lovely bride in the process. A son as well, but that was another story entirely.

How material greed always came back to haunt a man, Alexandre thought as he strolled across the marble courtyard, destined for the stables. Those who wanted more eventually got it. They eventually suffered as well.

As had Sophie.

But he mustn't be so hard on his wife. She had wanted only the life she had once had before meeting up with him. She had belonged to the demimonde, the beautiful young socialites, that her father's position at court had granted her. Truly, it had been his fault Sophie pined for Paris and all its trappings while he could no more afford to decorate her bosom with sparkling jewels than a rose could blossom in the ice-frosted winter.

Sophie taught Alexandre a hard lesson. A night of debauchery comes at a price. A steep price that roped him with a wife, worry, and responsibility. Not that he considered responsibility for his children a hardship. Alexandre enjoyed family, had always desired such. The girls were an endless source of joy.

But never in his wildest dreams had Alexandre thought he'd end up in such an emotion-starved relationship. He had not loved Sophie in the passionate, romantic way he believed a man should love his wife. He had thought her a whore that night nearly five years ago when he'd sought to satisfy his carnal craving for a woman. She had played the part, batting her lashes and rubbing her generous breasts up against his arm. It hadn't been a surprise to wake in the morning to find she was gone. Though she hadn't ransacked his purse for payment. He'd thought that odd at the time. Until four months later, when Sophie Marie Cellier appeared at the Saint-Sylvestre château, her bags in arm and tears streaming down her cheeks. Disowned by her father and cast away, for she was with child.

Could Alexandre have turned her away that day?

Could he have stepped onto a roaring fire barefoot? No. But yes, Alexandre had stepped onto simmering coals that day he took Sophie into his life.

He'd learned much about love and the expectations of

women since then. Of course, he rationally knew all women were not of Sophie's caliber.

But he did love his girls.

And now he could not hear giggles coming from the stables. As he stepped toward the cool shadows of the manure- and straw-tainted horse stable, Alexandre slowed his pace when he overheard Janette's innocent question.

"Why do I miss my mama so much? Sometimes it hurts me right here."

Alexandre tensed his jaw and closed his eyes. He could sense Janette's movement to place her hand over her heart.

"Me too," Lisette's yawning voice chimed in.

"That's not a hurt." Alexandre saw the delicious pink tones of Margot's voice waver before him. "That ache you feel in your heart, Janette, is your mother's memory. Every time you feel it, you know your mama loves you. She'll always be with you, as long as you can feel her in your heart."

"Really?"

"Really."

"But what if my heart stops hurting?"

"There are other ways to bring your mama close to you. Tell me something you remember about her. Something good that makes you smile."

"You mean like when Mama would comb my hair and call me a princess?"

Alexandre smiled at Lisette's memories. His sweet princess with the twisty blond curls. She would grow to be Sophie's double. Already he noticed her quest for the finer things. And she did have occasion to pout until she got her way. Very much like her mother.

"And when Mama would wrap us in her skirts and let us swirl about the room like the queen at a ball?" Janette said.

"What marvelous times you had with your mother,"

Margot sang in her pink waves as the twins' giggles told Alexandre they'd started to dance about the straw. "Show me how you used to dance with your mama. Oh! Alexandre."

"Papa!" Both girls rushed to him and gripped a leg. "We were dancing for Mama!"

"I see that." He looked to Margot, who stood twisting her fists in her skirts, obviously not sure if she should have been speaking so to his children. "I wager your mama is smiling in heaven right now to see your happy faces." He tried to take a step, but the weight of his girls toppled him, and the threesome landed in the hay with a crackle of dry straw and a new barrage of giggles.

"Let's bury Papa!" Janette shouted as she dug into the hay and began to scoop it over his body.

Exhausted but also delighted, Alexandre lay back and let the troops have their way with him. The day had been long. His girls deserved his attention. And a certain enchanting young woman had become too irresistible to shield with his ancient armor of indifference.

Life just seemed too perfect.

Eight

In which the truth is divulged.
But confusion reigns.

After they'd both tucked the girls into bed, Margot followed Alexandre into his bedchamber. A single taper took light at his direction, and he went to shuffle in his desk drawer. "I've your wages."

She scanned the dark, sparsely furnished room. Books were scattered everywhere, and thick beeswax candles were placed here and there, some lying on their sides. A laceless linen shirt lay rumpled at the base of his desk and two pewter tankards sat next to that. Everywhere on the pounded dirt floor sat potted plants in all stages of growth. Many were toppled over, spilling dirt in messy little mounds next to the plantless pottery.

For as meticulous and careful as he was with his plants, that order certainly did not follow him to his personal space. All and all, though, this room seemed irrepressibly Alexandre.

" 'Tis not much, but enough, I hope, to encourage you to continue your watch over my girls. Until a permanent nursemaid can be found, that is."

It was good someone remembered she would not be here for much longer. For as the days passed, that fact seemed to be slipping further from Margot's immediate memory.

"I'm fortunate enough to have room and food here at the château, thanks to Cook. Money is really of no object to me beyond saving for my education and assorted accessories that should please me."

"Your education?"

"Yes, I have plans to attend the Sorbonne."

"Entomology?"

"Am I that easy to read?"

He gave a shrug. "Let's see, butterflies, pig mud, and orange blossoms—stars are a little out of range. . . . Just a guess."

She leaned over his desk and surveyed the assortment of texts lying open and marked with dried strands of grass and leaves. *Le Jardin de Plaisir* by André Mollet. *Herbarum Vivae Eicones* and *Architectura Recreationis*.

"The engravings are remarkable," she said, as she turned the top book and studied a watercolor of a Viceroy tulip. Crisp green and yellow and a sanguine violet flowed inside the black outer lines of the sketch. "It's almost as if I could pick the flower from the page and smell it. Did you color this yourself?"

"Yes, with great difficulty," he said, finally satisfied with his coin count and reaching to give her three livres. "For the week. I hope that is well with your duties?"

"Oh, more than enough." Margot let the coins jingle to the bottom of the pocket sewn inside her skirt, not bothering to count them.

"Why was it difficult for you to color the picture?" she wondered.

He stood and stepped away from the desk. Margot moved the book beneath the candelabrum to study the flawless strokes of cream and olive green that dashed up the stem of the flower on the next page. The bowl of the flower was a light butter yellow with vibrant streaks of violet skittering down from the top center of each wide petal. He'd carefully written the genus, *Viola*.

She noticed now that Alexandre had taken to pacing, his strange silence all too familiar, as at last evening's encounter beneath the stars. *I am not cursed or bedeviled. . . .*

Did his difficulty in painting stem from his odd perception of things? It was a curious notion to entertain.

Settling into the hard chair behind his desk, Margot reached back and pulled up an empty clay pot. He took it, with apologies for the disorder, and set it on a stack of books. She folded her hands on her lap and decided she would not leave until she got some answers. This man intrigued her far too much to simply ignore the urge that pulled within her. She must know him. She simply must.

Before it was too late.

"Tell me why you see the world so differently than I, Alexandre?"

"What makes you believe I see anything differently than you do?"

"The comments you make. You start to describe something, then catch yourself and change the subject. Please trust me. I wish to know you, if only because your silence leads me to believe you'd rather not associate with me."

"That's not true, Margot. I very much enjoy conversing with you."

"As long as you don't have to look at me."

"What?"

She shrugged. Perhaps he wasn't aware of his habit of never meeting her gaze. "Don't you wish to set me straight regarding the rumors of this affliction you possess?"

He stopped pacing. "You have heard rumors?" His expression grew more solemn and pained than usual as he raked a hand through his hair. "I had thought it only the girls who had mentioned it to you."

"Cook has heard them. She said your wife would discuss it often."

"Bother." He sat on his bed, his shoulders falling as quickly as his mood. "Sophie did rather like to talk." He popped up, hands on hips, and just stood there. It appeared his body was ready to begin pacing, but from his steel stance, Margot couldn't be sure. "Socializing was Sophie's occupation, gossip her forte. There wasn't much about me that seemed to please her. Not that I tried as hard as I should have."

Alexandre drew in a deep breath and expelled it. He didn't like to speak of his wife, Margot sensed it. She was surprised he was even admitting this much.

"I've heard no ill words about you. I shouldn't worry that your wife left a legacy of cruelty in her wake. But she did seem to let everyone know you have odd ways."

"This affliction that my girls speak of." Now the pacing resumed, his hands placed on either hip. Tall and lank, he commanded the room with his silent grace. Even the limp seemed so perfect on him. *But a pitchfork?*

"The girls have explained it's nothing to do with your limp. They said . . . well . . . Janette said her mother . . . stabbed you."

He shook his head and spread long fingers through his hair.

"Forgive me if I'm out of place, but your daughters—"

"Janette does have a tendency to blurt things out, doesn't she?"

"I did not cajole them. I wasn't even expecting such an announcement. Oh, I should not concern myself with your personal life. Perhaps I should leave." She stood and sidestepped a pile of empty pots. She had never been one to push, and it was plain he did not wish to discuss this. "Forgive me, Monsieur Saint-Sylvestre."

"Please, call me Alexandre," he rasped in a soft voice that certainly could be tempting in the mere glow of candlelight.

Margot curled her fingers toward her palms and tried not to look into his deep, dark eyes for fear of frightening him from a confession. How could any woman be cruel to this man?

"Sophie did indeed come after me with a pitchfork." He offered her a wry smirk. "I was kissing another woman."

So honest. "So your girls told me."

He gave her a look that seemed to say *What haven't they told you?*

"The other woman was my sister-in-law, Madeleine," he explained. "It was a chaste kiss of gratitude, though Sophie could have had no idea when she came upon us in the garden."

The garden. Margot smiled. The man would be nowhere else.

"She had a tendency to rage very easily. It doesn't pain me much, save in the winter." He smoothed a hand over his left thigh. "For some reason, the cold makes my limbs ache. But as you can see, it does not tax my work."

"That is good to know," Margot said. "I could never imagine you kissing a woman who was not your own wife for any other reason."

"Indeed?"

She flickered her gaze away from his. He had suddenly become whimsical in his demeanor, seeming to thrive on her sudden discomfort with a glee that made her nervous, on guard. Could he know she often found herself dreaming of kissing him? Did he ever dream of kissing her?

To start wondering on such an enticing scenario would surely occupy the entire evening and press her into a compromising situation.

"About your affliction, then," she pressed. "I should very much like to understand, if you would trust me—"

"It's of utmost difficulty to explain unless you yourself have it." He sat on the edge of his desk, which displaced a book and sent it sliding to the floor with a crash. He gave it no concern save to push the remaining stack of opened notebooks and texts away with his elbow. "Never in my life have I encountered another who sees the world as I do."

She could see the struggle within him, pulling at his heart, silencing his words, and in his dark eyes. Eyes that pleaded for her to leave him to his secrets but at the same time glittered with the urge to tell, spill his soul, and have it out in the open for once and for all.

"You can trust me," she whispered. "I've no designs on gossip; you should know that by now. I'm not like the other women here at the château."

"That is plain." His voice rasped out the statement, startling Margot with its deep longing.

Longing. The same feeling she had had the other night when she'd spied him showering. And just last night, when he had pressed that startling kiss to her palm. 'Twas as if some part of her, some deep, inner vortex that she was not aware of, would act of its own volition when the time was right. Thus far the time had been *almost* right, just enough to waken that tingling within.

But it was not right by him. In fact, he seemed nervous, apprehensive.

"Do you wish me to leave?"

"No, not at all. You do tend to bring up the most uncomfortable topics. I should expect as much from you by now."

She shrugged, appreciative of his knowledge of her ways. He had observed her. He knew things about her. The realization gave her a secret thrill. *Would the baron ever afford the time to get to know her?*

"I fear you may be too curious for your own good one of these days. But I shall grant you the truth of my *affliction,* as it were, so I may clear the rumors from your mind."

Finally she would learn what made Alexandre tick.

"Believe me, I've searched medical texts for answers, but I've not found notation of any of my symptoms. There are days I wonder if this is all in my head, the result of a skewed view of the world. Overactive imagination. I just don't know."

He rubbed his palms together, took a deep breath. The muscle in his jaw flexed, attracting Margot against all wishes to remain, well . . . unattracted.

"Since birth I've seen the world far differently than most. Though I wasn't immediately aware the way I saw and heard things was different until my brothers and sister began to tease. I just assumed everyone saw and heard in the same manner I did."

Intrigued, Margot leaned forward and rested her elbow on his desk, securing her chin in her palm. Her skirts slipped silently over her ankles. His body was close to hers. Verdant smell of earth surrounded Alexandre like a garden welcoming her exploration.

"You see"—he held both hands before him as if to frame an object far away between his fingers—"when I look at something, I do not see it as you do. Well, yes, I do. I do and I don't. Oh, to explain this is most difficult."

She touched his wrist, startling him. "Do try."

He closed a hand over her wrist gently, considering for a moment before releasing her. She still touched him. He would allow it.

"Quite simply, I see colors and shapes and often taste flavors in an object as opposed to what you might term, well . . ."

He looked about, twisting right and left at the waist. "Let's use the desk here as an example."

Margot smoothed her thumb along the narrow wood rim of the desk, fascinated, as he continued. He had chosen to reveal a deeply secret part of himself. So unconscious of shame or humility. The knowledge made her glow. Excitement rushed through her veins; her breathing grew heavy.

"What do you see?" he prompted her.

She studied the object before her and said, "A desk piled with books on botany, pens and inkwell, and two crumpled pages which I presume hold unsatisfactory drawings."

"And I see a vanilla streak piled with containers of fruity letters."

Stunned, she reexamined the books, studied the drawings of flowers. No sign of fruit. Not a single orange tucked in the brilliant green foliage, nor a cherry dangling in the drawing of a cherry tree. As for containing anything, well, she supposed the idea of the pages containing text . . .

"I don't understand. Do you not see a book?" She held up *The Garden of Pleasure*. "Does it not appear a rectangle with a smooth red leather cover?"

"Actually the color is jagged and cold," Alexandre offered astutely.

"Jagged and cold?" She thought about it a moment.

Alexandre observed Margot's struggle to understand. Here he was, revealing his deepest secret to a woman he had known all of a week. What was he doing?

He hadn't even thought to resist her innocent plea to know him. It had been years since he'd told anyone. Sophie, of course, had laughed at him, ridiculed him, and then beckoned him to keep his mouth shut lest he be accused of witchcraft. She had been so ashamed of his "affliction."

But Margot deVerona was a completely different breed of woman. He could trust she would not falsely judge him. He wanted her to know. He *must* be able to trust her. He had revealed too much to turn back now.

Alexandre found he held his breath as he awaited Margot's reaction. It must be favorable, it must—

"The color red is jagged and cold?" she said again.

"Yes." Anticipation made his answer a mere gasp.

She leaned back in the chair, her eyes flittering over the contents of his desktop, then murmured, "Well, that's just . . . peculiar."

He expelled his breath. Damn! The usual reaction. He'd expected so much more from this woman.

His fists clenching before him, he could not quelch the anger that had simmered for years. "Peculiar? *You* are calling me peculiar?"

She straightened. "What do you imply by that?"

"I merely mean that I find it difficult to comprehend a woman who chases butterflies in order to souse them, and one who spies on naked men—"

"I was not spying!"

"Oh? So you make it a habit to gaze upon naked men unawares?"

"That was quite an accident!"

"You cannot call me the peculiar one. Everyone thinks you're a witch."

"You said you did not believe such nonsense."

"Then why are you so quick to judge me?"

"I—" She cut off her retort and looked away, her eyes not fixing on a single object for more than a moment. "You are right. But I didn't mean for you to take my statement of peculiarity in such a way."

"Really." He snapped his arms before his chest. "And how should a man take a declaration of peculiarity?"

"You are too defensive, Alexandre. I merely meant—"

"I have every right to defend myself against feeble accusations and vicious names."

"There is nothing wrong with being peculiar. I would much rather be thought of as peculiar than when left with the only other option of normal."

"I rather favor normal myself."

"Normal is bland, boring, dull."

"Nothing wrong with being dull."

She touched his shoulder, and though he wanted to flinch, Alexandre stayed himself. His hard exterior, the armor, had been peeled away, and he hadn't time to re-fasten the leather straps. But he still wore the chain mail. One last raiment of protection.

He had thought she would not judge.

"What you've just described to me is so out of the ordinary. I need to learn more. You are a kind and elegant man, Alexandre. As close to normal as anyone should ever wish. I'm sorry to have used the word so loosely."

Kind and elegant? Alexandre swallowed. He'd never received such a compliment. Wasn't quite sure what even to do with it. His mail had loosened, and he felt as though it might slip away if he were not careful.

"Forgive me for raging. I have a tendency to be quite defensive after years of being persecuted by Sophie."

"I'll not do that, I promise. Please, will you tell me more?" She came around in front of him, her eyes glittering with the candle glow. A touch of her finger to his cheek felt like a winter snowflake melting upon his flesh. Delicate and magical. Too brief the sweetness.

He had been as quick to judge as he'd expected her to be. He'd blown up before hearing her out. Perhaps she *could* accept. Certainly he knew if he walked in her shoes and she were the one exclaiming such fantastical lies, he would be doubtful.

But they weren't lies.

Margot moved to the desk and lifted the herbarium text. "Tell me about this. What do you see?"

Very well, one more chance. The damage had already been done. But perhaps with careful repair work, a more exact explanation . . .

He took the book Margot held, opened it, and drew his finger down the page of letters. A multitude of colors flashed at him as he scanned the words. "If I were to read a line from this book, it may take me mere seconds."

He zoned in on the word *spade*. A pretty word for the glossy violet *P* and the elegant gold *D* framing it in. "Then again, it might take me over an hour for the explosion of colors that burst from the lines on the page. At times I become so passionately consumed with the beauty of each individual letter that the words lose all meaning and it is the blend of colors that captivates my very soul. It is only with great difficulty and stern concentration that I can do it."

He allowed her a long silence as she considered his explanation. Dark blond brows narrowed to the center of her forehead, and she screwed her lips into an interesting pucker as she traced her fingers over the words in the book he held. She was trying to understand. Desperately. But Alexandre knew that unless she could actually see through his eyes, it could be only fantasy for her. She might come to accept but never understand. Not completely.

Ah, but the fact that she had not turned and run conditioned this woman in his soul. He should not have raged at her. She was not like Sophie, who had first feared his different ways and then had grown to put them down, feeling he was genuinely afflicted and not up to standards as a normal man.

Margot, he felt, might never lower him with a misinterpreted summation of his character. *I'd much rather be thought of as peculiar.* She wasn't like anyone else. And up until then, *no one* else had ever interested Alexandre.

For some reason, he relaxed, felt not so apprehensive as when he had been in the past when his secret was discovered. This woman he could trust to not misunderstand or try to exploit his world. Such a refreshing experience.

"And what color is this word?" she asked, extending the book toward him with her finger pressed to a short run of letters.

"It is not so much the words," Alexandre said as he began to read. "Each letter is different in tone and succulence of color."

"Succulence? That sounds rather . . . delicious."

"Indeed. The word is *flower*. That one is easy enough. You see here, the *F* is easily recognizable because it is violet, a deep, fathomless violet that might drown a man if he were to fall into it. Yet the *L* is always rather difficult for me because it is a light golden hue, much the same as an *R.*"

She snapped the book back and pored over the page of what Alexandre knew—from what his brothers had told him—were simply lines of black letters on white paper. But what he perceived was so much different. And so much better.

Expelling a heavy sigh, Margot slumped against the stiff chair back and laid the book on the table. "I cannot understand."

"I would be a fool to ask as much of you."

She shot forward. "But I can believe."

Those words were so good to hear. Alexandre took a deep breath. Unconditional acceptance.

He'd never once in his lifetime come upon an individual whose sensory perception of the world and all its trappings was as confused as his. For all he knew, he might be the only one with such a gift. For truly it was a gift to have letters enhanced with color, and sound decorated with distinct and memorable colors. He had known nothing else. This was his world.

And he had just allowed Margot deVerona inside.

He leaned over the desk and drew a finger over the sketch he had watercolored. "The tulip is a mixture of variegated rectangles, with each variety of color and genus adding more or less points."

"Yes, go on," she said, eagerly flipping the page to another print.

For many minutes Alexandre described the prints he'd painstakingly colored, page after page, not fearing rejection or repulsion, in fact spurred on by Margot's passionate interest. Finally he stopped, both palms pressed to the surface of the desk, and waited for Margot's analysis of his crazy way of viewing things.

But she still wasn't ready to end the description process.

"I wonder," she mused teasingly. The pink tip of her tongue glanced out to moisten her lower lip. "What do you see when you look at me?"

Her liquid-blue eyes danced defiantly, hope-filled. The hard jewel color flowed into delicious waves of peace. He saw her features, her wide, inquiring eyes and bow lips and pert little nose, as all others would see them. Or so he assumed. But surrounding—and somehow coating—that beauty flowed the blue waves of peace, as if an aura encapsulating her body. "Serenity," he said. And then he quickly added, "Topped with a dollop of mud."

She quirked a brow, taking his description to mind with a blush and a smile. For such a thoroughly independent woman, he liked her sudden bursts of modesty. Almost as much as he liked her rambunctious verve. The same verve that had enticed her to spy on him the other night.

"And what of sound? You mentioned that earlier. Do you not hear words the same?"

"Definitely the spoken word *means* exactly the same to me as it does to you. Sounds the same, as well. But I have a feeling you've never *seen* a voice before, have you?"

She sprang to her feet. "Like the other day when I was talking and you started tapping the air before me?"

"Exactly. I've never fallen out of my protective concentration like that before. I've become quite good at guarding myself around others. I have developed a tendency to shun crowds for the overwhelming sensory overload."

"I couldn't even imagine. All those shapes and colors and sounds floating about you, and each relating back to the incorrect sense. I should become so confused if a color were to make a sound or a sound were to appear before me as a color!"

"I've never known life any other way. In fact, this affliction, as Sophie took to labeling it, is really my gift. I shouldn't wish to see the world the plain, flat way that has so often been described to me by my family."

"No, of course not," she muttered, awe widening her eyes, and brightening her tone. "Now, as for sounds."

"Would you like me to show you?"

"Do you think you can?"

"I should like to try."

Eager to share with someone who did not judge, Alexandre moved around behind Margot. It had been a long time since he had held a woman. And even when he had held Sophie, he'd never really allowed himself to relax, to enjoy the sensory experience of woman. It was so easy with Margot. Her hair smelled of nature just after a rainstorm, so fresh and new. The curve of her arm as he skimmed his fingers down her sleeve spoke of grace. The heat of her body alerted him to the sensations he was trying to ignore, had been successful in ignoring until then.

Mon Dieu, but he desired this woman.

But now was no time to mix desire with the pleasure of allowing this woman to discover him. He slipped his arms over hers and clutched the wrist of her left hand. "Is this the hand you write with?"

"Actually, I use both."

"Ah, yes, to keep in balance, eh?"

"You should give it a try sometime. I'll have your girls writing with both hands before the summer is over."

"Perhaps I could then employ them when it comes time to seed, twice the work done at twice the speed. You are indeed peculiar, Margot."

"But you like me that way."

He smiled. "I do."

"You servant of the devil, you."

"Yes, well, only on Saturdays."

"Alexandre, I do believe you made a jest."

At that, he could only chuckle. Where was his chain mail now? Most likely puddled around his ankles. He was totally exposed, more naked than he had been when she'd witnessed him showering. And to tell the truth, it felt . . . right.

"You make me relax, Margot. A good thing," he whispered against the delicate curves of her ear. To move a hairbreadth closer would find his lips upon her flesh. So close to surrender. To answering the long-muted desires that stirred within.

But not yet. He mustn't lose this moment.

"Now, I shall use your left hand, for it is the hand I use."

"What are you going to do?"

"I'm going to let you slide your fingers along the colored waves of your voice." As he said that, he slid his fingers over hers. "Now, speak, say anything. Just . . . don't stop."

"Hmm, well . . ."

He lifted her hand and placed it in the air before them.

The heat of his touch did things to Margot's insides that made it rather difficult to concentrate on talking. Suddenly the notion of touching sounds lost strength and was replaced with the notion of touching Alexandre. Or, rather, Alexandre touching her. Margot wanted to close her eyes and enjoy the scintillating pressure of his touch, the warmth that radiated from his flesh to hers.

"Margot?"

"Er, yes, speak. Let's see . . ."

His whispers entered her thoughts as haunting wisps. "Pink, the color of shell . . ."

"My name is Margot deVerona."

". . . ripples glistening in waves . . ."

"Your name is Alexandre." He danced her hand in the air before her, seeming to touch down in taps on what she could only determine were the pink waves he saw when she spoke. Fascinating. "You have two lovely daughters—"

". . . The ripples shimmer when your voice heightens in pitch. . . ." He danced her hand up a notch and stopped with her silence.

"They are Lisette—"

"She is an amber line." He bounced her hand gently.

"And Janette."

"Perfect cool balls of aqua," he whispered. Down their hands slid, as if on a child's play slide.

Margot's breast warmed as his caress drew firmly around her waist and he nuzzled his nose against her neck, still whispering commentary on the rising colors and glistening waves. She closed her eyes to envision the colors and saw before her syrupy waves of pink that indented with each touch of her hand and then sponged out as she left them.

"Speak," he whispered. "Tell me what you can see. Do you sense the colors?"

"I do see them. I think. They are like waves on the

ocean gently gliding beneath the sun. But pink waves."
She smiled. She could only imagine the sight, couldn't
really understand if Alexandre saw the colors in his mind
or if indeed actual, tangible pink waves formed in the
air before him.

"Your giggles coat the waves in gild," he whispered.
"And they are warm."

"Mmm, so are you." She tilted her head back to rest
against his shoulder. "I like hearing through your eyes.
It is a delicious experience." Her hand wobbled before
her. "I understand something now."

"What is that?"

"All your life you must have had to hide this from
others."

"Exactly. Or they would think me possessed, not right
in the head."

"Yes, yes, and because you have worked so diligently
to hide this gift, other aspects of yourself have also become hidden. Like your emotions, your feelings. It makes
such perfect sense to me now. Your shy glances. Your
fear of conversation. Yet, the twins. You are always laugh-
ing and carefree with them, because the girls accept you
so easily. There is nothing wrong with you to them, and
so you can be relaxed and yourself around them. That is
why your wife and you . . . well . . ."

Her hand ceased to glide in bouncing waves. She'd hit
exactly on the nail. And he didn't care much for hearing
it out loud.

"You've nothing to fear from me. I want to understand,
and I will. Never would I ridicule you for the man that
you are. Open up to me, Alexandre. Show your feelings.
You are safe with me."

His sudden movement caught her off guard. The kiss
he seared to her mouth stopped Margot's words cold. Or,
rather, stopped them hot. For hot and hard and greedy,
the kiss stole her breath from her mouth and teased her

senses to grasp once again for those dancing waves of color.

But as quickly as she could focus on the pure joy of having him kiss her, it was done.

He pulled away with profuse apologies.

Margot couldn't help but chuckle, even while she glided two fingers over her lips. "You mustn't apologize for allowing your feelings to show. Alexandre, that was fire and urgency and everything you were just feeling, was it not?"

He turned and paced to the window, gripping one hand in and out of a fist near his thigh. "I've overstepped the line between employer and employee. I should not have allowed the armor to slip. That was foolish of me."

Armor? Ah, yes, his shyness, the cold facade he'd developed over the years. Not about to let him escape this new venture into emotion and trust, Margot drew her hand down his arm and forced him to meet her gaze. "But it was you. Wasn't it?"

He nodded. "Yes, it was completely me. Perhaps . . . for the first time in my life." He offered a smile that danced between confusion and utter horror.

"This is me." Margot slid her hand along his jaw, directing his face down toward her own.

Her kiss was slow and experimental. The scent of earth shrouding his being, slipped into the background. The taste of wine and heat streamed from his pores, his lips, his tongue. The sound of his want purred deep in his throat, and the texture of his body grew hard against hers as she surrendered to her curiosity.

Yes, this might be scandalous, the nursemaid seducing her employer. Yes, perhaps she hadn't given Alexandre the proper amount of time to grieve his absent wife. And yes, she had gone beyond brazen in initiating such contact when her own virtue had already been spoken for.

But no, she would not deny her heart. And at that very

moment her heart demanded satisfaction. Bless her mother for instilling the quest in her soul; this was exactly who she wanted to be.

Alexandre broke away but did not breech the distance. "This isn't right."

"Why isn't it? Did you not want to kiss me?"

"I did. But your position—Margot, I am your employer."

"An excuse made up by a man afraid of his own emotions."

He opened his mouth to speak but let his lips fall together in silence. And then, "You deem to know much about me, Margot."

"I'm learning," she countered with a step forward. Their bodies touched at the waist, at the arms, the thighs, and hips. He teetered but did not step backward. "Does my interest in you threaten the security of the self-imposed privacy you've grown to cherish? Are Janette and Lisette the only females allowed to know you? To care for you? To touch you? You have just revealed a very private part of yourself to me, Alexandre. Why now can't I learn *this* part of you?" She touched his lips.

"Mademoiselle, I should warn you, impropriety lingers—"

"On these lips?" She stood on tiptoe and closed her eyes, pursing her lips but inches from his face. "Perhaps you should silence my words before impropriety has a chance to leap out."

Determined not to open her eyes, Margot felt a slow triumph as Alexandre seemed to relax, his arms settling and his rigid stance smoothing into a pose that brought his breath across her lips. *Please,* she begged silently. *You can trust me.*

Gentle pressure eased along her mouth. Not his lips. The firm press of his finger skimmed the plump center of her upper lip. Margot shuddered. She wondered what color he viewed her lips to be. Or perhaps they were a distinct shape or succulence? Didn't matter, he could study her body parts for as long as he liked.

Too soon she felt nothing on her mouth. She flashed her eyes open to find Alexandre studying the ceiling, following something. . . . "What is it?" Expecting to spy a large insect skittering across the ceiling beams, instead there was nothing.

"I cannot do this. Not—yet. Forgive me, Margot, you are the most delightful woman I have ever held in my arms, but I fear if I hold you too long I should never wish to let go."

He ran a nervous finger down the front of his dirt-smudged shirt and hooked it at his waist. Just as quickly, he retraced his path and cleared his throat.

"What is wrong with that?"

Alexandre flinched as she touched his shirtsleeve, her forefinger barely grazing his arm. "Margot, you are beautiful. I—"

Margot raised her chin and glued her gaze to his darting eyes. "Then what is the problem?"

He gripped her hand and led her to the door, opening it as an invitation to leave. "I—you must go now."

Too shocked to do any more than follow direction, she stepped into the hallway and turned to reply, but the door quickly shut. Margot stood there, hand raised to pose her question. A perplexing wonder popped into her head.

He said he didn't wish to let me go.

Then why had he?

Nine

The French Inquisition begins questioning.
(Yes, well, we are in France.)

The day was a hot one. High noon wielded a merciless sword of heat to Alexandre's work-stressed muscles. He lifted his straw hat from the lip of a wooden planter and plopped it on his head. The shade of a thick-headed orange tree beckoned. He surrendered to the cool allure of the shadows with little protest from his usually staunch work ethic.

For some reason, these past few days had seemed a little more relaxed, a little less tense than usual. When usually life should be met before sunrise, and followed and itemized, and practiced and labored over—no, lately it just seemed to simply *happen*.

Quite a new experience.

Alexandre leaned back, set his elbows in the dirt that filled the planter and fed the root ball with vital nutrients. Off in the distance the Swiss pond glimmered so brightly, he had to look away or be blinded by ten suns worth of light. A sharp sight that put the taste of copper on his tongue.

A bronze flower floated through the sky toward him, wavering and darting here and there. On second glance, it was a butterfly. Trying to give up the bad habit of sousing himself on eucalyptus, no doubt.

Suddenly the glimmering gold insect dropped. And landed on Alexandre's leg.

Careful not to dislodge the fragile butterfly from its spot, Alexandre sat up and bent to study the creature. A portion of its scaled forewing had been torn from the lace-edged upper peak. Might have been attacked by a bird.

The insect did not startle when he carefully lifted it by its fuzzy brown abdomen for closer inspection. Before meeting Margot, he might not have given the creature a second thought, would have merely brushed it aside and went on with his duties. But to recall how Margot had so gently caressed the insects beneath the eucalyptus tree, as if they were breakable treasures one must only behold and never destroy, Alexandre could not now disregard the butterfly.

He knew nothing about insects save a few genus names he'd picked up in various florilegia and herbarium texts. Whether or not this wounded soldier would survive such a bite was beyond him. Margot might know.

So she wanted to study entomology? Fine goal for a woman. Not unthinkable for one so bright and perceptive. So what was she doing here at court when she might be studying in Paris at the Sorbonne?

Seducing you.

And doing a rather fine job with the task.

A swish of skirts, the sound mossy in color, directed Alexandre's attention to the Orangerie entrance, where Margot appeared with smiling face and swinging arms.

"I just laid the girls down for a nap. They deserve a good rest after their jog around the château this morning. What have you got there?"

He patted the planter beside him, and Margot sat in the shade of the orange boughs. Opening his palm, Alexandre displayed the butterfly. "It landed on my leg.

Looks like it battled a bird, though I can't be sure who
to claim as the victor."

Margot's delicate touch brushed his palm as she studied the butterfly, her breath rasping across his wrist.
Worry over the winged insect fled, to be replaced by a
wanting hardness in his breeches. Damn, but that feeling
had taken him unawares. Not an entirely unwarranted
feeling though. Much the way he had felt when he'd
kissed her last night by the flicker of candlelight.

Damn good kiss, too.

"It's similar to the others, but it looks to be a male."

"How can you tell?"

She shrugged and pressed her fingers gently over the
abdomen as if one were to test the bone of their littlest
finger for fractures. "I can feel its sperm sac. Quite a
well-endowed gentleman indeed."

And if she should glance down to his lap she might
have reason to classify yet another hardened gentleman.
Alexandre held his grounded patient before Margot's face
to draw her attention away from his own . . . difficulties.
If a simple touch caused him this much disturbance—
hell, it had been a long time since he'd been aroused by
a woman's touch. Too long.

Ah, but it proved he was a man. A man who could
indeed feel again. And enjoy the pleasure of a simple,
unexpected kiss. Perhaps this matter of seduction wasn't
so terrible after all.

"I should think he'll survive if kept away from birds.
But how to do that is another question entirely."

Her careful study of the butterfly's body and gently
splaying open of its wings intrigued Alexandre. He
looked across her curly head and drew in a deep breath.
The quiescent scent of the orange blossoms did not disturb the vivid vanilla that slathered his tongue with every
thought of her name. Margot. Margot . . . "Margot."

"Yes?"

"Huh?" Alexandre shook his eyes open and focused on the grounded butterfly and its inquisitive examiner.

"You said my name?"

"I did? Oh, I did. Margot, er—so you said the girls were sleeping?"

"They were drifting off to Nod as I left their room. I think I'm going to take this patient to my room and keep an eye on it for a day or two. It was kind of you to save it for me, when you might have just tossed it aside as most men would do. Thank you, Alexandre."

She kissed him. He'd not a moment to gauge what was coming, and so her lips landed his quickly, softly. Like a butterfly falling into his clutches.

"Oh." She pulled back and granted him a flash of her sun-kissed lashes. "I seem to lose all professional protocol when in your presence, Monsieur Saint-Sylvestre. Do forgive me."

But her wink did not lend itself to sincerity.

As Margot rose and dashed for the hundred steps, Alexandre once again found himself lingering on the divinity of Margot deVerona's person. That a man such as he, widowed and certainly scarred by marriage, should even allow a woman to get so close to him—to kiss him even—was unthinkable.

That he had confessed his secret last night was the most remarkable of all. And she did not treat him as though he were afflicted today. She had not even mentioned it. How refreshing!

There was something about Margot deVerona that enchanted the hell out of Alexandre. And made things quite stiff.

"Lisette, wake up!"

Janette plunged onto the thickly stuffed velvet counterpane. The bed ropes creaked. Ruby's limbs splayed this way and that as the girl jumped upon the tester in an attempt to wake her sister.

"What is it?" Lisette snuggled deeper into the sheets until but the crown of her head showed. "I was"—*yawn*—"sleeping."

"You won't believe what I just saw, Lisette. You won't never believe me." She wriggled down next to her sister and lifted the counterpane.

Yawn . . . and *sigh.* "Tell me, then."

"I saw Papa kiss Margot! On the lips!"

"You're a silly bunch of weeds, Janette. Papa cannot kiss Margot because she is our nursemaid. Now go back to sleep!"

"Even ask Ruby."

Lisette peeked out from under the blanket, granting her sister complete awareness. And Ruby. If Ruby said it was so, then it was so. "Really?"

"For true and real," Janette gasped. "Their faces got real close and then they kissed."

Lisette pushed up and sat upon her pillow. She eyed Ruby, who was held straight out, arms' length, by Janette for interrogation, as was the usual drill whenever Janette needed to prove her words. Which was often.

Ruby didn't blink an eye.

Lisette caught her head in her hands, then, reason kicking in, she asked, "Was it Papa who kissed Margot, or was it Margot who kissed Papa?"

"What difference does that make?"

"Just tell me, Janette, which was it?"

"Maybe it was Margot who kissed Papa. But I don't understand—"

"If it was Papa who kissed Margot first, then that means he loves her. But if Margot kissed Papa, then it is she who loves him." Lisette paused, gave Ruby the eye, and nodded decisively. "It was Margot who kissed Papa."

"Isn't it fabulous?" Janette squealed. She took to hugging and rocking Ruby effusively.

"Papa cannot kiss any lady but Mama," Lisette commanded her jiggling sister. "It is not right!"

"Mama is not here to be kissed. I think it perfectly fine. It is the Princess of Practically Everything and the King of Oranges. Just like the story. Come, Lisette, say you think it good."

Lisette crossed her arms and thought for a moment. Finally she announced, "I cannot say just yet. I have to think."

"But the story—"

"It's a dumb story. Now get off the bed, and take that nasty Ruby with you."

"But—" Stricken by her sister's sour behavior, Janette and Ruby slid off the bed and went to sit on the floor by Papa's chamber door. "We think it splendid, don't we, Ruby?"

"And so the Princess of Practically Everything decided she would tend the gardens alongside the King of Oranges. Off in the distance the kittens bounced about in the blue meadow, chasing butterflies."

"A blue meadow?" Janette squealed merrily. "Margot, you are beginning to sound like Papa. There's no blue meadows."

"Certainly, there are—"

"Would a princess ever kiss a king?" Lisette suddenly interjected.

Margot paused and studied her curly topped pupil. A calculated glitter flashed in the child's eyes. Very different from any look she'd received from her thus far. Almost eerie.

"Well, certainly she might," Margot said, thinking a fantastical fairy tale could have any of its characters doing whatever they might choose. "And certainly the king may kiss the princess if he should desire."

How her tale had come to reflect real life. Or had she knowingly made it so? Certainly she had based a few of the characters on real life. . . .

"Has the king ever kissed the princess?"

Janette's eager question startled Margot so thoroughly, she had to stand and walk from the girls' bed to get her wits about her. This talk of kissing was a bit threatening. A strange feeling to receive from four-year-old girls.

"What about the queen?" Lisette continued what bordered on becoming an interrogation. Margot shouldn't wonder if the Inquisition were stuffed in beneath the girls' bed. "Shouldn't the queen be quite upset that the king is kissing a princess?"

"There is no queen. Not in my story." Margot rubbed her arms to alleviate the chill that had suddenly overcome her.

"I thought this was *our* story," Janette whined.

"Indeed, you are right." Margot had been the one to press the boundaries of what should have been a simple fairy tale. And now she was paying for it. Time to change the subject. "I think I recall Cook saying she needed taste testers for her blueberry tarts this afternoon. Perhaps we should leave our story for another day?"

"But—" Lisette started to say, but Janette's squeal of delight drowned out the blond inquisitor's question.

Saved from the inquisition, Margot thought as she followed the girls up the stairs to the kitchen. Now, where had that line of questioning come from? And why was she feeling so nervous when they were but innocent little girls simply being curious?

Because it is their mother who is the missing queen. You know it, her conscience whispered. *Children are very smart. They can sense the minute changes in their world.*

And by allowing herself to become close to Alexandre, Margot had disturbed Janette and Lisette's world.

Legs crossed, sitting in the wicker chair before the kitchen hearth, Margot cupped her chin in her hands. The twins had each taken a tart outside to sit and eat, for they wanted to watch Pierceforest truss up the boar killed on the hunt that morning. While fleetingly aware of Cook's striped gray skirts bustling to and fro, Margot's mind was on Cook's announcement of the fête to be held that night.

She loved a grand ball, even if it did require one to dress far fancier than necessary. There was still the crimson plush in her trunk that she'd yet to soil. Most likely she would have to wear that one for the baron's arrival. The duchess had warned her she must look her absolute best when greeting her future husband for the first time.

Well, she could hardly consider an imploring shout to become more feminine a warning, but surely the duchess had meant she must learn slowly, in her own time. Most certainly the baron should not approve of her becoming uppity, frail, or gossipy, as most of the court women were prone to.

Wonder, wonder, wonder . . .

For certain most women would be on the arm of a handsome rogue that evening. Margot had no qualms about attending by herself. Nothing at all wrong with that.

Though it would be nice to dance in the arms of a tall, handsome, dark-haired man. With arms so strong they could spin her about forever, then close her in an intimate hug. His deep obsidian eyes would see no one but herself. And when she spoke to him, he would become enthralled in an enchantment of pink waves.

A clang of metal against stone startled Margot out of

her wondering. Cook stood behind the pine table, her own chin cupped in a meaty palm, her head shaking as she eyed Margot with a reproving stab. "Wondering again?"

"He's simply a marvel," Margot spilled out. "I was just wondering if he might attend the fête this evening.

"He?" Cook straightened and crossed the floor. No gentle smile creased the folds of her face now. Only a deep concern that made Margot sink deeper into her chair. "If you tell me the *he* in particular is Monsieur Saint-Sylvestre—"

"What is wrong with that?" Springing to her feet, Margot dodged Cook's grasp and spun before the fire, her hands at her hips as she swayed to an imaginary dance. "It's not as if he's married any longer."

"Margot—"

"He's a very solid man, you know. Not so terribly handsome as to attract the court *precieuses,* though extremely charming. And even though he's rather slim, the space he fills, he fills well. So unlike that toady baron."

Margot was not about to let Cook's heavy exhalation work against her own dreams. She had every right to enjoy herself before she was married. What was wrong with dancing with a friend?

"The baron shall never know." Margot went to Cook and pulled her warm, pudgy hands into her own. "Please understand, I've no intention of harming Monsieur Saint-Sylvester. I want only to enjoy his company."

"It is not him I worry for, child. What of his children? You have allowed them to become attached to you, and in one month's time you shall leave them forever."

"I've allowed nothing, Cook. It is my job to watch after Lisette and Janette. They both know I am watching them only until their father can find a permanent nurse-maid."

Another silent reproof from Cook's eyes set Margot at defense. "What?"

"As I was dishing up their tarts, the girls told me they saw you kissing their father this morning."

Margot's sway halted abruptly, her skirts swishing against her ankles. "What?"

"You heard me. Did you kiss Monsieur Saint-Sylvestre?"

The girls had seen? Now, when had they been out of their beds? And which kiss—oh, that quick little peck in the garden?

"It was more a kiss of gratitude than anything." 'Twas a good thing they had not witnessed her brazen spying the other night. "What else did the girls say?"

"I'm a might concerned for Lisette. She doesn't favor anyone but her mother kissing her father. Though the bouncy dark one has already christened you her new mother. Don't you see, child? You're interfering in three lives, not just one."

"And what of my own life?" Margot wanted to look away, but Cook caught her chin and held her gaze. Such wisdom, gentle but firm, in her gray, heavy-lidded eyes.

"I know you seek the passion you will be denied with your marriage to the baron, but it's not wise, the path you've chosen. And you'll remember, you *did* choose to fulfill the marriage agreement. It's just a fairy tale, this dream of finding love before it is too late."

The Princess of Practically Everything and the King of Oranges a fairy tale? Never!

"Cook, don't be overly dramatic. I don't seek love, only . . . the kind of presence Alexandre has to offer."

"Presence? You don't know what you're talking about."

"Being with Alexandre is like being with an old friend or a cherished treasure." She mustn't elaborate beyond that. If Cook were to know that she often fantasized about kissing him and having him touch her . . . "I like spending time with him." *And kissing him.* "The girls as well. And I won't be denied this pleasure. I simply won't!"

Enough of the heavy condescension. She had a piglet to feed and a ball to plan for.

Ten

Enchant me not . . .

Sometimes children have a way of putting things *just so* that it makes it impossible for a father to refuse them anything.

"But you must attend, Papa," Janette had whined in a sleepy voice that was punctuated by Ruby's shaking head. "Margot will be there all by herself. You cannot leave her to sulk around the potted o-lander all evening."

"What if she should nod off and fall into one?" Lisette had added in manufactured horror. "Your trees, Papa!"

Very well, then. Just a moment or two, to ensure Margot did not nod off in one of the potted oleanders. Or, rather, *o-landers,* as Janette pronounced it.

The king insisted on lavish surroundings and the illusion of a completed garden. So the entire crew of gardeners and workmen had paused from their usual duties to assemble an outdoor ballroom behind the palace on the southern terrace, circled in potted orange trees and potted box shrubs. Pewter luminaries sparkled everywhere, and great papier-maché moons and stars were strung from an overhead lattice ceiling that gave the illusion of an enchanted midsummer's eve. Gardenia scented the air, thanks to generous vines of the braided flowers laced through the canopies. And relegated to a far corner was a froth of red-blossoming *o-lander.*

All to impress the king's mistress, Louise de la Vallière. Alexandre had never really understood man's need to impress a woman in order to lure her into his arms. If she was interested, she would come to him. No need to put on airs and boast falsely of amorous deeds. He much preferred a woman to like him for himself. Not that fortune had stroked him in that aspect of his life.

But, he had to admit, for the first in a very long time he had stirred up confidence and revealed that secret part of himself to a woman. And she had not laughed or ridiculed him for a fool. It was a good feeling, this surrender to trust. What Margot did to his self-confidence was indeed rather interesting. She made him forget that he must be on guard. So much so that he was actually out socializing tonight. In a manner of terms. Certainly he was there only to please his daughters.

Tucked amid a chorus of silk- and satin-clad fops, a full wine goblet in hand, Alexandre smoothed his other hand over his own ill-repaired doublet of plain blue plush. Sophie had insisted more times than he could recall that he must have at least one of the new style in long coat; doublets were passé. He'd never gotten around to such a task, finding parties and invites easily avoidable when he'd lived at the Saint-Sylvestre château with his brothers. Vaux had boasted smaller, intimate parties, of which Sophie had attended without notice of his absence. She had been possessed of a way of shining when surrounded by extravagance and the sparkle of jewels and wit. Had he attended those parties with her, she might never have noticed.

It was just as well. Alexandre was sure his repertoire of plant genus and fertilizing methods would bore even the most scholarly within the snap of a finger.

He eyed the military row of orange tubs he'd lined up

that afternoon to create a border around the dance floor. If the duchess Bouchet moved two steps backward, she would collide with the weakest of the trees and surely cause it grave damage. He quickly extricated himself across the crowded floor and slid behind her, unobtrusively forcing her forward as his ankle slithered across her jewel-laden hem.

From his vantage point he could keep a keen eye on all the bordering tubs. Now, if only he could concentrate on one thing and avoid the mixture of dancing shapes and colors that glimmered and slid in globs before his vision. It was difficult to sort out the voices and the laughter. Laughter especially was vivid and bright and always lingered in his vision in waves or dancing sticks far longer than the actual sound. Heap upon that the dulcet colors of feminine charm and the dark geometrics of a gentlemen's seduction, and Alexandre found walking a straight line difficult.

Perhaps he'd stayed long enough. A glance away from the crowd zoned Alexandre's sight on a perfect round orange hanging low in one of the top-heavy trees. Concentrate, he coached. The sweet smell of fruit and the smooth color. Citrus taste of star-shaped points. He could call the flavor to his tongue, feel the points prickling across his palm as they so often did when he bit into an orange. *Concentrate.*

What was that? Shimmering over the pointed smell of the orange, a vivid color surged ahead. Alexandre turned to scan the crowd. It was then he saw the pink waves dancing off at the edge of the dance floor.

The knowing face of Titania, sprung straight from *A Midsummer Night's Dream,* paused in her dancing and looked directly at him. She flashed a lowered lash, an averted glance of her eyes, and darted behind cover of the king's crown.

Alexandre rubbed his eyes. He checked his goblet—

still full save one sip of the driest, most miserable wine he had yet to taste.

He scanned the crowd's loud squares and darting lines and boggled colors in search of the sweet vision. Patience walked a thin line. But until he assured himself of what he had just seen . . .

Ah! There. Titania. A teasing flirt of lashes across the crowded floor of glittering costumes. A pair of wigged heads surged before the woman, and when they had passed she was again gone.

"I am quite tired when my eyes begin to play such havoc." Alexandre pressed thumb and forefinger to his scalp. "Certainly my senses have been run through this evening."

He slugged a good portion of the wine, his throat constricting in rejection of the foul brew, but he managed to choke it down. Not so terrible as the initial sip. In fact, this wine was beginning to bloom.

It had been years since he'd imbibed, relaxed, let his guard down to simply enjoy himself. That had been the eve of his daughters' births. He, Armand, and Adrian had walked to the edge of their father's land and crouched down in the grass to toast his good fortune of two healthy girls and—for the moment at least—an exhausted and blissfully silent Sophie. One interesting aspect of a good drunk was that Alexandre's senses were dulled, not as perceptive as usual. Which would certainly be a boon this evening.

He finished off the goblet with great flair.

A zing of sensation moved up his left arm. Alexandre spun around. Margot giggled and flashed him the teasing fairy-queen grin he'd witnessed from across the floor. "You're looking rather befuddled."

He summed up her appearance. Not quite as elaborate as the other women in their jewel-studded silks and wigs. No, she was a match to his plain dress and simple hair.

A burgundy plush bodice barely concealed her ample bosom and cut an enticing curve above her hips. But it wasn't the gown that caught Alexandre's eye. It was that pale-winter's-snow bosom. Every breath she took teased him with the notion that her nipples might spring free of the bone-stiffened velvet to taunt and tempt. How she radiated a vibrance beyond that of any fine jewel or cloth the women at court could ever dream to wear.

"I'm here at my daughters' request."

"Really?"

"And to what honor do I owe the privileged company of the most beautiful woman this eve?"

She blushed like a deep exotic peach, sweet and tangy. He could taste the flavor on his tongue. And that had nothing whatsoever to do with his confused perception. No, Margot's blushing cheeks were just that appealing.

"You owe Cook for the kindness of allowing me to bed Lisette and Janette in her chamber this eve, close to her watchful eye. I plan to bring them to their own beds before I retire for the night."

"I shall accompany you."

An elegant brow lifted above her right eye. "Really? I don't think I need assistance in retiring this eve. Unless you insist?"

He caught her teasing insinuation and hadn't even realized he'd worded his statement so. "I mean the children."

She shrugged and began to move backward, the teasing grin and mischievous spark to her eye returned. "I don't," she said, and the dance of her voice enticed Alexandre to follow her.

She deftly slipped between two tubs of orange trees and moved as if following a trail of fairy dust over the strips of sod that surrounded the makeshift ballroom until she rounded the corner of the château and stood in the lacy shadows of the iron-latticed balcony.

Intrigued beyond rational thought, Alexandre joined her in the alternating lines of shadow and candle glow. The confusion of the crowd released hold on his muddled senses. Now only Margot's scent tempted in hums of violet. Rose, perhaps, for that flower often held a purple cast in his vision. "You lead me astray, Mademoiselle."

"Ah, but how easily you follow."

The touch of her finger beneath his chin lured Alexandre forward. Unhampered by wide petticoated skirts, he stood close enough to warrant a worry of propriety, but far enough away to make his body ache for just one more step.

"Do you wish to kiss me?" she challenged him.

"Perhaps."

Around the corner the sprightly jaunt of harpsichord and fiddle led the dancers into a minuet, while here in the shadows the thud of Alexandre's heart pushed him forward to touch Margot's lips with his own.

"Yes," Margot gasped as she pulled him to her body and boldly answered his tentative kiss.

She tasted of fruit, perhaps the sugared strawberries pyramided upon the lavish tables this evening. The flavor mixed with the dry wine into a pleasing champagne of sensation. While his taste had never confused itself with sound or sight, the smell of Margot's perfume danced about his vision in violet columns. He closed his eyes. The vision softened, so he might see the violet column if he wished it. But he did not. Instead, he concentrated only on the bold challenge Margot's kiss commanded of his heart.

She gave a little whimper, prompting him to open her mouth and trace her upper lip with a lingering slide of his tongue. Like touching heaven. He held an angel in his arms. 'Twas a good thing the twins had been successful in talking him into attending the fête this evening.

This was the first kiss Alexandre had ever really enjoyed, wished to never end.

"I can feel it in my bones," she murmured against his lips.

"What's that?"

"This kiss."

Alexandre released a heart-thudding sigh. "I can too."

He slid a hand up through her hair, relishing the soft texture of the unpowdered strands of satin and silk. When had he ever the privilege of touching such softness save that of his own daughters?

"Can we kiss again," she wondered, "for a very long time?"

To be wrapped in an endless lazy embrace with this enchanting woman seemed a dream he might never have. He mustn't have. He didn't deserve such undiluted happiness.

"You are unsure," she said. "Oh, I know this is terribly wrong of me. You've only just lost your wife, and here I am seducing you—"

"Are you really? And I don't smell the eucalyptus anywhere near." Her smile was shy, but it spread to her eyes.

"What are you thinking, Alexandre? Are you angry with me for kissing you?"

Angry over a kiss? "A kiss from a fairy queen should never make a man angry."

"Fairy queen?"

"You've caught me up in your magic, this enchantment you've spun me into."

"I've enchanted you?"

He'd never known enchantment until then. And the thought of being pushed away from the feeling was rather dire. But this woman confused his own sense of right and wrong so desperately. 'Twas an altogether different confusion from that of a noisy crowd. Much more personal, singular . . . devastatingly right.

But it was still difficult to answer the call and surrender completely. The chain mail had been picked up from the puddle around his feet. He didn't exactly wear the tunic of protection, but he did still carry it with him.

"Alexandre?"

"What?"

"You don't seem well. It's the party, isn't it? I don't know why I didn't realize sooner." She turned to survey the buzz of guests who conversed and danced beneath the glittering papier mâché stars. Brightly clothed tumblers jumped and contorted upon great gold balls, much to the delight of the king's mistress. "I imagine you must see such an array of voices right now to literally drive you quite mad."

Alexandre felt the tension ease out of his muscles. He relaxed against the wall and pulled her close. All things were right standing in this woman's embrace. A woman that understood him. Such a rare and delightful treasure.

She looked down at their embrace. "You wish me to stay?"

"I wish you to release me, Mademoiselle of the Pink Wavy Voice, before I find enchantment a delicious captivity not much worth leaving."

She pressed close and whispered, "You don't sound very convincing."

"Kiss me once, Margot. Then I must return to check on my children."

"Yes," she uttered absently as her lips drew near to his. "I suppose the princess cannot have the king so quickly. There must be struggle, trials to overcome, and goals to first accomplish."

He did not understand what she mumbled, but it ceased to matter as the fairy queen pressed a beguiling morsel to his lips. This kiss was soft, brief as a dragonfly's landing upon a sun-striped pond, yet it reached into his very soul. So light, yet confidant in its touch. *I have you now,* it whispered. *You cannot flee.*

"I will go," she said, and with a quick kiss to his forehead from her soft, moist lips, she spun about and hurried inside the château, away from the party.

Alexandre sighed and pressed his palms to his face. He squeezed his eyelids tight.

What was happening to him? All his life he had diligently worked and studied and sketched and observed. And always he protected himself from the ignorance of others. He lived a God-fearing life, filled with long, weary days of good, hard labor. He loved his children and had given his wife a good home. He never questioned his existence, nor did he challenge the ineffable. He'd never once given in to daydreams.

I have you now. . . .

Yes now. And now he found himself wishing he might be the star of Margot's next dreamy state of wondering. Also, he wondered just how long it would be before he could acquire another of her kisses.

"They fell in love?" Janette's giggles echoed up from beneath the tent of bedsheets Margot had fashioned while the girls had earlier bathed in the wide copper tub.

The announcement that the King of Oranges and the Princess of Practically Everything had fallen in love seemed to please the raven-curled twin immensely. It was the attitude of the other girl that warranted further investigation. Lisette, upon hearing about the love, pulled the bedsheets over her face and now lay there, completely still and silent.

"Love is a good thing, of course," Margot tried to explain. No reaction from Lisette. She might have been playing Ophelia floating down the stream, morose and livid. "Is there something troubling you, Lisette? Are you tired?"

"Tired," agreed the voice from beneath the sheet.

Yes, most surely. The day had been long, what with helping Cook tidy up after the party preparations. Follow that with an hour in the stables, playing with the new piglet, and both girls had yawned all the way through their baths.

"Good eve to the both of you," she said, and leaned over to tuck Janette in beside her mummified sister.

"You'll come back, won't you, Margot?"

"Of course. I shall return in the morning. Your papa will be in his room soon if he is not already." She waited for Janette to lie back, but the child perused the notion for a moment, then gave a great sigh. "What is it, Janette? I can stay here until your papa comes in for the night."

"Mama once kissed us and told us she'd come back—"

"But she never did!" Lisette's little head appeared from under the sheets, startling Margot with her exclamation.

"Lisette's right," Janette pouted. A glimmer of a tear formed in her eye. Her lips quivered. "Mama didn't come back. She promised, Margot. Why didn't she come back?"

"She lied to us," Lisette hissed.

"Oh, girls." Compelled to wrap the fragile kittens in her arms, Margot nestled on the bed between the two. Lisette remained rigid. Janette's entire body quivered, waiting for permission to release. Had she never cried loud, angry tears for her mother?

"Why?" Janette gasped. "Didn't she like us anymore, Margot?"

"Oh, dear, no, girls. I'm sure your mother loved you both very much."

"She didn't love Papa," Lisette said.

"Now, how do you know that?"

"She said so!"

Had their mother ever said such a cruel thing, or was it more that the girls had read the body language between their parents?

"I want Mama to love Papa," Janette quivered. "And I want her to love me and Lisette. We weren't bad, Margot. We really weren't."

"Of course you weren't. You two are fluffy little kittens. You aren't bad, just curious!"

She pressed Janette's head to her breast and smoothed a hand over her hair. Snuffles filled the room, brave and restrained.

"Just cry," she said. "Your mama will hear you in heaven."

"She will not!" Lisette flung herself against the bed pillow, but Janette, thick streams coating her cheeks, wanted to believe. "She will?"

"Yes. She might not be able to come back, but she can know your heart. And it's your heart that makes you cry."

"I miss Mama." And Janette's pain flooded out in loud, gasping sobs.

Comforting with a hand to the child's brow, Margot wiped tears and offered nods to reassure. It was good for Janette to cry. As for Lisette, who remained fixed, facedown in the pillow, she would cry when the time was right.

Minutes passed before Janette's sobs turned to stuttering sniffles, and her eyelids blinked heavily beneath a scatter of dark curls. Kissing Lisette's brow through the sheet, Margot lingered a moment over the child's soft purrs. Two little kittens nestled in the thick feather bed, their eyelids like soft alabaster shell, their lips two fallen bows from a cupid's quiver. They smelled delicious. Of innocence and salt and home.

Margot's youngest brother, Maximillian, was but six, but she could still recall the scent of his hair after the rain had washed away the dust and play grime. Sweet and fresh. Distinctly boy.

A throng of longing for her siblings' laughter and hugs and kisses—even their tears—thrummed through Margot's breast. She pressed an open palm to her bosom and located the heavy beats echoing inside her body. Much as she had grown to enjoy her freedom, she did still miss her family. In her heart.

She traced a stray wisp of hair out of Janette's face and left the children, knowing they would be well until their father returned for the evening.

Closing their chamber door silently behind her, Margot scanned the dark hallway, eventually picking up the laughter and violin song from the party. She had been surprised to find the cautious gardener socializing. Well, he hadn't been in conversation. More likely protecting his precious nursery of trees.

She liked standing in Alexandre Saint-Sylvestre's arms. She liked kissing his lips. She liked looking into the dark gaze she had successfully captured and was learning to tame.

She would like to imagine doing so much more with him.

Eleven

*Do you know the rich pay a pretty pistole for
those restorative mud baths?*

Squeals echoed across the grounds of Versailles during
the afternoon break from construction. In the wake of
the squeals floated various feminine squawks, male
oaths, and the tinkling giggles of Lisette, Janette, and
Margot as they dashed after a renegade piglet acciden-
tally set free from the stables.

Margot kept her peripheral sight on the twins and their
darting little hamlet as she paused just long enough to
check the lone woman who sat upon a garden bench, her
toes thrust straight into the air to avoid the piglet's rocket
path. "It is just a piglet, Madame. No harm done."

"No harm?" the woman bellowed in a voice much surprising for her petite frame. The star patch at the corner
of her thin lips pointed to deadly green eyes. "The king
shall hear of this when he returns from the hunt!"

Dismissing the woman's angry huffing, Margot hiked
her skirts up and took to running. The piglet's path took
it straight toward the Orangerie, which could be reached
only by descending the hundred steps.

Ha! Their prey would be stymied! If not become dinner. The king would never allow such calamity without

punishment. Margot prayed she would once again escape His Highness's notice but reasoned she would be most deserving if she were banished from court after this escapade.

Janette's laughter had become a belly rumble as Margot gathered the girls into her arms and the threesome stood atop the hundred steps, watching the piglet descend the stairs in a crisscrossing, hop-skipping manner. The little porker could certainly cover territory. He was already halfway down, showing no signs of slowing or giving up on his coverage of each and every step.

A mop of dark hair popped up from the bottom stairs of the Orangerie. "Alexandre! The piglet!" Margot called as she took the stairs, one twin gripped surely in each hand.

In a clatter of garden implements, and after deftly sidestepping a wooden bucket filled with pond water, Alexandre limped into the chase just as the piglet landed on the grassy stretch that led directly to the Swiss pond.

"He'll drown!" Janette called as she watched her father and the piglet scamper closer to the glimmering pool.

"Pigs are afraid of the water," Margot reassured her as she hastened behind the running twins. She hoped.

"Not the pig," Lisette chastened. "Papa! He cannot swim!"

A splash of pond water erupted into scattering droplets, pig squeals, and male bellows. On the contrary, pigs were not afraid of water. A spiral of pink pig tail bobbed upon the surface as a sniffing snout headed toward the opposite shore. For all the splashing and squealing and cries from the twins, Margot could not make out curled pig tail from groping human fingers. Surely the pond could not be so very deep at the edge?

Plunging to her knees at the shore, Margot caught Janette around the waist before she could lean too far forward and fall into the algae-frosted waters. "Stay back, girls."

"But Papa needs to be rescued!" Janette wailed. Ruby beat the air with flailing limbs.

Lisette pulled her sister away and into her arms. "Margot will save him."

Or maybe not.

One step forward on the slick shore grass and the soft soil beneath Margot's feet shifted, pulling her down and into the pond in a *swush* of billowing skirts and pig squeals. A wodge of mud splashed her face. But a moment of panic quickly became calm. Margot immediately realized the pond was shallow and she could easily sit without the water breaching her shoulders. She glanced her tongue out and spit the grit and algae from her lips.

"Got it!" Alexandre declared victoriously as he surfaced and somehow held ten pounds of squirming pink flesh in the air with both hands.

In the next instant the pig soared over Margot's head and toward the girls for the hand-off. Stretching to deliver his catch, Alexandre lost footing and landed most unceremoniously in Margot's lap, his hands bracing themselves on either side of her arms and the sucking sound of mud securing his fists.

"Good going, Janette," he called over Margot's shoulder. "Tuck him in your skirts and cradle him tightly. Yes, that's it!"

While the girls giggled over their catch, Margot found herself in a most interesting position. An ooze of mud spilled down her back and another eased its way up her skirts, settling into places she'd be most surprised to find mud in later. But as Alexandre worked his fists in the mud, it seemed the thick substance had in mind only to draw him closer until he literally lay upon her outstretched legs, his face perfectly aligned with her own.

"Pardon me," he said. "It appears we are in a most compromising position."

"Certainly, we are," she added as comically as he had chosen to make his remark. Above and behind her, she could just see a half dozen courtiers who had gathered on the south terrace above the Orangerie to watch the spectacle. "The king shall have my head."

"How did the little monster escape?"

"Janette was feeding him over the railing when Ruby fell inside the stall and she had to open the door to retrieve her. I was helping Lisette brush out the horses, so I did not see until it was too late. Forgive me, it was all my fault."

His smile beamed. "Nonsense. I was just considering a swim."

He whipped his head back to disperse the trails of muddy water that flowed down his face. Looking much like a drowned pig himself, he succeeded in loosening one hand, but the loss of hold had him plunging his fist for purchase. Which he found against Margot's shoulder.

"Hell, I've gone and made a disaster of your dress," he commented on the mud that oozed from his hand and all over her shoulder and down the front of her bodice and between her breasts.

Now she had mud in every unimaginable place.

"You don't think my plunging into the pond damaged it enough?"

He shrugged. "Damned ugly color, isn't it?'

"You don't like my pink silk?"

"I don't believe I've ever seen it looking pink. There is usually mud or dirt or some disgusting substance all over it. Why did you come in? I had the slippery little beast."

"Your daughters told me you could not swim. I thought too, well . . ." Embarrassed now that it was quite obvious the man did not need help, Margot felt her face flush warm, even sitting in the cool depths of the water. "I thought perhaps you might need rescue."

"I thank you for your consideration." His breath hushed close to her lips. Dark eyes glittered with teasing play. "But I'm not sure rescue is what I desire from your company."

The urge to plunge forward for a slippery kiss struck Margot hard. But she maintained propriety, knowing the courtiers still watched.

"I find I'm quite stuck," he said. Margot could feel his attempts to pull out his other hand. "If I could get purchase on the bank . . ."

He reached beyond her head for a thick tuft of grass, which brought his chest up and his lips a little too high for her delight, but he could still kiss her on the top of the head if he wished. He worked his feet, which Margot could hear were suctioned deeper down into the mud with every step.

Alexandre lifted one leg out of the water to display his bare foot, the muddy hose dangling from his largest toe. "Perhaps I was in need of a new pair of boots." And then he toppled, landing his knee between her legs and his face right before hers.

Seizing the moment, Margot slid a muddy hand up behind Alexandre's head and pulled him to her kiss. Pond grit coated their connection, but he did not make an attempt to pull away.

"Mmm," he murmured against her lips.

"My kisses are displeasing to you?"

"On the contrary, I rather favor the vintage, a subtle blend of silt and algae."

It was only the sudden cheer from Janette that stopped the couple. Alexandre jerked his gaze up to the girls.

"The King of Oranges has kissed the Princess of Practically Everything!" Janette declared as she began to spin circles on the lawn with the piglet swaddled tight to her gut.

"The King of Oranges?" Alexandre questioned Margot. Myriad droplets from his hair rained upon Margot's eyelids and cheeks as he hovered over her. "And the Princess of Practically Everything?"

A diversion was needed to rescue her from explaining, and a diversion she was granted. Margot managed a shrug and felt her entire body begin to slide. Gripping anything she could seize hold of, Margot yelped as the soft earth behind her became a mudslide. "We're going to need a pole to get out of here," she called above Alexandre's struggles to gain purchase.

"Or we could swim to the dock," Alexandre managed to say, with a splashing, flailing arm pointing toward the south side of the pond, where a wooden dock had been placed for the king's use.

"But you can't swim!"

"I know this!" he said, and then Alexandre's head disappeared beneath the surface of the water.

The twins were exhausted. It took little more than Margot directing their dirty clothing to the floor in a puddle around their squiggling toes and motioning to the copper tub filled with tepid water to incite a bath. The dented old tub was certainly seeing plenty of use lately. Ten minutes later, both girls glistened. Even Ruby was looking a little fresher—soggy but clean.

"No time for the story tonight, girls."

"But we must," Janette protested.

Lisette murmured, "The king . . . he kissed the princess . . ."

Margot heard Lisette's whispers even as the child's head hit the pillow and she closed her eyes to purr. Indeed, the King of Oranges had kissed the Princess of

Practically Everything in plain view of the entire court. But Margot could not worry what gossip might be fluttering from ear to ear just then. All that really mattered to her was Lisette's odd actions. As tired as she had been, she'd flinched from Margot's efforts to help wash and dress her. Something bothered her. But Margot could not be sure what.

"Sweet dreams," Margot whispered as she first kissed Lisette's lavender-smelling brow, then Ruby's cloth head, and then Janette's closed eyelids.

Reaching across Lisette's tiny figure, Margot gripped the heavy drapes and pulled them closed to block out the red glow that remained on the horizon.

"Now, for my next patient," she said as she rose and shook off a shiver. Her own clothes were still moist. She hadn't taken the time to change, for she wanted to get the girls immediately out of their muddy things. "And then I'm next. What I wouldn't give for a steaming bath right now."

She tapped on Alexandre's chamber door, and a distant sneeze prompted her inside.

Looking rather like something that had been dunked, sloshed around, and spat out upon the floor, Alexandre sat in the middle of the candlelit room, a linen wrapped around his bare shoulders collecting the moisture from his hair. He still wore his muddy breeches but had removed his hose—well, his remaining stocking—and both feet soaked in a small basin with steaming water.

"Cook sent Pierceforest with hot water after filling the girls' bath," he said with a shrug and a sniffle. "It feels good, but I'm still freezing."

What a sweet, incapable man. Certainly intelligent, but quite out of his league when presented with domestic challenges. Margot crossed to his side and lifted the linen from his shoulders. She began to pat his head dry. "Of course you're cold. Have you no mind to strip these wet things off? You'll catch your death sitting here in this moist."

"You said rain does not give the fever."

"Rain, no, but to sit and stew in this cold room."

A grand sneeze lifted his feet out of the water, and they landed with a grand splash. Hot droplets splattered Margot's toes, heightening her own craving for warmth.

"Sophie used to . . ." He sneezed again. "She used to take care of me. You must think me an utter imbecile. Here I sit, waiting to freeze to death, when the most basic of care must be given me by a female."

"Nonsense, that's what we women are for." Margot laid the linen over his head and hugged him close to her breast as she coaxed the water out of his soaked locks. The damp cloth felt cool against her breasts, like pressing ice over ice. "We're here to care for our men—er—any man who should need caring for, as the case may be."

Already claiming him as your own now, eh? What was the name of that man? That other . . . oh, certainly you recall that other. Didn't he have a title or something?

"Have you a robe? The shivers will go away once you are completely dry. If you could slip out of your wet breeches, I'll see to washing them and return them tomorrow."

"In the bottom drawer of the armoire," he said on a teeth-chattering shudder. "The girls get along to bed?"

"Sleeping like angels," she called from the armoire. "Clean angels."

A thin cotton robe lay compressed at the back of the drawer. When Margot snapped it firmly, it lengthened to a wrinkly sheet of brown and cream stripes. Never worn, obviously. Did he never lounge before going to bed? Certainly not with the hours he kept. Most likely he would come inside, wash, eat, then plunge right into bed. When did the man take time to indulge? Did he ever indulge?

Alexandre really needed some time to just sit back and relax . . . enjoy life.

"That will do," he said as she held it before him, her thoughts a million miles away.

Feet still firmly planted in the basin of water, Alexandre pulled the towel from his shoulders. Long strands of midnight hair flowed over his shoulders and across his chest. Muscles forged by hard labor flexed with every movement, capturing Margot's interest like no butterfly ever could. His pectorals were defined and thick, stunningly firm. Most likely from chopping wood. A jagged line veed down his chest, outlining the cut of his shirt, as his neck and face were bronzed a nice shade of brown. Down to his elbows his arms were comically pale, his hands also pale, most likely owing to gloves.

So captivated was she on his chest that Margot did not notice the tug at the robe she still held before her. "Huh? Oh! Yes, the robe. I shall turn my head." She did, and waited. But she did not hear a thing.

"You want me to strip?"

"You need to remove your wet clothes."

"Perhaps I can do this myself."

"It isn't like I've not seen you naked before. Oh!" Should she have brought that up?

"Yes, indeed, I suppose you have."

She heard the *click* of his breech clips. Well, she'd gone beyond embarrassment. Again. But the notion to flee was not even a glimmer of a thought. Cold, wet fabric slid over his long legs and landed with a squish next to the water basin. He slipped both arms through the robe, and when Margot turned to look, he stood before her, bare legs jutting from the robe and arms splayed.

"Do you shower in the winter?" she wondered, chin cupped in hand.

"Unfortunately not. There are some things, such as

freezing temperatures that a man should not expose certain bared body parts to."

Alexandre's hair had chilled and now glistened in midnight blue and black in the candle glow. Fighting off her own shivers, Margot threaded one hand under the heavy mass of his long hair and slid the towel between his robed back and tresses. She squeezed hard, then worked the towel over his entire head. When it felt as though she would get no more water in the towel, which was now thoroughly soaked, she dropped it to the floor and began to work her fingers through the tangled masses.

The pressure of Alexandre's hand on hers strafed through Margot's breast. This shiver she knew was not from the cold. "You needn't," he said.

She drew her fingers through the length of his hair, which traveled clear down to the middle of his back. "It'll tangle if I don't comb through it. If you'll allow me?"

He still held her wrist and now brought it around to press against his face, also blessedly warm. "You're like ice, Margot. *Mon Dieu,* but I've been so unkind, sitting here, allowing you to care for me, when you've nearly gone dead in the extremities. Come."

He stepped out of the water and turned to look her over. "You've still mud on you. You look like a drowned pig!"

"I will bathe when I return to my room. I'm sure Cook will have some boiling water left."

"But you should leave right now."

"Yes." She shrugged. "I suppose." But her body did not turn for the door. "I just, well, I like spending time with you, Alexandre. Caring for you and the girls." She reached and touched his cheek, then spread her palm to draw his warmth into her flesh. "It comforts me to know the three of you are well."

He closed his palm over her hand and drew it away

from his cheek. But he did not then lead her to his door as Margot suspected he might. Instead, he pried open her fingers and pressed a kiss to her frozen flesh. Instant thaw. A circle of heat blossomed beneath his kiss and radiated outward to slide across her wrist and up her arm. It reached her face in a scintillating shock of goose prickles and an encompassing flush of heat.

"You are too kind," he said. He kissed the tip of one finger, and then the next, each contact nudging Margot's temperature up a notch. "It was pure fortune I happened upon you that first day, sousing butterflies. And there was that incident with the pig snot."

She'd forgotten about that. How foolish he must have thought her. Not that she had done anything remarkably upstanding since then to change that opinion . . .

A kiss to her pinkie finger sparked the simmering flush to a raging fire. Margot drew close enough to feel the heat radiating from the length of Alexandre's body. Even with her skirts soaked to her thighs and the mud beginning to crust in those assorted private places, she had never felt more beautiful than at that moment.

Candlelight reflected in the obsidian orbs of his eyes. Margot could see her own face reflected in the depths. Her smile smiled back at her.

"I've become soused by your presence, Margot. I crave your nearness, your conversation, your sweet smile. Even when you make me speak of things I'd rather not. And when you insist on studying my naked body parts."

"Forgive me, I—"

"Never."

A kiss to her wrist elicited a surprising moan from deep within her throat. Did he know what his touches did to her? Could he possibly fathom that she'd fall to her knees and pledge fealty to him for life if only for another and another of his well-placed jewels?

I like Papa's sliders.

"I want a slider," she whispered.

"Do you now?"

She nodded, trepid in her boldness.

"Do you know I reserve my sliders especially for those I care about?"

"Oh." She looked away, but he touched her chin and moved her eyes back into his dark gaze. His lips were hot. Firm as they touched her forehead, lingered there between her brows for a moment—just long enough for her heart to fall off rhythm—and then the slow slide of his lips traveled the length of her nose.

"Alexandre, I—" Could she be so bold? There was no question. The feeling leapt to her heart and fled her thoughts on a sigh. "I think I love you."

He paused, his lips lingering close to hers. Such warmth in his dark eyes. And no fear. That was a good thing after she'd just spouted something she should not have. Love? Did she really mean such a declaration?

He did not pull away and push her from the room. Instead, he paced toward the window, where the night was blackened by the reflected light of the room.

"Love."

"I think so," she said, feeling the emotion of the word surge in her breast. "Yes, I do. I *do* love you, Alexandre."

"Love is a most bold declaration, Mademoiselle."

Mademoiselle? Oh, dear. That was not a good word.

"I do not mean to startle you, Alexandre—"

"No, no," he said with a raised hand, "you do not."

A heavy sigh lifted his shoulders, and he turned around to face her. It was impossible to read his face, for the grim line of his lips could mean anything from calm to interest to anger. Margot began to wonder if she should have acted on her bold desires.

"I have never really known love," he said, "save for the girls. You can make all the assumptions you wish regarding Sophie—"

"I assume nothing." She clutched her arms before her chest to waylay the shivers, but the confrontation did not preach relaxation or calm. Instead, her every bone tingled with expectation, with the desire to have her declaration matched with equal enthusiasm.

"I did not love Sophie. I thought I made that clear to you."

"You did, but—" She knew he did love his wife. In a certain way.

"Love is a difficult emotion to grasp. Unless it comes freely and is not forced, it can never be true. Margot, I—"

"No, please." She rushed to him. She had stepped over the line. Again. It was too soon. "I expect no reply in turn. I simply wanted you to know my feelings. I was foolish, perhaps."

"No." He smoothed his thumb along her cheek, brushing the end of her brow. "It pleases me, your announcement."

"It-it does?"

Her head framed between both of Alexandre's hands, he kissed her long and deeply. She felt as though he were mining her soul to judge her honesty, and she opened completely to show him her eagerness to give trust. Never had she felt so taken by a man, so mastered by his control. So wanted. Needed.

Supporting her with his hand behind her back, he drew his kisses over her chin and down her neck. An urgency tipped his actions. Drying strands of Alexandre's raven hair fell over her shoulders and skimmed her décolletage with cool, feathery strokes.

With some coaxing he pushed her sleeves down to completely expose her shoulders; a few motions at her back and he'd opened the ties of her stays. Her bodice loosened, freeing her of the tight torture device and exposing her breasts to his hot tongue.

He laved over her cold flesh, coating it hot and wanting in his wake. Margot felt her equilibrium give free. She reached and gripped the back of the chair but could not prevent her body from swaying. The motion pulled them both down to the floor, Margot's head landing upon the wet towel she'd used to dry his hair.

But it also startled Alexandre out of his ministrations. He shook his head, as if clearing the muddle, and looked aside. "What am I doing? I mustn't."

"Oh, yes, you must." She slid her fingers over his shoulder, groped to keep him on top of her. "Please, Alexandre, I shall freeze without your touch."

"Then you must go to your room and remove these wet things."

"Might I remove them here?" she gasped.

The room became very still. He did not answer, only studied her face, her pleading look. He reached up to twine his fingers through the ones she'd tangled in his hair. The candle sandwiched between botany textbooks on the desk, sputtered and reduced the glow of the room in an instant. It was guttering out. A few more minutes and they would be lying on the floor in the dark with nothing but the upset pots of dirt and flowers surrounding them.

"Margot, you know what will happen if we go further."

"We needn't do everything. This night I desire only your hands upon my flesh."

"You believe any man can touch you without wishing to join with you?"

"You wish to make love to me?"

He shook his head solemnly. His jaw flexed as he sucked in his lower lip. An indecisive moment. And then . . . "I cannot. Not yet. Margot, you jump so quickly from one event to the next. First it is a kiss and now it is lovemaking. You must slow down."

"I don't want to."

"But I need to catch up."

"You wish to?"

He drew in a breath, exhaled, and then, "Yes."

Twelve

Lisette, queen of discontent

Alexandre had surrendered to his staunch beliefs and allowed the twins to skip out into the light rain shower that pitter-pattered the marble aisles of the Orangerie. Margot sat next to him on the wooden base of a tree planter. She had removed her shoes and hose, tossing them without a care to the ground. Now her toes wiggled in the rain, dancing to the joy of the twins' laughter.

"Watch me, Papa!" Janette did a sort of single-footed hop-dance between two boxed lindens and with a grand heave of her arms landed with both feet in a burgeoning puddle. Skirts, arms, and face were thoroughly soaked. As well as Ruby.

"That ragged old doll," Alexandre said with a chuckle. He leaned back on his elbows and nodded encouragement to Lisette's pleas for him to watch her ballerina twirls. "There are days I believe I've yet a third child named Ruby for her constancy in Janette's life."

"Be thankful she's a rather quiet child," Margot mused with a toss of her head, which dispersed her curls across Alexandre's arm. "And most agreeable."

The shimmer of hair across his inner elbow drew Alexandre's attention. Silk on dirt-encrusted flesh. An unthinkable combination. Last night they had come so close to making love. Too close for him.

He still wasn't ready. Margot was moving too quickly. What was right? What was wrong? He'd never known the emotion of first love, had never really thought it would come to him. And was that really what this was? First love? Or something else, like lust or despair searching for an outlet? He just didn't know.

He stretched his arm out, his fingers glancing over the tumble of Margot's curls that skimmed the dirt surface of the pot. A rainfall of sunshine at his fingertips.

"Don't you love it?" Margot asked.

No, not lust, nor despair. This had to be love. It just felt too good to be anything else. "Indeed." He thought to clutch the sunshine, capture it in his hand, crush the gorgeous strands between his fingers like fresh sprouted flax waving in a summer field.

"I wish it would go on like this forever."

"Forever," Alexandre mumbled the word. Forever meant so many different things to so many different people. *To have and to hold Sophie forever* . . . To him it had always meant a little less than satisfaction. A little less than happiness. Just a little less than he had ever hoped for.

Dared he hope now?

Margot turned and bent so their faces were close. "Wouldn't you like it to go on forever?"

This moment, this sketch in time featuring giggling girls and a sunshine rainfall of silken hair and delicious pink words? *"Can* it last forever?"

"Alexandre, what *are* you talking about?"

"The same—" What was *she* talking about? "You're talking about the—"

"But the rain, of course!" She twisted her lips into a pretty pout and flashed a glittering wink at him. "What did you think I was talking about?"

Certainly not the rain, Alexandre thought now as her sparkling eyes awaited his response. He had been out of his senses just then. Dreaming of forevers and sunshine rainfalls. Rain? "But of course, the rain."

Don't even dream, he cautioned himself. *It cannot be.* It was too soon for him to consider a relationship with another woman. Certainly Sophie deserved a respectful mourning period. But Alexandre could not deny his emotions.

But to continue to dance around them so? If only he could receive a sign, something that would let him know it was all right. *Go on, embrace these feelings.* Far too much to hope for, let alone even consider.

He sat up, finding Janette and Ruby danced a jig around Lisette's body, seated as an island amid a puddle. "Certainly it will be a task cleaning the girls' things this evening. Perhaps we should call them in."

"Nonsense," she whispered strongly in his ear.

Alexandre turned to the pink shimmer of voice, but Margot dashed out into the rain before he could catch the whisper on her lips. She spun once, her plain wool skirts swirling like rose petals billowing to catch the sun. The rain goddess lifted her arms above her head, her fingers splayed to worship the rain. Drops glanced off her lips and splattered her cheeks. She lifted one arm straight up, closed her eyes, and stood like a statue, funneling the water down her limb. With a graceful movement she rolled her head back from shoulder to shoulder. Total surrender to the element.

Alexandre gazed up the delicious curves that arched and stretched before him. The rain saturated and hugged Margot's clothing into a living statue of curve and flesh and temptation. He skated his tongue along his lower lip. The minty sharpness of the rain heightened his senses and whetted his appetite. But 'twas not rain he desired to consume until his senses were drunk upon the pink waves of happiness.

A lithe hand glanced out and Margot's fingertips beckoned from her sensual rain dance. "Come," she enticed. "Dance with me."

The notion to rationalize, to seek excuses, did not come. Alexandre looked down to find he already stood. But dance? With his limp?

The touch of Margot's rain-wet hand to his sent a burst of cool mint through his senses and flashed brilliantly in his eyes. Like a flash of destiny exploding in an instant and then shimmering away to reveal what he desired.

Margot de Verona.

Drawing his hand up Margot's arm, Alexandre slipped his fingers through the wet mass of her hair and cupped the back of her head. He drew close. Close enough to feel. *Close enough to fall.* Close enough to—

"Kiss her, Papa!"

Margot did not look away at Janette's enthusiastic declaration, only smiled at Alexandre's nearness, beckoning with her eyes.

She'll put a spell on you, that one.

"The King of Oranges must kiss the Princess of Practically Everything," Janette explained.

"The King of Oranges?"

Margot shrugged. "A fairy tale. Using one's imagination is a very important skill," she defended against his raised brow.

"Kiss her!" Janette pleaded, though Lisette, Alexandre noticed from the corner of his eye, now sat on a box planter, silent yet fiercely observant.

"And who might the King of Oranges be?" he asked the rain goddess in his arms.

"Perhaps you." Another shrug. "Though I shouldn't put significance in a child's tale. It *is* merely fiction."

"Of course. And I shouldn't expect that you would in

any way resemble this Princess of Practically Everything?"

"Oh, not nearly *everything,*" Margot exclaimed with a hand to her breast. "Perhaps . . . mmm . . . very much. But certainly not everything."

Alexandre looked down to find Janette stood very close, Ruby clutched expectantly to her chest, the duo of wide child eyes and dull glass eyes fixed to his and Margot's embrace. Such hopefulness captured in his daughter's stance.

He looked to Margot. Intermittent raindrops *splished* from her nose and *splat* onto his lips. He glanced his tongue out, tasting the cool liquid, then eyeballed his shorter companion. Such pressure! Two eager females waiting his action.

And one was not to discount the eagle-eyed gaze of the all-seeing Ruby.

"Shall we?" Margot offered after Janette, this time, whispered her plea for a kiss.

At that moment Alexandre's heart leapt before his brain to claim the victory. "I shouldn't wish to disappoint the masses." He leaned forward to kiss the Princess of Not Practically Everything but Certainly Very Much.

Amid Janette's cheers and the splashing of her toes in the puddles that surrounded, Alexandre thought he felt Margot's heart beat in his own heart, its thud, powerful and swift. Like his. But he couldn't be sure if it was as reluctant as his own. Or *had* been as reluctant.

Margot's kisses contained something wonderful. Something ineffable, like clouds and rain and sun and pinkness. It made Alexandre want to learn the composition so he might become master of the elixir. But as he pulled away from the passionate pink power of Margot's kiss, Alexandre again noticed from the corner of his eye his Lisette. Head down and lower lip thrust out.

"Ah! But the rain makes us silly!" Alexandre forced

himself to leave Margot and slip and slide over to Lisette, where he lifted his daughter into his arms and spun her around. An amber giggle slipped from her lips, curving the pout into a smile. "One more spin and then it's in to dry off. Come, Janette, you're next!"

Silly, eh?

Margot lifted her shoes and hose from the ground and with a wistful sigh stood waiting beneath the orange boughs until Alexandre had spun his daughters a few more times.

So he had thought that kiss silly? She had thought it nothing less than magical.

Certainly Alexandre Saint-Sylvestre needed some straightening out. The man did not know a gesture of passion when it jumped up and pressed its lips to his.

"I shall just have to see to changing that," Margot said decidedly as the trio scurried toward her, all giggles and squishing footsteps.

After they had returned to his room and dried off, Margot settled the girls on the end of Alexandre's bed with their studies. The rain was barely audible within his bedchamber, but it did still drip from his hair. Recalling last evening's venture into seduction over a wet head, Alexandre discreetly squeezed the water from the tips of his hair and decided he must busy himself or become completely distracted by the single curl that fell down Margot's forehead.

Stepping backward, he nearly toppled a pile of empty seedling pots. Decision made. He would see to a much-needed straightening of the room. But as Janette produced answers to Margot's mathematical queries, Alexandre's pots remained in a jumble upon the floor as he paced, his attention fixed to his daughters' teacher.

He wondered if Margot realized that when she was

listening her eyes were brighter than the sky on a clear day that featured but the one fluffy white cloud. Hmm. He paused in his stroll, pressed a finger to his lips, and . . . wondered.

Margot glanced up from Janette's count to twenty. Her eyes met Alexandre's. *Caught in his perusal.* Alexandre shrugged and slipped his hands down his thighs. With a sigh he wandered to the desk, where he made to put the jumble of texts and notes in order. A glance up found Margot smiling sweetly at him. He looked quickly down.

"Now you must write the numbers one through twenty," Margot said as she stood and directed the girls. "When you are finished, I'm sure Cook will have supper, from the delicious aroma that slips under your father's door."

"And now for you," she said as she approached the desk, her hands astutely on each hip and a wicked smile curving her mouth. "Doing some straightening?"

Utterly at a loss as to where to even begin the monumental task, Alexandre shrugged and set a sketch of a tulip in Margot's outstretched hand. "Of a sort. I wonder I might require a secretary at times for the jumble that becomes my desk."

"How do you find anything?" she said, not really interested in the answer it appeared, for her engaged tracing of the line drawing she held. "You said it is difficult for you to color your sketches?"

"Only for the great pleasure working with the colors gives me. I have rather fallen behind." He spread his hands over the notebook filled with colorless sketches, drawings he intended to someday publish as a folio of botanical studies. "You don't color in your little notebook?"

She shrugged. "I've never had the paints. I wouldn't know how to begin mixing them." She glanced to the wooden crate on the floor, where he kept the fat, cork-stoppered vials of powder, pure pigment of malachite and sienna and vermilion.

"Can we stop now?" Janette wondered loudly with an uncharacteristic huff.

"Have you written twenty yet?"

No response save two hearty sighs.

Margot suddenly leaned forward, conspiratorial in her flickering glance to the girls and then back to Alexandre. "I'll organize your desk for you and straighten your pots and sweep out the dirt."

He raised a brow. There must be some condition hiding behind the secretive tone of her voice.

She reached and drew a finger along his hand, tracing the line of his thumb to the sensitive flesh that veed between it and his finger. "If . . ."

If? He knew it.

"You could see to allowing me to experiment with your paints? I would like to put color to paper on some of my sketches."

He closed his eyes and focused on the teasing trace of her finger along his hand. A purlicue, that was the scientific term for the slight web of flesh between a person's thumb and forefinger. Such a pretty name for a part that was, at this moment, so sensitive. . . .

Alexandre opened his eyes to find Lisette's attention aimed on the illicit action between him and Margot. Abruptly he pulled away and went to the girls, consciously blocking Lisette's vision and clearing his sudden guilt at the same time. "I shall consider it," he said back to Margot.

He offered his summer-capped princess his hand and lifted her off the bed, spun her into a whirl, then planted a slider from the middle of her brows down her nose.

"I love you, Papa." Lisette clung to him, her little legs wrapping around his waist and her arms latching to his neck. She cast Margot a venomous pout. "I'm tired of lessons."

"Me too!" Janette and Ruby sprang up and started bouncing on the bed in protest. "We want to eat!"

Just catching Margot's rolling eyeballs, Alexandre fought the regret at his sudden detachment from her attentions. Lisette had needed him just then, he knew that. Gripping Janette's hand, he helped her to leap and sail from his bed. When Ruby was offered up, he tapped the doll on the head in affirmation. "Run along to the kitchen, then, the three of you."

"I'll be right along," Margot called as Janette sped into a dash.

Halfway to the door Lisette halted, her little gaze holding the leeriness of an adult twice betrayed. "You're not coming now?"

"I just want to straighten a few things for your father," Margot called as she adjusted Alexandre's books. "Run! Cook might need some testers for this evening's apple tarts before she sends them on to the king."

The mention of tarts removed the pout from Lisette's face, and the blond girl allowed herself to be pulled along by her sister's eagerness.

"They adore you," Alexandre said as he closed the door. "You needn't begin your organizing this very moment, Margot. Run along with my girls."

"You want me to leave right now?" She couldn't help it. Fighting her desire had gone beyond difficult; it was now impossible. They were alone. A man and a woman who had touched each other and kissed each other. He'd kissed her breasts last night. What she wouldn't give for such surrender on his part again.

Margot stepped before Alexandre and lifted her chin to meet his eyes. "Alexandre," she breathed, "I want to be your lover."

The loss of his smile jolted Margot to her senses. What had she just said? *Mon Dieu,* what she had just said!

But she had meant it.

Even as he backed away from her, Margot followed Alexandre's confused retreat. "I care for you," she said. "Don't you care for me as well?"

"Caring does not require a carnal pact."

His thighs connected with his desk, dislodging an open-faced book. Margot sprang to catch it before it hit the floor. Closing the sketchbook, Margot pressed it to her chest and peered into Alexandre's darting gaze. She'd be damned if she would allow him out of this discussion with his way of avoiding confrontation by pleading the poor, innocent widower.

Margot set the book down and placed her hand to the side of his cheek. Minute stubble tickled her palm. He gripped her wrist but did not pull her away.

"Margot, what happened to taking things slowly?"

"I'm sorry, I lose all rational thought when I am alone with you." She touched the purlicue on the hand that he'd secured around her wrist. "I just cannot *not* touch you."

"Yes, well . . ."

"Well what?"

"Did you *not* notice Lisette just now? And earlier. How she sat there bravely, acting disinterested, when I could see inside her little heart was being torn apart by the sight of you and me embracing. She is not comfortable with seeing her papa kiss another woman."

"But—"

No, Margot had not noticed Lisette. Janette had been so thrilled at their kiss earlier. She had just assumed Lisette's testy attitude was from hunger. But then, she had been testy last evening as well when she'd burrowed herself beneath the sheets. . . .

"Oh, *mon Dieu,* I am being so cruel. I did not give

her actions much thought beyond simple childhood crankiness. It is to be expected. One moment a child can be the height of happiness, and the next a lung-stretching tantrum might overtake. But of course, she must believe her papa can kiss only her mother."

"Indeed."

"And do you feel the same?" She drew her finger down his jaw and it lingered just a glance away from his lower lip. He gripped her hand to stop her action.

"While there are days I can still feel Sophie's overbearing presence, as I have explained to you, Margot, we did not have the usual loving relationship. There was little physical contact. Though I'm sure there were times the girls did see us kiss. Rarely." He drew in a sigh and exhaled heavily but decisively. "Margot, I like touching you and kissing you. I've already said as much. But your announcement—"

"That I wish to be your lover?"

"Yes. It—I don't know exactly. . . . Hell. What do you want me to say?"

"I want you to say yes." Melding her body against his, their clothing a fine barrier to heat and muscle pulses, she lifted her chin to coax his attention. "I want to know you." He dipped his head into her palm, unable to resist as she drew her touch along the side of his face, his eyes closed. "I want you to know me. Intimately. As a man can know a woman. I desire you, Alexandre."

Her voice caught on that last utterance. Margot knew her request was more cruel than kind. This man simply had too many things to worry about, what with finding a new nursemaid and tending his own duties to the king. And now she was heaping yet another decision upon him!

"Forgive me, I am being a fool."

With only a quick exit in mind, Margot fought the reluctance in her bones to sever her contact with Alexandre but finally pulled free. She made it no more than three strides, when she was embraced from behind.

Alexandre clung to her, spread his hand around her waist, and drew it up to press her shoulder against his chest. His unbound hair, still damp, tickled her neck as he nuzzled against her collarbone and breathed a lusty exhalation against her flesh. "I want you to stay."

Now? Tonight? Forever?

"I've never done this before," he whispered in her ear. "Never have I been forced to confront my feelings like this. I've always wrangled them into a tight ball and buried them away, deep within. You've dug into that tight wad of emotion, Margot."

"I didn't mean—"

"No, I like this—this . . . uncertainty. It's new, bold, exciting. I'm not sure what will come next, where my next move will take me, why or when I will react. But it feels good, Margot. Will you just let me hold you so I can ride this feeling?"

"If I stay, I can't promise I'll be satisfied with a simple embrace. The girls are waiting for us. Lisette . . ."

"Just give me one moment," he whispered into her ear. "One moment of nothing but you, Margot."

Thirteen

Closer . . . yet still a star's journey away

Another rainy day. The splatter of drops against his window felt minty and blue in his mouth. A good sensation, complemented by infrequent thunder blasts that rolled across his tongue like so many little metal balls, tickling and cold.

Drawing his hair back, Alexandre tied a length of black ribbon around the thick mass at the base of his neck. A man should just chop off the entire mess for all the trouble his unruly hair gave him, were it not for the sweet recollection of Margot's fingers running through the length. And Janette's insistence that it must remain, for certainly Ruby finds it most romantic.

Ah, but what to do today? It had rained for three days. Much as the king protested, no man could work in the mud. Alexandre scanned the floor of his room, running his eyes over the pots of seedlings and toppled dirt containers that had easily avoided his bewitched thoughts last night.

What a joy this impulsive and carefree woman was to know. How she lightened his heart when he had almost thought the pulsing organ might fall from its position in his chest for all the heartache that had befallen him lately.

Margot deVerona's presence touched his heart, lifted it back up, and placed it where it belonged. Still he could feel her touch upon it. Warm and right.

I want to be your lover, Alexandre.

Sophie had said much the same that first night in the Paris tavern where he'd sat down, ordered ale, and closed his road-weary eyes. *I want to be your lover,* whispered in icy round tones now in his thoughts. Sophie's voice.

He hadn't resisted. But should have.

And now he did resist the plea a second time. But felt he should not.

Alexandre squatted near the red clay planter that contained a tulip bulb. Its foliage had pushed up through the surface just the other day. He smoothed his fingers along the tender new leaves. When finally it bloomed, he could then sketch a study of the flower that was supposed to bloom in pink with deep green streaks.

This had been a gift from Le Nôtre for Alexandre's excellent work at Vaux-le-Vicomte. He'd given the bulb to him three days after Sophie's death, having found Alexandre sitting alone in the stables, a pitchfork in hand, all thought to spike up some straw for his flower beds erased by the sudden emotion of loss.

It had hit him so suddenly. He'd been thinking only to protect his daughters from the moment he'd learned of Sophie's demise, couldn't bother with his own emotions, for surely he should not care about a woman he did not love.

But on that third day following Sophie's death he had come to grips with the fact that he had indeed loved Sophie Marie Saint-Sylvestre. Certainly not in the romantic, passionate way of lovers, but in a grateful and endearing way. She had been a part of his life. Though they had both followed their own courses, the twins had connected them.

As fragile as that connection had been, Alexandre did mourn Sophie's absence.

Was it wrong now to even consider favoring another woman? It had been mere months since his wife had passed. Surely he must maintain propriety and mourn for—what?—six months, a year?

Weeks earlier Alexandre could have easily accepted the year as his punishment for indifferently destroying Sophie's life.

Now a year was unthinkable.

His emotions had been set free by Margot; he did not want to stifle them now. All his life he'd hidden behind a facade of indifference, even of shyness, in order to protect himself from the ignorance others would have of his gift.

Margot had accepted him without question. And if she did question, it was the eager curiosity that sparkled madly in her eyes and only made her all the more attractive to him.

Alexandre could imagine spending a lifetime with the curly topped beauty. Wouldn't Lisette and Janette be thrilled about that?

Janette would. She'd not once questioned Sophie's absence since Margot stepped into their lives. But he still was uncertain about Lisette. She had balked around Margot since the evening Janette had encouraged their kiss in the rain.

Could he hold off his feelings for another woman because his daughter could not yet accept him and Margot as a couple? Certainly he must give Lisette the time she needed to grieve Sophie's death and entertain the idea of her father loving again.

Or could he perhaps continue with the relationship while keeping it from Lisette? Who knew how long the child would need to come around?

Standing, Alexandre went to the windowsill to locate

a good spot for the tulip pot. When the rains dissipated, the sun would grant this little plant much-needed light, as Margot had spread sunshine over his and his daughters' lives.

I want to be your lover.

Could he risk making love to Margot and redoubling his past mistakes?

Truthfully? He wanted to. He desired the woman beyond all reason. Those soft blond curls did not remind him at all of Sophie. They were inexplicably Margot. Holding her in his arms was a sweet surrender, touching her breasts and kissing her . . .

The pot settled onto the sill with a heavy clunk.

"I must strive to keep her fully clothed the next time we meet. It is the only way," he tried to convince himself. "Until I've the nerve to ask for her hand."

"So the Princess of Practically Everything fell in love with the King of Oranges, but there was one thing standing in her way. . . ."

"The villain," Lisette pronounced in a perfectly horrid voice, which was promptly followed by twin giggles.

"Indeed, the villain." The child was most eager to introduce that character, wasn't she?

"He was a most dark and evil man," Margot narrated, clawing her fingers before her in graphic display. "A toad who could mount his horse with one great froggy leap and snap up pretty little kittens with his long tongue."

Both girls gifted Margot with utterly horrific expressions.

"But he dressed very well," she added, which released them from their tension. "He was . . . a baron. The Baron of Blunders. A most imposing figure he cut. Tall and pale with a huge bellowing gut. Yes, indeed, quite hideous."

Margot shuffled out from between the two girls on their bed and stood. "There is always evil the good people must overcome in order to learn and grow before the story can end."

"But why must there be evil?" Janette said on a yawn. "Why can't it be all good and the king can marry the princess and the kittens shall live happily ever after?"

Margot sat on the edge of the bed. Yes, why couldn't life be as simple as happily-ever-after? Surely for some people it was. Princesses and kings perhaps.

"Do you really think we'd like to listen to stories about perfect people and perfect love? I'd much prefer a bit of adventure myself. A frenzied dash through a thunderstorm as compared to a lazy day under yet another perfect sun."

"I like the sun," Lisette growled sleepily. "The rain makes my curls wilt."

"Yes, well . . . indeed." A bit too tired herself to argue any moot points, Margot gave a reiterating tuck and kissed the girls' heads. "Tomorrow we will journey into adventure. We shall put our princess to the test to see if she has what it takes to deserve a kind man such as the King of Oranges."

Janette answered with a snore; Lisette, a heavy sigh. "The king is very kind. But what happened"—*yawn*— "to his queen?"

Margot glanced at Alexandre's chamber door. A line of gold candle glow traced the bottom of the oak door. He'd spent most of the day inside after the noon rains had begun. She'd avoided talking to him for fear that it would all come gushing forth. *It* being the intense craving for his touch. The want for his kisses. The need to give herself to him. The desire to become his lover. *Before it is too late.*

His queen? "This king hasn't yet found the right woman to be his queen."

"Oh."

Margot stood and straightened the girls' dresses inside the armoire and placed their shoes in neat pairs. Finding Ruby sprawled at the end of the bed, she tucked her next to Janette's shoulder.

"He's still awake," whispered a small voice. Lisette always did linger on the edge of sleep, while Janette pretty much went dead to the world as soon as her head hit the pillow. "Papa likes talking to you, Margot. It makes him happy."

She reached and squeezed the little fingers extended across the velvet counterpane. "I like talking to him too." But she could not forget Alexandre's worry about Lisette not accepting their closeness. "But what of you? You were sad the other day when I kissed your papa. I don't want to make you sad, Lisette."

"I was thinking of Mama." A wash of tear glossed her eyes. "Mama is the only one Papa has ever kissed. When he kissed you, it made my tummy feel grumpy. Right here." Lisette pressed a hand to the exact place on her body where her heart pumped, far from her stomach. "I like you, Margot. And I know Papa likes you, because you make him smile."

Alexandre's smiles were a rare treasure that Margot felt privileged to have discovered. She leaned forward and pressed a kiss to Lisette's head. "If my getting close to your papa is going to make your heart—er, your tummy hurt, you must tell me, Lisette."

"Do you love Papa?"

I think I love you. She had so foolishly confessed to Alexandre yesterday. Immediately following, she had questioned the bold declaration. But the answer had been easy. Yes, she did love Alexandre.

But love was deep. It was emotion. It was . . . forever.

"I . . . I'm not sure. I haven't even thought about that." A forever she could not give Alexandre and his daughters.

"Then why did you kiss him? In the story the princess never kisses the king until the very end; then they live happily ever after. It's always that way. It can't be any other way."

In fairy tales. But reality was so very different from fantasy. Much as Margot did love Alexandre, she knew it could never be. And she mustn't allow Lisette to believe it could be so. "Sometimes adults like to kiss each other because it makes them feel good."

"Like when Papa gives me a slider?"

"Exactly."

"But you will love him if you kiss him again, won't you?"

"Oh, Lisette." That a four-year-old child could challenge her so made the flesh on Margot's arms prickle.

"Go on, Princess," Lisette said on a hearty yawn, and a lackluster gesture toward her father's chamber door. "The king"—*yawn*—"waits."

"By your leave?"

"I grant"—*yawn*—"my leave."

Margot stood and stepped over to the chamber door. She placed her palm upon it, aware of Lisette's sleepy attention falling upon her in the darkness.

Indeed, she did hear a scratching on the other side of the door. He was drawing in his botanical notebook. Designing images of the plants that peopled his world. Surely a painstaking process, for his perception of colors must make it difficult to reproduce on paper.

It might take me an hour to read one sentence, for the mixture of colors and pure beauty of each individual letter will capture my attention. . . .

Alexandre had overcome insurmountable odds to stand where he did today. How difficult it must have been to study his books and learn the various plant species when such concentration was required. And to do so without revealing to others the secret part of him that might label him outcast and different.

Alexandre was a different man. Delightfully, devastatingly different.

He would never make demands of her, never declare in a gruff voice that male children were required to keep him satisfied. Never would he dump her at a palace in expectation of her gaining domestic skills and ladylike manners in order to please him. Alexandre asked nothing of anybody beyond the same respect he gave his own daughters.

Could she interfere in his life more than she already had?

I want to be your lover. That was all she could be, his lover. For she had been promised to someone else.

Reluctance never felt so strong, so real, as if it coated the door with a sticky substance that held the wood locked within the frame.

She would only hurt him if she were to make love to him and then leave to marry the baron. And what of his children? Did she risk creating false hope in their little hearts by continuing this relationship? How then might she hurt them when finally she left? For she must leave.

Do this for yourself, Margot, you want to know love.

"No," she whispered to her evil conscience. "How selfish."

"Margot?"

Had he sensed her presence?

Fearing another call might wake Janette, Margot slipped inside Alexandre's room. He rose from his desk, the fine ripples of linen pillowed up at his elbows slipping soundlessly down his forearm to bunch at his wrists. One limping step forward. And an outstretched hand.

His look said it all. *Come to me. Let's begin.*

Margot took a tentative step forward. Her conscience raged inside her skull, vying to topple her brave steps and send her fleeing. *Think of the girls. You mustn't give them false hope. You can never stay with this man.*

He touched her jaw, smoothed a finger over her lips. *I do want him. Can we not just share this moment without then expecting something more? Can it not be simple?*

"Simple," Margot whispered as his lips fell upon hers.

He kissed her. She kissed back. But Margot's thoughts were focused on the lack of warmth that should be caressing her body. Alexandre's hands were not exploring her waist, running up over her breasts, mapping out her sensitive spots. He did not move to make the kiss any more than his mouth pressed to hers. Something toiled inside the man's brain. Something that vexed Margot beyond all reason. It could not merely be his fear of Lisette getting upset over their relationship.

"W-what is it?" she whispered as he pulled away and paced to his desk. When Alexandre turned, the eerie illumination thrown up from the candle sitting on his desk shadowed his grim expression.

"I am just trying to keep the pace slow, as we agreed."

"Oh. Yes, but—"

"Margot, I have spent much time considering your request that we become lovers."

"I expect nothing in return," she rushed in. "I would never ask for a commitment—"

"Be that as it may . . ." He gripped her shoulders and eyed her with a gaze more parental than that of a potential lover. "You are not thinking rationally, Margot. I do want you, I do. But what if a child were to come of our union?"

The surrounding air became heavy upon Margot's shoulders. It suffused her lungs and made her body feel like a lump. A child. She hadn't thought of the consequences, beyond the fact that she may never continue her relationship with the man. Margot would not dream of chaining Alexandre to her heart with such a ploy as a child. It was an impossible notion.

Oh, but what could she do? She wanted him, wanted to make love with him desperately.

There were ways to avoid conceiving. She had heard rumors. Hmm . . . She would find out exactly what was required to have relations without having children. Yes, she must. Then Alexandre would feel safe and she could enjoy his passion.

"You take on a certain pose when you're wondering, you know that?"

Looking up from her cupped chin, Margot smiled. "My wondering pose. Janette has taken it on in her perusal of insects during our nature walks. Lisette has developed her own wondering pose, which features a raised brow and intense little eyes."

"I like what you have done for my girls, Margot. You shall have children of your own someday. Children that will thrive under their mother's inquisitive and wondering wing. But I shouldn't wish that to come until you are ready for it." He tilted her chin up into his gaze. "And especially not until you are first married."

Fidgeting with the top hook of her stays, Margot shrugged. "I understand. I would never think to burden you with another child when you've already such a—"

"I love my children. They are not a burden."

"I didn't mean it—oh." She stepped forward and touched the satin cord that had secured the neck of his shirt, being careful not to touch the exposed flesh beneath. "Forgive me. The twins are gifts from heaven. I know you love them. But I also know you've much work and not enough time in the day to give them all the attention you desire. I enjoy your company, Alexandre, but I would never make demands on a man's heart when it is already stretched to all ends."

"I don't mind a little tugging on your part. You are all right with this?"

"I suppose I must be."

He quirked a brow. "You suppose?"

"I'm not sure what this really means. Is this where our relationship ends?"

"No, no." He cuddled her into his embrace and pressed his cheek to the top of her head. Scent of earth and musk coated him like a sweet perfume. "I don't wish to end a relationship that I cherish more than my own job."

"Really? But your work, it is your life."

"You have also become my life. We just need to slow down, take things very carefully."

"Is that possible? Every time you kiss me. . . . I feel so . . . I don't want things to stop. I want to race forward. It's as though I can see the beginning of the rainstorm, it is within a few strides, if only I could run fast enough. I don't know if that feeling won't come upon me again. But I do know I don't want your kisses to end. Alexandre, what must we do?"

"True, we have gone beyond mere friendship."

"I give you my word I will do nothing to chain your affections to my own, Alexandre. I want only to know the joy of being close to you."

He lifted her hand and kissed her knuckles slowly and with utmost attention. "I wish it could be different, but for right now I am too worried of the results should we make love. And there is Lisette. She mustn't be forced to abandon her feelings for her mother, nor must we steal them from her. But you must never forget that I care for you, and that is why I am doing this."

"It will be difficult. But I will do whatever you ask."

"Will you leave me now?"

Damn, but that was a hard request to swallow. But if she wanted to prove her willingness to comply with his wishes, she must. Margot stretched up on her toes and kissed his forehead. She held her lips there for a moment, closing her eyes against the pain of parting. "I'll see you tomorrow morning for breakfast?"

He nodded. He held her hand for a long time as Margot slowly walked away. She almost thought he wanted her to stay, but finally he released her and, clamping his arms to his chest, turned to the window.

Slipping inside the subtle quiet of the outer hallway, Margot slumped against the wall and closed her eyes. "I will find a way, Alexandre. I want to be with you. In every possible way."

A bright star winked and disappeared behind a heavy matting of clouds. Someone was keeping an eye on him.

Alexandre hated having to pull away from Margot just when they had come so close. But had he not, the night would not have ended with a chaste kiss and an *au-revoir*. No, Margot would have woken in his arms tomorrow morning, her sweet body melded to his, his arms wrapped possessively about her.

Alexandre fisted his hands. To even think of her body lying next to his! Flesh and heavy breaths and panting kisses. The image shuddered through him like an awakening. He wanted Margot deVerona. He needed her. His body wanted the release. His heart demanded the affection. What held him back beyond the feeble excuse of an unplanned child?

That his soul had been scarred by his first marriage would forever haunt him.

And while Alexandre may give a notion to considering that Margot was more right for him than he might ever imagine—he even believed she might think the same—he was no fool. He could not allow himself to revisit previous mistakes. If he were meant to have a child with Margot, it must come after they were married—a marriage that would happen if and when he ever felt ready for commitment.

There was the possibility that nothing would happen should they lie together. But he couldn't take that chance. Not now. He just . . . didn't have the time for more responsibility. He couldn't ask Margot for her hand when he had nothing to offer but days away from her side.

But how much longer would the king's project continue? It gave a reason to years, perhaps even decades of work. Would he never have the time to care for a complete family, to fall in love?

Fall in love.

Alexandre smirked. To even think such words meant only that it had already happened. He'd been speaking around the notion last night when he'd told Margot he'd never known the emotion before. Drumming up any excuse not to face the reality that perhaps he held love in his arms in the form of Margot deVerona.

But the fact that he didn't want to release her from his arms frightened him more than revealing his sensory gifts.

Marriage.

Should he ask? Was he ready?

Fourteen

Once upon a time a princess plotted to win a king.

The slimy cavity of bone and flesh creaked in protest as Margot eased a handful of Cook's rosemary stuffing inside the freshly butchered goose. Eleven more slippery patients, lined along the kitchen's table, awaited the same treatment. Thankfully Cook had done the "deed" earlier, for the idea of having to take an animal's life—dinner or not—made Margot shudder.

She scooped another handful of moist bread crumbs and spices from the large iron kettle and eyed goose number two. All afternoon she'd pondered the idea of exactly what it would take to assure Alexandre that he could risk making love with her. While she hated reducing the act to such clinical thoughts, it had to be done. It could happen no other way.

And it must happen. There was no question; she must know what it was like to lie with a man she loved before succumbing to a loveless marriage. And that man must be Alexandre, for she did love him.

While her mother had coached Margot through the domestic duties of life and taught her morals and letters and had even been the one to instill in Margot an insatiable curiosity, she hadn't more than a few words regarding the carnal relations. "The man shall lead the way" and "A wife gains more virtue than she loses by submitting to her husband" were about all she had had the time to offer between nursing small children and seeing to the meals and the laundering.

And while Margot knew exactly what actions were involved in the act of making love—she had stumbled upon the duchess more than a few times during the act, though she hadn't been seen—the information Margot really needed just wasn't there.

Setting fowl number three in front of Cook, who then trussed the beast with a few quick motions and mounted it on the roasting spit, Margot reached for another naked bird and let out a sigh. "Cook?"

"Tiring of the work already?"

"Oh, not at all. I've had my hand up a goose's hindquarters more times than necessary, but I do know my work."

"I must say, you do. A woman of many talents, you are, Margot. A fine catch for any man."

"I should like to be caught."

Cook's giggles, always so high and bubbly, never did match her physique, where one might expect a ribald belly rumble. "You're already caught, child. Mustn't go confusing your dreams with reality, much as the fantasies may seem more appealing. I just pray the baron . . ."

"Yes?" Margot clung to Cook's trailing thoughts.

"Let's just say a smart woman like you needn't be tied down by infants and chores. Pray the baron loves you for the dreamer you are, Margot. Pray the man wants to watch you soar, as I have been witness to your flights."

"I fear the toad shall be most pleased to see me shackled to a bed with a half dozen infants scampering about and yet another in my belly. All of which must be male, as he has stipulated in the marriage contract."

She had reluctantly signed the contract months before,

even though the original agreement, as drawn up years ago by her mother and the baron's father, had many cross-throughs and changes. Nicodème de Verzy had sent along the new version for Margot's approval before he left on a venture across the Irish Sea.

The stipulation that her education should be paid remained. But a new line had been added that a male child shall be conceived as quickly as possible. Margot twisted her thoughts over that one for days before finally signing. Of course she would bear her husband children. There was certainly no way she could ensure the child would be male, but the stipulation regarding her education had glossed over that worry.

Goose number four slipped across Margot's skirt in protest of its treatment, but with some quick fingerwork she rescued it before it took a featherless flight to the floor.

"How I would love to soar. But what if I should find a man I truly love? A man I really . . . care for. Someone who I know cares for me. Someone who wants to watch me soar."

"Child, you must give up your romantic notions on Monsieur Saint-Sylvestre."

Margot glanced up from her slippery work to find Cook eyeing her. The woman could stab a person with an admonishing word without opening her mouth.

"We've become very close."

"I don't want to hear it. You are impossibly stubborn, Margot deVerona."

"I care for him, Cook." She shoved the stuffed goose aside and with a heavy sigh caught her chin in hand. "And he cares for me."

"The man is merely confused. He needs you to look after his children. His heart has been broken by his wife's death—"

"He never loved her. You told me yourself what a cruel woman she was. Alexandre has told me much the same."

"Has he now?" Cook secured another slippery fowl and shoved a handful of stuffing inside. Rather forcefully, Margot noticed.

"I've no designs on the man, Cook; you must believe me. I know in but a few weeks' time I'm to be carted away to some horrible castle to be set up as housemaid and breeding machine to a toad."

"If you think your fate will be so horrible, then it most certainly will. What happened to your positivity? You're a girl who grins at the most dire challenge with a sparkle in your eye. You can make this marriage to the baron anything you wish it to be."

"I'll concern myself with that when the time comes. All I want right now is Alexandre."

"No!"

"You know I'll not take a care to your protest," Margot said on a stubborn lift of her nose. "I've decided I want to know what it is like to lie with a man who loves me before I must be forced to lie with one who does not."

Cook's fist pounded the table. A squishy crack spurted gobs of stuffing on the woman's grease-smeared apron. The goose was still attached to her hand "So he loves you now, does he?"

"Well . . ." Margot hooked her elbows on the table and caught her chin between her hands. A chunk of stuffing oozed across her cheek.

Cook pushed the trussed goose aside and hooked an elbow on the table next to Margot.

"You won't tell my mother, will you?"

"And why shouldn't she know her daughter has intentions of destroying a match she wished for you? Should the baron discover your liaisons with the gardener, he'll have the man drawn and quartered, and then he'll cast you in rags back to your mother. Would you risk ruining an innocent man's life in the pursuit of your own selfish passions? And think of those precious girls."

Lisette and Janette had become attached to her. They had most likely forgotten Margot's statement of watching after them only until a permanent nursemaid could be found. As she was also beginning to allow that pertinent fact slip her mind.

"I have considered them."

"Obviously not enough."

But what about *her* needs? Her desires? She must have a chance to experience love. She must!

"Perhaps the baron will not know. I can put up a great and glorious production on our wedding night, and he'll never be the wiser. Oh, Cook." Margot gripped her wrist and decided she must tell all. She could trust Cook. "I want to make love to Alexandre. He wants to make love to me."

Cook's eyes flared, as did her nostrils. She looked ready to go into a diatribe, but instead she just settled.

"We almost did," Margot whispered. "But he cares about me so much. He doesn't want to get me with child."

"He doesn't want to get you with child, or he doesn't want to find himself as a father again?"

"Cook, you do know he married his wife only after he found out she was pregnant."

"You should not have such information."

"He told me himself."

"Exactly! You've become too close to a man when you start discussing things better left to the privacy of the bedroom."

"Indeed."

"Oh, Margot." Cook let out a hefty sigh at Margot's arrogant reply. She raked her pudgy fingers back through her hair, dispersing crumbles of stuffing through the gray strands. "I did not know the man was forced to marry.

'Course, that does go a long way in explaining that mismatch from hell. The poor man."

"Yes, and now, don't you see, he's frightened to death that it might happen again."

Cook's hand felt heavy and cold as she clamped it gently over Margot's hand. "Then you must release him of such a fear."

"No! You said yourself that I should find a man who wants to watch me soar. Well, I think Alexandre might be that man. Oh, Cook, there must be ways. I want to lie with him without fear of getting a child."

"My dear, sweet, passion-swept Margot." Cook smoothed a hand over Margot's shoulder and with a kiss to her nose leaned back and crossed her arms over her abundant breasts. "There's no changing your mind?"

Margot shook her head.

"I must give you benefit, you are smarter than you look. Most women don't give a bother for such thoughts such as preventing an unwanted child. I pity Beatrice, who spends more time visiting the witch under the hill than she does in a man's bed."

"The witch under the hill?"

Suddenly conspiratorial, Cook shifted her gaze from the doors to the windows and back to Margot. "The laundry maid who's always swinging her hips into any man's path goes there to lose her baby. Three times at least since I've been here. Wicked woman."

"She—to lose her baby . . ."

Cook made a slashing motion across her throat, the implication obvious.

"That's horrible! An innocent child not even given the chance to breathe its first breath? I would never dream to do such a thing."

"I should pray not. But one can never be one hundred percent safe when indulging in passions." She gazed a hard, glittering eye upon Margot. "Do you know that?"

"Surely I do. Perhaps. Well . . . no."

"Oh! No, I cannot allow you to do this. Banish all thoughts of Monsieur Saint-Sylvestre from your mind now. This instant."

"Done." Margot flinched but braved Cook's discerning gaze. Finally Cook nodded and shoved another goose Margot's way. Conversation ended.

But a new plan was forming.

Afternoon found Margot and the girls seeking Alexandre in the stables. Cook had packed a basket of goodies for lunch. Fresh goat cheese, raspberry preserves, rye bread, wine, and apple cider. Pierceforest interrupted their lunch, a mischievous grin on his face. Janette was the first to spy the wiggling lump tucked inside his leather vest.

"What's that?"

Alexandre was just ready to admonish Janette for her curiosity, when a *mewl* and a furry head popped out behind the dirty vest.

"A kitten!" Lisette sprang up from their makeshift lunch on a straw pile and clutched at the furry little treat Pierceforest handed her.

"There's a whole mess of 'em at the other end of the stables."

Janette's glee virtually screamed from her wide brown eyes.

"I could show the girls down there for a spell," Pierceforest offered. "If you don't mind, Monsieur Saint-Sylvestre?"

"Oh, please, Papa!"

Alexandre smoothed a hand over his braid and cocked a parental frown upon his girls. But he could not disguise the smile in his eyes. "As long as there are not additional members in the party on your return."

"Yes!" The girls scampered ahead, while Pierceforest bowed and tossed a wink to Margot. "I won't let them become too attached."

"Good luck," Margot called as she gathered the uneaten bits of the girls' lunches. There were but a few swallows of wine left in the bottle, which Alexandre accepted and slugged back.

"You really think they'll be able to leave the kittens?"

"No, but perhaps it wouldn't be so terrible to have one scampering at the girls' feet. Nothing wrong with a playmate."

"Don't you think Ruby would become terribly jealous?"

"Ah, I hadn't considered the wily-eyed Ruby."

"You are such a good father."

His blush appeared to surprise him so much that Alexandre pressed the side of his hand to his forehead to shadow his flushed cheeks.

"You mustn't be ashamed of it."

"I'm not. It's just, I'm not used to receiving compliments."

"I thought you had come to expect the unexpected from me?" She reached and pulled his hand from his face. They twined fingers and clasped hands with an absent ease. "Speaking of the unexpected . . . your girls . . . the other day they said something that disturbed me."

"What is that?"

"Lisette said that their mother left them one day. She just climbed in a carriage and rode off. She promised to return for them, but Janette said she never did come back. Alexandre?"

A touch to his arm found his muscles tense, a glance to his face, his jaw tight. He shook his head, pleading her retreat, but Margot could not.

Compelled to comfort his hurt, she embraced him. He

did not push her away, only remained stiff, his eyes still closed. His body shuddered inside her embrace. Muscles tensed under her touch, and she thought to almost hear his heart pump. Margot knew he was fending off a storm of emotion as best he could.

"Shall I go?"

He shook his head adamantly. *No, stay,* he silently said.

The wind swished the leaves outside the open stable doors, so distant the sound, as if the trees were a million leagues away. All the emotion Alexandre had kept bottled up over the years was so close, so tangible, it hung in the air like the moment before the rains, heavy and graspable.

"I had hoped the girls would forget their mother's leaving," he finally said. *"Mon Dieu."* He let out a heavy exhalation, and Margot felt his body wilt against her embrace. A motion to break free coaxed her to move away. *Grant him space.*

He pressed the heels of his palms to his eyes. "The memory is so horrid."

"Then you mustn't speak of it." Frantic to change the subject, Margot scanned the open stall they sat in, seeking diversion. The girls' giggles were distant; they were blissfully unaware of their father's pain. "I should refrain from constantly bringing up this topic. If I could take back my foolish words—"

"No." A proud man he sat, his long legs crossed at the ankle before him, tormented by a past not of his choosing. "You are curious. That doesn't bother me. I have shared a deep secret with you already, I shouldn't fear exposing myself any more than I already have."

"But you needn't."

"What of your needs?" He touched her hand, twined his work-roughened fingers through hers once more. "You need to know me completely, don't you?"

"I would like that."

"Then I will grant it. It is the least I can offer after my refusal last night."

"Oh, Alexandre—"

He silenced her protest with a hand. "I want to give of myself to you, Margot. But you must allow it to come gradually. Little by little. We will come together." He kissed her nose. "I promise you that. But today I will tell you all that you do not know about my departed wife and me."

Feeling as though she had pried a wedge into his soul and forced it open for her own perusal, Margot formed another protest on her tongue, one last chance to allow him some privacy. But she didn't speak it. The urge to know him completely overwhelmed. She could not fight it.

"Sophie and I had reached a point where we'd decided to no longer live together. Less than six months ago." From where he sat he scanned the horizon, shaggy with immature trees and all stages of construction. "I could not fault her for wanting to leave Versailles. It is a mess at this stage. She did not care for the little rooms I have in the Orangerie. Didn't like to be so close to insects and dirt and other dreadful substances. 'I attract nature something foul,' she'd always say. Well, you've seen the disarray of my room."

"I like the mess. It is you," Margot offered.

He granted her a half-smile. But the grim line quickly returned. "She really did deserve far better. Fine furnishing and clothes, fancy coifs and elegant cosmetics. I tried my best." Now he turned away. A sigh lowered his shoulders.

"When she wanted to move back to Paris—without me—I agreed. I knew she would thrive in the city. And even though I believed the open space of Versailles was what the girls needed in their younger years, I also knew Sophie would see to their education and upbringing. She left for Paris to find a home. When she returned, I knew it would be for the girls. And nothing else.

"Four months ago Sophie returned."

Only four months that his wife had been out of his life. And Margot had deemed to tamper with the fragile skein of his emotions. Cruel of her. But it could not have been prevented. Not as long as she continued to follow her heart.

And she always followed her heart.

"It was the middle day of a seven-day fête Louis had given for Louise de la Vallière. I was up on the south terrace, trimming the box hedge. From there, I could see Sophie's coach arrive. A cloud of dust fumed around the carriage wheels as I stood there, hands limp at my sides. I knew Sophie would not exit until the dust had settled. I also knew I would not step one foot forward to meet her, for that would only quicken the minutes before my daughters must take leave of my arms."

"But they would visit?" Margot asked.

"Not Versailles. We had agreed that I would travel to Paris every other week to visit the girls. But it was not to be."

His body stiffened against the arm Margot had wrapped around his waist. It was coming. The horrid confession that he needed to tell and she so desperately didn't want to hear. But she also did want to hear.

"The carriage door creaked loudly; it was a black, crumbling sound. I could hear it even at that great distance. So hideous how it felt in my hands. You know, the color?"

She nodded, understanding completely.

"I saw Sophie's violet-gloved hand slide along the door and her head popped out. She wore a new hat trimmed in frothy violet plumes. That was her favorite color. Horrid color, isn't it? Just too loud for my taste.

"As our eyes met, I could feel my wife's disgust choke

in my throat. Disgust for the lands, the life she'd been thrown into, disgust for me.

"She stood upright, stepped onto the top platform of the little folding steps, and then I heard the snap. The mechanism, I would later learn, was rusted and old. Sophie fell without a scream, breaking her neck instantly as she hit the ground."

"Oh, Alexandre."

His staying hand cautioned her silence. He'd come this far and he could not stop now. The corner of his mouth quivered as he spoke. "And do you know I stood there for one moment longer. I kept running the scene over in my mind. She has come for my girls. And now she is dead. And now they are mine. And why did I punish her so?

"That is all I will ever remember about my wife. Why did I punish her so?"

With yet another sigh Alexandre slipped from Margot's embrace and caught his head in his hands, his elbows catching upon his knees.

Punish? The man hadn't an admonishing bone in his body. "It was not your fault. It was you who suffered the severest punish—"

He stopped her with that perfectly sad look; grim mouth, and tear-glittering eyes. Margot swallowed. She wanted to embrace him, to bleed his pain into her own body so he could finally be free. But this was not her pain to have. It was his. And he must be allowed the sadness, the memory, the pain.

"I'm sorry," she offered. "We are not to question His great plan for us, mere mortals. But perhaps the two of you were brought together for a specific reason, to experience pain."

He smirked.

"And now it is over."

"It will never be over." His jaw held tight, Alexandre's eyes glittered with an unusual malice. "Can't you see?"

"No, I—"

He swept a hand toward the far stables, where Pierceforest had taken the twins. "Perhaps you should see to the girls."

"I could not—

"Leave me!"

"But, Alex—"

"Please!"

Margot stood, took a tentative step backward—then stopped. "No. No, Alexandre." She plunged to her knees and spread her arms around his shoulders. His body remained as rigid as the cold hardness she had just seen in his eyes. "I will not leave you when now more than ever you just need to be held—"

"I cannot," he muttered, and made to push her away.

But he did not use his strength as she spread her arms around his and beckoned him closer. Margot held fast. She had no reluctance. Now was right. She felt it. Alexandre's quiet sobs touched her heart with the tragic burn of regret and guilt.

"It was my fault," he said, clutching her, his fingers gripping her hair in squeezing clutches. "If I had not chased her away, she would never had reason to return."

"You could never chase anyone away. You said yourself, it was this place."

"I could have moved to Paris with her. Then she would have never been in that carriage."

"You could have no more left your life's work than the stars could twinkle next to the sun. Your wife's death was an accident, Alexandre. Tragic, yes, but it could have happened to anyone. It might have happened to the person who rode in the carriage the day before, or had Sophie not fallen, it might have happened the next day. You could not have prevented it."

"I should have raced to meet her. I should have been there to catch her, Margot. There is nothing you can say to make it right. It was not right! It was all wrong! We should have never married in the first place!"

Sharp silence sliced through the airy stable, lifting the tip of Alexandre's braid against his arm as he sat there, staring off into the sky, his back melded against her body.

Margot's heart beat rapidly. No more so than his heart must beat, she knew. Or perhaps Alexandre's heart could never again hold a steady, strong beat for the guilt that weighted it down and twisted it with the horrid memory of his wife's death.

That he had not wanted to marry Sophie was obvious. That it could have happened no other way was also clear. "You would never have abandoned her to raise your children on her own."

"No, I could not have," he said with a shake of his head. A heavy sigh dropped his shoulders. But with his next inhale Alexandre pulled himself straight, pushed a sleeve up his arm, and threw off the raiments of sadness. "Now you know all."

Indeed. Such a brave man. "I love you for trusting me enough to share yourself with me."

His embrace surprised her in its immediacy. He clung more than hugged. Surrendered his anxieties in the melding of his body against hers. "I love you for allowing me the courage to do so. I feel better now."

"Truthfully?"

"Yes. Rather as if the proverbial weight has been lifted from my shoulders."

"I can see it in your eyes."

Beneath her tender touch Alexandre's mouth wriggled up into a shy smile, straightened briefly, then grew to a strong arc. "This enchantment thing is certainly a lark."

"But I am no witch."

"No, never. I think it takes an entirely different species

to work such a spell of enchantment. The genus *Devero-nus margoticus.*"

She giggled, which sparked a chuff of laughter from him. Racing to touch his mirth, Margot traced her finger from end to end of the curve on his lips. "If this is what enchantment looks like," she whispered, "I'd better go brew another batch. I treasure your smile, Alexandre."

"You have put it there."

So she had. "I think I know how to keep it there."

"How so?"

A kiss. A perfect, lingering kiss beneath the bare rafters of the king's stables. Out of eyesight but within hearing range, the twins' giggles punctuated the silence between Alexandre and Margot as their desires chased away the sadness of his confession. Heartbeats pounded. Fingers twined. Margot curled a slippered foot around one of Alexandre's legs as he stretched out along her body and lowered her head to the straw-covered floor.

She knew all now. He had trusted her and had opened his heart to reveal his darkest torments.

Now, if only she could be as honest with him.

Fifteen

Midnight madness

He stood outside the kitchen door, hand poised to rap on the plain oak plank, when the notion that he would wake Cook as well as Margot stayed Alexandre.

It was nigh past midnight, but he'd not been able to sleep after checking in on the girls. The essence of Margot's being lingered in the girls' room, in the folds of the bed sheeting, in the curls of his daughters' hair. Everywhere Margot deVerona called to him. Seduced him with an invisible mist of temptation.

He had to see her—to ask her—but he did not want to wake Cook and risk a round of gossip in the morning. Not that his kiss in the Swiss pond the other day hadn't sparked a few nudges and winks. If Stephen were not in Paris begging his father for yet another stipend, he might have rankled Alexandre for days.

Alexandre meandered down the dark hall to the outer door and stepped onto the crushed stone that wound its way to the south terrace. Full moonlight drowned the grounds in eerie illumination. Statuary took on a muted pewter glow. The pair of lions perched at the head of the hundred steps each carried a pudgy-faced cherub upon its powerfully muscled hindquarters. Strength and softness.

He mused how remarkably close that defined his relationship with Margot. But it was she who possessed the strength. She had not allowed him to accept the blame for his wife's death. And he knew now that he had not been to blame. Yes, an accident. He had known that. Accidents happen all the time and no one can truly be blamed. But until he'd heard it from Margot's lips he had never wanted to believe it.

He mustn't be so hard on himself. For the sake of his girls he would try not to be. From this day forth. He must begin anew. And there was one way to do that.

There, upon one of the lion's backs, sat Margot, a passenger riding sidesaddle, her arm around the cupid who commanded the lion with a mischievous tug to its reins. For a moment Alexandre fancied the stone lion standing regally on all fours, its two riders clinging to its mane. With one leap it would take to the air. Margot's laughter would shower the sky with new stars of the pink, wavy brand.

His boots crushing the stones in horridly loud steps, Alexandre winced as he crossed the terrace, but Margot did not turn at his advance.

"You are not afraid of a stranger's footsteps approaching in the night?" he called as he closed the distance.

"I knew it was you."

"My limp sets an unusual pace."

"That, and who else would be looking in on the Orangerie at this hour?"

Alexandre hefted a foot up onto the lion's hindquarters and looked off across the Orangerie to the Swiss pond. Moonlight glimmered on the surface in silver waves that felt cool in his mouth and formed columns in his sight. So vivid, without a second thought he reached out to run his fingers along the sensation.

"Describe it to me," Margot said as she lifted her hand

to spoon inside his extended fingers. "How does the moonlight feel upon the water?"

He curled his fingers through hers. The sensation of flesh to flesh coiled inside him, stirring his desires. *Marriage?* Could he ask her? Every portion of his being said, *Yes, this feels so right. It can be different. Better this time. Real.*

It is the only way to begin anew.

Alexandre shaped Margot's hand as if to caress a glass tube. A tube he could feel, as tangible as the ground beneath his feet, and he knew it was an impossibility for others to even imagine. But Margot had already spread wide her mind. He could tell or show her anything and she would consider before judging.

Honest trust. There was no other way to describe the feeling she granted him.

"Imagine a glass cylinder," he said. He moved to stand behind her, lifted her left hand, and formed the same grasp upon the moonlight. "It is pleasantly cool, like an iced dessert on a hot summer day. You can run your palm up and down its length for about the distance of two handbreadths. The ends are not sharp or jagged; rather, they segue into the nightscape, leaving your open palm kissed by the breeze."

"Doesn't this glass tube block your vision in a way that makes it impossible to determine it is actually the pond you are looking at?"

"No. It's difficult to explain. I see the pond and see the tubes at the same time, superimposed upon my vision over all, so to speak. It is all one object, and yet I recognize it as a pool of water, as do you."

She turned and propped her chin upon the cupid's stone head. "I should wonder for endless days."

"You needn't try to understand," he said with a tousle of his hand over her curls. "Your acceptance alone is such a gift to me."

"Do you ever wonder what it would be like to see the world as all others? In plain colors and sounds that only come from a spoken word instead of an inanimate object?"

"Often." Fallen into reflection, Alexandre paced to the edge of the deck that overlooked the Orangerie and propped his hands at his hips. The breeze that rippled the moonlight upon the pond blew through his loose hair. "My sister Mignonne used to try to explain things to me. She would become so frustrated when I insisted that an apple was dulcet and that her horse's footsteps cantering across the pounded high roads were red."

Closing his eyes cleared away the sensations and shapes that were his natural vision and hearing. There were times Alexandre had wished for normalcy; even the thought to be deaf or blind would be better than to try to exist in a world where no one could understand his point of view and always labeled him some terrible thing: *afflicted*.

"I wised up in my teens. As the calling to study botany became more intense, my own life became clear and real. It was quite obvious I would forever possess this unity of the senses. This is how I was intended to be. And so I accepted and became cautious to keep it to myself. It is a pity others cannot place colors and textures to a voice or taste."

"I like seeing the world through your eyes and ears, Alexandre."

He'd not been aware of her movement. Now Margot embraced him from behind and rested her head upon his shoulder. Her fingers clasped around his chest and he reached up to weave his fingers through hers. Desire rushed forward, knocking down all previous walls he'd erected. They belonged together. There was no denying the truth.

Yes, the time was right.

"I sought you out tonight to ask you something." He

turned and lifted her chin. Moonlight shimmered across her delicate features, romancing with her blue eyes, her rose-pink lips. "I love you, Margot."

She parted her lips to speak, but he pressed a finger to them for silence. He must speak now, while his emotions were at the fore. He knew the truth would shine. The girls loved Margot. He loved Margot. What he must now say was the way things were to be.

"I should wish you to become my wife."

"Alexandre," she said on a gasp. "But—oh." She glanced away, her gaze fleeing his.

"Margot, I mean it, I—"

"Oh, no, Alexandre, you mustn't. You are doing this only because you think it is what I want."

"Nonsense, I want to marry you—"

Now it was her turn to silence him with a gentle fingertip. The moonlight caressed her golden crown in a cold embrace. No more romance. This was reality.

"You think if we are married it will be all right to make love. To have children. Alexandre, I don't want to have children right away. You are not ready for another child either, I know that. But that doesn't mean I must wait years to have pleasure, does it?"

"You don't wish to marry me?"

She stepped back until he could no longer make out the glitter coruscating from those hard blue eyes. Had she purposely stepped into the shadows?

"It is too soon for you," she offered in a voice that was not at all pink. More a deep maroon. An unsure color that clogged in his throat like a lump.

"But the girls, they love you as well. They need a mother—no—I mustn't put it like that. I'm not asking you to marry me so I will have a permanent nursemaid, believe me."

"I know you are not." Overhead, clouds slithered across the face of the moon, darkening the night as deeply as Margot's voice had become. "You are too kind to even consider such a notion. But it is your kindness that shall once again lead you into a bad situation if you continue to act only to please others."

"You believe our marriage would be a bad situation?" Ready to spout an argument, Alexandre quickly adjusted. "But, of course, we've known each other only a few weeks. And here I am, a man with children, requesting you sacrifice your freedom—"

"Oh, no, don't use such a harsh word. Sharing my life with you and the girls would never be a sacrifice." He sensed a quaver in her voice. It matched the nervous shiver in his heart. "I should think it a gift to be your wife and a mother to Lisette and Janette. A gift of which I am not deserving. Oh, Alexandre, why did you have to ask me to marry you? I cannot . . . can never."

Crushed stones cudgeled in crisp clicks under her frantic feet. "I just wanted to know the passion, the excitement of lying with you. . . ."

"We can," he rushed in. She was becoming agitated and tearful. This was all wrong. He must fix it! "Whenever you wish, Margot. I want you too. I just wanted all things to be right by you."

Tears glistened in silver streaks across her cheek. "They can never be right." She turned and lifted her skirts to dash toward the palace.

Clutching his chest, Alexandre pressed his fingertips to his shirt. The sudden pounding deep within, it hurt desperately. A new ache was born in the shade of Margot's haunted voice. *They can never be right.*

What had he done?

Plopping as grandly and as disgustedly as she could onto the wicker chair, Margot melded her spine against the curved reeds, then caught her chin in hand. A great sigh was necessary.

Cook did not look up from her chores. She sat before three wooden buckets of vegetables, at the moment de-papering plump, juicy gooseberries.

Another sigh did not produce the much-needed inter-ested look from Cook.

She should not burden the woman with her troubles. Heaven knows, Margot owed Cook her firstborn for all the kindness the woman had granted her since she had come to stay at Versailles. And never a request for a return favor. So beautiful in her grace and wisdom, and completely unselfish, Cook was.

"Very well, then," Cook said as the pale-veined golden marbles funneled out of their crisp pods to land in a pottery bowl. "What in all the wonders is troubling you today, my lady mischief?"

"Oh, Cook!" Margot stood and made a theatrical swish over to the table. She sat upon the high stool and spread her upper body across the end of the long table, dramati-cally displaying her discomfort. "The most horrible thing has happened."

"I've just washed the table, child. Do remove your body before mud and pig snot or something else disgust-ing falls from your person and into the king's supper."

"Sorry." Margot righted herself and brushed her hand across the immaculate table.

"There's another basket of gooseberries by your side," Cook said, her implication crystal clear.

Margot pulled the basket onto her lap and plucked out a crackly berry. The papery pod easily released its treas-ure, but she had to snap the stem from the berry. Who could think to work when she had such thoughts burden-ing her mind!

"Out with it, then, before you bring on a sigh so great, you blow the kitchen into the Swiss pond."

"He's asked me to marry him, Cook."

"I know he has, and it's about time you've wised up and accepted that fact."

"What? Oh, no, not the baron. Monsieur Saint-Sylvestre."

A sharp *chunk* of wooden bowl against knuckles preceded a surprising oath from Cook.

"I had not thought he had become so enamored of me."

Berries forgotten, Cook crossed herself, then pressed both palms together to plead to the heavens. "Forgive her, Lord, she's but a foolish child."

"I am not foolish! Just . . . impulsive." Margot toyed with a renegade berry. "But I should wonder—"

Firm fingers closed over Margot's toying hand. "You'll do no more wondering, Margot deVerona. Look what a tangled mess all your wondering has gotten you into. You are engaged to the Baron de Verzy. In a very short time the man will arrive to take you away from here to his own home. Where you will then serve him and grant him the children you agreed to give him in the contract you signed with your very own hand. You must tell the gardener before you break his heart. Though I dare wager you've already done a fine job of tossing his heart about. And those poor girls, do they know about their father's proposal?"

"No!" Margot hastened to answer. "And I've already told him I could not marry him, so you needn't go on such a verbal rampage."

"But you didn't tell him why."

Margot looked to the well-swept floor to avoid Cook's all-knowing gaze. "How could I, when he was looking so charming and sweet beneath the moonlight. I cannot break his heart, Cook. I care far too much for the man to ever hurt him."

"Every day you do not tell him of the baron is another

twist to his soul. Don't you see you've already begun the damage? It can only worsen if you do not confess. And if you do not, I believe I shall."

"You would not!"

Plucking up a gooseberry, Cook slipped away its crisp jacket, nonchalance in her attitude. "I shouldn't wish to find myself in such a position, but if needs be . . ."

"No, no, I shall tell him. I shall tell him!"

Margot pushed away from the table and began to pace the floor. Behind her, Cook's shelling took on an erratic pace, with berries hitting the bowl and plinking across the table at such a speed to beat a mounted rider to Paris. When Margot stepped on a renegade berry, felt the ooze stain her thin slipper, she stopped and let out a frustrated grunt. "I did not mean for things to get so out of hand! I merely wanted to know what it was like to love a man. I did not think he would decide to propose to me."

"If you're not careful, you'll have two husbands instead of just the one—"

"The one perfectly horrible, ugly, nasty toad of a baron!"

"Now, child, just because you deem him unacceptable to look upon does not mean the future cannot promise great joy. Is it only the visage that must please you?"

"Certainly not! Look at Alexandre. He's got that delightful limp. His face is fine and proud but not overly beautiful so as to distract. It is what is inside Alexandre that makes me love him. He's more appealing than that sword-swinging, ale-swigging baron."

"And have you seen him swig ale?"

Margot could only shrug and hope Cook would not question further.

"I fear you've gone beyond help, Margot. What you need is a miracle. Or a damned good spell, for that matter."

"Of course! I wonder if—"

"Oh, no, no, no." Cook thrust an admonishing finger between the two of them, arrowing the finger directly to the tip of Margot's nose, where she gave a reproving tap. "I'll not even have you wonder."

About the previously mentioned witch under the hill? Margot thrust her nose away from the tap. "I should never."

"You would."

"But I will not."

This time Margot passed Cook's perusal with a proud stance and a sparkle to her eyes before the woman went back to work.

Pleased with her secret revelation, Margot sat before the table and folded her hands. She had things to do. Things that did not involve toting two small girls across the country to find the rumored witch beneath a hill.

"What's brewing in your wonder-cache now?"

"Nothing at all."

Cook raised a thin gray brow.

"I thought you had plans to market in Paris today?"

Seeming leery of the sudden conversation change, Cook's eye lingered on Margot's face before finally saying, "Indeed, I've run clean out of flour. But I've so much to do here, I've sent for Pierceforest."

"You're going to send Pierceforest to market? You remember what happened last time—he came home with rotting fish and maggot-infested flour. Someone must accompany the man—oh, but *I* could ride along with him."

"Nonsense, I need you here in the kitchen today. I've peas to shell and vegetables to chop."

"Simple tasks for small hands."

"The girls?"

"Yes!" Jumping to Cook's side, Margot threaded an arm around the flustered woman's shoulder. *Act quickly,* she thought, *before she has too much time to think.* "Oh, Cook, please let me go to Paris. I can pick the freshest items for you and the ride there and back will be just what I need. Some time to muddle on this whole situation."

"There's no muddling to be done beyond devising the gentle words required to release Monsieur Saint-Sylvestre from your tangled net."

"Tangled? Cook! You really think me a wicked person who would lure a man into my traps?"

With a hefty sigh and a sorry shake of her head, Cook's grimace softened to a gentle smile. "No, child. You're just struck, is all. You couldn't have seen it coming even with that fancy telescope you tote around in that little case."

"Struck?"

Cook left the berries alone and clasped her hands about Margot's. "Love struck, Margot. You've been pierced by Cupid's arrow."

That sounded nice. Rather exotic even. Margot smiled.

"Pity the arrow didn't pierce the baron's head. It would make things much easier for you if he were dead."

"I should never think such things!"

"Indeed not. But perhaps an injury to his brain that would prevent him remembering he's a fiancée stowed away at the king's château, eh?"

Margot gifted Cook with a generous hug. "I do love you, Cook, much as your wondering leads you to some strange notions."

The ride to Paris was quick at Pierceforest's direction to the two-horse cart, but an hour's journey to the gates of St. Denis. Having been in the city only a few times in her life, Margot was immediately taken aback by the pungent aroma of the streets. No, aroma wasn't quite the correct word, more like miasma.

Horrid, horrid smells assaulted her from all sides as

she followed Pierceforest through the market on the rue du Ponceau. Her slippers would surely have to be destroyed for the animal droppings and rotting substances that she stepped upon. It was disgusting. But not enough to distract her from selecting the best flour, and not a sack filled three quarters with larva-infested millet and topped off with a fine powder. No, she dug her hand down into the sacks at three different vendor's stands until she was satisfied her purchase would be worth the price.

Pierceforest trailed behind her, his arms slowly filling with Cook's list of supplies. By noon she had completed her task and, selecting a baguette, some fresh goat cheese, and a bottle of wine, she and Pierceforest dined al fresco in the back of the cart before setting off to the château.

"Looks like rain," Margot commented with a glance to the sky, only to receive a nod from the ever-silent Pierceforest. "I know the sky is clear as holy water, but it won't be much longer. Do you smell it?"

Another noncommittal nod from the man.

"Pierceforest, stop the carriage."

"Whatever for, Mademoiselle deVerona?"

"I want to walk."

"The château is still a league off, and you said yourself it's to rain soon."

She jerked the reins from Pierceforest and with a firm tug brought the horses to a halt. "I wish to walk. I've some botanicals to gather for my studies. Tell Cook to expect me in a few hours."

"But in the rain, Mademoiselle?"

Margot shushed out her skirts and turned to march off the pounded high road and into the meadow of coltsfoot that painted a great swash of bright yellow before and all around her. "Hurry along, Pierceforest," she called back, "before the rain catches you and the flour is dampened."

His face screwed up in a mixture of wanting to rush after her and plop her back down on the seat next to him and wanting to protect his precious cargo. Cook would curse him to high heaven if he returned with flour paste. And he'd been on the receiving end of the cook's evil eye many a time, Margot knew.

If she continued her brisk pace, he'd ride on. Which he did. A click of his tongue inside his cheek, and the horses stirred in their harness and plodded onward.

Rain? A secret smile tickled Margot's mouth. Certainly not. The sun was high, the air dry and clear.

Now, to find this supposed hill that hid a witch in its belly.

His horse's hooves clicked dully across the checked marble court sandwiched by the north and south wings of the king's old hunting lodge. By rights he should have ridden directly to the stables to see his mount was brushed down, but he had wanted to survey the gentleman's château that the king had plans to convert into a grand palace.

Behind the rose brick walls lay royal finery of a match to no man's most exotic dreams. An easy disguise to the filth and recklessness of its past. Nicodème's father had served Louis XIII two decades before as Master of Horses. Then the lodge had been exclusively dedicated to men and their passion for the hunt. Not even the queen had been allowed entrance to the hallowed halls of virility and male pride.

"Times do change," Nicodème muttered as he turned his mount toward the stables. "My wife shall know her place. On her knees before me."

Sixteen

Toadstools and dragon guts and mouse toenails and . . .
one gorgeous grinning witch, darling

Musty odor of burning peat carried through the odd
little clay-tiled dormers set into the domed ceiling of the
cottage. Margot had not seen any ditch fires before stumbling upon the hill. Rather, it was two hills sunk deep
within an outcrop of oak, and the house was sandwiched
between the blue columbine-frosted hills like a magical
cottage no one could see until they'd stepped right on
top of it.

While unobtrusive from the bark- and rush-bound
outer walls, Margot had let out a great gasp as she
crossed the threshold and entered what could only be
called the realm of all that glitters and delights.

Inside the circular cottage the walls, coated with the
greenest moss she had ever seen, danced with animated
little spots that upon closer inspection proved to be toadstools of the most fanciful colors imaginable. Over Margot's head, ropes of dried rosebuds strung across the
ceiling in exotic display reminded her of an Arabian
harem. The most delicious fragrance filled the small cottage. Indescribable, but so sweet she could taste the air
on her tongue.

As Margot stepped forward a few awestruck inches, her hair was tickled by long, hanging strands of braided herbs and shells whose mother-of-pearl innards glittered in the glow of at least a hundred candles. Chirps of tiny birds could be heard but not seen, for perhaps the winged creatures homed in the moss-papered walls amid the growing toadstools and fluttering wings of butterflies freshly birthed from their opaque chrysalides.

The floor, more moss, so tight and verdant that it might have been crushed velvet mixed with the softness of a newborn's sigh, squished as Margot journeyed beneath the dazzling spectacle.

Even more dazzling was the woman who was supposed to be, if rumor would have truth, the witch under the hill. She could not possibly be!

Hair brighter than rubies swirled and curled and danced upon a slender face with sharp gray eyes and a pursed rosebud mouth. Her nose was so fine and pale that could Margot not see nostrils, she might wonder were it not there at all. Silver dust shimmered on her eyelids; one might never really know if it was laid there by a thick powder puff or if it was indeed the footsteps of a curious fairy.

"You have come to speak to the witch under the hill," the woman stated plainly in a deep, glamorous voice that Margot associated with a wizened sage.

Under the hill?

"Under, above, between." The woman dismissed Margot's unspoken thought with a splay of her elegant fingers. More silver dust skittered down her wrists and the back of her hands. Rich violet plush flowed over her shapely figure in waves that seemed to undulate a rhythm of their own. A chain of impossibly fine silver danced around her waist, glinting madly in the candlelight.

"I've come to seek help," Margot said as strongly as she could. She was not frightened or leery, just . . .

stunned, standing inside this capsule of glittering treasures. This was not a witch's lair but a fairy queen's boudoir.

"Appearances do not deceive," the witch offered in what seemed like a wisp of sugared wind from over Margot's shoulder. "If you believe it, then it certainly can be."

Words very similar to Cook's encouraging "You can make your life anything you wish. . . ."

"Are you a fairy queen?" Margot blurted out. Why not? It certainly seemed possible.

"Fairy, witch, sorceress. Labels mean nothing, darling. I am Charesse. Now, enough of the ogling and avoidance. You've come to me with a desire burning in your breast. Release it into my hands."

Margot stared at the woman's splayed hands, so long and delicate yet reassuringly powerful in their grace. She pressed her own hand to her stomach and summoned the courage to release her worries. "I need to prevent a child from being conceived."

"Ah! You speak of seriously good magic, darling." The woman—Charesse—drew a long black fingernail under a strand of colored pearls that spun from the ceiling to the wall and then back to the ceiling a half dozen more times.

Margot drew her eyes away from the curve of the woman's hips and found her irrepressible curiosity stopped at her breasts, high and round and so, so exposed. "Magic is good, isn't it?"

"Eh, it can be." Charesse gave a graceful wave, a gesture more fitting of a grand dame seated in a private salon with dozens of male admirers surrounding her, before tracing a finger along her ample décolletage. "But I, darling, do not practice the good magic."

"Oh." Feeling rather spellbound by her surroundings, she could offer nothing more than that at the moment.

Margot settled into a chair directly behind her legs. On the table before her glimmered a frayed damask cloth woven of deep azure and gold threads. And upon that—

"Is this your crystal ball?" Margot reached but did not touch the iridescent globe of glass perched upon a mother-of-pearl base.

"It is my gazing ball, darling."

"What do you do with it? Can you see the future?"

The witch seated herself across from Margot. With a suave glance of her silver-dusted eyelids, she replied coolly, "I gaze into it. What do you think?"

Margot regarded her smug expression. Very well, she had asked for that one.

"Now, tell me more about your reason for venturing to my abode, and I shall listen to see if I desire to assist you in your endeavors."

"But if you don't practice good magic—"

"Your request may command a touch of the dark. Go on." She flicked an impatient splay of fingers at Margot. "Tell."

"Very well. I'm desperate." Margot leaned as far across the table as she could get so she needn't speak too loudly. "You see, I am in love."

"Ah, love." The witch sat back and crossed her arms over her bosom, a strange smile drawing her bright red lips into a glossy bud. 'Twas a Cheshire grin belonging to the cat that ate the mistress's supper.

That she was such a beauty did not comfort Margot. She wanted a witch; how could one expect this woman to know spells and incantations if she were not a hag and green with warts?

Silence hung as the twosome exchanged gazes. Margot's uneasy, the witch's grin so knowing.

"What is it?" Margot turned and checked behind her. Maybe the witch stared at an invisible familiar that would do away with the silly woman who came requesting a spell that would not allow babies to fix in her stomach so she could make love to the man she desired. "Why do you stare at me so?"

"Love is a most noble cause for any venture into deception."

"I don't wish to deceive anyone. I just want to make love to a man without getting with child."

The witch raised a perfectly groomed red eyebrow. "You come requesting a pessary?"

"I . . . think so. . . ." Whatever was a pessary?

"I don't prevent babies, darling, only destroy them after they are made."

"But that's horrible!"

"Isn't it though?" The witch ran a lacquered nail under her ruby lips, gazing at Margot with eyes that glittered at once a thousand colors and then no color at all. She took great joy in her words. They were as much jewels as the glittering objects surrounding her. "Perhaps you are in need of a potion that will ensorcel this man into forever being your love slave? He will go insane with passion and will constantly hunger for your lips, your breasts, your sex."

"My lips, my—my . . . breasts," Margot mouthed, caught in the witch's web of charm. What could be so terrible about having a love slave? A man who desired only to please her. "My . . ." Margot perused the final one for a moment. Her sex? Oh!

"I shouldn't think so. Certainly not." Fidgeting with the damask cloth, Margot tried to push away thoughts of Alexandre hungering for her most private body parts. It just wasn't . . . well, it wasn't thinkable. Not yet.

"You wish to singe the hairs from his body? How about a spell of boils? Perhaps you wish to put a permanent kink in his man muscle? That should prevent babies, darling."

"You are most horrible!"

"It's a living," the witch said with a shrug and a flit of her fingers to the pearls hanging above.

"I shouldn't have come here."

"Curiosity is a deadly adversary, isn't it? You will not leave with words of this visit on your tongue." Charesse stood, and when she did, Margot noticed a mangy gray cat skitter out from under the woman's long, violet skirts.

At least she had a familiar.

"Not really," the woman said with a nod to the cat. "He comes and goes as he pleases."

Margot clutched her throat. Had the woman just read her mind? She looked to the witch, who turned and sorted through her polished crystal jars upon a shelf, seemingly unaware of Margot's thoughts. But was she?

"I should wonder." Catching her chin in her palm, Margot crossed her legs and watched as the witch lifted crystal lids and poked her nose in and out of jars containing various substances that did not sparkle or gleam like the rest of the room, but instead seemed to melt and sludge and ooze up against the sides of the glass. She was preparing the spell that would make Alexandre's man muscle develop a kink; she just knew it. Oh! But she should have never come here expecting her troubles to be resolved. She should have remained at the château and wondered on this herself.

She wanted to make love with Alexandre. Just once. To know what true love felt like. To forever cherish being in love and receiving love.

Perhaps Alexandre would never even have to know of the baron. Never.

"Oh, but he must know your heart." The witch turned and eyed Margot. A flash of quicksilver starred in her eye, seeming to spear Margot in the heart. "How can you claim love for a man if you will not open your very soul before him and display your goodness as well as your mishaps and failures? Hasn't he done as much for you?"

Margot jumped from her chair and approached the witch on moss-padded strides. "Can you read my mind?"

"No." She pressed her hand to Margot's breast, her lacquered nails clicking delightfully. "But I can read your heart."

"Well, it's a fine thing for you to be preaching goodness, when you claim with grand pride to be a purveyor of evil."

The witch tore her hand from Margot. A spike of pain pulsed behind Margot's rib cage. Had she just—

"Just because I do my job, and do it well, does not mean I don't know a good soul from a bad one. You, darling, possess a good soul. Much as that does not at all surprise me."

She pressed a hand upon Margot's breast again and closed her eyes. Drawing in a deep breath through her nose, the witch sighed. "It is a curious and proud heart. But it can be selfish at times."

"Self—" Margot snapped her mouth shut.

Of course, she was being extremely selfish. She had considered as much before. She had no right to take the girls' father away from them, or to intrude upon their mourning for their mother.

But she had no intention of taking Alexandre away from anyone!

"What about my happiness? Doesn't a happy heart make for a happy life?"

"Indeed." Opening her eyes, the witch beamed a serene gaze upon Margot. "But I'm afraid I cannot help you, Margot deVerona. You've already found the answer you seek, but one must journey to the end to discover they already possess the beginning."

* * *

A grander entrance could not have been commanded of the king himself. Cook and the girls looked up from their corn-shucking adventure as the click of shiny boot heels ascended the stone steps onto the kitchen floor. A tall man with broad shoulders and a glorious mane of straw-colored hair, strolled the floor from door to hearth, taking in the surroundings without so much as a *bonjour.*

Silver fixings on his sword belt clicked against the gold buttons tracing his gray velvet doublet from chin to waist. Glamour blossomed on his smooth, unlined face. Perfectly shaped pink lips pursed and perused. Quite a pretty man, though not in the least feminine. No, a finely handsome catch if ever there was one, Cook deduced, feeling a bit of a spring flush color her cheeks.

A wave of lavender drifted from the blond god to Cook's nose. *And smelling so fine.*

Finally he pronounced himself satisfied with the kitchen with a nod and a plop onto the wicker chair by the hearth. He drew up one foot and rested his ankle across his opposite knee. Long, graceful fingers eased over the extremely pointed tip of his glossy jackboot.

"I am the Baron de Verzy," he announced grandly. "And I've come for Margot deVerona."

Seventeen

Enter, the villain

Janette's sharp intake of breath alerted her sister, who also drew in a gasp.

"I've been told I could find her in the kitchen," the man said. His glittering eyes made a casual sweep of the room. "Though I do find that rather odd."

"The Baron of Blunders," Lisette whispered *sotto voce*.

"Shh," Cook admonished. She slid off her stool and wiped her hands on her apron. "My lord, it is a pleasure to meet you. I've heard so very much . . . er . . . about you." Yes, but she had expected a toady old hunchback to come crab-walking it in here. Not this delicious ray of sun and sinew.

"And what has my devoted fiancée told you of me?"

"Devoted? Oh. Er . . . well, perhaps not as much as I might think." Devoted? Where did this man get his information? Too nervous to concentrate, and a trifle confused, Cook's fingers became entwined in her apron. "And so you've come for her now, have you?"

"Indeed." He stood and preened a hand across the velvet of his sleeve.

The man was a tall one. Very nearly as tall as Monsieur Saint-Sylvestre, Cook wagered. The two men should meet eye to eye. Though, eye to eye was one thing the two would never agree on, should it come to Margot.

And where was the wondering little fool right now? Bother.

"I had thought I might arrive a few weeks from now," the baron said as he strode the floor stones before the hearth, "but my adventures were abruptly cut short by loss of nearly half my traveling companions to the pox. Dreadful malady. Mars the flesh something horrid. I kept my distance and coated my skin with an ancient elixir especially created for the queen of Egypt, so you needn't worry that I might carry such a disease on my person."

"Oh, no, never," Cook gawked. This man poxed? She would fling herself before the inflicted soul to protect him from such a fate.

"Precious girls," the baron remarked. A stride found him looming over their cowering heads.

"It's the Baron of Blunders," Cook heard Janette whisper.

The Baron of Blunders? Must be some fairy story Margot concocted with the girls. Best to shuffle the two out before someone started getting nervous. Cook looked down at her fingers, red and shaking as they twisted inside one another. Nervous?

"We're twins," Janette piped.

"Twins?" The baron gave a curt, one-syllable laugh. "But I thought twins always looked alike?"

"You're just not looking very close," Lisette snipped, and turned back to her cob of corn. Then she added decisively, "Such a blunder."

"Ah. No wonder I prefer little boys." The baron cracked a trying smile at Cook. "Girls will be girls, eh? So, where is Mademoiselle deVerona?"

"Where? Oh." Where indeed? Vex the girl to the bone. What to tell the man? It wouldn't do to announce Margot was missing, for she hadn't returned with Pierceforest from market. Certainly the baron would be angry to know his fiancée was not being properly looked after. But she'd never been one to twist her tongue around a lie. "My lord, surely you wish to rest and refresh yourself before meeting Margot. After the long journey here?" Avoidance, on the other hand, was a much simpler matter. "Dear, is that a travel line I see creasing your forehead?"

"Do tell!" The baron grasped his forehead. Vanity had nothing over this peacock. "Perhaps you are right. The road wearies a man."

"I feel certain rest would serve you well, and it will also give Margot a chance to . . . prepare to meet you."

"Ah, yes, she must have such expectations. I shouldn't wish to surprise her, when she must prepare for our first meeting. Could you show me to a room?"

"Er . . . yes." First she's covering for the wayward wonderer and now she's to do servants' duties as well? "I believe Pierceforest might still be lurking out in the courtyard, I'll just show you to him and he'll see that you're settled in, my lord. Can't be meeting your beloved with the road's exhaustion hanging on you, now."

"Indeed not. But you will inform Margot that I've arrived?" he asked as Cook shoved him toward the door.

"Of course I will." She closed the door behind the primping figure of strength, beauty, and downright sensuality and blew a stray hair from her nose. That had been too close for comfort.

Where was the girl anyway? Pierceforest had returned from Paris hours ago. Gathering botanicals? For what reason? It just didn't make sense.

As the appearance of the Baron de Verzy made no sense. What Margot had not told Cook about her future husband!

"A toad, eh?" Fitting a fist to her ample hip, Cook peeked through the window and spied the long, rhythmic strides of the summer god come to earth as he crossed the courtyard behind Pierceforest. "Margot de Verona, you've got a lot of explaining to do."

Cook would appreciate the basil Alexandre had cut that afternoon in an attempt to prune what had become a wild bush. Le Nôtre's idea to create a potagerie was right on, though the man did not foresee it happening for a few more years, when the grounds could be cleared and the final building plans were settled upon. No sense in divesting in a grand plot when it may fall victim to the king's whims. For now the garden of simples, as the English called it, served Alexandre well in his study of herbs and Cook in her fine feasts. Though he much preferred it placed far away from the officious smells of the menagerie when it found its final home. 'Course, there was much to be said for the abundant supply of fertilizer close at hand.

Alexandre's boots crunched across the loose stone carpeting the south terrace. Rather windy day for late summer. Margot must have kept the girls inside, for the thick stone walls of the château kept the rooms comfortable. But he'd missed them for lunch. Food tasted ever more satisfying when served by his girls and accompanied by Margot's delicious smile.

Perhaps there had been a reason. After his failed proposal, Alexandre wasn't sure how Margot felt about him. Clutching the basket of basil in one hand, he turned to enter the kitchen, when a man's voice called him around to the back of the château, where the shadows arabesqued the ground in filigree design.

"I must say, you're the first servant I've seen in hours," the man called as Alexandre approached.

The tall velvet-and-lace-festooned man shielded his eyes with a flat hand. A courtier gone astray? His gray doublet felt tangibly bumpy on Alexandre's tongue. Hideous color. He pressed his tongue to the back of his teeth to fend off the sensation, but with little luck.

"I've been looking to have my mount stabled, and there isn't a lackey in sight. And I've been given word the king is to St. Germaine."

"Indeed, he left last evening for the hunt." Alexandre joined the man in the narrow slash of shade hugging the walls of the château. He would keep his eyes from the man's clothes. Made it easier to digest conversation. His voice was a rather bland mix of cream and yellow lines. Nothing offensive as long as he didn't inhale. Lavender, Alexandre presumed from the musty floral that clouded around the man in an invisible horde. How much scent could one man endure?

"I've a post to deliver directly to His Majesty's hands."

"I believe the king's party plans to return in a few days."

The man threw up both hands in exasperation and turned to kick the wall. "Some luck I've ridden into. Not even a proper party to greet me upon arrival, an encounter with those horrid rodents, the king is away, and now this extended stay. Damn!" He hitched his hands at his hips and with a toss of his head splayed a great mane of hair over his shoulders.

Vanity at its best, Alexandre thought.

"My horse is the chestnut roan. You'll see to him, then?"

Alexandre smirked and fingered the rich, velvety leaves in his basket. The soft texture overwhelmed the bumps riding his tongue. "I'm afraid not."

"What sort of outfit is this? Servants refusing orders and the master out on the hunt? I must say, I've quite tired of Versailles, and I've been here but two hours. And now I've to remain another two days?" He gave the wall another kick and strode past Alexandre. "The roan stallion," he repeated, obviously expecting action.

In too much of his own mood to worsen it by challenging this lackwit with the way of things here at the hunting lodge, Alexandre cautioned his inner need to stand up against him. Calm and cool always hold the upper hand. "I am the gardener, Monsieur. I'm afraid I cannot see to your horse, though I'm sure a lackey can be located somewhere around here."

"My lord."

"No." Alexandre offered a shrug. "It is only *Monsieur.*"

"I mean"—the man turned and cocked his head, which dispersed a spread of hair across his shoulders. Any woman would be proud of such tresses—"it is *my lord.* Me. I am the baron de Verzy."

"Ah, forgive me, my lord."

"And you are?"

Certainly none of your concern, Alexandre thought of the pompous blowthwart. "Alexandre Saint-Sylvestre. Simply . . . Monsieur."

"Naturally," the baron said through a tight jaw. "I haven't looked forward to this visit to Versailles since I knew it was coming. And now that it has arrived, I despise it even more. Two days until the king returns?"

"I believe so. Perhaps you can leave the post with a trusted adviser?"

"No, my uncle charged me with its safe delivery. He and the king are old companions. I suppose that means I've time to see to my horse myself, then."

"I could fetch Pierceforest. He might stir up a lackey for you."

"That would be most kind of you, Monsieur. Now"—he removed his gloves and slapped them smartly against his thigh—"since I do have a few days of leisure, perhaps you could tell me about the women here at Versailles?"

* * *

Close to nightfall Margot stepped onto the dusty grounds laid before the Versailles stables. Disappointment clung to her shoulders as she strode wearily across the marble courtyard. She'd lodged a musketball-sized pebble in her satin slippers about half a league back, and had taken to slipping off her shoe, emptying it, slipping it back on, only to have to empty it after yet another twenty paces.

Now she didn't care that her left foot was bare and dirty and scratched all around the ankle from the spiny nettles. Nor that her right shoe was thoroughly worn on the sole and her skirt hem might never come clean for the dust and grass stains.

She cared for nothing beyond a nice relaxing bath steeped with the neroli oil she had started in Cook's pottery jar. Oh, but her tired bones required soothing and her senses needed to be seduced from the day's hardship of walking all the way to the witch under the hill, only to be refused for such a *good* request.

Some witch she was with her fine plush gown and sharply carved cheekbones. Not even a single wart! Did the woman expect that anyone would believe her claims to magic, let alone trust a spell from one so unwitchlike?

"Most likely the rumors of her performing abortions and love spells are completely false," Margot muttered as her feet stepped onto the cool marble inside the château and she forced her aching limbs toward the kitchen.

Next time she would ride to the witch under the hill. Rather, the witch *between* the hills. Bother, was she already planning another trek to the glamorous mystery of a woman?

"I shall have a more worthy request next time," she said decidedly. "Must think things through. Perhaps there's a way of presenting my request so it appears much more evil than it truly is."

Anytime you wish to interfere in a man's life it is evil!

But how could seeking a safe method to make love harm anyone? Alexandre would appreciate her efforts. He had made it known he wanted her. My God, he wished to marry her!

What had Charesse meant with her mysterious statement that Margot already had the answers. That she must journey to the end to discover she already had the beginning?

"She just wanted to vex me. Crazy fairy witch!"

She punched the air, but that action pulled at the aching muscles in her back. Margot groaned. "Maybe I'm just making things more complicated than they need to be."

No. Things were already thoroughly and completely complicated.

Pausing before the kitchen door, Margot looked over her disarray. No more than usual; at least not from what Cook had already seen of her. She smoothed a hand over her droopy curls and bent to slip her shoe on but found her left foot was swollen and tender, so she tucked the shoe in her skirt's waist and drew on a lackluster smile.

The kitchen was quiet and dark, no sign of the twins, though a kettle did bubble heartily over the hearth. Hunger gripped. Chicken pie, Margot divined with a sniff and a hearty sigh. She would eat her own portion as well as clean away any remainders tonight.

She tiptoed to the table, where the pie crocks were pressed with freshly kneaded dough, and traced a careful finger around the crimped edges of the first pie, which sat waiting thick chunks of chicken and crisp garden peas and carrots and the special mixture of spices that Cook used to work a masterful spell over the whole.

"Oh!"

Startled by the shriek, Margot toppled forward, catching her hand in the pie dough. When she tried to ease her fingers out of the sticky substance, it only clung all the more. She turned her body and twisted her arm, hiding her disaster with a careful pose as Cook came barging through the outer door.

Like a bee dodging from one flower to the next, Cook bustled across the floor before Margot. "Where have you been, child? This is most horrible, most horrible indeed. I've been all atwist!"

"Is it the girls?"

"The twins? No, I've seen them to their beds. Woman, you are mess! We must see to straightening you up right away!"

Still trying to work her fingers out of the dough, Margot reached out with her clean hand to silence Cook's frantic skittering, but the woman grasped her wrist and yanked her toward the hearth.

The pie crockery scraped across the table and landed with a crash on the floor. Cook spun in a swirl of flour-dusted skirts. Heavy globs of dough oozed from Margot's fingers, one huge globule landing with a dull splat on the crockery-littered floor.

"Sorry," Margot managed to say sheepishly. "You startled me when you came flying in. Forgive me, I didn't mean to be gone so long."

Cook was not listening. In fact, she disregarded the mess on the floor with a cluck of her tongue and another jerk of Margot's hand. With one deft swing she twirled Margot around and landed her against the hearth wall. Held still by one of Cook's meaty hands, Margot couldn't figure what was going on until the woman dipped her apron in the boiling water and squeezed it out with a roll against her thigh. Then she took to washing Margot's face!

"I shall bathe soon . . . enough!" Margot got out behind the hot cloth that felt rather good when she really thought about it.

"He's coming!" A male cry funneled into the kitchen as Pierceforest peeled into the kitchen and circled the long table, his hands raised in the air. "He's coming!"

"Out with you!" Cook shushed the idiot toward the door that led into the hallway.

"Who's coming?" Margot wondered as she bent to pick up the broken crockery before anyone could step on it. "What is going on?"

"He's here," Cook said as she crooked an arm through Margot's and lifted her straight.

Margot spit at the cloth as it grazed her lips. "Who is here?"

Defeated, Cook dropped the offending artillery and let out a hefty sigh. "The baron—"

"The toad?" Oh, *mon Dieu!*

"Toad?" Cook gripped Margot by the chin. She rounded a curious eye on her. "And just when have you laid eyes on this toadish old man you are always whining about, hmm? Tell me, Margot. I'm most interested."

"Well . . ." Why Cook's sudden interest in the man's appearance? Wasn't the very idea that he was here—to take her away—bad enough? "Well . . ." She twisted her fingers into her skirts.

Cook slapped at Margot's fingers. "Speak up!"

"I haven't actually ever laid eyes on him."

"I thought as much."

"Why do you say that?"

"Hmmph." Cook toed the crockery pieces on the ground, easing them into a tight pile with a few kicks. "The Baron de Verzy is one of the most handsome men I've dared laid eyes on. He is not old and wrinkled but fair of visage and spirit. He did not lay a single warty hand upon his weapons as you've so vividly described, but walks with esteem and challenge to his gait. He's a god, Margot. Why have you lied to me about him?"

"It appears you've developed quite the penchant for the man. Why don't you just marry him?"

"Because it is you who agreed to be his wife in exchange for an education. And here you are, every day defying the trust you granted him by swooning over the gardener and seeking love potions from a witch."

"It was not a love potion, merely a—"

Cook quirked a brow.

Margot worked her lower lip with nervous nips. "It's not important."

"Indeed. Now, you haven't even met the baron and already you've created such a nightmare about him that you might never know for sure what the man is like."

"I shouldn't care if he is as handsome as you say. It is not the outside that I must live with for the rest of my life, it is what is inside a man that will ultimately make me happy. I've told you my heart, Cook."

"Yes, well, it is a fine to-do to have a nice outside, for that is what you will wake up to for the rest of your days."

"There is not a single thing wrong with Alexandre's appearance!"

"Nor the baron's! Margot"—Cook settled from her rage and placed a hand on Margot's forearm—"I'm just asking you to use an open mind when you meet the man for the first time. You've already created this image of an ogre. Well, now you must toss that to the wind. Start anew. You did agree to this bargain of your own free will."

"I did." Margot hung her head. Perhaps the creation of the baron's image had been a way of distancing her fate from reality all along. She knew what must be.

But she hadn't known Alexandre Saint-Sylvester when she'd agreed to marry the baron. Things had changed.

"Ah, it smells divine in here!"

Margot froze at the deep male voice. It did not belong

to Joffroi or Pierceforest or any of the lackeys who dared broach Cook's kitchen. And that scent . . . lavender. It was quite forceful. It must be *him*.

She dared not turn around for fear that to finally look upon the man—her future husband—would forever seal her fate with the touching of their gazes.

Cook bustled over to him. "You had a good rest, my lord?"

"Indeed. Though now I'm hungry and ravenous thirsty. You there!"

Margot cringed.

"Fetch me some wine."

From the corner of her eye Margot saw the baron's black boots as he plopped onto the wicker chair—her chair—and crossed one boot over his knee. Still she did not move. Could not. 'Twas as if his voice had iced over her veins. To move would shatter her resolve.

"Is she daft? Fine lot of misfits the king's got here at the château. I never did find a stable hand; had to brush my horse down myself. I said wine," he enunciated slowly.

Margot could feel the heat of his words blast her in the back of the head. Just enough to make her feet move a step.

What was Cook thinking right now? That Margot should spin about and introduce herself? That she should have sent Margot packing that first day she'd lost her job as the duchess's chambermaid.

Cook skirted past Margot, hefted a brown bottle of wine from the rosewood rack set against the east wall, and gave Margot the evil eye before popping the cork and handing it to the baron. "I see you met our gardener earlier."

The baron had spoken to Alexandre? Horrors!

"Indeed, I'd mistaken him for a servant. Now, where has that woman gotten herself to?" the baron barked before swigging back the wine. "You said she would be back after I'd rested. I'm bored. I need company."

Margot, now clinging to the table, wishing upon wishes that she could just climb under one of the pie-crusts and bury herself away from life, still could not bring herself to turn around. Of all the ways to meet her future husband . . . looking as if a pig had dragged her across the countryside.

"Mademoiselle deVerona?" Cook said on a faltering note.

"The woman sent here months ago to serve the duchess Ducette? You made it seem as though you knew who I was talking about earlier. Are all the servants in this godforsaken hunting lodge daft?"

Enough. Margot could not allow Cook to be treated so. She spun around—choked on her own breath at sight of the broad-shouldered, golden-maned god seated in the center of the room—then recovered what little resolve she had left.

"I am she," she managed to say in a surprisingly strong voice. She flicked her fingers, but the dough gobs remained.

Sky-blue orbs of crystal, perfectly placed upon a raw-chiseled face, turned and observed Margot's silly actions. She froze. Inside she wondered if that color of blue was even natural on a human face, so exquisitely lucid and deep the color.

"You are . . ." The baron struggled for words, then finally spit out, "Whom?"

"Mademoiselle deVerona." She curtsied, and in the process of bowing her head a sprig of bright yellow coltsfoot fell to the floor.

The baron looked to Cook. Back to Margot. Then pointed a long, straight finger at her. "You?" His steady gaze drew a quick map over her body from tangled hair to grass-streaked skirts to wiggling dirty toes. "Ha!"

A rumbling thunder of laughter exploded on the room and shocked Margot so thoroughly, she jumped. Cook, on the other hand, merely slumped onto the stool before the table, planted her elbow quite unaware in a piecrust, and caught her forehead in her palm.

Eighteen

*Beware a promise made in haste,
for it is binding and true.*

The pure strength and unceasing force of the baron's laughter made Margot grip her fingers into fists at her hips. *Damn the vexingly handsome man!* How dared he laugh at his fiancée with such obvious lack of respect for her own feelings.

She had not laid eyes upon the man until that moment. The marriage agreement had been delivered by proxy. To judge from the changes made to the contract, she had always pictured him toady and old. What a horrible trick life was playing on her now.

Not that she would allow this pretty knight errant to bruise her feelings with his idiotic display. She would show him just how much his laughter was worth.

"My lord, I hardly find this an appropriate greeting." She had to raise her voice to be heard over his continued humor. "If you've a condition that reduces you to fits of laughter, I might be informed so I may know to expect such in the future."

Slipping both hands through his glistening flow of hair, he finally settled to a maroon-faced calm. Damn, but the man was a pretty sight to behold. Tall. Well muscled. And that hair, why, it practically gleamed.

With a thrust back of his shoulders he continued. "Of course, do forgive me, Mademoiselle. I had no idea I would find my fiancée in such a state. Surely you have been victim of most foul circumstance to find yourself in such . . . disarray. The duchess send you out for hand-dug truffles?" He smirked, let out a little laugh. "I do recall your attached request to tote along that damned pig. Thought it rather bizarre at the time, but now . . ."

He grazed his eyes over her, blatant in his disgust.

"You are a fortnight early," Margot said, slapping her arms across her chest and lifting her chin as nobly and proudly as possible. "Would I had known you were to arrive this early, I might have prepared by . . ." She glanced to Cook, still muddling at the table, who offered no rescue from her situation. Elbow pie, anyone? "Well, I might have saved the truffle hunt for later," she finally replied, sweeping her palms across her soiled skirts.

"Again, I beg your forgiveness, Mademoiselle de-Verona, I most certainly should have sent advance word of my arrival. But now that I am here, we shall make the best of things until I am able to leave. I've a message to be delivered directly to the king's hand and have learned he will not return for a few more days. So it seems I've leisure on my schedule. Most frustrating."

Indeed! A few days with the baron at Versailles, so close to Alexandre, yet by all means he must be kept away from him. How, now, would Margot explain the baron to Alexandre? To the twins?

Oh, the baron's arrival had taken her completely off guard. She had much hoped to be prepared for him when the time came, with the twins already expecting a new nursemaid and Alexandre knowing her reason to agreeing to marry the toad.

Toad? How she'd let her foolish, wondering mind twist

that one all to blithers! Margot cast a sly glance over the baron's figure. How one man could pack in so many stunning qualities and not be a bronze god immortalized in a royal garden was beyond her. Nothing whatsoever toadish about him. Unless he was one of those enchanted toads the princess had to first kiss before revealing his true beauty. But he'd already been kissed, for the warty raiments had been discarded.

Hmm . . . Such broad, straight shoulders. Perfect shelves for the golden shower of hair that curled ever so dashingly upon his head. And those wide hands with long fingers, most likely used to stunning advantage when touching a woman's—

He will hunger for your lips, your breasts, your sex. . . .

"You may run along and change into more fitting dress," the baron announced as he strode the floor, taking caution to avoid the broken pie crockery. "Do up your hair properly and scrape that mud from your face. We shall dine together this evening. It'll give us a chance to discuss our future."

Our future. Those two words wrenched her out of her scandalous fantasizing like no jar to the head could ever do. Margot choked back a scream. Her heart threatened to punch right through her chest and declare mutiny. The only other in that *our* should not be the man pacing the floor just then. It should be Alexandre.

"Margot."

She sensed that Cook had spoken, but Margot could not focus, for her thoughts ran the gamut. She had been so wrong to assume the baron would be an ogre, a toad, a rotting old man. But no, she would never judge a man by his appearance. Breathtaking as the baron was, Alexandre was still the most handsome man she knew. He stood proud and elegant, as enticing in his charm and physical appeal as the baron.

The baron ceased his pacing, his back to the two women, and scanned the outer courtyard through the window. He flexed both arms back as if easing out a muscle, then pulled his arms forward, which strained the gray velvet doublet nicely across his bulging biceps.

Margot sucked in the corner of her lip. Think Alexandre, she coached. Alexandre is the man who has captured your eye. He has muscles just as large as the baron's. He's long, beautiful hair, kind eyes, and a kind heart. Everything she desired . . .

. . . would soon be taken away from her.

As Margot touched the twins' chamber door, she listened carefully, then slowly opened it and crept into the twilight-glittered room. Most likely Alexandre had tucked the girls in tonight. Cook had told her she'd explained to Alexandre that she had sent Margot to Paris on an errand. He probably thought her still away and had assumed the night duties without a thought. Certainly he might expect she was angry at him after she had refused his proposal. Oh, why had he done such a thing? It would only make her leaving all the more difficult.

"Margot!"

"Shh," she whispered as she tiptoed across the room and settled on the feather-stuffed bed. Both girls plunged into her arms and laid sloppy kisses to her dirt-smeared cheeks. Ruby clonked her in the gut. "Be quiet or your papa will hear. I'm sorry I wasn't here to tuck you in, girls, but I was on an errand."

"The Baron of Blunders is here!" Janette pronounced in wide-eyed dismay.

"He really is," Lisette chimed in. "We saw him. He said we didn't look at all like twins."

"Nonsense." Margot ruffled Lisette's ringlets and tapped her on the nose. "If the two of you had the same color hair, I should be calling you Janette right now and might even wonder if you"—she lifted Ruby and addressed the wood-faced doll—"are Lisette."

Janette giggled, which prompted Margot to shush her again. "I don't want your papa to think you do not take to his tucking in very well. You must be quiet little kittens."

"But, the baron." Janette would not drop the subject. "He's come to take the princess away."

"Is he really here to take you away, Margot?"

Lisette's soft question, combined with Janette's wide black eyes, were a mighty combination of guilt. Regretting the fact that she had allowed the girls to become so attached so quickly, Margot coaxed both slender sets of shoulders back against their pillows and kissed them on their foreheads. A stream of silvery moonlight highlighted their lash-dusted eyes and innocent yet silently strong worries.

"I certainly hope not" was all Margot could say.

"But we love you," Janette began in what might become a wail. Margot rushed to hug her and tucked Ruby close to Janette's neck.

"I love you too. Both of you."

"We're the kittens," Lisette began somberly, "and you are the Princess of Practically Everything."

"Well . . ."

"Papa is the King of Oranges, and the Baron of Blunders has just come today. In the story the baron wanted to take the princess away from the kittens. Tell us that's not the way it goes, Margot. Please, you must."

"Yes, you must," Janette softly reiterated.

Already she could feel the devastation of a child's heart breaking. Margot wanted to rush a healing palm to the odd little fissure that would soon rend into a large crevice if things were to happen as they should.

She must honor her agreement to the baron, leaving

Lisette and Janette to fend with a new nursemaid. Perhaps they would adjust quickly. She'd not known them for more than a few weeks.

Glorious fool, her conscience chided. These girls love you. As you love them. You cannot leave without breaking their precious hearts. And if it must be done, it must be done with care and a gentility that will ease them over the pain.

"I want you to be my mama."

Margot would develop her own broken heart soon enough. "Oh, girls, that would be the most wonderful thing in the world."

"Then you will be?" Janette wondered. "Will you marry Papa?"

What must Alexandre be feeling this very moment? Surely he must be upset over what had transpired last night. If only she hadn't been forced to refuse his proposal. Nothing would please her more than to become Madame Saint-Sylvestre and mother to these sweet girls. Oh, but she had been such a fool following her heart instead of logic these past few weeks.

"Girls, there are some things . . . some grown-up things that I need to take care of before I can even begin to think about marrying your papa."

The elfin child looked up from Margot's embrace, tears reddening her eyes and puffing her face. Janette sniffed. "What things? Don't you love Papa?"

"Yes, very much. But . . . well, I have made an agreement with the baron, promised to marry him. It was all done long before I ever met my two precious kittens."

"Why would you do that, Margot? Why would you marry another man, when you love my papa?"

"I didn't know your papa when I agreed to the baron's proposal. But believe me, I do not love the baron in any way."

"Then why would you give him your heart?"

Margot adjusted her weight on the bed and pulled Lisette onto her lap. The smell of blueberry pie lingered in her blond ringlets.

"You must not marry the baron!"

"I agree. An education would mean nothing if it required selling my heart. But I'm afraid I don't know what I can do now."

"Why can't you just tell the Baron of Blunders to mount up and ride off?"

"It isn't as easy as that. I signed a paper stating I would do as he wished. It is a binding contract that cannot be broken."

"You can't just tear it up?"

Could she? For a moment Margot's heart raced with hope. If only things could be so simple. She shook her head. "I'm afraid not. The marriage contract is in the baron's possession."

Lisette sighed and stuffed her fists under each arm, thoroughly as disgruntled as Margot felt. "This is a problem."

"Indeed."

"How would the King of Oranges and the Princess of Practically Everything solve it?"

"I don't know, dear. I wish that I did."

Even in the darkness Margot could see the tear jewel glimmering in the corner of Janette's eye. One blink liquefied the precious gem and skirted it down her plump cheek to splat upon Ruby's head.

"You must understand, an agreement was forged by our parents when I was just a little girl like you two. I've promised to stand by the baron's side and give him the children he wishes. In turn the baron promised to pay for my education. And that is something I want more than anything in the world."

"Even more than Papa?"

"Even—" The word stuck to the end of her tongue,

keeping the rest of her reply safely silent. Should she lie or tell the truth? Certainly lies were not allowed, not to a child. But the truth . . . Did she even know the truth anymore?

You love their father, you know that you do.

"There is nothing more in the world that would make me happy than to be with your papa always. And you two, of course. I will do what I can."

"No . . ." Janette's tears flooded from her wide eyes, and Lisette turned to smooth a hand over her sister's head.

"The princess won't leave her kittens," Lisette said in a most brave voice. "Will she?"

It hadn't been a tearful question, more a challenge to even dare to break their hearts.

"I will try my best," Margot said.

"You mustn't leave us like Mama," Janette said through restrained sniffles. "Mama never came back. You cannot leave us, Margot, you cannot!"

"I won't." Margot closed her eyes at her sudden thoughtless outburst. Words pulled from her soul by two little beings that loved her so unconditionally; they did not need more heartbreak in their lives. And Margot desperately wanted to stop up the bleeding crack in her own heart. "I promise you I will not leave you. But the two of you must now make a promise to me."

"Anything," Lisette said, and the two bobbed their heads eagerly.

"You mustn't tell your papa about the Baron of Blunders and the King of Oranges or anything else in our story. I cannot give the story a happy ending if your father finds out."

"But the King of Oranges can help," Janette pleaded. "He is a king. And kings have more power than barons. Even *I* know that."

"Janette, your papa is not . . ." Margot recalled for a

moment Alexandre's statement that his daughter's voice appeared in round balls of aqua to him. How magical and yet very fragile. No, she could not do it. Could not allow the harsh reality of her world to harm these girls any more than it may already have. "Your papa is the king of my heart. And I promise the two of you I will remain true to him, as I shall remain true to my two little kittens."

"You won't leave with the baron?" Janette asked with a sniff and a pouty lower lip.

"I shall not. Now, I want to hear the two of you promise me your silence."

"We promise," they chimed.

Margot tucked the worn counterpane up around their necks and kissed them again, belatedly remembering to buss Ruby's forehead just as Janette was about to remind her, then she tiptoed out of the room and closed the door.

She blew out a breath that traveled up all the way from her toes. "What have I done now?"

She had just promised the unpromisable.

Thinking he had heard a noise in the girls' room, Alexandre pressed an ear to the door to listen before entering. He had only just heard Margot's request for the girls to make her a promise. What sort, he hadn't been able to decipher through the door that separated their bedrooms.

So Margot finally made it home from her busy day in Paris. Thoughtful of her to stop in and kiss the girls goodnight. Perhaps it was a promise to have sweet dreams. He could expect nothing less from Margot and her whimsical ways.

Popping his head out the door leading into the Orangerie, Alexandre just caught the melon swish of her skirts as she hurriedly departed. Well, if he must say, she was nearly sprinting. Where was she off to in such haste? And without a moment of time to bid a good eve to him?

But of course, she most likely did not want to face him after his disastrous proposal.

He leaned against the door frame, crossing his ankles and arms, and pricked his ears to just make out the disappearing melon tones as she took the hundred steps. Perhaps she was tired after a day in Paris and sought her own bed. The journey to the great city and back would be enough to tax any woman.

Yes, that was it. She had forgotten the proposal. As he must. The two of them must simply pretend it had never been spoken. He was willing to if she could. But he would not allow their relationship to stale. From there they would move ahead, confident in each other's trust.

It was well past supper, though Alexandre had yet to stop into the kitchen and sample the tasty treats he'd smelled all afternoon. Chicken of some sort, he could tell by the curves. Perfectly done and roundly tempting.

With the girls already dozing, his stomach did protest lack of attention. Perhaps he might invite Margot to share a late meal and a bottle of wine.

Spurred by the notion of a romantic evening with his fairy queen, Alexandre dashed inside his room and shuffled through the crates on his floor. Glassy clinks helped him navigate the wine crate in the darkness that did not grasp the single-taper glow from his work desk. He had a half dozen bottles of Beaujolais that he'd been hoarding for years. The last of his father's honeymoon stock. Each of the Saint-Sylvestre siblings were given six bottles upon Antoine's death. Alexandre had obligingly opened one on his wedding night, feeling the occasion certainly demanded some sort of celebration. Sophie had taken one sip and complained of its dryness.

As he lifted a dusty amber bottle and smoothed his fingers over the narrow neck, Alexandre recalled his befittingly horrific wedding night. He'd still been in a state of shock at finding himself promising to love, honor, and cherish a woman whom he'd initially thought a tavern whore, one to service his needs while on a venture to Paris to purchase botany books. Then to learn four months later that same woman was really of the demimonde, who admittedly had been slumming it that night. In search of a man so different from the fops who'd courted her. Something different.

Indeed, he had been something different. For never had Alexandre done such a foolish thing. He'd courted two women in his lifetime; both he had abstained from seeking his pleasures out of courtesy, honor, and respect. There had been only that one other woman, Rexene, whom Armand had introduced him to at a fête on the left bank. She had been his first. Sophie had been his second.

Not a particularly long list of conquests for a twenty-seven-year-old man. But enough; for his earlier experiences had worked only to put a bitter taste in his mouth for the amorous delights.

Until now.

Now the acid aftertaste of his past experiences had begun to recede, to be replaced by a much sweeter substance: Margot deVerona.

As much as Alexandre wished to not become involved with another female, that same force worked as a counterbalance, making him desire Margot in equal amounts to his wariness. He could not fight this feeling. And he would not. Sophie no longer controlled his every thought before he had it, his every move before he made it.

He was a free man. A man who could make his own choices.

Marriage? He'd been out of his head last night. Simply wishing to please and in return be pleased. Perhaps it was a boon, Margot's reaction. She was the wiser of the two of them, knowing it was too soon for marriage.

But a romance? The time seemed right. Alexandre's heart craved as much.

Dinner and wine, and after that . . . some kissing and touching. Alexandre drew in a deep breath. Yes. Long hours of kissing and snuggling and touching and tasting . . .

Thinking to find Margot in the kitchen, perhaps helping Cook with clean-up, Alexandre, wine bottle in hand, skipped up the hundred steps and crunched across the south terrace. The night was clear and fragrant with the undiluted freshness of nature. It had been over a year since he'd been so unconscious of his limp. Now it was barely there and quite pain free. Such a lark!

The kitchen beckoned with a welcoming glow. Half a dozen thick tallow candles flickered across the stone walls. The aroma of roasted fowl and rosemary and the corn flour used to make Cook's famous biscuits lingered. Margot was not sitting at the table, eating, nor was she plopped in the wicker chair before the sizzling embers in the hearth.

Cook spun around as Alexandre's heels clicked closer. "Monsieur Saint-Sylvestre, I was wondering when you'd come to eat. I've saved you a plate: chicken pie with vegetables chopped by your own girls' hands."

He spied the plate sitting on the table. The curves of the chicken assaulted his nose with a surrendering feeling. This was what a true home smelled like. Welcoming and happy, and never should a child worry for his next meal. Not that he had ever to worry for his meals when he was a child. Until of course, his mother passed.

After his mother's death, his father's frequent work stints to the king's musketeers had kept him from home for long periods of time. Armand, barely fifteen, had had to take control of the household and see that the siblings were fed and clothed in their father's absence.

Pity Armand had been forced to ride the high roads

to support the family. Alexandre would not hear of accompanying his brother on his midnight raids. But he hadn't balked at accepting coin to purchase his books for study. To this day he felt guilty for that. But he assuaged that guilt with the knowledge that Armand had never harmed his victims or threatened them with a pistol.

Wrenching his thoughts from the past, Alexandre approached the table and gave Cook a thankful nod. "This is very kind of you. I should think if a man did not show for dinner, he would deserve to starve. I was wondering . . . perhaps Margot hasn't eaten?" He lifted the wine bottle. "I thought we might dine together."

"Oh!" Cook pressed two water-wrinkled hands to her cheeks. "I mean—oh."

She corrected her surprise quickly. Curious.

"Actually, she's, er . . ."

Alexandre followed Cook's darting glance to the adjoining door, where he knew Margot shared the cook's bedchamber, and back to the door leading into the main halls of the château.

Then it dawned on him. "Forgive me, of course, she must have already retired. The day has been a long one, and with Margot's travel to and from Paris—"

"That's it!" Cook declared, seeming quite pleased with Alexandre's explanation. "She's gone to bed. But I could wake her if you wish?"

"Oh, no." Alexandre fingered the edge of the plate, disheartened that his plans had been thwarted. "Perhaps tomorrow."

He set the wine on the table and seated himself before the plate. Now the curves of the chicken had completely disappeared and he saw only the golden crust of the pie round, roasted to what might be a pleasing taste but, to him, lacked the curve of enjoyment. "I think I'll eat in my chambers if you don't mind."

"That would be best," Cook offered, then virtually swept him out of the kitchen with plate and wine bottle in hand.

Before he could turn and offer thanks, the door closed behind him, and Alexandre sensed more than heard that Cook put an ear to the door to listen.

Food-laden plate balanced on his left hand and wine bottle swinging near his knee, Alexandre had to wonder. This was beyond curious. Why, it touched on the peculiar. Hmm . . . perhaps Cook was merely fending off interruptions to Margot's well-earned sleep? Or what of the unthinkable? Had Margot told Cook about his idiotic marriage proposal? Was Cook now fending off his advances at Margot's request?

"I've been such a fool," he muttered. "Surely she will never forgive my improper proposal."

With a sigh Alexandre trudged back down to the Orangerie and dined on cold chicken pie and no wine.

Nineteen

He might be a blunder, but, goodness, can he kiss!

Red overwhelmed the bedchamber the baron had been given. From the red-sashed angels that dotted the mu-raled ceiling to the red burned-out velvet wall covering to the red damask on the chairs and bed curtains and bedding.

Margot had reluctantly foregone the notion of a bath and had quickly scrubbed face and hands and legs and had Cook lace her into the crimson velvet gown. But the idea that a bath would be much more enjoyable than spending a tension-laden meal with this man lingered as she crossed the floor.

The baron directed her to an intimately sized table and seated her, then took to lighting the candles.

"My lord—"

"Please," he said as he blew out the tinder. "You must accustom yourself to calling me Nicodème when we are alone."

"Very well, Nicodème." It felt odd to speak his name. A name she would use every day for the rest of her life. Much more harsh in texture than the delicious ring of *Alexandre.*

"Of course, *my lord* is certainly demanded when in

company," he added with what he might have thought a sly wink.

Margot took the one-eyed flicker of lash more as a warning. Beneath the pale beauty, something darker lurked. She wasn't sure why that thought came to her, but it did.

He still wore the gray velvet doublet, buttoned up to mid-chest to reveal only a slash of lace beneath. Margot noticed she had taken to breathing through her mouth, for he did like to lavish on the scent.

"I hope you are hungry. It appears your cook has sent enough to feed half a dozen healthy men. I shouldn't wonder if it would take two dozen of your sort to eat as much."

Margot paused, her fork hovering over the flaky crust on her chicken pie. "My sort?"

The baron arched a brow, his fork in midair before his lips. "Well, you are rather thin and frail."

"I'm nothing of the sort." She set her utensils down, finding the baron's lack of consideration most vexing. "I'm sure I could eat you under the table any day."

"Really?" His cherub-bow lips pursed beneath a glittering blue gaze.

Now, what had she said to provoke such a ribald grin from the man?

Oh!

"That remains to be seen." He took up the silence with a slice of his knife through chicken. "But I must admit, I am disappointed. Your hips are painfully narrow."

"My—my . . ." Too puzzled to even finish her sentence, Margot slid her hands over her skirt, mining for the bones in question. There they were, just where God had placed them. Too narrow?

"You're far from the good breeding stock I had expected." Nicodème slurped a healthy slug of wine over his lips and scanned the table, finding a plump corn biscuit to his liking. "I should wager you'll have a difficult time passing a child through those hips. Dread painful, to be sure."

"How dare you speak of me as if I am a brood mare."

"But you are aware I expect children?"

She raised her hands to her waist. "Of course I am. The adjustments to the marriage contract were quite clear. I just thought it would be . . ." What? Different? A little more romantic than being told one hadn't wide enough hips to birth children? Margot had known all along this marriage was merely a business arrangement. On both their parts. She'd had no expectations. Until Alexandre Saint-Sylvestre had walked into her life.

"Margot?"

"Huh?"

"That pose is most unappealing for a woman of such small visage. You should keep your hands from your face. The oil from the meat will stop up your pores and cause boils."

What a romantic man! "Forgive me." Margot clasped her fork as if ready to stab. Eager to keep her other hand occupied, she grabbed a biscuit. "As for my hips, perhaps I'll fill out after a few years at the Sorbonne," she offered, well aware her tone was snide. "Days spent sitting idle and reading from books should certainly provide the cushioning my hips might require."

"My dear, your schooling shall come *after* the first child is born."

"After!" Her corn biscuit exploded in her fist, dispersing chunks all over the table.

"Margot!"

"That was not part of the arrangement. How dare—" She slammed her fork on the table. "How can you possibly expect me to tend my studies with an infant to breast? Oh, no, my lord, that is quite out of the question.

I must tend my schooling before delivering an infant to your hands."

"We shall discuss this later," he said with a snap at his biscuit and another swallow of wine.

"I want to discuss it now."

"You challenge your place, Mademoiselle. You must abstain from speaking so loudly. Women should not be so bold as to command such admonishment from their husband."

"You are not yet my husband."

"You foresee not filling the position as my wife?"

I wish. Margot slumped against the stiff chair back. The baron pierced her with that remarkable blue gaze. 'Twas rather annoying not knowing whether to swoon or poke a finger in his eye.

Certainly any woman should be pleased with Nicodème de Verzy as her husband. As far as outer appearances went. And certainly most women should also have no trouble providing their husband with a child as soon as possible.

But how could she tend her studies with a bleating infant in arm? Margot had learned well enough with seven younger siblings that babies required attention. A large amount of attention. There would never be enough time for study when soiled nappies required changing and mouths required feeding and little minds required play and hugs and rocking and singing and cradling and tear wiping, and—oh!

"I'm not sure I understand your reason for choosing me in the first place," she prompted.

The baron leaned back, stretching his arm out across the chair back, a peacock in his pride. Delicate lace danced around his wrist and framed the long grace of his fingers. The blue of his eyes romanced the candlelight. So delectable. "You know as well as I this marriage was not a choice on either of our parts. What reason do you need?"

"I have to wonder why you do not just choose one of your current mistresses, someone you already enjoy a relationship with, to provide this child you so desperately require. Instead, you travel halfway across France for a waif with narrow hips."

"You assume I have mistresses."

"You do not?"

He shrugged and smiled around another hearty bite of chicken. "It is not the wife's privilege to know such things."

"Oh! How impossibly vexing you can be. I only wish to understand your reason for claiming a woman you have never before seen, until now, to conceive and raise your children. 'Tis not as if you've mentioned love to me, so I should come to believe it unnecessary. One woman is as good as the next. Perhaps someone with wider hips?"

"Much as I prefer buxom women with long, dark hair and thick red lips and plump breasts just made for suckling—" He swished back a gulp of wine, dashed his tongue over his lower lip, and grabbed another biscuit, quite unconcerned that his comments were so ribald. "That is what I would prefer. You were chosen by my father, and I will honor his wishes. Your mother birthed eight children. Why should a man not expect the same from her daughter?"

What an ass. It was becoming easier with every word the baron spoke to remember she did not wish this marriage, handsome face or not.

"For as inadequate as you've explained me to be, I just assume you might seek a more fitting candidate. You were able to make changes to the marriage agreement. Surely you might be able to insert a different name where it calls for wife."

"You will be my wife. Get that through your small, thick head."

Margot bristled, punching her fists to her hips and straightening proudly. "Better to be small and thick than tall and daft."

"You press the bounds of polite conversation, Mademoiselle."

"My lord, I have been known to speak my mind. Always."

The baron leaned across the table, the movement flashing a fiery warning at her in the reflection flickering in his eyes. "And I have been known to tame wild horses with a well-wielded whip."

So he thought to intimidate her with threats? Well, it would not work! Margot tucked her shaking fingers under her thighs. She would not show her fear. She did not fear him. Too much. "I believe I've had enough of wine and chicken."

"Not enough to add even a sliver of padding to those damned hips."

She stood and made to leave, but the baron swept into her path and gripped her by both shoulders. An invisible wave of rank odor quavered under her nose, but Margot could not place the origin. It was quickly overwhelmed by lavender. "I'll be away most of the day tomorrow."

And what do I care, she wanted to blurt out but held her tongue. Surely such control must have some merit. Where had that awful smell come from?

"I want to ride out, see if I can locate the king's hunting party so I don't have to endure another day idling here at the lodge. I'll return for another shared meal."

"Of course, you mustn't allow me to wither away," Margot said, but her words were cut off by a surprise kiss.

Stunned but too tantalized to even think to push the man away, Margot could only close her eyes and notice the ease with which the baron pulled her close. Her body fit up against his, limning his hard lines with her own curves. He was as tall as Alexandre, and she had to tilt her head back to catch his brute kiss and not lose it.

All the distasteful words the baron had spoken over supper disappeared with the wine-flavored taste of his kiss. This was indeed a potent way to end one's day; enveloped in the strong arms of a god.

But her peek into Olympus ended as abruptly as it had begun. The baron nudged her away to look into her eyes, a wicked grin spiking dimples in both of his cheeks. Dimples! How irresistible could a man be?

"To our future," he said.

"Our future," Margot mumbled, still beguiled by his kiss.

"And to many strapping sons."

"Sons? Yes, certainly, of course," Margot muttered. At Nicodème's direction she stepped out into the hallway and mindlessly curtsied to the baron as he closed the door behind her.

"Sons," she muttered again as the floor beneath her moved and she found her body propelled forward. "Yes." She brushed her fingers over her lips, a hot rush of desire coursing through her body at recall of his masterful kiss. Never had she received such a commanding kiss. He'd completely controlled her thoughts, her emotion, her staunch efforts to not like the man with that hard morsel.

Margot's body connected with something solid. She stepped back, blinked, then pressed her hand and forehead to the heavy oak door that led into the kitchen. So taken she'd been by Nicodème's kiss, she'd actually walked all the way from his room to the kitchen in a lovesick daze.

"Fool!" she chided herself, hugging her arms as though a chill wind had breezed through the lodge. But the only thing that had breezed into her life was a baron with devastating blue eyes and stunning kisses.

Perhaps a son would not be so bad? She could nurse a babe and read from a textbook at the same time. Field studies and experiments could be conducted with an infant tangling in her skirts and pulling to be lifted—

"No! What are you thinking?" She pushed her fingers up through her hair and caught her forehead in her palm. "One kiss from the man, and all of a sudden you've become his love slave?"

Perhaps next she would be considering the witch's spell that would have him hungering over her body parts!

"What about true love?"

And what about the promise she'd made to Janette and Lisette about never leaving them?

"Oh, this is a fine mess!"

Her social calendar was definitely filling up. Much as she should have refused, Margot did not. A note had arrived in her room that morning, inviting her to lunch in the loft above the stables. A graceful *A* had signed the note.

And just what color is his A? Margot thought as she began her ascent up the rickety wood stairs to the loft. "Wonder, wonder—oh!"

Pulling herself up onto the loft floor, Margot tiptoed over scattered rose petals. Everywhere red and pink and yellow curves of sweet-smelling softness carpeted the floor. Purple violets dotted the carpet as vivid accents. Her skirts stirred up the tender petals, and she felt them slither across her ankles, enticing kisses of nature. The loft was small, no longer than two beds pushed end to end and about as wide as a man measured from nose to toes. A dormered window was horizontally striped by strips of thin rosewood, and beneath the window lay a display of goblets and wine and cheeses.

"Are you pleased?" Alexandre's hands spread around her waist and hugged her from behind.

"No," Margot whispered. She felt him tense. "I'm enchanted. This is too lovely, Alexandre. You've created a fantasy up here."

"You are not still angry with me?"

She spun in his arms and traced the grim line of his lips. "Whatever for?"

"My foolishness the other night. I frightened you away with my proposal. It was hastily made. I did not mean to press you into something more serious than we both desire."

"It was not foolish, Alexandre, only premature." A marriage proposal and a marriage agreement. How complicated her life had become. But she didn't want to think about the other one, the god with the devastating kisses. Was it possible the man might simply cease to exist if she gave him not another thought? For now Margot wished to put all effort into her relationship with Alexandre. For that was the only one that mattered. "We must not speak another word on that. Promise?"

A relieved sigh hushed over Alexandre's lips. "Agreed."

Good. One sticky problem swept out with the rushes.

"But come, sit over here by the food," he directed, and helped her to the floor. "Now for the pièce de résistance." He raced to the stairs and returned with a long, narrow dowel. It worked well to push the rosewood slats over the window up into their pocket. Sunlight streamed through the window and sparkled in silver and aqua in the globes of the goblets.

Margot gasped and raised to her knees. "It's perfect. I've never seen such a fine blue sky. Oh, I wish I had brought my telescope. I imagine one could see a kestrel's flight leagues away."

Alexandre settled next to Margot and brushed a pile of rose petals aside to reveal her leather valise. "I had Lisette sneak into your chambers. A little covert operation. I hope you do not mind. She was dreadful careful."

"Lisette would be. Thank you."

He had dressed in his finest, Margot noticed now. Blue velvet doublet, the same he'd worn the night of the party, and black breeches. Most likely Lisette had tamed his hair into the braided queue that filed down his back, and he might have scrubbed for an inordinate amount of time on his hands until only the faintest evidence of his labors remained.

The telescope forgotten, Margot observed as Alexandre uncorked a dusty bottle of wine. That muscle flexed in his jaw as he worked at the cork. There was just something about the movement, the pulse of his strength that so enticed her.

"My parents' honeymoon stock," he said as he began to pour. "Are you hungry?"

Margot dipped her cheek into his beckoning hand. "Only for your touch." She pressed a lingering kiss to the sensitive flesh in his palm, flicked her tongue out to tease the purlique. How a simple touch to that little web of flesh worked like a switch, activating his desires and firing up his passions.

"Are you sure you won't taste something?" He plucked a violet pansy from the edge of Margot's skirts. Her lashes fluttered and her lids closed as he drew the petal across her lower lip. "Open your mouth," he whispered. Margot did, and Alexandre slipped the petal inside, pressing it gently with his fingertip against the hot mound of her tongue. "What do you taste?"

Mmm . . . Margot closed her lips over the stem and concentrated on the fine silken petal saturated against her tongue. A hint of sweetness, followed close by a spicy flavor surprised her. "Cinnamon," she whispered, and opened her eyes.

"I've never eaten a flower before," she offered. "I never thought you could."

He plucked another petal and tickled it across her forehead. "Some flowers are edible. They can be quite tasty sugared and placed on desserts." Scintillating tingles followed in the wake of the petal's journey down her nose— like one of his precious sliders—to her mouth. "Open," he whispered.

The petal sealed to her tongue and Margot tasted a new flavor. Saltiness, as Alexandre pulled his finger over the tip of her tongue, moistening it to slicken his journey back and forth over her lower lip. Too soon, the delicious taste of his touch was gone. The fragile wisp of nature melted away in her mouth.

"Your whispers are of cinnamon," he said in a deep, lingering voice. He kissed her chin and drew an exploratory finger along her jawline.

"And what of my kisses?" Margot wondered.

The heat of his touch abruptly left her face. Alexandre reached behind her to the plate of food and produced a soft, plump fruit. "A peach." He took a hearty bite of the peach and chewed it up without so much as an offer to her.

"Really," Margot said, pouting. "How can you be so sure?"

Alexandre's eyes danced across her sullen expression. With a wink and a cock of his head he drew his forefinger over the exposed flesh of the peach, drenching his digit in the dew of the fruit.

Peach juice slipped into her mouth as he painted his finger across the plump mounds of her lips. A decadent thrill ran over her shoulders, like tiny imps scampering through the grasses. What this man did to her senses.

Her entire body reacted to his touch, silently pleading, screaming for more, more, and more.

"Your kisses"—his whispers heated the dew on her lips—"are the sweetest by far."

Their lips connected, then opened to invite the dance of passion. Alexandre's tongue dove deep within to taste Margot's peach-flavored whimpers. As close as they physically were, Alexandre had become a part of her in spirit as well. So close, she felt that to never see him again would be like ripping out a piece of her heart and leaving it to wither in the sun.

It must not happen. Could she possibly prevent such a horror?

"Margot, you do something to me. Your kisses, they release this fierce wanting within me. Never have I so desired to do such things with a woman. To taste her, to touch her, to know her."

Margot's eyes flashed open. "To know me?"

"Perhaps," he said as he reached to the floor. He produced a ruby rose petal and slithered it across Margot's exposed décolletage.

What was he doing? It felt like seduction. It looked like seduction. It tasted, mmm, did it taste of seduction. But he'd denied her request to make love. And then had requested her hand in marriage, only to now confess it mere foolishness. He was so conflicting in his actions, it was hard to know how he wanted her to react.

Though she knew exactly how she wanted to react.

The path of the velvety petal painted a scintillating trail across Margot's breasts. *Follow your heart,* her conscience whispered. *It is what is right. You haven't much time left. . . .*

Inside, her heart pounded. Her senses sopped up every minute touch, every gentle breath, and her mind surrendered to the moment. She felt her spine go limp and

Alexandre's hands slip around her back to lower her across the petal-strewn floor.

"There is something I must know," he whispered as he idly flicked the rose petal up her neck and under her jaw. "You said when I first hired you this would only be temporary. That you would care for the girls until I could find a permanent nursemaid."

She had. But now that impossible promise to the twins cleaved to her conscience.

"So I assume that meant you would not be at Versailles for long?"

Not for long? *Try one more day.* Unless she could make the baron disappear or at least convince him that she definitely wasn't bride or mothering material. A difficult task thus far. For as long as the baron continued to surprise her with his devastating kisses, she would never retain a plan of action long enough to enact it. Oh! Was he such a powerful force against her feelings for Alexandre?

"Margot?"

"Um, no, I hadn't planned to stay much longer. . . ." *Just kiss me again,* she wished. *Erase all thought of Nicodème de Verzy.*

"I see." Defeated, Alexandre pressed the rose petal to his own lips, still lingering over her, but it seemed his thoughts had retreated from the present to an inner cache of troubles. "And marriage is certainly out of the question. I suppose if I offered you higher wages, you might not reconsider?"

"Oh, Alexandre, it's a little more difficult than that. I do love the girls, and I would enjoy nothing more than to care for them indefinitely, watch them grow—"

"Then do so." The rose petal forgotten, Alexandre pressed close, trapping her in an expectant gaze. "I promise I won't ask you to marry me again. But please, just stay. For the girls. F-for me as well."

"For you?" Was he saying—no, he couldn't actually be. "Alexandre?"

"Margot, I must admit I've taken a liking to your presence."

Just a liking?

"Hell, it's more than a liking, I think of you first thing in the morning when I rise, and count the minutes until I see you appear in the Orangerie with the girls at your skirts. And when I sit in the darkness of my room at night, I"—he sighed—"I wonder what it might be like to share the darkness with you."

"You've certainly changed your mind since the other night, when you sent me away from your bed."

"There is still good reason to avoid the carnal pleasures. Until we both can be sure, Margot, I don't want you with child. Believe me when I say I shouldn't blink an eye to commit to you if it should happen, but I know the idea of marriage frightens you."

More than he could ever know. Oh, when would she confess? She must soon.

"Alexandre, there are . . . well, there are things . . ."

No, she wasn't prepared to tell him about the baron. Not now. Later. If she could have some time to herself to figure the best way to reveal her fiancé. Perhaps, even—could she hope—she might be done with the baron by then.

"I need some time to think," she announced, rising to her elbows and signaling her need for space. Space? Hell, she wanted to entwine her limbs in this man's and kiss him forever. But she could not do that until everything was made right. Alexandre Saint-Sylvestre did not deserve her betrayal.

Was it too much to hope that she might know love for but a moment before it would be forever swept away?

"I've perplexed you," he said, standing and offering his hand to help her up.

Margot stood next to him and brushed silken rose petals from her elbows, then flicked a few from Alexandre's doublet. The blue velvet skimmed cool beneath her fingers. Tilting her head up, she kissed him on the chin, for he did not move to bend to her. "Indeed, you have perplexed me. But it is a good vexation. Can you accept that I need time to muddle this over?"

"You'll consider remaining a nursemaid to the girls?"

"I-I will."

Another impossible promise.

"And"—he absently gestured through the air—"starting a relationship with me?"

Oh, but he pleaded so sweetly.

"I have been thinking of nothing but since the moment I laid eyes on you." The truth for once. The devil take her for her other lies.

He afforded her an embarrassed smile. Margot smoothed the end of his braided hair from over his shoulder and down his back. They had come to terms that she desperately hoped she would be able to keep. She must. For she loved this man. And yet, if she spent one more moment in his arms, she would spoil it all.

"I should see to the girls now. They'll probably wake soon."

"Of course."

"But first"—Margot levered herself up on tiptoe and landed Alexandre's mouth with a long kiss that did not part his lips but instead counted his heartbeats against her own—"tell me, does my kiss have a color or a sound or shape?"

"It is pink," he said with a smile. "A cherry pink that would tempt the finest painters to match its hue. But I daresay it would be an impossible quest." He brushed his thumb over her mouth, the usual kindness in his eyes now molten passion. "The only way to experience the color is touching, feeling, and releasing one's worries."

"You do seem much more relaxed than when we first met."

"It is because of you. Thank you, Margot, for adding a new shade of pink to my life."

Twenty

And ye harm none, do as ye will.
(Well . . . that's the way it's supposed to work.)

A new shade of pink?

The man certainly had a way of putting things, of making her feel so . . . guilty! Something had to be done. There was simply no way Margot could marry the baron de Verzy. The contract must be torn up, changed, burned! She'd come to Versailles with the intention of learning who she was, who she wanted to be.

And now Margot knew with certainty that she did not want to become the baroness de Verzy.

Fists pumping at her sides, she skirted a thick tangle of brambles and tumbled down the side of the columbine-speckled hill. A squirrel with cheeks full of nuts bolted upright to sit on its hind legs and study Margot as she fumbled with her skirts and untangled her feet from them. Blowing a renegade strand of hair from between her eyes, Margot then stood, curtsied to the curious nut-nibbler, and knocked on the door that led into the realm of all that glitters and delights.

* * *

The sun had held reign in the sky for well over two hours when Alexandre spied his daughters marching out of the Orangerie. Lisette's fists swooshed her skirts in rhythm to her military steps, while Janette and Ruby lumbered rather lazily behind.

Alexandre swiped his arm across his forehead, pushed back sweat-drenched strands of hair from his face, and called to the girls, "Where is Margot?"

"We don't know!" Lisette huffed. She stopped, planted one fist on each hip and shook her head furiously to display the tangle of curls that jagged and jigged all over her head. "We've been waiting a very long time for her to come and dress us and comb our hair."

Alexandre now noticed Janette's skirt hem was tucked in her left stocking and her dress was on backward.

"I'm hungry too," Janette said with a yawn. "Where's Margot, Papa?"

"She left us. I just know it," Lisette spouted.

"Come, come, girls, you mustn't get so riled. Scoot over here, Janette. Let me fix your dress for you. And, Lisette, sit on the tub here by me and I'll fix up your hair."

Janette squiggled her arms out of the blousy sleeves and jiggled around inside the gown as he held it by the shoulders and then laced up the back for her. Where could Margot be? She hadn't mentioned last night that she'd be late.

"Perhaps Cook has her working in the kitchen and she isn't able to get away."

Lisette merely huffed and slammed her arms over her chest.

"Why don't we ask Ruby?" Alexandre suggested. He'd seen the girls on many occasions consult the silent sage, never really sure what the answer was that they seemed to read in her milky glass eyes but recalling that they always abided by what she had to say. It couldn't hurt to lighten the mood a bit.

"Yes," Lisette decided as she stood and spun her sister around. She lifted Janette's arms, displaying Ruby between the two of them. "Ruby, is Margot helping Cook as Papa said?"

Alexandre found he held his breath as his daughters stared with wide-eyed anticipation at the doll. Could he ask it his own question? *Does Margot love me? Do I love her?*

"She is." Lisette looked to Alexandre, gave him an accepting nod of her head, and patted Ruby on her crown.

Janette turned to Alexandre. "Ruby says she's in the kitchen."

"Then you girls had best skitter on up there and break your fasts with Margot. Run along now. And bring the comb, Lisette. I'm sure Margot will have you looking a princess in no time."

Aqua giggles and amber shouts surrounded Alexandre in a succulent shroud. To bask in his daughters' happiness put him in the most perfect place. The day would be a good one. It could be nothing less when greeted with laughter.

Ah, but what might Ruby-the-All-Knowing have said regarding his feelings toward Margot? Did he really think he might love her?

He pressed a hand over his heart, sensing the steady beats, the quiet rush of blood inside. And then he closed his eyes and wandered deeper within, beyond the beat of life and to the very essence of himself. His soul.

The soul of Alexandre Saint-Sylvestre was an ancient and mysterious thing. There were times he knew that every step he took was right. Every motion, every thought, moved him in the direction he was meant to go. And then there were times when he wasn't sure where he belonged, didn't know how to accept the treatment life served him, just seemed to follow the ways of the world with hope of not falling off.

Margot fit inside that portion of his being that knew exactly where it was going. Like a missing piece pressed into place upon his heart. She fit in his soul. Perhaps she had lived there all his life, and only now he recognized her part in his existence. This was true and pure love. And if she was not ready to marry, he would find another way to win her heart.

Request for a hate spell was greeted with a glossy-red grin and an invitation to be seated while Charesse poked about her jars and baskets of oddities.

Margot, her heart beating faster than rampaging stallions, tried to calm her nervousness by focusing on the brown wren that was currently plumping up its nest in the wall next to the doorway. It would tuck a narrow strand of straw into the thick green moss, weave each end carefully for a tight fit, then flutter to the floor, where someone had laid a neat pile of shredded straw.

The woman thought she practiced black magic, but Margot sensed she was far too kind to ever kill an unborn child. Surely the rumors Cook had heard were just that. Beatrice had lost her babies without Charesse's help.

At that thought the witch cast Margot a knowing glance.

Margot didn't miss a beat. "You said before if I believe it, then it certainly can be."

No answer for that one. The witch snapped around, cocked her head as if listening.

"Isn't that so?" Margot wondered.

"Quiet! Listen."

Margot stared angrily at the woman as she closed her eyes and lifted a hand in the air, her forefinger thrusting heavenward. "They come!"

"Who?" Margot managed to ask as she watched the woman shove the table aside. The tattered damask ripped, and the gazing ball rolled but did not shatter as it landed on the moss floor. With one guttural heave the witch ripped the moss from the ground, sending dirt flying. Beneath lay a wood floor. And an iron ring.

"They've been watching me for weeks, darling." The witch tugged the ring and lifted a secret door. "You will do to follow me if you wish to breathe long enough to confess love for another man to your baron."

"They?"

"No time for questions. Take the stairs carefully. But quickly!"

Margot let out a squeak as Charesse pulled her down into a dark passageway and closed the door over their heads. Dank and must filled her senses. The lucid skitter of rodent feet opened her ears wide. Why was this woman forcing her into this cold, dark cell?

"I want to go back up," Margot whined, feeling the walls close in most coffinlike.

"And risk being burned as a witch?"

"What? Who is up above?"

"The cardinal's men. Mazarin has been drooling for a good hanging for some time. Ever since that poison he'd requested didn't work. Actually made the woman more amorous, vex me to the bone! Why don't people just suffice with the sword or pistol when they need someone dead?"

Margot clutched the witch's arm. "I can hear their footsteps!"

"There is a path to the opposite side of the hill," the woman instructed as she groped for Margot's hand. "We can run and maybe make it to the forest if they spend any amount of time searching my cottage."

"But they'll see the toppled table!"

"Indeed. So—will you stay or will you come with me?"

Stay and risk being accused of witchcraft—*you're not a witch, you're a butterfly souser*—or follow and risk being ridden down in the fields and then accused of witchcraft. "Have you another choice?"

"Come, child!"

The pounding of boots above her head stripped away Margot's reluctance as she followed the witch down the black path.

"Maybe she's gone to the north side of the king's land to see if there are any blueberries left," Cook offered to the two sullen faces who sat opposite each other at the table.

Their bowls of strawberries and fresh cream hadn't been touched. And in an oddly quiet yet stern ceremony, the tatty little rag doll had been soundly trounced upon the head, then laid facedown on the table just out of reach.

Fine time for Margot to go and get herself missing, Cook thought. Had the baron caught her up and was keeping her occupied? No, surely Margot would have seen to the girls. Besides, Cook wagered the baron did not rise until the sun was well high in the sky. He didn't look a person to arise early. Most likely Margot was off . . . somewhere. Some—

Oh, no! A sickening quell birthed in Cook's gut. She wouldn't have. Gone off to that damned witch under the hill again?

No. Not after her last adventure, and after Cook had admonished her. Why, Margot wouldn't dream to—

"Bonjour, lovely ladies!"

Startled from behind, Cook nearly dropped the pitcher of cream when she felt a man's arms encircle her waist from behind and gift her with a generous hug. There was only one man who dared greet her so casually. So amorously. *Him*.

Her heart pounding in her throat, Cook turned, and with a fluff of her hand to her hair welcomed André Le Nôtre back from his vacation to Italy.

He kissed both her cheeks and paused in his kiss to her forehead. Cook drew in the scent that wafted from the man's flesh, rosemary and lavender, his own personal blend.

"My plump little clove of garlic, your cheeks rose as bright as those delicious strawberries." Hunger burned in his pale gray eyes, but it was not for her culinary delights. She knew that as sure as the spring flush colored her cheeks. "But what is this!" His hand slipping unobtrusively into Cook's shaking grasp, André approached the table and pouted his question. "Two sad faces? How can two little girls be so sad in the presence of my famous smiling strawberries?"

"Smiling strawberries?" Janette tilted her bowl toward her to study the contents.

Lisette sighed.

"We were just looking for their nursemaid," Cook offered. She squeezed André's hand, giddy beside the tall, lank master of gardens who wore an amorous question in the squint of his gray eyes. No, Margot could not go missing today. The wondering fool must be home tonight. For tonight . . . was for her and André.

"I rode through Paris on my return," he said as he pushed Janette's spoon close to her fingers. "There was a great fuss going on in the courtyard before the Louvre. Do you girls want to hear something mighty frightening?"

"André."

He shushed Cook with a gesture and turned back to

the girls, dramatic flair seasoning his words. "There are witches afoot."

"Witches?" Lisette offered sullenly.

"Indeed. They were mounting the dunking chair above the Seine as I was passing through. And two this time, they say!"

"Come now, André, you mustn't stir the girls up so. We're worried enough—"

"What does a witch look like?" Janette asked around a slurp of strawberry and cream.

"Oh, I think they're something nasty to behold," André said, great dramatics lifting his hands to gesture. "Warts and purple hair and—"

"Purple hair." Lisette shook her head as if to convey her utter disbelief in his fabrications. Certainly nothing could pierce her sullen mood.

"Yes, supposedly that nasty old witch under the hill has finally been caught."

"The witch under the hill?" This time the jolt to her heart could not be attributed to her lover's entrance. Cook gasped out a response. "You said there were two?"

"Indeed, quite a catch."

"And did you see the other?"

"Only briefly, as they were dragging them inside the Louvre for questioning. She was a might beauty, blond curls, punching fists, and all. Perhaps too sassy for her own good."

Not what Cook had wanted to hear. Gripping André's shoulder for support, Cook waved a weak hand toward the door. "Quickly, girls, run, find your papa!"

"Damn these hundred steps!" Cook huffed and struggled and bent and stepped and eased her way down to the first platform. Having gone less than a third of the way but using all the breath allotted her on this day, she slumped on the cool pink marble and wheezed the summer air in and out. "Where is that man?"

Leaving André without explanation and a hearty bowl of strawberries, Cook decided she could not abandon the twins to run this errand alone. Margot's life may depend on expediency. She scanned the rows of orange trees down to her right. It was impossible to see inside the Orangerie, for the shadows from the high sun darkened the doors set beneath the south terrace.

Cook pressed a hand to her beating heart and drew her gaze down the remainder of the stairs and out across the finely manicured lawn. "Ah!" Alexandre stood at the edge of the Swiss pond, his daughters to either of his sides. By the time she was able to lift an arm and start waving, the girls had noticed her and came running, followed in tow by their father.

"We found him, Cook! Have you fallen?" Lisette was the first to arrive, and like the studious little sweetie she was, she pressed the back of her hand to Cook's brow. "You're very hot, and all wet!"

Janette joined her sister, Ruby equally interested from the crook of Janette's arm.

"Girls," Cook gasped. "Run along into the kitchen and fetch me a ladle of water, will you? And do tell Monsieur le Nôtre to help himself to some more strawberries!"

"Le Nôtre has returned?"

"Yes, this very day. Now, Monsieur Saint-Sylvestre, I've desperate need of your ear. Please, girls, do hurry along." With a reassuring gesture from their father, the girls ran up the steps. "And do take your time returning!" Cook called in their wake.

"What is it? Are you hurt?" Alexandre knelt beside her, checking her sweaty brow as Lisette had.

"I've been running, is all. Monsieur, you must listen carefully," she gasped and heaved, trying to catch her breath. But until she saw Margot's face, she might never

breathe correctly again. Finally in one deep breath she
was able to say, "Margot is in danger."

"Danger?" He chuckled. Actually chuckled! "Whatever could the wayward entomologist have gotten her
pretty head into today? More pig mud? A grand shower
of butterflies?"

"Monsieur Saint-Sylvestre!"

"Very well, go on, Cook."

"She's in Paris. I feel certain she's been arrested."

"Arr—" He snapped his jaw shut at Cook's silencing
hand.

"André rode through Paris on his return."

"André?"

"Monsieur, will you hear me out?"

"Sorry." But he could not hide a grin at her slip in
speaking her lover's Christian name.

"He told me two witches have been arrested."

"Witches—what does that have to do with Margot?"

"I can only assume that once again, for reasons quite
beyond my understanding, Margot traipsed over to the
witch under the hill."

"The witch under the—again? What? Whyever would
she have reason to do that?"

"It's of no import, Monsieur. What is, is if that was
the witch who was arrested, Margot might very well have
been arrested alongside her."

"Impossible. Witches do not exist. Even if they did,
Margot is most certainly not a witch. Though she did
have me believing in her powers of bewitchery—"

Cook gripped Alexandre's sleeves and pulled him into
her breathing space. Serious consequences would befall
any man who did not heed her gaze. "Be that as it may,
Monsieur, you must ride to Paris immediately. André said
one of the women had blond curls. A sassy blonde." She
quirked a brow. "Remind you of anyone?"

Alexandre swallowed.

"You know what they do to women accused of witch-craft?"

He didn't even bother with a reply. Alexandre started for the top of the steps.

"And hurry!" Cook called. "Bring her to me immediately. The baron awaits!"

The click of Alexandre's boots upon the marble abruptly stopped. Cook glanced upward to find him standing at the top of the stairs, clenching the cupid's head that rode the lion's back. He turned. "The baron?"

The heavy beats of Cook's heart stalled with a massive thud. "Don't tell me Margot has not yet mentioned the baron de Verzy to you?"

"The baron here to deliver the king a message? What does he have to do with Margot?"

His boot steps clicked down to her side. Cook looked up into Alexandre's blank face. "Hell."

She patted the stone beside her. "Well, you'd better have a seat. This will take some explaining. But be quick about it, our Margot's life is in danger. You need to get to her soon. That is . . . if you still desire to rescue her after you've heard what I must tell you."

"I am not a witch!" Margot yelled as the guard who'd escorted her and Charesse from Mazarin's office to the dungeons in the Louvre manacled her wrists to a cold stone wall seeping with damp.

"She is not a witch," the real witch replied coolly as she toed a wedge of slimy straw scattered in the corner of their iron-barred cell.

"You are a witch," the guard replied as coolly. "And witches are known liars."

Now, how would she challenge that statement? Everything she said would be considered a lie, and a lie would be taken as truth! "And just how do you intend to prove I am a witch?"

The guard tipped up his plumed hat and gifted her with a greasy, black-toothed smile. "We'll dunk ya."

"Dunk me?"

"Aye, if you float, you are a witch. And if you sink, you are not."

"But—" Margot sputtered. Reasoning fled. There was only one thing she knew at this moment. "If I sink, I'll be dead!"

"Aye."

Twenty-one

She had wished only for a bath.

What Cook had told him . . .

How could Margot do such a thing to him? To keep such a secret after he had revealed so much to her. It was very obvious she'd had no intention of ever telling him about the Baron de Verzy. She'd used his affections so cruelly.

Or had she thought to break things off with the baron as Cook had reluctantly, almost as an afterthought, mentioned? No, certainly not. Margot had been well aware of her fate with every kiss they had shared. Her silence was equal to Sophie's trick of declassing herself the night she had conceived. Margot had reduced herself to Sophie's level.

Yet he found himself riding to her rescue. When he should just let her burn at the stake for her cruelties against his heart.

"No," Alexandre blurted out as his mount clicked swiftly over the cobblestones. He gained the aisle of buildings in the Louvre that were dedicated to Cardinal Richelieu and dismounted. Much as rational thought pleaded a routine case, his heart would not allow the verdict to be called. He would not judge Margot until he'd heard her reason for keeping her engagement a secret. A woman like her, filled with mystery, might certainly have a reasonable explanation. He hoped.

He would reconcile his own hurt feelings later. He'd invested in this woman. The girls had invested in her. And reconciliation would be impossible if the other party were dead.

"I must find her."

Tipping his hat to a soldier that exited the Louvre, Alexandre tied his horse to a wooden hitching post and took the steps three at a stride. Fortune played her hand, and a very familiar green voice greeted Alexandre from the side.

"Captain Lambert!" Alexandre rushed to his brother-in-law and they exchanged the obligatory kisses to the cheek.

"It has been months," Chance said. "And what is this?" He flipped a finger through the frothy black plume that jutted from Alexandre's hat. "Looking a dandy, even?"

"The girls must have stuck that in there." He also wore the velvet doublet he'd donned yesterday to impress Margot, for it had been at hand. "I've an emergency, Captain. There's a woman in dire need of rescue."

Chance's expression hardened. He gripped the hilt of his sword. "Tell me everything."

Most unsuccessful the day had been. The king's hunting party, rumored to be stabled at St. Germaine, was not there, with no information as to where they currently were. The stupid lackeys Nicodème had questioned in the stables could tell him only that the party was most likely on the way back to Versailles.

Not taking the road he'd traveled, directly south from St. Germaine. Where could they be? It was but a four-hour ride from there to the hunting lodge. Nicodème had given up in disgust after his horse had taken on a stone from the road. He'd had to walk the beast back to Versailles's stables, a good half a league in the humid heat of the day.

He should have just sent a lackey in his stead to fetch Mademoiselle deVerona and avoided this godforsaken journey altogether. A fine welcome he'd received upon his arrival. A fat cook and two rodents. And then Margot, covered in dirt from toe to ear.

Nicodème was seriously toying with reconsidering the notion of marriage to the country waif. His father had gone on about Mistress deVerona's mothering skills. Surely her daughter would have much the same. And so what if he must pay for her education; 'twas a mere scoop out of an endless keg of riches. Riches that had been forged decades before during the tulip craze brought over from Holland. Nicodème's father had told him he'd bought low and sold high, never ceasing to be amazed at the exorbitant prices the ugly flowers brought in.

But riches? None that Nicodème had yet to see.

Shaking the wet from his clothes and hair, Nicodème strode down the hallway toward the fragrant kitchen, where he would most likely find Margot. Either there, or down in the Orangerie with those girls.

Girls. The very word oozed like sludge through his thoughts, gritty and distasteful. He had no way to ensure Margot's first child would be a boy. For her sake, it had better be so. He didn't relish carnal relations with the mud-coated waif any more than necessary. And a boy was certainly necessary to carry on the de Verzy name and secure the remainder of Nicodème's inheritance.

As he pushed open the heavy oak door and stepped

down into the kitchen, the squeaks of two rodents lifted Nicodème's hopes. Margot must be here.

"My lord!" The cook dropped her wooden spoon in the wide iron kettle and with some effort pushed her hefty mass up from the hearth to waddle over to him. "I expected you'd be off the entire day. What are you doing back so soon?"

Nicodème ripped his arm from the cook's possessive grasp and smoothed a hand over her finger marks crushed into the velvet sleeve. A wary eye found the girls cowering together at the pine table, their eyes wide, as if with fear. Good. The female sex had better learn its place when he commanded the room.

"I was unsuccessful in locating the king's hunting party. My horse took on a stone, and I had to walk three leagues to be sure. I'm tired and rather peckish. Is Mademoiselle deVerona about? I thought she tended the rodents—er, girls."

"Margot?" Cook stood before him, her hands behind her back, a curiously evasive expression keeping her eyes from meeting Nicodème's. She acted as though she couldn't comprehend the meaning of the name.

"Yes, Margot. The moppet of a woman with the blond curls and a curiously misfit way about her. My future bride?"

"No!"

Nicodème spun to determine which of the girls had squeaked out that protest. Both sat innocently staring at him, their pudgy lips rimmed with a blackish-blue substance. Fingers stained the same color rested on the table before what might have been blueberry tarts before they'd become infested with rodents.

"No?" Nicodème approached the table, measuring his strides and stretching his shoulders high and wide. Delight shuddered through his system as the girls shrank close together until one might not part them with a pry-horn and a herd of oxen. "What do you mean"—he pressed his knuckles to the tabletop and leaned imposingly closer—"no?"

The dark-haired one sniffed back a tear. But it was the blond rodent who huddled her sister closer and barked out a surprisingly confidant answer.

"She means you cannot have our Margot! She promised she would not leave us."

"Girls!" The cook shuffled over to the table and scooped the blueberry disasters into her hands. "You'll be finishing your tarts in my room. There's no reason to go spouting silly notions at the baron."

Nicodème placed a firm hand on Cook's shoulder. He could feel the woman stiffen beneath his palm. The appropriate reaction. "I'll not have them leave this room until the impertinent one explains what she means by Margot's promise to never leave."

Still gripping Cook's shoulder, he leaned down to eyeball the now noticeably shivering girl. "Why would Mademoiselle deVerona make such a promise when she has promised me she will be my wife?"

"I—" Lisette swallowed. Her head shook miserably as she looked from Nicodème's steady gaze to Cook's and then to the chamber door that was but a dash away. "I—"

"My lord, this is most inappropriate." Cook broke free from his grasp and succeeded in shuffling the girls away from his clutches.

Nicodème followed the cook to the chamber door, intent on wedging his way past the woman and into the room to question the rodent's mysterious comment, but the door squeaked shut and he succeeded only in slamming into a jiggly gut of flesh and flour dust. He wasn't about to allow the group success over him.

Pressing his hand against the wall over her shoulder and pinning the woman in, Nicodème said, "There is something going on here. Something most suspicious.

And I think the blond one holds the answers to my questions."

"I'll not have you interrogating that innocent child," Cook countered in a gruff voice that coaxed Nicodème to step back. "Margot is simply gone to market—"

"Again?"

"Yes. She will return . . . soon." The cook pushed by Nicodème and waddled over to the table, where she began to scour the stained tables with a cloth. "My suggestion to you would be to sit and wait."

"Perhaps I'll ride to Paris."

"And risk missing Margot completely? No, you'd best sit down and have a tart, my lord. It might sweeten you up a bit, though I wager it would take a whole pie to soften your sour edges."

Nicodème raised a finger to retort, but instead he strode out of the kitchen and pounded his fist against the wall repeatedly.

What must death be like?

Cold water lapped at Margot's bare toes. Her slippers had been removed before two burly soldiers bound her into the river-slickened chair. From her peripheral vision she'd seen the soft leather shoes instantly grabbed up by a toothless old woman. She could hardly curse the blatant thievery, feeling that at least someone could use them.

It was certain she would no longer have need for shoes.

The stench of foul water, brewed by waste, dead fish, and centuries of dumping an assortment of refuse into the Seine, curled up Margot's nostrils. A strange buoyancy dizzied her mind. Every few ticks of her heart, her toes dipped into the water and then were jerked out. Her skirt hem soaked up the water, weighing the fabric down upon her shaking knees.

To die this way will be so horrid. She would not be granted the peaceful demise of old age, or even the quick blow of a well-placed dagger or musket ball. Surely drowning would be the longest, most painful way to end her life. As the brown water rose above her chin, she would panic and gasp, filling her lungs with water and losing the last bits of precious air. She would not even be allowed the opportunity of the death struggle, for her hands were bound behind the makeshift wooden chair and her feet were strapped tightly to the roughly hewn legs.

The chair, fastened upon the end of a long log and connected at the shore to an iron-pinned mechanism at the corner of a shed that housed a hydraulic pump used to distribute water to the Louvre and the Tuileries, could be levered up and down by two strong men. Both men waited eagerly now for the signal from the man in a black robe and white Venetian lace. A priest who'd hastily declared her guilty of witchcraft after noting the evidence that she'd been found in a suspected witch's home, so surely that made Margot a witch as well. The priest had scoffed at the notion of waiting for the law to intervene. The king was away, leaving Mazarin to rule the city. And Mazarin would not suffer a witch to live.

That was, Mazarin had a bone to pick with a witch who had not satisfied his murderous desires.

"This is the people's right!" the priest loudly declared, eliciting an uproarious cheer from the crowd of dirty-faced men and women and barefooted children. There were even a few well-dressed ladies with men on their arms who'd stepped out of their carriages to witness the horrific sight.

Thoroughly traumatized after witnessing her accomplice's dunking, Margot fought the screams that vied for release. The red-haired beauty had gone under without so much as a flinch. Not a single bubble of air had risen to the surface as the crowd quieted to look over the wave-less waters.

Die with dignity, shimmered somewhere deep within Margot's gut. *As the witch had. You know they are wrong, but it is too late.*

At least she had been granted the emotion of love.

"Alexandre," slipped out of Margot's mouth. A prayer to no one but herself.

She would never again see him. This situation would not even be happening had she not foolishly entertained the idea of loving Alexandre in the first place. It was all her fault she found herself skimming the broth-colored waters of the Seine.

But did she deserve such a fate for trying to alter her own destiny? Hardly. Perhaps a good thrashing and a promise never to interfere in a family man's life again. But death by drowning?

The log bobbed, soaking Margot to the knees. Cheers from the crowd sounded like ocean waves crashing in her head. Margot closed her eyes and began to pray.

The next dip of the log buried her waist deep in the chill waters. They were purposely doing this slowly to prolong her suffering and spike up the crowd. Some entertainment.

"Witch! Kill the witch!" echoed in the back of Margot's prayers.

"Please forgive them," she whispered, her lips moving as rapidly as her heartbeats as the waters caressed her shoulders in a squeezing crush. "Forgive me my indiscretions. I should have accepted my fate. The baron isn't so terrible. . . . Oh! Yes, he is!"

As her head went under, Margot fought her better senses at holding her breath. But survival instincts won, and she slowly bubbled up her breath, gasping for a new lung-full as the chair rose completely out of the water—

quickly—and then back into the muffling depths of the river.

One last thought flickered in her mind as she could no longer hold her breath. *I have broken my promise to the girls.*

Twenty-two

The two musketeers—
and one confused botanist—arrive!

Margot and the other suspected witch had been taken immediately to face punishment. Without so much as a trial? Had the entire city of Paris gone insane in the king's absence? With Mazarin behind the ruling, Alexandre could believe it. Apparently they hadn't even bothered with torture. Just straight to the chair.

Leading his two cohorts into the pack of bodies before them, Alexandre thanked the heavens he and Chance had also run into Armand, his eldest brother. Now they were three, and every extra sword counted.

The crowd gathered around the *château d'eau* situated at the edge of the Seine was woven as thick as wool, and no less offensive in shouts and odors than decades-old wool soaked in stable droppings and left to rot.

Alexandre's precise senses immediately became overwhelmed. His vision stormed with colors and shapes of every size and shade. Odors birthed on his tongue in distasteful points and razor-sharp angles. Nothing round or sweet about this crowd. If he were to remain for much longer, the confusion would only increase, and he would do Margot no good by fainting. Which was what would happen.

Yes, yes, a fine hero he'd make. And all because he couldn't process sensory articles in the manner of the masses. Now, if Margot were chained in a dungeon all by herself, things would be simple. No distractions. His concentration would not be in question.

As it was, this challenge was unavoidable.

Determined to succeed, Alexandre followed Chance's lead as the man shouldered his way through the crowd. Armand, right behind him, clamped a hand on Alexandre's shoulder. Alexandre gritted his teeth and tried to concentrate on picking out the wavy pink lines of Margot's voice among the fog of gray haze and sharp, battling shapes.

"Up ahead!" Armand shouted over the cacophony, and pushed Alexandre onward. "They've already dropped the chair!"

Alexandre's gut clenched at his brother's statement. Was he too late? Did Margot already swim in the Seine? But she would not be swimming! He stumbled, but Armand's sure grip caught him under the arm.

"Concentrate," Armand said. He knew well what a crowd did to Alexandre's senses. "We will get to her. The river is but ten paces away."

Nodding understanding, and drawing from Armand the stalwart courage that the man possessed in an infinite amount, Alexandre drew in a breath and pressed onward. But the river's edge provided no hope.

"She's underwater!" Alexandre shouted. He made to rush forward, but a blow to his chest stopped him in his tracks. He had not been touched by any in the crowd. 'Twas the emotion of sudden loss that beat at him mercilessly. Pressing a fist to his aching heart Alexandre gritted his jaw and surveyed his next move.

Chance had already jumped on top of the dunking

mechanism in an attempt to weigh down the end. He had to climb up the smooth, debarked timber, for the counterweight was as long as the end that dipped into the river, and the drop to the Seine was a good ten feet.

The crowd moved in on the threesome, trying to drag Chance down, but Armand brandished his sword, as did Alexandre, and they were able to fence away a small perimeter around the hideous death machine.

"The witch must die!" shouted the crowd. An angry bruised fist punctuated the cry.

Alexandre spied a priest in lacy vestment fleeing along the shore toward a waiting carriage. Painful red squares bobbed over the sight, so sharp Alexandre winced.

"Let her drown!" was the call that pulled Alexandre from his state. Another blind shout, "What are you doing?" accompanied a barrage of boos and hisses.

"I need help," Chance managed to say as he clung to the end of the log, his weight not enough to counter the chair that held Margot beneath the water. "Stand off!" Chance shouted to the crowd. "I am Captain Lambert of the king's musketeers. How dare you take justice into your own hands. By order of the king, this woman must be released."

A nasty whine whistled out and smacked Alexandre in the gut with its dripping crimson tone. "She's already dead!"

"No!" Alexandre lunged to catch a wary onlooker under the chin with the tip of his rapier.

"Alexandre!" Armand shouted.

No, Alexandre thought. *I will not draw blood.* But he could not endure this mindless violence for one moment longer.

As he held his threat steady, one thing came to mind. One horrible truth. One way to rescue. He must say it, much as the truth would stab him more fiercely than his own rapier.

"She does not float," Alexandre said to the man he'd speared with his steel. He assumed what little courage he had left and growled, "So that proves she is not a witch."

"Indeed," the man awkwardly agreed, and stepped away from Alexandre's sword. "It must be so!"

"She does not float!" Alexandre yelled above the din, and the crowd suddenly quieted. "You have murdered an innocent woman!"

"Grab that rope there," Armand directed Alexandre, taking advantage of the crowd's sudden realization of what was happening. "Toss it up to Chance, and he'll run it through the iron grip. . . . Yes—now, pull!"

Alexandre on one end of the rope and Armand on the other, they both forced the log down to the ground. Chance scuttled to the end of the log to put his weight into it. The strength of three men worked against the pull of the heavy waters. A *shush* of water and a grand *aahh* from the crowd signaled the chair rose from out of the sludge-colored Seine.

Alexandre could hear the water dripping onto the surface of the river—it possessed the same minty sharpness as the rain, but it was the most horrible blade ever. He knew that Margot was above. He didn't want to look. Could not.

But he must.

"Turn quickly," Armand directed. The brothers pressed the end of the log around, bringing the chair, and the motionless, wet, slumped body of Margot to the shore.

While there were shouts of joy over murdering the witch, half the crowd had dissented to sad observation that indeed she must have been innocent, for she had not floated.

"I'm going to let go!" Alexandre shouted to Armand, and received a positive nod.

The chair clunked to the bank. A sodden head of blond

curls, now washed to streams of dirty gold, lolled back across the chair. Livid flesh blossomed around Margot's closed eyes and lips and nose.

Alexandre dashed his rapier through the ropes that bound her legs and arms and the triple band about her shoulders. *Damn them all!* How could anyone float when tied to this horrific contraption?

She fell like a sack of market flour into his arms. Heavy and wet and lifeless, her lips blue, her fingers, when he lifted her hand to his lips, cold twigs.

"He cannot take the witch with him. She must be drawn and quartered and burned at a crossroad!"

"She is not a witch," a woman's voice in the crowd argued. "She did not float." The crystal-blue globes formed by her voice oddly reassured Alexandre. She would hold off a revolt. For a moment.

Chance and Armand moved into position behind Alexandre. The captain swept his sword and dagger before him in a wide arc, holding off the crowd like a pack of savage wolves not willing to leave fresh meat. Armand, his back to Chance's, poked an aggressive soldier in the thigh.

Alexandre pressed his face to Margot's cold cheek. Inside he felt as if he had taken the chair alongside her, so tight his throat had become, making his breaths gasps. "You won't die on me now, Margot. Not before I've had words with you. Dammit!"

Never let her go. Squeeze the life back into her. Do . . . something!

He lowered Margot to the ground and turned her to the side. The Seine gushed from her lips. Following the stream came chokes and heaves. As her body cringed and bent, she struggled to breathe. Her fingers flexed and grasped and clutched at his leg.

She lived! Alexandre smoothed his hand over her back, reassuring her that he was near.

"Alex . . . ," she tried to say though gasps and wheezes. "I'm . . . innocent. . . ."

"Don't speak, my love. I'm here now. You are safe."

"The witch . . ." She coughed and flickered her eyes open to look up into his. "She really was a witch. She floated . . ."

Alexandre smoothed her hair away from her face. "Where is she?"

Margot turned her head toward the Seine. "She didn't float for long."

He glanced over the river. No sun glimmered on the liquid surface. It was dull brown and evil in its design. Minutes earlier, a witch had died in these waters. Dread shivered up his neck and tingled over his scalp. Margot's fate might have been much the same had Alexandre been a moment later.

"I must get you out of here before the crowd turns against us. I've only two backups. It won't be long before they demand their hideous festivities be completed."

She might have answered, or it might have been a huge sigh of relief. Alexandre helped Margot to her feet, then bent to heft her up over his shoulder. She hung like a lifeless rag doll, hardly a burden upon his shoulder.

Signaling to his brother to take the lead, Alexandre sprinted out of the crowd behind Armand, realizing he hadn't succumbed to confusion after all, so intent he'd been on saving Margot.

That she meant the world to him was a new truth.

But that she could not be his pierced his heart and ripped steely claws down the muscle.

Margot clung to Alexandre, both arms wrapped around his waist, her cheek pressed to his back. He'd not spoken a word since they had exited the gates of Paris. She could feel tension in the set of his body, rigid upon the horse, the plume in his hat tickling her face.

Of course he must be angry at having to rescue her from such a ridiculous situation. She would allow him that. But she desperately needed a kind word just then. A gentle caress to smooth across her wet hair. She had felt death! Truly she had given up her last breath beneath those murky waters, only to have it restored by Alexandre's savior touch. A distant savior.

Alone she felt. Never had she spent so much time so close to the one man she desired beyond all other desires. And never had she felt so utterly alone. Within her desperate grasp sat a warm, feeling body. But he might be a statue for the chill his presence gave her.

Without warning their bobbling journey came to an end. The growing palace of Versailles loomed in the distance, still a half-league away. A mist of smoke curled over the main lodge like a beguiling witch's brew. Perhaps Cook's supper. Here, beside a copse of orange maples, Alexandre dismounted without a word and pulled Margot from the horse's back.

"How do you fare?" he asked, but it seemed forced. Almost as if he were making a polite remark, urged on by a stern parent.

"I'm alive," she said with a weak smile. He did not smile in return.

He began pacing, finger to forehead, hand on his hip. The black plume in his hat, which had tormented Margot's nose all during the ride, now fluttered with every step. Perhaps the girls had sneaked a feather into their father's hat. He might be quite unaware it even decorated the brim.

"Dammit!" He whipped the felt hat from his head and slammed it onto the ground.

Margot stiffened at this uncharacteristic action.

Oh, hell, what did she expect after such a glorious

rescue? She owed him her life. More than her life, she owed him . . . the truth.

He turned and marched over to her, his right fist hovering before him, his jaw tensing. A stomp of the ground raised the dry soil in a cloud at his feet. Just when it appeared he might turn purple from the tension that strained his face and fist, he spoke. "You do know that I love you, don't you?"

Margot had to run the statement over in her mind a second time. It had been issued with such sharpness, she wanted to be sure she had actually heard a statement of adoration and not a declaration of hatred. "Er . . . yes, I do. I . . . think?"

"You know I love you—dammit all to hell—for I just told you the other day!"

"Of course I do," she hurried in, not wanting to further outrage him, for might he declare something beyond love with such passion brewing in his veins. Though she couldn't possibly believe it was a love passion. "I love you too, Alexandre. Please, you must forgive me for what happened today. I never intended—"

"Cook said this was your second visit to the witch under the hill?"

Meekly bowing her head, she nodded. "Actually she lives between two hills."

"Why?" He gripped her by the shoulders. All the fiery energy that had once compelled her to him like a butterfly to eucalyptus now frightened. But he had every right to anger. And every right to the truth.

"I went there the first time . . ." She looked away, though he did not release her. "To secure a birth preventive. For—for us."

"Margot?"

"It was after the first time I confessed I wished to make love to you and you explained your fears. I only wanted things to be perfect, Alexandre. I didn't want you to have to worry about anything. But the witch would not perform such acts of charity. She preferred evil spells."

"And was that the sort of spell you returned for today? Something evil?"

"Oh, Alexandre." Courage drained out of her body, flooding over the ground and sluicing out her pride with it. Now the true betrayal must be revealed. Though she couldn't fathom it, even more she could not comprehend hurting such a kind and gentle soul. "I went for a hate spell."

"A . . . hate spell?"

"Not for you," she rushed in. "I love you."

"You cannot!" He sliced the air with his hand and fixed his gaze upon her eyes. She tried to see the kindness, and, yes, it was still there, but it was laced with pain and sadness from betrayal. "If you really cared for me, you would have told me about the Baron de Verzy."

Mon Dieu, he already knew. But how? The girls? Cook?

"All this time you've been trying to seduce me. When you knew you were betrothed to a baron. Of all things!"

Her deception revealed, Margot could not bear the heavy weight of truth. She slumped into a tangle at Alexandre's feet and buried her face in her wet skirts. "I should have drowned!" she sobbed. "A fitting punishment for the cruelties I worked on the only man I love."

"Love?" he scoffed.

"Forgive me, Alexandre. I had no right to keep such a secret."

The touch of his hand caressed her head. Much gentler than she had expected. "Then why did you that night I told you my secrets? I gave you opportunity to share your own."

"I was afraid. I didn't want to lose you, when I had just found a trust that was so fragile. Oh, I'm so sorry."

Wanting to pull his hand into her grasp, Margot fought the urge, for she had no right to demand any tender sentiments from this valiant man. He had known about the baron before coming to rescue her. *Yet still, he had come for her.*

"Cook told you?" she said through sniffles.

"Yes. Le Nôtre returned with news of two women having been arrested for witchcraft. Cook guessed it might be you and sent me along to Paris, but at the last moment she mentioned the baron was waiting for you."

Margot's head shoot up. "He waits for me?"

He nodded and looked toward his home. "I'm to return you to the château posthaste."

"He must have plans to leave. But he cannot; he waits for the king. He said he would be two days."

"I passed the king's hunting party on the way to find you. They were just arrived at Versailles."

"No, I cannot go. The hate spell was for the baron." She plunged forward and clung to her savior's body. "Please, Alexandre, I do not want to marry the baron. It was an arranged marriage."

"Obviously you agreed to it."

"Of course I agreed when I had no thought but to satisfy my own selfish desires. I wanted to secure my family and my education."

"Doesn't sound selfish to me."

"But it is, don't you see? I had no idea I would ever fall in love. Please, don't take me back to that man's arms. Not . . . yet."

Alexandre turned and paced toward his horse. He fingered the saddle, for all appearances set to mount, when he turned and gestured she sit. "You'll go nowhere until we've talked about this and I know all there is to know about Margot deVerona's secret life."

* * *

The news of Margot's betrothal worked to pull Alexandre down beside her in the shade of a majestic orange maple. Leaves fallen from the tree were moist and leathery and did not crunch as they would in another month.

The entire time Margot had been growing into his life, loving his children, loving him, she had known she was promised to another. This was extremely difficult to learn.

But then the real reason she had gone to see the witch under the hill, between the hills—whatever—stunned him even more. She had been seeking birth prevention so the two of them could make love with no worry of a child coming of their union.

"You purposely sought to make love with me before you married the baron? I don't understand, Margot. Most women might consider such a ruse only if they wished to become with child because their betrothed did not serve their needs. But you were going out of your way, and into the Seine, to make sure a child did not happen. Explain this, please."

"Oh, Alexandre." Her skirts had dried now, as had her hair, which was quite messy, the curls all scattered haphazardly atop her head. She knelt before him and stretched her skirts so she could place one knee to either side of his legs and sit upon his thighs. "I love you so much."

Pink waves . . . delicious after the angry sensory barrage of the Parisian crowd. He wanted to touch them. But steeled himself.

Alexandre stretched his arms back and leaned on his palms, distancing his desires from the need for truth. "As you've said many times over. But it still does not change the fact that you were trying to seduce me for some . . . selfish reason that is beyond my grasp."

Her pale eyes glittered with tears. "It was selfish. I

cannot believe that was really me doing such things. Holding so little regard for your feelings."

His heart wanted him to touch the glistening jewels and wipe away her pain, but his conscience demanded real answers. No more lies.

He had to close his eyes when she began to speak. Avoid the pink waves of temptation, but the clear tones of her canorous voice wavered behind his eyelids in smoky wisps of pink.

"I wanted you to be the first." He felt her palm press against his chest. Still so cold. The river had bled her of vitality. "The first man to make love to me. You are the first and only man I have ever loved. I wanted to take memories of your kindness and love with me into a marriage that I know will never harbor love. The baron wants me only as a breeding machine for heirs. He had a stipulation added to the marriage contract that until I produced a son, I would not be granted money for an education. How could I possibly succumb to that fate without first knowing what real love could be like?"

"You might have told me—"

"Would you have lain with me had I told you I was betrothed to another man?"

Probably not. Though, who knew? He was completely smitten by this woman. So much so that he now realized she had not deceived him, as he had thought. She was only a frightened young woman reaching out for one thread of security before all threads were forever severed by a loveless marriage.

"I would have had I known your intentions," he said, as sure of his words as he was sure of his love for Margot.

She sank into his embrace. "You are too kind to me, Alexandre. By rights you should drag me back to Versailles tied behind your horse."

"Never," he brushed across her ear. "I may not like

the fate that awaits you, but I'm consoled to know that I might have been the first."

"I should wish for you to be the first . . . and the only."

"That cannot be."

"I know. You shall always live in my heart. . . ."

She sniffed and broke into a storm of tears. Every crystal drop worked like a tiny dagger spiking into Alexandre's heart.

"I don't want to marry that horrible baron."

"Come, come." He smoothed a hand up and down her back, rubbing gently as he did when one of the girls had had a nightmare, or Janette had lost Ruby. "The man doesn't look all that horrible. I'm no judge of a handsome face, but even I could see he was appealing. Of a sort. Though he does use rather much fragrance."

"I don't care for a handsome face and broad shoulders and magnificent hair when they are but exterior glitter to a dark soul. I shudder to think what will become of me should I give birth to a girl. He's such designs on a woman's position. He had promised me an education with the signing of the marriage vows, but now I fear he will renege on that."

"You agreed to marry the man for an education?"

"You know how much I desire knowledge, Alexandre. I thought the marriage would be bearable if I had a vocation to occupy my lonely days. I don't want to be one of those helpless, stricken women who are virtual slaves to their husbands. I want to use this." She tapped her skull, setting her curls aquiver. "I want to know that I can make a difference, that I can fend for myself if need be. That I will not rot in some dingy old castle with infants dangling from my arms and swinging from my skirts."

"You need to always have a wonder in your mind."

He touched her brow and smoothed his fingers along the narrow ridge. "I understand."

What would become of this bright star if her predictions for the future came true? To be stifled by the loss of love, the denial of freedom? This woman was meant to shine, to follow her dreams and chase her desires.

"Oh, Alexandre, I love you. I want you. And the girls! I've harmed them terribly, haven't I?"

He hadn't even begun to think of the impact this information would have on the girls. They would be heartbroken, shattered. It would be Sophie's death all over again.

"The girls will eventually accept," he reassured her. Though his empty words did nothing to reassure his own breaking heart.

"No, Alexandre, I—I made a promise. It was horrible of me. I did it to calm their fears." Her gaze flickered to the side. Blinking away a huge teardrop, she said, "I promised I would never leave them."

Oh. So she had promised them their greatest desire, knowing it was simply a lie. "I see."

"No, you don't see." She gripped his shirt. "I want to keep that promise. I must."

"But the baron . . . Perhaps this man can give you what no other can offer? He *is* a baron, he must be moneyed. He can offer you fine dresses—"

"And what should I do with a fine dress but immediately soil it and bring the baron's wrath upon me? Do you want to let me go knowing I shall be beaten daily?"

"Margot, you are jumping to wild conclusions."

She released his shirt and nodded, catching her forehead against her hand. "I know."

Easing his palm over her shoulder, he imparted his warmth into her chilled flesh. "You will never want for a thing in the baron's care. And how can you be so positive that he will not grant you the education?"

"He wants me with child as quickly as possible. Education will come much later, or perhaps never if he is to keep me with infants to breast. I do love children; don't read me incorrectly. But I am too young to confine myself to motherhood right now."

"The twins—"

"The twins are not bleating infants in need of constant supervision. I love Lisette and Janette. There is nothing the baron can offer me that I haven't already received from the short while I've been a part of your little family. You know me well enough to realize I've no desire for material things." She touched his hand and pressed it to her lips. "The only thing I shall want for is you."

"Don't say that. You will always have me. Here." He touched her breast. "In your heart."

"That is not enough."

"Don't make this harder than it must be, Margot. Please."

He pulled her close and began to rock. A child's comfort that always eased his own worries. He could rock Lisette or Janette for hours, it seemed, though oftentimes it was no more than minutes when he might find a purring child asleep in his arms. If only he could rock this woman's worries away. And chase his away as well.

But the fact remained, the baron awaited Margot. Cook must be having a hell of a time occupying him.

"He waits for you."

"I know. He must deliver a message to the king and then be off. With me."

"Yes."

Their eyes did not meet. Too much pain in that.

"We should bid each other adieu now."

Alexandre stood and helped Margot to her feet. "No good-bye. Adieu is too final."

She nodded, a shiver exaggerating her actions. "Very well. But will you give me one last kiss before we climb upon your horse and the world shatters to a million pieces?"

He smoothed a hand across her cheek and smudged a tear trail into his palm. "A kiss will only make our parting all the more difficult."

Her expression changed from grief to sheer horror so suddenly, Alexandre felt as if he'd literally smacked her across the cheek with the back of his hand.

"I cannot," he offered, the pain of such words splitting his heart in two. "You ask too much of me."

She nodded understanding and walked to the horse. Alexandre remained, firm upon his ground. Margot's nod worked much the same as his refusal for a kiss. He felt the sting of her silent acquiescence burn through his cheeks. At that very moment his heart fissured. The tiny crack that had been pried into its armor upon the death of his wife now split and allowed a new emotion to creep out. It oozed over his soul, coating it with an ugly blackness that erased any trace of pink waves.

So this was heartbreak.

He didn't favor the feeling at all.

Twenty-three

Kitten tears and baron juice

Slumping into his chair, Alexandre caught his forehead in his hands and closed his eyes. His entire body felt heavy and bruised. Very different from the tired achiness that would end a long day of labor. He'd never thought heartbreak could prove such a profound weapon against his muscles. A hot warmth pooled in the corner of his eye. He pressed the heel of his palm against the tear to stop its descent.

Behind him, he heard the subtle creak of the door adjoining his chambers to the twins' room. He hadn't the heart nor the strength to turn and chasten them for leaving their bed. Perhaps it was just the wind, or a wayward spirit, or a settling structural beam.

All he could see behind his closed lids was Margot's face, surrounded by unruly curls of sun and her ever-present smile. When he studied her features from behind the darkness of his eyelids, he did not see the geometrical shapes or colors or lilting waves that so commonly coated his senses. Pure Margot lived within his memory. Her visage, her smile, her tender kisses, her wondering pose.

Her admission of love.

He wanted to embrace this vision and shelter it away from the rest of the world. No one must have her. She belonged to him. *He* loved her, not that pompous baron who had claimed an eldest child years before in hopes of a hardy brood of male children in return. Margot had been made exclusively for Alexandre. Her lips fit only his. Her body melded as if a missing section of his soul against his own body.

He should have granted her final request. A simple kiss.

Ah, but that would have been the coup de grâce to his wounded heart. (And he'd never been a man who could stand bravely before the firing squad.) He'd taken the coward's way out when refusing her that kiss.

Had he been a fool as well?

He heard a whisper behind him, "Do you suppose that is Papa's wondering pose?"

Wondering? A brief smirk traced his lips and disappeared as quickly. If only they knew.

"I don't think so," Lisette answered quietly. "It looks more like his sad pose."

How easily a child could read the truth in others. Swiping his sleeve across his eyes to clear away the tears, Alexandre turned with a forced smile and spread his arms wide to beckon the girls. "Come."

They snuggled onto his lap, Ruby clonking him on the jaw as her owner found the perfect nest under his right arm. Such abuse he had received from Ruby over the years. The thought put another true yet quick smile on his face.

But Lisette's amber voice threatened to discover the fount of tears that bubbled just behind his eyes. "Don't be sad, Papa. Margot is not lost anymore." She smoothed a tiny hand across his cheek, spearing a renegade tear with the pad of her finger. "Why are you crying?"

"Why didn't Margot come tuck us in and say our

prayers with us tonight, Papa?" Janette laid her head on his shoulder and wiggled her bottom to further root out her nest.

All he could do was to hug them and rest his head upon the valley of their joined heads. He'd surpassed some difficult moments with his daughters over the past few months. This one promised to be the most challenging.

"Doesn't Margot love us, Papa? Why didn't she come tonight?"

Within a single fortnight Margot had assumed the title of loving caregiver. She fed the girls' souls with her own whimsical ways. They in turn had opened their hearts to let her in. A possessive and needy place, the heart of a child. But unconditionally true.

Could Margot ever fathom the impact her leaving would have on his girls?

"Papa?"

He must tell them now, before they might see her leave in the morning.

"Margot will no longer be able to care for the two of you—"

"What?"

"But she must!" Janette exclaimed. "We love her! And she promised—"

"Now, listen, girls, Margot has been promised to another man. The man who wants to marry her has come to the château to bring her to his home, where they will live together and have children of their own."

"But we're her children now," Lisette whispered in horrified disbelief. "She said that we could be her children if we wanted."

"And we want to be," Janette agreed. "Why can't she marry you, Papa?"

"She was promised to this man years ago. Long before I met her, you understand."

"But she made a promise to us too, a promise to never leave us!"

"You do love her, don't you, Papa?"

"Yes, of course—" Caught in the middle of his own heartfelt declaration, Alexandre paused but a second before speaking the truest words he had spoken in his entire life. "I love Margot with all my heart, girls. But it is too late. I wasn't even aware she was betrothed."

"What's betwothered mean?" Janette managed to ask as she smoothed Ruby's skirts across Alexandre's lap.

"It's means she's supposed to marry a man she doesn't love," Lisette piped up before Alexandre had a chance to open his mouth. "The Baron of Blunders!"

Janette's own face screwed into the same horror that held Lisette's face in shock.

"The man's name is de Verzy, not . . . Blunders?"

"It's just like in the story, Papa. The Baron of Blunders has come for the Princess of Practically Everything. He's a big, awful, ugly man who's going to take Margot away and never let us see her again."

"Now, how do you know he's big and ugly?" Alexandre wondered.

"Oh, we seen him when we were eating Cook's tarts. He walks around with his nose pointed up, looking like that ugly redheaded rooster does when he prances around the chicken coop. Anyone who would take our new mama away from us just has to be big and awful. Oh, Papa, is there nothing we can do?"

. . . our new mama . . .

They'd already laid claim to Margot.

As had he.

Only hours ago Margot had been his. She had been the girls'. She had been free.

"And now the kittens will never see the princess again. Never ever!" Janette wailed.

"Kittens? Girls, what are you talking about? If this is some silly story Margot has been telling you—"

"It's not silly, Papa," Lisette cried. "We are the kittens and the baron is the villain and Margot is the Princess of Practically Everything. Oh, Papa, it's all coming so horribly true. The story Margot has been telling us. It's simply awful, simply awful."

"Girls, now, you mustn't get so upset. It's very late and you both should be sleeping. I'm tired myself. Will you let me tuck you into bed and promise we'll talk about this again in the morning?"

"No more promises," Lisette pouted. "They make me sad."

"Come, Lisette, you mustn't hold Margot to a promise it is clearly impossible for her to keep."

"Then she should have never said it."

True. But he could completely understand Margot's irrepressible desire to give the girls all they should wish. It was akin to refusing his own heart.

Alexandre stood and shushed the girls back into their room. They climbed upon the fluffy tester bed and Janette pressed a finger to his chin. "But how will the story end? We hadn't finished it with Margot."

"Girls, I don't know anything about princesses and barons and kittens. Perhaps you'll make your own ending in the morning." He kissed them on their foreheads and tucked the counterpane up to their chins. "But do make it a happy ending, yes?"

"Yes, Papa," they muttered in the heaviest, most heart-wrenchingly violet voices. "Good night."

He left their door open a crack and peeled the shirt from his arms as he crossed the floor to his bed. Barons and princesses and kittens? How Margot had pleased the girls with her fantastical stories. Unfortunate she would not get to finish this story before being whisked away by . . . the horrible . . . Baron of Blunders?

Alexandre paused before stepping into bed. The Princess of Practically Everything? Now, when had he heard that before?

"I should have slipped some nightshade into his tart last night."

"Now, Cook, we've already had one close call with the angry Parisian mob because of witchcraft. No sense in tempting fate."

"I was wrong before." Cook's stirring in the hearth kettle had become dizzyingly speedy. With a huff she suddenly pulled out the wooden spoon and gave it a sharp smack against the fireplace. "A woman shouldn't have to marry a man she does not love!"

Margot tucked her knees up to her chest, her nest in the wicker chair feeling uncomfortably chilled this evening. "You know as well as I that it happens every day."

"But it shouldn't happen to the Princess of Practically Everything."

Margot regarded Cook.

"The girls told me the whole story last night. It's so very much your life, isn't it, Margot?"

"I'm not a princess."

"Nor is Monsieur Saint-Sylvestre a king. But the fact remains, there were never two people more meant for each other."

"Now you take my side."

Cook laid a gentle hand upon her shoulder. "I'm so sorry."

Unbidden tears moistened Margot's cheeks. "Things will work out."

"Will they?"

"I hope so." She drew in a deep breath and felt a minuscule rush of hope. Just enough to strengthen the conviction in her words. "They will. The story can't have an unhappy ending. Can it?"

"No, child, it cannot." With that, Cook turned back to her stew.

Margot didn't even think to catch her chin in palm and drift off to wondering. All the wonders seemed too distant to grasp at the moment.

A slash of sunlight warmed his nose. Sun? He'd overslept. Hell, the gardens needed watering and he had to meet with Le Nôtre at the north terrace before noon and—Margot was still leaving.

Alexandre slumped against his flat feather pillow. To the devil with the plants and his duties. Today was no day to disregard with mindless work. Today the woman he loved would leave his life.

Behind him, two quiet whispers slipped through the heavy oak door. Alexandre stood, stretched out the kinks from a fitful sleep, and realized he'd fallen asleep with his breeches on. Touching the door, he paused as Lisette's amber waves danced before his vision. He pricked his ears to listen. The girls had taken his idea of ending the story literally.

"When the King of Oranges found out the Princess of Practically Everything was being taken away by the Baron of Blunders, he said, 'I will not have it!' "

Janette's giggles were muted, most likely behind Ruby's head. "Was he a handsome king?"

"Oh, yes. Long, dark hair and sleeves rolled up to reveal strong muscles."

Alexandre checked his arms. He always rolled his sleeves up to keep them from becoming soiled. Hmm . . .

"Ruby finds his hair most romantic," Janette swooned.

Yes, he'd heard that one before.

"I shall rescue the princess and the kittens."

Alexandre leaned against the wall and crossed his arms over his chest, savoring his daughter's imagination.

"The king was standing nearby," Lisette narrated, "in the royal orange grove."

"Oh, yes!" Janette clapped.

"He heard the kitten's meows and pulled a fat orange from the tree above his head and ran to the palace, where the Baron of Blunders was fighting to get his horse to leave. 'Take that!' the King of Oranges yelled. He threw the orange at the Baron of Blunders, and it hit him right in the face."

"In the face!" Janette cheered. "And orange juice spread all over his head and his body and all over the ground. And the baron cried, 'I'm melting, I'm melting.' "

Alexandre tried to control his smile. Such imagination. But an orange, eh?

"So the baron began to melt," Lisette continued. "Into a puddle of orange juice and baron juice."

Janette paused. "What color is baron juice?"

"Purple," Lisette answered as if anyone who did not know were a fool. "The King of Oranges ran up the stairs and set the kittens free, then he ran down to the carriage and pulled the princess out and gave her a big kiss."

"Yuck."

"They must kiss. The ending won't be happy unless they kiss."

But of course. How could he have been such a fool? They must kiss for the ending to be happy.

And he had denied Margot that kiss.

Alexandre swung the girls' door open, catching them huddled in the center of the bed. Their bright eyes widened and their little fingers flew to their mouths. "Papa!"

"Girls." He stepped inside and hooked his hands at his hips. "I've been thinking."

"Yes, Papa?" They were both obviously stunned that he'd not yet admonished them.

"I believe . . ." he said, pressing a dramatic finger to the air before him, "I've a princess to rescue."

"Yes!"

He caught both girls in an arm and spun them around the room.

"But I'd best get going before the Baron of Blunders spirits her away. Can you two manage with your clothes and hair this morning?"

"Yes, Papa!"

"Good. Dress, then on to the kitchen to break your fast with Cook. I must go and kiss the princess and make a happy ending."

He dashed into his room and thrust his arms into his doublet. Boots and gloves, and . . . his rapier. Alexandre opened his door and paused at a call from the girls' room.

"Rescue the princess, King of Oranges!"

"I will," he said to himself with a burst of confidence. "I won't return until she is mine."

Alexandre crossed the short stretch of cobbled path and neared the grand doors that entranced into the south wing of the palace, when he paused, mid-step, hands on hips.

Who was *he* to tell Margot what she could do and could not do? And who was he to try to take her away from a life that might prove beneficial to her? The baron had money to judge from outer appearances and from the little Margot had told him. He could give Margot anything she should wish, including an education. While Alexandre had nothing beyond the dirt encrusted beneath his fingernails and two emotionally needy girls.

Not to mention his own emotional needs.

The baron could gift Margot with fine clothes and servants. While Alexandre mightn't afford a new dress for Margot for years to come.

The baron could put her up in a fine apartment in Paris, take her traveling to see the world. While Alexandre could offer only the humble chambers he held in the servants' quarters beneath the ground. As for traveling, he hadn't the time, nor the desire really.

The baron could open Margot's eyes to any number of wonders by financing her education. While the only knowledge Alexandre could grant Margot was that of common sense and learning such as an apprentice might acquire.

So what did he have to offer Margot that the baron could not?

Feeling alone and quite out of place standing in the eerie morning shadows of the château, Alexandre looked up to the sky. High above, the moon 'twas but a pale ghost of the night. With her telescope and wondering eye Margot possessed the moon and the stars. What more did she need?

You do love her, don't you, Papa?

Indeed. Love. She needed love. A love she might not find in the eyes of the baron de Verzy. And, dammit, he, Alexandre Saint-Sylvestre, wanted to give her that love.

Thrusting his chin up, Alexandre marched onward.

She had gone beyond trying to contain her tears. Now, with cheeks soaked and her eyes stinging, Margot struggled to keep up with Nicodème's pace as the man's hard leather heels clicked out of the château and onto the marble courtyard. His lavender cloud was wearing thin. More and more she caught the scent of perspiration and stale body foulness when in his presence.

There, a step down from the black and white checkered courtyard, waited a coach and four, the horses pawing the ground and jingling their fixings. A grandly liveried little man waited duteously by the door, as if a miniature pawn plucked from a chess board and placed there by a giant's hand. She had little time to pack, stuffing her dresses and shoes in her bag. Cook had rushed behind her with Grandma's valise, but she hadn't been able to place her notebook.

"Tears shed for your gardener, no doubt?" Nicodème remarked with a kick to the bag, which tumbled from her shaky grasp.

Cook had had no choice but to finally tell Nicodème that Margot was in Paris last evening, and that the gardener had gone looking for her. He'd made a remark this morning upon meeting her at dawn that he would not call the gardener out, for he suspected the man had not gotten the pleasures he had sought from her. Margot had defended with an angry growl that Alexandre was no more than her employer.

"I cry for the girls," she said now. "I cannot leave without bidding them farewell. Please, my lord, they will be heartbroken."

Nicodème's careless swing sallied her bag up on top of the carriage. The driver leaned back to secure it with a leather strap and buckle.

"I'm sure their father will explain matters." Nicodème's grip returned to his sword hilt. The rising sun glinted in his eyes. They were reddened, as if from missed sleep. "The man is aware that you are promised to me?"

"Indeed I am."

Margot faltered at the sound of Alexandre's voice, crisp and challenging in the echoes of the marble courtyard. She turned as the sound of a sword being drawn out from a leather sheath cut the air.

"What now," the baron muttered, plainly showing his peevish mood. As he stepped toward Alexandre, he shoved Margot back, and she had to catch herself against the carriage exterior. "What is it, gardener? Did you come with my fiancée's final wages? I'll take them, if that is the case. Margot worries that your rodents—er, daughters—will be upset at her departure. You will ease their discomfort, won't you?"

"It is rather difficult to change the minds of children," Alexandre said as he closed the distance between him and the baron by two sword lengths. "Once their hearts have been promised something, they'll not let it go so easily."

Mon Dieu, he spoke of the promise Margot had made to the twins. Fool that she had been!

But what was Alexandre doing here, his hair tousled from sleep and in but shirt and breeches, as if he'd dressed quickly. And wielding a sword? Though he did not draw it on the baron, he stroked the marble squares with the tip in an arc before him.

As if drawing an invisible line and daring the baron to step over it.

"A promise?" The baron turned to Margot, raised an inquiring brow, then turned back to Alexandre. Casually he paced before the daring arc Alexandre still mapped out, commanding the game board with an imposing confidence. "Now, what sort of promise would a woman make to two little girls that would have their father standing before me . . . threatening me with arms—"

"This is not a threat," Alexandre said, snapping his rapier up to his face in a salutatory manner, then swiftly dashing the blade through the air. "But a challenge."

"Alexandre, no," Margot breathed. Her heartbeat quickened to a dizzying pace. Her knees felt weak, and so she clung to the carriage door as she yelled, "It cannot be!"

"A challenge?" The baron's laughter further worked to stir up Margot's nausea. "You challenge me? A mere gardener whose hands are stained with the filthy earth challenges the baron de Verzy to a duel?"

"I do."

Alexandre's confidence surprised Margot. But at the same time it frightened her silly. The baron stood grandly, his feet planted, his shoulders squared. He matched Alexandre in height but bypassed the gardener when it came to images of warriors swinging heavy artillery in battles. Did Alexandre even know how to handle a weapon?

"Ha!" The baron's curt guffaw echoed through the courtyard. A flip of his head dispersed his locks gloriously across his shoulders. "And in whose name is this challenge issued, Monsieur? Is it for your children and their weeping little hearts, or is it issued from . . . someone else?"

Desperately shaking her head at Alexandre, Margot tried to capture his attention, but he would not grant her his eyes. That she should fling herself between both men and end this idiotic confrontation right now pried at her judgment.

"I fight for the lady's hand," Alexandre said.

'Twas her heart that stayed her in place.

"She does not love you. It is I to whom her heart belongs, and I return the favor."

"Our marriage agreement does not require love," the baron barked as he ceased his pacing and unsheathed his sword with little flair. "But it does require the honoring of said agreement. Margot deVerona is mine, Monsieur Saint-Sylvestre, there is nothing that can change that. But if you still insist upon matching steel, then by all means I'm not the one to back away."

"Winner shall walk away with Margot," Alexandre countered as he eyed his opponent and drew into engarde stance.

The baron matched Alexandre's challenging pose and said, "Agreed. As the loser shall die."

"No!" Margot screamed.

"Stand off!" the baron shouted at her as the men engaged blades. "Best you'd run and inform the cook that the rodents shall be in need of a full-time nurse, for their father shall come to his death this day. Touché!"

Margot trod the ground that jutted up against the marble courtyard. The baron would not be so cruel as to kill Alexandre, knowing he had children. Would he?

Most certainly he did not care a whit should he orphan the twins.

"Alexandre, please," she begged. "No good can come of this. I must go with the baron."

"Do you not love me?" he called as he feinted, then dodged to avoid the baron's return lunge.

"I love you more than the world!" she yelled, clutching her hands tightly to her breast. "You will break my heart if you were to die. Please, Alexandre, end this duel and live to love your daughters."

"Listen to her," the baron growled as he expertly stalked Alexandre like a bull pawing the ground before the matador. "Surrender your weapon and I'll turn and walk away. I'm not so cold-hearted that I'd orphan your children. Even if they are girls."

"I will not sentence Margot to the life of hell you have planned for her."

Alexandre bent at the waist, thrusting his blade blindly forward as the baron's sword skimmed his shoulder. Blood stained his shirt, quickly blossoming at his right shoulder. Margot stepped forward, but her toe hit the marble floor, setting her off balance. He was not badly injured, only a cut.

"Your hell is my paradise," the baron said. A guttural heave and gritted teeth accompanied his thrust, and he forced Alexandre back against the carriage. "The woman is being paid well for her services."

"Find a real whore to fulfill your demands for an heir," Alexandre retorted. He could not move forward, for the baron, heaving and sweating, held him at bay. "There are a dozen women at every tavern along the way to your home and a dozen more who would gladly give you a child for less than the price of a fancy meal."

"But I want Margot." With that, the baron raised his sword above his head and swung.

Steel *whoosh*ed the air, slicing it with a perceptible scream.

But no, 'twas the scream of a child.

Margot swung her attention to the door at the end of the château, where Janette and Lisette had appeared. Cook followed close behind, her jowls jiggling as she scampered out, but not close enough to grasp the twins.

"Papa!"

Before Margot could reason the situation, her arm was roughly jerked and her body faltered. The baron hefted her up under her arms and legs and carried her over to the carriage. As he shoved her inside, she saw but a glance of Alexandre's inert body, lying half on and half off the edge of the courtyard. But 'twas the vivid crimson stain flowering his gut that prompted her scream.

"Be off!" Nicodème shouted to the driver. The carriage bobbed as the baron stepped up inside.

"No." Margot lunged for the door, but Nicodème caught her around the waist and threw her with such force against the opposite seat that she passed out.

"Papa!" Janette fell to the ground by Alexandre's head and pressed her palms to his cheeks. Bright red colored his shirt on the shoulder and his stomach. Had the Baron of Blunders killed the King of Oranges? "No, no, no, no!"

"Girls, come away from here," Cook gasped as she

huffed up behind Lisette's figure, who now stood frozen, watching the retreat of the carriage. "Oh, bloody saints, he's bleeding!"

Cook plunged to the ground by Alexandre and with quick triage determined the shoulder wound was just a cut. But his stomach . . . "Run for Pierceforest, Lisette. Hurry!"

"Papa cannot die. Please, Cook," Janette begged, still holding her father's head. Sniffles quickly burgeoned to glugging sobs.

Placing one hand gently over the wound on Alexandre's stomach so as to keep the sight from the girls' eyes, Cook turned. Lisette stood still, her eyes fixed to the dusty cloud that the baron's departure painted in the air. "Lisette, please, you must run find Pierceforest. Lisette?"

"She promised," the flaxen-haired sprite whispered. Stolid and fixed, a single orange clutched in her fingers, Lisette finally pulled her gaze to Cook's. "She promised she would never go away."

Twenty-four

What did you expect?
She did sign the agreement.

Armand looked over his brother's inert figure. He and a quiet yet strong Pierceforest had laid him on the kitchen's table and Cook had taken to sewing up the wound in his gut with thread drawn from her mending basket.

Armand had arrived an hour before. He hadn't a chance to speak with Alexandre after their rescue of the woman from the Seine and wanted to check up with him. Never had he seen his brother so fiercely determined over a woman. "He's going to survive?"

"A sword to the gullet isn't usually so kind," the robustly fleshed cook commented as she tucked her sewing supplies away. "But I probed the wound. Didn't feel as though anything partial to life had been damaged. I think he'll mend well. Though I do want him off my table soon, I've biscuits to roll out. Girls, run outside and fetch me a bucket of rainwater, will you?"

Janette cast a wistful look toward her father before leaving. Lisette remained planted in the wicker chair, her knees drawn up to her chin and her eyes fixed to the table where her father lay.

"They grow so quickly," Armand commented of his nieces. It had been months since he'd seen his brother's children. At Sophie's funeral. Neither of the twins appeared to have lifted spirits since then. "My son is toddling about my wife's skirts right now. Keeps her quite busy."

"They can be a handful," Cook said as she studied Lisette's pose. She cast a worried glance to Armand, then decided it best to leave the child be. She turned and perused the table, running a thick finger under her chin. "Perhaps you could help me lift him?"

"I'm . . ." The patient's voice suddenly cracked, and he lifted a hand. "Fine."

Armand leaned over his brother's chest and smiled at his attempts to move. "You always were the one to collect injuries like a tax man collects coin."

"Armand?"

"I had to come see how things went with your lady. But it appears not so well as I had expected."

"Margot." Alexandre eased himself upright and swung his legs over the side of the table. He gripped his bandaged gut, then straightened, testing the pain with a grimace. Red squares. "Where is she? Tell me the baron did not leave with her."

Armand looked to Cook, who could only shake her head miserably. At that moment Janette trudged back in. "Papa!" Cook made it to the rescue just as the water bucket was released.

"You're alive!" Janette pronounced with a swoosh of her arms into the air. She made to leap into Alexandre's arms, but Armand quickly caught her up.

"Careful, little one, your papa has been hurt. You must be gentle with him."

Alexandre smoothed a hand over Janette's hair and gestured she climb up on the bench so she could stand face-to-face with him. He pressed a kiss to her forehead and slid it down to the tip of her noise. Her giggle was a welcome elixir to his heavy heart.

"I love you, Papa." Janette clung to Alexandre's chest.

"And Lisette?" Alexandre looked to Cook, who nodded toward the hearth.

"She's been like that since we brought you in. Won't talk or even take to one of my blueberry tarts."

Alexandre looked to Armand, who shrugged, then held out his arms to Janette. With a nudge she allowed her uncle to swing her into his arms.

Alexandre stood and walked to the chair where his daughter sat, a frail rag doll stiffened in the sun. He touched her brow with a gentle whisper and followed with a kiss that slid down her nose. "I will bring her back."

"No promises." She pouted fiercely.

"No promises, only truth." He smoothed a fingertip down a long, shiny curl. So like Sophie in her ill-tempered moods. Pouty lips and clenched fists. Alexandre kissed her forehead again, and Lisette slid her hand inside his fingers, gifting him with a silent acceptance.

"You think you can bring her back?"

"What matters is that you believe I can."

"I do, Papa." Her eyes brightened. "The King of Oranges can do anything."

In her story the King of Oranges *could* do anything. But that was just fiction. Wasn't it?

Ah, but it was Margot's story as well. And more than anything else, he wanted to be a part of her story.

"How long have I been out?" Alexandre wondered now.

"A good hour." Cook handed Ruby to Janette, who'd been abandoned on the floor like a wilted flower at sight of her father sitting up. "Gave me something of a fright. Thought you were a goner."

His face nuzzled into Lisette's curls, Alexandre looked to Armand. "Brother, I've another favor to ask of you."

Armand eased his palm over the hilt of his sword. "Anything."

"I must go after Margot."

"Oh, yes!" Lisette cheered, causing Alexandre to wince and reach for the wound on his shoulder.

"You're in no condition to go anywhere," Cook reprimanded, wiping her fingers on her apron. "It'll be straight to bed for you. Don't worry, I'll look after the girls."

"I cannot." Alexandre stood. He found that as long as he didn't bend, the wound in his gut did not tax him terribly much. It did have a nasty red squareness. Very solid and sharp on the corners. And it felt as if that square sat right within his stomach.

"Girls." He held his hands out and both slipped their fingers through them.

Never more determined in his life, Alexandre relayed his plans to the room. Pride surged up from his heart to quicken his words. "Margot's promise of never leaving you is still good. 'Twas the baron who broke that promise. She did not want to leave, and I must now see she is returned to where she belongs."

Alexandre paused, feeling the bitter slide of doubt trace the back of his throat. There were the obvious arguments to his plan. Margot would be much better off with the baron's money to see her through life. She *did* agree to marry him. The baron certainly was not in the wrong. He'd run through them all a dozen times over in his thoughts, building his doubt to an incredible head.

But that doubt was tamped down by Alexandre's knowledge of Margot's desires. He had had the privilege of seeing inside her heart. Free-spirited and true, she could never be happy if he were to leave her to the baron's whims. A breeding machine of male children was what she would become. That would not make her happy.

But what of her family? If Margot refused the baron's proposal, surely he would demand the bride price be returned. With seven children still at home, Margot's mother desperately needed that money.

"What is it?" Armand asked. "I can see the love in your eyes, brother. You must do this. You know I will be right beside you."

"I want to," Alexandre started cautiously, gauging his words so he would not disturb the girls. "But I'll need money. Margot's family must be looked after. She's seven siblings. And there is Margot's education. She mustn't be denied anything."

Armand quirked a brow. "There're always the high roads."

"Don't even consider it." Alexandre ripped his hands from the girls' grasps and paced away to the hearth, where he fixed his stance and stared at the glimmering flames. The smell of burning wood sliced blue arrows across his vision. He closed his eyes and sought inner strength, the answers to the impossible.

"I was merely jesting." Armand's hand settled upon Alexandre's good shoulder.

"I know you were, brother. But the fact remains, I cannot give Margot the life she can have with the baron."

"The Baron of Blunders is an evil man!" Janette interjected.

Lisette joined her with matched *humph*s, their arms slamming across their chests. "You must rescue the princess," Lisette pleaded.

"The princess?" Armand wondered.

"Of Practically Everything," Alexandre said. "But

she has denied the claim to everything. Though she will take credit for very much."

Now he could not fight the grin that tugged at his downcast mouth. Margot truly was the princess who could rule over more than very much. Practically everything included his daughters, his heart, and his soul.

"I've some money set aside," he said decisively. "Probably no more than a few years' stipend for Margot's family, but it will serve. Girls?"

Both gave him a wide-eyed yes, papa?

"I love Mademoiselle deVerona," he said, realizing that if he truly did, then he could not stand back and see her wrested away by a man she did not love. Finances would work out with faith and trust. "Do you both love Margot?"

"Oh, yes, Papa!"

"You must get her back!"

"I will." He pushed a sleeve up his arm. Vigor surged through his system, sparking the drive to succeed in his conquest. "I must go immediately, before it is too late. The baron already has an hour's advantage. Armand, will you ride with me?"

"You needn't even ask. I'm ready to ride."

"Cook? Would you mind watching the girls? It may be a day or more."

"Of course not! My Lisette's a fine chef, and Janette is an expert taste tester. We'll be just fine, won't we, girls?"

"Go rescue the princess," Lisette declared grandly.

"And bring us home a new mama," Janette said.

At that comment Armand looked to Alexandre, the question in his eyes very obvious. Alexandre offered a shrug, and that irrepressible smile only grew wider. "I am in love. One mustn't question their heart in times of desperation, only follow where it wishes me to go."

"Then we must be off," Armand announced. "Before your woman marries the wrong man."

"Please, just a few moments is all I need."

Nicodème remained stiff-faced at Margot's pleading to stop the carriage. Nature called, and most desperately. With the rocking and joggling of the carriage, she was near to fainting with trying to control herself.

"I shall soil my skirts," she said through gritted teeth.

"How eloquent you are, Mademoiselle." A brisk tap to the carriage top with his sword brought the wobbling box of damask and lacquered wood to a blessedly quick stop.

Margot plunged out onto the ground and darted for the forest that lined their travels. Eloquence be damned, she was in a hurry.

"Don't be long!"

Certainly she would not be, for Margot sensed the impatient baron would seek her out in less than a minute if she did not return.

Relief found, she took a moment to catch her breath against the plush moss-covered trunk of an elm tree. For two hours now they'd traveled a brisk pace. 'Twas as if Nicodème thought Alexandre were right behind them.

But Margot's last glimpse of Alexandre, sprawled on the ground and bleeding in assorted places on his limp body, told her there would be no rescue attempt. Her fate had been decided with a slice of the baron's sword.

Her fingernails dug into the thick bark. But that pain was minuscule to the wrenching twist in her heart. Lisette had stood as if a statue watching their retreat. Margot knew exactly what it was that had held her to the spot: the breaking of her promise.

Not only had she destroyed Alexandre's life, she had

toyed with the twins' hearts as well. How could she have been so foolish to have ever entangled herself in their lives? It wasn't right. The girls had endured enough heartache. And that she had been the cause of so much of it shamed Margot immensely.

"I can never face them again," she said of the image of two innocent souls that had been tainted by her own greedy desires. "Pray God they can forget my betrayals. And their father . . . that he may someday love again . . ."

"DeVerona!"

"Coming!" she called, but, as suspected, the baron was on her like a jailer seeking an escapee.

Nicodème wrenched her wrist and tugged her across the tall grasses that lined the road. "Night soon comes. We'll have to find an inn to stay, and give the horses a rest. We should be to Reims by nightfall tomorrow. And then we can wed."

"So soon?" Margot cried as she was forced up and into the carriage with a rough hand to her backside. She landed on the seat with an ungraceful plop, and her shoulder bruised up against the opposite wall. "Why such a rush? You have me now. As you pipe, I must dance."

The baron closed the door and shouted to the driver to move on, ignoring her question.

"You have won!" she declared.

"He is still a rival," Nicodème said with a glowering look over her.

"Alexandre? He is not. Reims is dozens of leagues from Versailles. I shall never see him again."

"I love you more than the world!" the baron mocked the words she'd screamed during Alexandre's standoff with Nicodème.

Margot glanced aside.

"No reply to that one, eh? Perhaps, then, you can

explain this." Nicodème whipped something out from inside his doublet, a small notebook—her notebook. No wonder she hadn't been able to find it. He flipped it open to the page where she had rendered Alexandre's face in ink. Kind eyes. Lustrous hair. Immense heart.

"Where did you get that?"

"Doesn't matter. But I will keep this as a reminder to never trust you."

Margot felt as though she were being singed by a lick of flame, cast like a torch from his eyes. If this were any indication of her future with this man, she wished for death by childbirth. At least then Nicodème would have his child, and she would be released from the hideous prison of his ridiculous rules and demands.

A square hand thrust out and gripped her chin. The flame in Nicodème's eyes reached all the way to Margot's soul. It hurt. So desperately.

"Tell me you did not lie with him."

She shook her head. "I did not."

"But you wanted to."

She drew a firm upper lip. To answer truthfully would only draw the battle line between them more deeply.

So be it.

"I would have gladly given myself to Monsieur Saint-Sylvestre."

He released her with a rough jerk. Margot touched her chin where his fingernail had slashed a stinging line through her flesh.

"It makes me proud to say I shall never truly be yours in bed, for always the image of Alexandre's face shall be in my mind when you are rutting between my legs."

This time 'twas a slap that silenced her bravado. Nicodème clutched a tight fist before her, seething. Margot cringed, but the second blow did not come.

"And if he is dead?"

"You would not! He has children!"

The baron's grin cracked a wicked arc upon his ugly handsomeness. "Then know it is your obedience to my wishes that holds the gardener's life in the balance. If you do not obey me, I shall see to it that bastard is buried beneath the very ground he tills, making orphans of those superfluous children of his."

"I despise you!"

"And I you. But it was not I who made things this way. My hate for you has been born of your own stupidity. Remember that when my anger beats bruises into your flesh."

With that, Nicodème crossed his arms and settled back against the seat. He hooked a boot on the opposite seat next to Margot's thigh. He did not blink, keeping his gaze focused on her, until finally Margot closed her eyes and slunk into the corner of the coach.

She had really done it now. All the torment, all the pain, that would come for the rest of her days, as the baron had stated, was entirely due to her own stupidity. She had given her fiancé reason to distrust her, to despise her.

But at least you did know love.

One small light to cling to.

"How much longer, how much longer . . ."

Margot paced the creaking floorboards of the surprisingly clean room the innkeeper had shown her and the baron to after they'd arrived in Cherchez. Clean water in the pottery bowl had been a welcome splash of refreshment after the long ride. Even the fact that there was a bed and not a mere straw-covered pallet was encouraging.

Though every time Margot allowed her vision to wander to the clean white linens that dressed the narrow trundle bed, she could only imagine what horrors the night would bring with Nicodème's return.

He'd left over an hour before, with the intention of going below to have a few tankards of ale. He offered to have wine sent up for Margot, but she declined, feigning a weak stomach after the ride. Now, if she could just continue with that ploy and convince the baron that she was in no condition to share his bed this eve, things would be all right.

At least for this night.

But already Margot's nerves were plucked by the occasional laughter from below. Laughter fringed with drink. Laughter she knew all too well to belong to the baron. He would be drunk by the time he mounted the stairs and stumbled into the room.

And she had no escape. The room was on the second floor, a precarious jump to the ground. Margot would be a fool to risk such; and after attempting to open the window, she discovered the pane was stuck well into the frame from years of whitewash and grime.

She was trapped, unless she thought to slink down the open staircase that angled one wall of the tavern without catching Nicodème's eye. Hardly worth the risk. For all seats within the tavern had a plain view of the stairway.

And if she were to succeed in such an escape, what would she then do? The baron would come looking for her. She did not know northern France. She could elude him for only so long.

She'd signed her life away by agreeing to the marriage, and now she must face the consequences. Good or ill.

Wishing now she had asked Nicodème to have the tavern maid send up some bread and cheese, Margot flopped onto the flat feather-stuffed mattress and let her shoulders fall back into the stale crush. She blew a curl of hair from her eyes, but it only landed in the same position upon her right eyelid.

"I wonder, wonder, wonder," she muttered, staring up at the ash-coated ceiling beams. "But what do I wonder about?"

There was certainly nothing fantastical or interesting to spark the wheels of her wondering mind here. 'Twas nothing but bare floor, the guttering flicker of a single candle, and a bowl of tepid water. Below lurked a cavalcade of assorted dandies, soldiers, and laborers, all men—not a place Margot cared to broach or wonder about.

She rolled onto her stomach and rested her chin on a fisted hand. "I wonder how *he* is doing?"

The baron could not have killed Alexandre. The thought was unbearable.

Margot clutched the linens near her head and turned to smother her streaming tears in the folds of white cloth. "Please don't let him be dead. For the sake of the girls . . ."

Wood slammed against wood as the chamber door swung wide and the clomp of Nicodème's mud-crusted boots took the floor. Margot sprung upright, remembered her aversion of being too near the bed, and dashed to the wall by the window.

The Baron of Blunders stood in the glow of the doorway, shoulders squared. A spittle of spirits drooled down his chin, and he cracked a wicked grin. For about three seconds. Equilibrium worked a tipsy spell on his body, luring his sizable bulk forward and back and to the side. But he didn't stumble as he gained Margot.

"What do you want?" she hurried out. "Get away from me, you're filthy drunk!"

"I might be drunk"—Nicodème slapped a wide palm against the wall just beyond Margot's shoulder, pinning her between it and his body—"but I'm not filthy. Yet!"

If his breath was not filthy, then Margot would like to know exactly what he considered such. On second thought, scratch that desire, she wanted nothing to do with upping the stakes on how disgusting a man could be.

Tentatively she pressed a single finger to his chest, hoping to waylay his swaying body and steer his breath away from her face. But he quickly snatched up her feeble defense. The smile that twisted his lips could have curled a seal's hide silly.

"I've a surprise for you."

"Oh . . ." She managed a grateful smile. "You really shouldn't have. Perhaps another tankard down in the tavern with your friends?" Yes, the notion of sending him to an oblivious stupor might prove most beneficial. If Nicodème passed out, he could not touch her. What's more, an unconscious Nicodème would provide a moment of respite from his horrid breath.

"Come with me."

"Where?"

"Don't question your betters, wench. Just follow me."

As her wrist was pulled through the doorway and down the narrow hall, her body had no choice but to follow. What did he have in mind? They weren't headed toward the stairs.

The baron knocked on the door at the end of the hall, then immediately opened it and entered without so much as a by your leave. As he yanked Margot inside the small, candlelit room, her mouth fell slack at the sight of the man sitting by a plain table, slicing through a loaf of dark bread.

A priest.

The baron slapped Margot heartily across the back and announced, "Tonight we marry."

* * *

Well past midnight their horses slowed to a walk as Armand and Alexandre entered the village of Cherchez. Wasn't more than a blacksmith and a flour mill with a few lights spotting the upper windows of a large tavern.

"I don't think the baron would sink so low as to stay at a tavern," Alexandre commented as he pulled his horse to a stop next to Armand's black Andalusian. "There are no carriages." He knew the carriage the baron had left in belonged to the royal stables. "I wager the king will not take kindly to the man borrowing one of his rigs."

Armand surveyed the road that stretched ahead into a black haze. "Chatillon is but a league away. It's four times the size. Perhaps that is where they have stopped. I seriously doubt even that man would ride the whole night through. Horses need rest sometime."

"Indeed. Shall we ride on, then?"

"It's your call, brother."

Though he much preferred to bed down here, right in the middle of the road if need be, a league was but another half hour's ride. And if that meant finding Margot tonight, then he'd ride on.

"Let's be off."

As the priest's required query "Does anyone wish to speak against the marriage between these two young lovers?" rang in her head, Margot glanced out the window and saw two riders sitting in the weak light of the tavern's glow. Their faces were away from the tavern, but there was no mistaking that midnight hair flowing over both the riders' shoulders and the sudden jerk when the taller, slenderer of the two slumped in the saddle. As if wounded.

"Alex—"

The stinging suction of the baron's hand clamped over her mouth. He pressed his face close to hers, glanced aside to the window, showing her he, too, had seen, then motioned to the priest. "Continue."

Outside, Alexandre hitched his heels into his horse's flank and rode away from Margot's life.

"Do you mean to call me slave as well as wife?" Margot said as she watched her new husband twist a length of rope around her wrist and the bedpost. It took him forever to get a good knot started. His fingers were obviously numbed by alcohol. More than twice Margot thought he'd pass out if only he'd allow his body to answer the wavering call of inertia.

"Just making sure you're here in the morning," Nicodème slurred. Long strands of blond hair stuck to his face with sweat and booze. He'd lost any handsomeness Margot had ever felt he possessed. Even those devastating kisses now only promised reviling disgust.

"I'm afraid you won't have your pleasures with me this night"—he paused, belched, then finished—"though."

"Truly, I am disappointed."

"Really?" He popped his head up from the floor, where he had knelt to slip off her shoes.

Margot pressed a foot to his chest and nudged. "No." A simple push is all it took to topple the swillpot of a man who was now her husband. His head pounded the floorboards with a dull thud.

Much like the sound of her heart as it slipped from her chest and plopped to the floor. Nothing would ever again be right. She had succumbed to the devil's bargain and had gotten the shortest stick.

For a moment her heart had soared to see Alexandre sitting outside—so close, yet leagues and leagues away. The baron had hidden the carriage around back in the stables, and Margot realized now that had been a well thought out plan. He had expected Alexandre to follow as much as Margot had prayed Alexandre would simply be alive.

Alexandre was alive.

And now Margot was not. Today her heart had died.

Twenty-five

Once upon a white kitten's imagination . . .

The facade of Castle Verzy stirred images of pale wraiths and ax-wielding armored knights in Margot's imagination. Immediately following the vision of bloody battles and moaning ghosts came the horrifying chill that this desolate, black-faced, crumbling castle was to be her home. Surrounded by nothing but wind-burnished land and a wide moat that might have dried up centuries earlier, and not a tree or blade of green grass in sight.

"There was once a formal garden out back," Nicodème commented as the carriage rolled to a stop before the stone bridge that crossed the yawning moat. "It's nothing but sticks and rotting vegetation now."

The comment was made so casually, almost offhandedly, that Margot jerked around to study the baron. "It is a shambles. You said you were to sea, what—four months?"

"About that."

"How could the servants allow it to become so rundown?"

Nicodème jumped out of the coach, setting it to a wild wobble upon the well-sprung wheels. Borrowed from the king's stables, Margot wondered now if the king was even aware of such a loan.

"I let the servants go before leaving," Nicodème said as he strolled toward the bridge, not even bothering to offer a hand to help Margot from the carriage.

Already realizing that she would have to look after herself, Margot lifted her skirts and stepped down. The ground billowed in a froth of dry dust around her hem, making her wonder if the rain even bothered this dismal little patch of land. *La Champagne Sèche,* this northern section of Champagne was called, literally meaning dry champagne.

How would she live without the rain?

"Château Verzy-à-l'eau," the baron said with a grand sweep of his hand.

L'eau? What water? Where?

Nicodème started across the bridge, casting the coachman a thankful gesture as the chess piece of a driver tossed Margot's bags to the ground.

Her last connection to normalcy, to—why, to reality—rolled away as Margot stood fixed to the ground, her bags smashed up against her legs exactly where the coachman had tossed them. There were no servants. There appeared to be no stables that she could see. Where was the baron's horse, a coach? Was there no way of leaving this place?

She turned at the waist, wanting to call to the coachman as he snapped the leather reins across the horses' backs, but her voice felt as dry as the land. She was the baroness de Verzy now. She belonged here, at the baron's side. Her mother had wished it so.

For good or for ill, as the priest had sternly directed.

Pressing her hand to her gut, Margot turned to find the baron observing her.

"Are you ill?" he called peevishly.

Most certainly more ill would come of this union than good.

Then again—Margot lifted her chin and plastered a smile to her face—life is always what one made it. As Cook had said, she could make this situation as foul as she wished, or try to understand the baron and his ways and reach for the goodness that was so obviously and desperately needed in this barren corner of land.

"Not at all," she called, and bent to lift her bags. *Just getting my bearings.*

Not bothering to offer assistance, the baron strode toward the castle and kicked open the door, which was, not surprisingly, unlocked.

"Watch that last step," he hollered back as Margot stepped onto the stone bridge. "Hurry along!"

The bridge was no wider than a man measured from nose to ankle, but even so, Margot had to fight the dodging equilibrium that teased her to peer over the edge and down into the moat. 'Twas a long fall. Numerous loose pebbles did not make the going easy. When she was but two strides from the castle door, a huge stone moved beneath her feet. Margot jumped and landed on the castle floor just as the stone slid and wedged precariously between two supporting stones.

Releasing a nervous breath, she vowed never to use the bridge again. If she had to build wings from the feather-stuffed mattresses to fly down from the tower, she would to avoid this horrid entrance. Surely there was a way around back that led to the rotting flower garden?

Abandoning her bag at the door, for she sensed Nicodème's hasty pace would leave her alone at the door all day if she did not follow, Margot skittered after him. Her skirts stirred up dust from the floor; heavy dust that might have been a layer of wool to knit sweaters, so thick it was. It seemed more like four years' worth of neglect than just the four months.

The unmistakable squeak of a rat hastened Margot's steps until she fell in behind Nicodème's long strides. Too many things to wonder about already, and none of them a particularly enticing wonder.

"I'll give you a quick tour," he said, and spun around, stopping suddenly.

Margot plunged into his chest with a grunt.

He slipped his fingers up through her hair and lifted her face. "Then we can consummate the vows." With that he leaned in for a kiss that was as unavoidable as the plague. Last night's liquor tainted his breath into a horrid brew. The more Margot struggled, the more it seemed to spur him on. As though he thought she enjoyed sucking on his putrid lips!

"Please," she said as she pushed against his solid chest. "The ride has been long and I am exceedingly weary."

"You're not going to wheedle your way out of the wedding nuptials, now, are you?"

"Oh, never." Not until she figured a way to do exactly that. " 'Tis only that I request rest and a reprieve, perhaps . . . a day or two to settle?"

"Two days?"

She shrugged sheepishly, clasped her hands under her chin, and fluttered her lashes. "A day and a half?"

"You forget your position."

"I'm not going anywhere. You will not lose me within the day and a half." *Unless she slipped and fell down that horrid moat.*

"One day," he barked, and turned to start up a darkened stairway. "I'll show you our room, and then you may explore on your own. I've to see to Planchette, who is riding behind us with my horse. The stable needs attention as well. Will that suit you, Baroness de Verzy?"

"Certainly."

One day of reprieve. *Thank the heavens.*

Now, if only the King of Oranges could locate the Princess of Practically Everything in time.

Our room. Ha! The first chance Margot got, she intended to locate an additional bedchamber and claim it as her own. Exclusively her own. She would not share the baron's bed every night. Not even the devil and all his seductive wiles could convince her of that. But she seriously suspected the availability of additional rooms with completely structured walls was scarce.

The baron's whirlwind tour had taken Margot through the kitchen, which was simply a small room with an empty hearth and an ancient table split down the middle from age and perhaps a sharp blade. A medieval blade did hang on the wall in the entrance hall, which gave further wonder as to when this castle was last occupied. The keep was brimming with rats. The baron had, wisely, not opened the door after pressing an ear to it. The garderobe was, well, not smelly. But the echo of rats coming up from the moat was enough to ensure Margot that she would use a chamber pot. If she could find one.

Our room was about the only one with four walls and a hearth that looked as if it might have been used within the last decade. A canopied bed mastered the large room. The bed curtains were a faded azure damask, and the gold fringe was torn from the hem more often than it was sewn to the fabric. Two chairs were pressed to the cold stone wall opposite the door, and a twelve-pointed rack from an elk hung crookedly above them.

Indeed, the mattress was stuffed with feathers, as she had hoped. When she sat upon it, the squeak of tiny inhabitants sent Margot straight upright. Further inspection proved three nests of mice, if not more.

At least something had found this castle habitable.

"How has the man lived in such conditions?" she wondered, chin in hand as she paced the wreckage of Nicodème's life. "Surely the castle must have been ransacked while he was away. But . . ."

Nicodème had not given any clue that the condition of his home distressed him. In fact, he had casually lifted the fallen bed canopy and tossed it over one of the posts to display the marriage bed to Margot during the tour. A pat to the dusty counterpane only put a gleam in his emotionless blue eyes.

Margot shook off a shudder of revulsion. She must lie with this man. It was going to happen. Soon. *Don't think about it. Just . . . don't.*

As far as she could determine, there were but a half dozen pieces of furniture in the entire castle. With no servants, the firewood had not been stocked, nor was there any discernible food in sight.

Truly she had stepped across the stone bridge and into hell. And the resident devil was tall and blond and mightily handsome. But didn't the devil always disguise himself in the most luxurious of vestments to attract his minions?

"This is insanity!"

Riled, and not about to become a maid as well as a wife to the pompous, vainglorious baron of . . . well, indeed, he was the Baron of Blunders, to have lured her here with false promises and the power of a bargain that might not have any power at all.

Did Nicodème de Verzy even have the money he'd promised her mother as bride price? To look at his home, Margot would guess he did not. And what of the money he'd promised to put forth for her education? Had it all been lies?

But why? 'Twas obvious the baron wanted her only to produce male heirs. But what good was an heir when the man had nothing to leave the boy?

No. Margot battered down her raging thoughts. Surely

there was a rational explanation to all this. Quite possibly Nicodème had put things in storage before his journey. Or indeed the place had been ransacked, and with the baron's riches he would see to replacing things posthaste.

But what if it were true?

Margot rushed to the glassless window and looked down over the stables that were in the back court. The west end of the clay tile roof was caved in. The gay whistle of a man without a care carried up to her tower room. Nicodème had removed his doublet, the same gray velvet one she'd seen him wear every day. A dirty shirt hung on his lank frame. It looked like a peasant's discard. It had holes in it. Big, sweat-rimmed holes. So filthy . . . one would think it smelled—and to disguise that smell a man might use an inordinate amount of scent.

Margot gripped the windowsill with tight fingers. Could he be poor?

Nonsense. She shook her head. He'd been traveling for days to retrieve her from Versailles. He was merely in need of a bath, his clothes a good scrubbing.

On the other hand . . . She followed his stroll across the dusty ground, his arms swinging. That shirt looked as though it had seen a four-month tour on ship and another four months beneath the sea.

Hmm . . .

"I think the Baron of Blunders has some explaining to do."

Furious, Margot beat a path outside to the stables.

"You are from the king's stables? What is your name?"

"Planchette, Monsieur."

They'd happened upon the slim young man two leagues north of Chatillon. The man's gay tune had carried even over the pounding of their horses' hooves. A fine tune to greet the day, Planchette had stated as Alexandre had ridden up alongside the horse and cart. A simple wood cart but unmistakably borrowed from Versailles for the royal seal branded into the wood on both sides and the brass-spoked wheels.

"The Baron de Verzy promised me ten pistoles when I arrive at his castle with his horse and supplies," Planchette offered with a swat at an insistent insect.

Alexandre exchanged glances with his brother. This was a chance they could not pass up. His brother knew it as well.

Armand dug for his purse and tossed it to the man. "Take that and my brother's horse, which belongs in the king's stables as well."

Without a blink the leather strings binding Armand's purse were unknotted and coin spilled out upon Planchette's hand.

"We will see the baron's horse and supplies to his estate. It is in Reims, you say?"

Planchette's quiet humming ended in a shrill whistle. "There's over twenty pistoles here!"

"Best you'd ride now," Alexandre said as he slid from his mount and offered the reins to the man. "Before my brother remembers he's a wife and child to feed."

"Indeed. *Merci,* Monsieur." Planchette dismounted, blindly offering Alexandre the reins, for he still marveled over the amount of coin in his hand.

"You said it was in Reims," Armand said again.

"Yes, Reims. Three leagues northeast of the town in *la Champagne Sèche.*" In less than a minute the man was off on the king's horse, coin jingling at his side. He was no fool to think twice about such an offer.

"That was a lot of money, brother."

"I figure you're good for it." He tipped the brim of his hat up, squinting in the sunlight. "Besides, when a woman is concerned, a man should not count coin, merely hand it over. That is one thing my wife will never let me forget."

The blithe giggles and carefree essence of the girls had disappeared upon the dusty trail of their father's departure. Cook, having attempted to coax the girls to try her gooseberry pies—just a spoonful, if you will—shoved the pastry toward the center of the table and took up Janette's morose figure onto her lap. Ruby dangled in her lackluster grip. A heavy sigh lifted the child's chest and sunk her body against Cook's bosom.

"Now, come, girls, your father will soon return. He's a strong man. You needn't worry so about him."

Lisette looked up from the fix she'd held on the floor for the past half-hour. She was the braver of the two, not a glimmer of tear in her eyes, as was a constant now in Janette's. Cook wondered if it might not be better for the child to break down and have out with all the torment that was wrapped up inside her little body.

Oh, but she wasn't at all sure how to handle children beyond feeding them. Margot was so good with them, always planning nature walks and making up stories. Hmm, perhaps that might prove an entrance to their sad little hearts.

"What about that story you two have been making up with Margot?" Cook tried to put as light a tone as possible on her voice. "Have you any more? Perhaps you could finish telling it to me?"

Lisette gave her sister the look they so often exchanged. Mental exchange of their thoughts in a way only twins could understand. It was so serious, it frightened Cook.

"It just wouldn't be right," Janette muttered. She lifted Ruby and stared at her wooden expression. "It's changed."

"How has it changed?"

"The last time we told it, the baron was left in a puddle of baron juice," Lisette volunteered as she caught her chin in her hand. No whimsical wonders in that pose, only sadness.

Though the subject of that man was the last thing Cook wanted to discuss, her own curiosity got the better of her. "Baron juice?"

"It's purple, you know," Janette said with another shoulder-lifting sigh.

"What's purple, dear?"

"Baron juice," Lisette sliced out sharply.

"Dear. Hmm . . . well . . . stories are meant to be changed. Perhaps the purple juice wasn't as sour as it should have been and he recovered sufficiently."

"To steal the Princess of Practically Everything away from the King of Oranges," Lisette dramatically declared. "It wasn't supposed to end that way. The Princess of Practically Everything belongs with the King of Oranges. The Baron of Blunders must be stopped."

"Well, then"—Cook seized upon the opportunity— "perhaps you should see that he is stopped. So where would that leave the story? Let's see now . . . The baron stood up and wiped off the purple juice."

"And the orange juice," Janette added.

"Orange juice?" Hadn't a clue how that had worked into the story, but if so . . . "Indeed, the, er, orange juice as well. And now the king is off to rescue the princess at this very moment."

Janette turned in Cook's embrace and flashed an eager expression up at her.

"So tell me what happens next," Cook said, encouraging Lisette with her silence.

"You really want to know?" the blond sprite wondered.

"Most definitely. But you must promise me a happy ending."

"It will be!"

So Lisette crawled upon the table—Cook shoved the pie out of reach just as a small slipper nearly dipped a toe into the crust—and she crossed her legs and began her tale.

"When last we saw the Baron of Blunders he had swept away the Princess of Practically Everything and carried her off to his evil castle by the sea."

"Does he really live by the sea?" Janette wondered.

"I don't know, Janette. It's a story." Flustered at the interruption, Lisette pressed the coils of her hair, then took a breath and started again. She punctuated her tale with hand gestures and widened eyes. It was difficult for Cook not to smile. "The Baron of Blunders stuck the Princess of Practically Everything high up in the tower filled with spiders and bugs."

"Oh, poor Margot," Janette moaned.

"You must remain silent if you wish me to continue," Lisette said, hands propped on hips.

"Now, Lisette," Cook chastened. "Perhaps not so vulgar with the descriptions?"

Lisette huffed, rolled her eyes heavenward, but continued. "The King of Oranges was set on rescuing the princess and bringing her home to tend the two little kittens."

Janette glanced up to Cook, an eager smile brightening her intent face. A kitten if there ever was one.

"The king rode off with his . . . the—the man was called . . . hmm . . ." Lisette thought for a moment, wrinkled her nose, then finally declared, "Well, the man was Uncle Armand."

Obviously not thrilled that she hadn't been able to conjure a fairy-tale title for Armand, Lisette brushed it off with calm disregard. "Now, the king and Uncle Armand arrived at the baron's dark, crumbly castle and walked up the stone bridge. It was a long, wriggly bridge, and pebbles fell with every footstep they took. Uncle Armand looked down just as he stepped onto the castle step and said, "It's a long way down, a man could fall forever and ever and ever. . . ."

Now was no time for his limp to act up. Alexandre took the stone bridge with stealthy steps, gritting his teeth at the ache in his thigh. One careless step and his equilibrium would be thrown off.

A moat had once surrounded the dilapidated castle, but the waters had dried long before, leaving a cavernous seam below. With Armand breathing down his neck he measured his strides. Pebbles dislodged and made the going rough.

"Careful," Armand cautioned.

"I'm being careful," Alexandre called as he jumped and landed the step before the castle door. He reached out, gripped his brother's hand, and pulled him forward.

The last step dislodged a thick boulder that tumbled down the side of the ravine.

Alexandre swallowed, thinking that he'd just stepped on that very boulder a moment earlier.

Armand gripped the door pull and leaned forward, peering into the vast slice of emptiness carved below. "It's a long way down. A man could fall forever."

". . . and ever and ever—"

"That will be quite enough, then," Cook reprimanded, jarring Lisette out of her chanting.

Janette seemed to enjoy the story, as macabre as it was, so Cook settled to listen, thinking at least it kept the girls busy.

"Once inside the castle, a chill ran down the King of Orange's back. . . ."

* * *

Alexandre shook off the chill and gave Armand a look. *What have we stepped into,* they both said in exchanged silence. *And is Margot really here?* The place was abandoned, dilapidated. What man could have possibly lived here, but for over a century ago?

"You're sure this is the right place?" Armand wondered as he scanned the space around them, up the three-story-high walls and across the rubble-strewn floor.

"If Planchette's directions were correct. Surely there is another entrance, perhaps a more serviceable part of the castle. We've just come in on the wrong side. The baron is here. I can feel it," Alexandre said. "And so is Margot."

"Can you feel her presence with your senses?"

Alexandre knew Armand was questioning his ability to see a remnant of her in a colored shape or flavor. "No, it's not like that." He pressed a hand over his heart. The hole ached, awaiting Margot's piece to be placed there. "It's deeper, much deeper."

Of course, there were also the telling footprints dashed through the dust on the floor.

"So the King of Oranges and Uncle Armand walked the dusty floors of the castle, following the footprints. It was very dark, but holes in the ceiling where tiles had fallen from the roof allowed the gray sky to splatter here and there. There was a rat. And another rat!

"Uncle Armand took a step and yelled.

" 'It's just a spiderweb,' the King of Oranges said. . . ."

"I hate spiders," Armand said as he wiped the thick gray webbing from his face. Alexandre pulled it from his brother's hair. "I think I'll use this." Armand unsheathed his sword and began to journey forward, slashing a path through the clotting of webs.

"They came upon a winding stairway that was dark and cold and very, very long," Lisette narrated, lowering her voice to an eerie whisper.

Cook leaned forward, propping her elbow on the table and catching her chin in her hand. Janette followed suit. Even Ruby had found her way to the tabletop and now sat at Lisette's knee, gazing intently upward.

"The King of Oranges and Uncle Armand slowly climbed the stairs. Spiders skittered down the walls, making Uncle Armand jump and poke at them with his sword. But the King of Oranges was brave and determined. He could hear the screams of his princess just above, and he started to run."

"Why is the princess screaming?" Janette pleaded.

"Yes, why?" Cook frantically blurted out.

"Well, she's with the Baron of Blunders, who is the villain," Lisette explained matter-of-factly. "And you know what villains do to princesses."

"No." Janette picked up Ruby and asked, "Do you know, Ruby?"

"Well, honestly," Lisette complained, "if you're going to keep interrupting."

"The screams have stopped," Cook threw in, cautious to keep the tale from becoming too macabre. "Because the villain suddenly fainted."

"He did?" Janette wondered.

"Yes, he did!" Seeming to like that thread, Lisette quickly added, "And the King of Oranges and Uncle Armand opened the door to find the princess waiting with open arms. The King of Oranges ran to her and kissed her and they lived happily ever after."

Janette popped her head up. "That's it?"

"That," Lisette said, rubbing her palms together satisfactorily, "is it."

Twenty-six

Actually . . . this is how it really went.

"I don't understand you," Margot said as she paced the pounded-dirt stable floor. There were no horses, though it appeared Nicodème expected one to appear any moment from out of the ether. He vigorously worked a pitchfork against a crusted stack of what might have been four-year-old hay, so gray it had become.

"This apparent obsession you have with begetting an heir," she continued, ignoring the grunts of her husband's labor. "And yet your seeming lack of finances. Why is the castle in such a shambles? And where are the servants? Surely you must have left someone in charge while you were away. I find it difficult to believe one would be so reckless with property—"

Nicodème threw the pitchfork to the ground. It clattered, setting Margot's nerves on a very narrow edge. He stalked toward her. Just when she thought he might snort and paw the ground, he halted, tossed his hair back with that patented flip of his head, and let out the sigh of all sighs. "You talk too damn much."

"Hmmph. Get used to it."

"Remember your place, woman."

"Slave-wife to the baron of the end of the earth?" Margot muttered, keeping her voice low so Nicodème would not hear. Alexandre would never dream to utter such words, *Remember your place.* He was too kind. Oh! Perhaps she might have been better off to have never met Alexandre Saint-Sylvestre and his twin daughters? Certainly their joy and kindness had spoiled her. How now would she adjust to the conditions of her new life?

But maybe she didn't need to adjust. There were some questions still unanswered. "About the condition of your estate—"

"Very well, I'll tell you." He punched a fist into his opposite palm and began to pace before her.

"So I am right? You do not have money?"

He nodded his head in what could be interpreted as a yes.

"How dare you!" She flung her fists before her, stretched them wide, not sure what to do—punching him would only serve her a return punch. Damn! "You have made promises to me and my family that you cannot keep?"

"Will you close that infernal mouth of yours? If it is to flap as such in the coming days, I wonder should I return to sea."

"Well," Margot huffed, and clamped her arms across her chest. And then she muttered, "I certainly wouldn't stop you."

"I will tell you all if you can see to remaining silent while I do."

Only a shrug would suffice, but Margot delivered the gesture with as much vehemence as she could muster.

"It all started on my eighteenth birthday. My father died that day."

So he was starting with pity. Well, she would not grant him one ounce of the fickle emotion. Her father was dead as well. All parents had to pass on sooner or later.

"Before he died he said he had two very important things to tell me. First, that we were quite rich. I knew the tulip market had soured years before I was born, but Father made millions on those damned flowers and sold just in time. Millions!" He turned and thumped the air with a fist, seeming aghast at the mere volume that word held. "Can you imagine so much from an ugly little flower?"

Margot defiantly held her stance. Her father had told her all about the tulip insanity when she was a little girl. How he had desired just one Viceroy tulip to hold and then sell for an outrageous sum, as so many had. It would have certainly made his ill-paying position as a wheelwright much easier to bear.

"Yet, there was bad news as well. My father thought to direct my future with the news that he had secured a bride for me. The woman he truly loved, your mother, had a girl."

"My—my mother?"

"Yes, and because he could not marry that bitch because she was below his station, he instead promised his son to her. Can you believe such a thing? That a man would give his son as a love token to a dirt-smeared country chit?"

Margot shrank from the baron's accusatory tirade. He easily made her feel as low as a snail, and not much more appealing than the slimy lump. But . . . her mother and Nicodème's father? That didn't make sense. *Maman* had never once mentioned anything of the sort.

Find out who you are, Margot, before you become something you are not.

Had she really had an affair with Nicodème's father? But Papa . . . Had she loved Nicodème's father more than she loved Papa? Impossible. Her parents had always been very loving, sharing hugs and kisses often. Well, as often as Father's demanding work schedule found him at home.

" 'I promised her a bride price,' my father said in his dying breath. 'I spoke to her mother and she told me Margot is quite precocious and wishes to go to the Sorbonne. I've put aside a stipend for her education, which you will give to her upon your wedding day.' A stipend!" Nicodème's boot toe pounded the stable gate, setting the rotting wood to a rattle. "But where were my millions? I wondered."

Indeed, where was the baron's money?

"Father gave me an allowance. A very generous allowance, but it was a mere pittance to what I could have had, *should* have had."

"What did you do? You spent the money, didn't you? As well as that set aside for my education?"

"Indeed, I did." He crossed his arms over his chest and closed his eyes as he recalled. "Wine, women, and the sea beckoned, and I followed. Only I became bored after a few months. And . . . a bit lonely."

"And most likely stripped clean," Margot commented.

"Indeed, I was broke again. There was only one way to solve that problem. I sent to my aunt to invite you to Versailles so I would not have to travel all the way across France to get you." The duchess Ducette was the baron's aunt, Margot had known as much. "And now I am not alone."

"So you married me for . . . companionship?"

"You do think quite highly of yourself, you know that?"

"But what of this child you insist upon having?"

"It was my father's last request that I provide him with a grandson he could be proud of."

"But don't you see? You think you've got trouble

now without a sou to your name. A child will only make things doubly worse. How will you support a child? It needs food and milk and clothing—"

"Ah." A slender finger punctuated the air between them. The baron's grin turned greedily charming. Had his father used much the same charm to convince Margot's mother into forming the alliance between their children in exchange for a sum of money? Or had she truly loved a man other than Margot's father? "You haven't heard all, my stumble-brained wife."

Margot kicked the wooden handle of the pitchfork. "I shall not take kindly to such verbal abuse."

"You've to put up with it for only a short while."

"And I will not bring a child into this world when there are no finances to support it."

"But there will be millions, don't you see?" He squeezed a palm over each of her shoulders and leaned close, imbuing her with his odor. Not a trace of lavender remained to hide the stench of sweat. Clever disguise; the aura of riches achieved with but a splash of scent and a pretty exterior. "My father refused me the brunt of my inheritance until I could prove worthiness. I must become a family man and produce a male heir to carry on the de Verzy name. Only then will my aunt and uncle release my many millions to me."

"So my child—"

"Our child will make me a rich man."

If greed possessed a color, it held the shimmery vibrance of a perfect set of blue eyes. Deceptively alluring, but beneath the shine beat a heart of blackness. 'Twas as if she were looking through Alexandre's eyes at that moment. And the colors put a sour taste on her tongue.

Prying Nicodème's fingers from her shoulders, Margot stepped back and stumbled. Her stays constricted, and she felt a dizzy rush wobble her surroundings as she sank to her knees, clutching the stable post as she did.

She meant nothing more to this man than a means to riches. And to know that it was her mother who put her in this situation . . .

"Why me? You could have easily married any woman to get this family you need."

"Believe me, I thought of that. Both before meeting you and after our first distasteful encounter in the cook's kitchen."

Distasteful? Who was he to speak so, the foul-smelling beast of a man!

"But it's not so easy to find a virgin who's had experience with children."

"Why is virginity so important?"

"Well, if you don't know—"

"Was a maidenhead required as part of this twisted bargain as well?" No, her mother could not be so cruel.

"Not in written form. But there are advantages to having a clean wife."

Clean? Margot gasped for air. As she had suspected, she had been reduced to a brood mare. How could *Maman* have done such a thing to her?

No, no, she would not think ill of her mother. She could have had no idea what a foul man Nicodème de Verzy would grow to be. Surely *Maman* might have loved Nicodème's father—even if she had not, Margot could never fault her for making a bargain to bring much-needed coin to the deVerona household. She would not blame her for anything. Never.

"I'll not risk exposing my child to all sorts of diseases and such when it comes gushing forth into this world. Do you know what horrid pox whores carry on their person? It's hideous for the boils and pus—"

"If you know so much, perhaps I should fear my own

health. What proof have you that you haven't contracted a horrid pox in your travels?"

"I am clean! As you will soon enough see." He gripped the waistband of his breeches and adjusted them. Margot looked away. The thought of even looking at him sickened.

"Of course, I also favor your blond hair and blue eyes. Combine that with my rather favorable features"—he combed long fingers through his golden mane—"and together we will create a stunning little creature."

"You cannot even call them by name, can you? A babe is a creature, a girl a rodent. A child means nothing to you if it is a girl. What will you do if I birth eight girls and not a single boy?"

"You really don't want to know, do you?"

Nicodème's honesty had become too much to bear. Nicodème de Verzy had thought this out well, and he knew exactly what boundaries he could push to get exactly what he wanted. She was nothing more than a pawn who would not receive any payment in kind for her suffering.

"W-what of my education?"

"What need I for an educated wife?"

"That was part of the agreement!"

Nicodème gripped her dress, his fingers slipping behind her bodice and skimming one of her breasts. "Try to make me give you one single livre."

"I hate you!"

"Ah, but you are my wife." He pressed his fingers together, pinching her nipple. "And that is all that matters. Now, I believe it's time to lift these dirty skirts of yours and start my trek to millions."

They had arrived at the top of the stairs, the last place in the castle yet to check. This had to be the baron's bedchamber. If Margot were not behind this door . . . well, then, this was the wrong castle.

But the feeling of urgency racing through Alexandre's veins only increased with every step up the dust-quilted stairs. *This is the right place. She has walked these halls, these stairs.* He just knew it.

"Are you sure you want to do this?" Armand whispered from over Alexandre's shoulder.

Alexandre pressed his palm to the door and secured his other hand over the hilt of his rapier. "I have to. She needs me."

"And what of you, brother? She has lied to you. Betrayal holds a cruel sword."

The weight of Armand's hand on Alexandre's shoulder felt like the judge's pound of the gavel. Deciding, final.

What of him? Yes, Margot had betrayed him. But what Armand did not mention was that he'd survived a betrayal of the same sort. A betrayal of the heart. Could Alexandre, after all the struggle he had endured, now survive?

He needed Margot deVerona more than two little girls needed a mother, more than the world needed another entomologist, more than the trees in the Orangerie needed his attention. Margot's vitality for life had become his. She had filled that hole in his soul and made his navigation of life a mindless ease. He needed Margot . . . to continue breathing, to face life, to have a receptacle for the tremendous amount of love he wanted to give.

And beyond the need there was the desire to spend the rest of his days sitting at her side, watching her wonder, gliding his hand along her pink voice.

"We belong together. I can feel it in my heart. I've never felt this way about a woman before, Armand. Is it possible? To survive a betrayal?"

"It's not only possible, if she is the one for your heart, it is necessity."

"She is the one."

"Well then, let's do it."

Two seconds of matched eye contact conveyed the plan. Alexandre whispered a count to three, and, shoulders first, the brothers stormed the door.

The old door gave with ease. Alexandre plunged inside the chamber, his rapid footsteps not halting until the bed caught his weight. Numerous squeaks and motion under his hands alerted him to the bed's inhabitants.

"By the saints, it's infested!" He lunged and drew out his rapier. Then he pulled back, realizing what he'd just done. Prepared to battle the rats?

"Empty," Armand said as he strode across the room, lifted the tattered curtains aside with his sword, and released them in a puff of dust.

Damn. Had they ridden all this way only to storm the wrong castle? Alexandre eyed the elk head on the opposite wall, staring like a demon at him. The eye sockets were bare and black. Much like his heart would become if he did not find Margot.

Where was she? What was the baron doing with her at this very moment?

Alexandre pressed his eyelids closed. He didn't want to think of things like that. But he must. If he was to get to Margot in time, he must continually remind himself of her danger.

"Down there," Armand said, beckoning Alexandre to the window with a gloved hand. "Is that her?"

Below, on the barren dirt ground, a woman walked from the tile-roofed stables toward the back of the castle, her fists pumping near her thighs to quicken her steps. Blond ringlets bobbed with every angry step. Her

mood was palpable even up here, three stories above
the ground. Margot deVerona absolutely seethed.

The sight made Alexandre smile.

He sped for the door, Armand on his heels. The open
staircase gave his aching limp little bother as he descended, for his sights were set on a reunion with Margot. She would be his. He would steal her away from
the baron before the man had a chance to discover Alexandre had been at his estate. And then they'd marry
and spend the rest of their days together.

Angry shuffles on the ground floor signaled Margot's
entrance into the castle. Indeed, there must be a back
entrance. Alexandre landed the last step just as her
crimson skirts swished into sight. Her fist working angrily before her chest, she suddenly noticed him—
screamed—and pressed her back to the wall.

Frozen by her reaction, Alexandre stayed his brother
just behind him with a cautious hand.

"Alexandre?" Her expression went from shock to
surprise, then to an odd worry in the matter of a second. "You're here?"

"Yes—"

"You're not supposed to be here!" she raged, pumping her fists against the wall behind her. "Oh!" She
slipped her fingers up through her hair and turned the
direction she had come. "It's too late!" And then she
ran away.

Ran away?

"Now, that was peculiar," Armand stated soundly.

"Peculiar." Alexandre worked the word on his tongue
while trying to make sense of what had just happened.
"Peculiar . . ." Rather a gray word if he should define
the most prominent letter. "Peculiar . . ."

Well, that's just . . . peculiar. She'd said as much that
night he'd revealed all to her. But she hadn't run away

or declared him afflicted. She had endeared herself to him that night. Had accepted his peculiar gift . . .

"No, I am the peculiar one," he said, his thoughts racing from the past to the present. "She's just the one who wonders all the time. Armand, come, something is wrong!"

Locating Margot was as easy as following the skirt swishes through the dust. So many odd turns and steps and dead ends. She had tried them all in her aggravated state, and Alexandre followed them all. 'Twas a damned labyrinth, this castle. But soon the smell of dry air and dirt told him they were close to an outer wall.

Loud maroon sobs arrowed straight for Alexandre's heart. He followed the tangible pain outside to a shuddering body of crimson plush and sun-kissed curls. "No, Margot, please don't cry. I'm here."

He embraced her, but she did not react in kind. Hands pressed to her face to hide her tears, and her sobs continued, her body shuddering against his. A touch of his hand to her cheek directed her face against his shoulder.

Was he too late? Had the baron ravaged her?

"It's all right," he said into the twisted curls on her head. "Everything will be fine, you'll see. I'm here."

His words did no more to cease her sobs than did they encourage his own aching heart. What could he say to silence her fears? To silence his own? The baron had not been defeated. He might be lurking somewhere, watching him and Margot play out their affections for each other.

Where was that bastard?

"Armand, have you seen—"

"I expected as much."

The arrogant shout pulled Alexandre around. Exiting the stables and caught in the bright glare of the noon sun, the baron approached on long, purposeful strides.

Dirty cream-colored triangles formed in Alexandre's vision as the baron shouted. "Unhand my wife, gardener!"

Wife?

A shudder in Margot's shoulders stirred her head up from his shoulder and she met Alexandre's eyes.

"Wife?"

She sniffed and nodded. "It's too late."

Twenty-seven

*You can knock him down,
but that doesn't mean you walk away with the prize.*

Margot whispered quickly in Alexandre's ear as the baron approached, "He's not going to give me a single sou for my schooling."

She knew her husband approached with malice in his step, so she slipped out of Alexandre's embrace and made to placate the approaching beast.

Margot, her hands pressed to Nicodème's shoulders to keep him from advancing on her wounded hero, turned to find Alexandre still faced the limestone wall of the castle. His fingers arced into claws against the stone. His words were so pained. "When did you get married?"

The baron took a step, but Margot pressed her back to his chest. Much as she despised standing this close to him, it did stay him to the spot like an admonished puppy.

"Last night," she said in answer to Alexandre's query.

"At the very moment you passed through Cherchez," Nicodème added with the most satisfying curdle to his tone. "Pity you weren't able to join the festivities."

"There were no festivities," she snapped.

The other man moved to Alexandre's side. Keeping his dark eyes fixed to her and the baron, he muttered something in Alexandre's ear. Dark eyes and curly black hair. Could this man be one of the brothers Alexandre had mentioned?

"I will ask you to leave my property," the baron announced as he slipped a hand around Margot's waist and held her to his body. His stench overwhelmed. Certainly it had been months since the man had seen a bath. "You wouldn't want to be in my way. My wife and I have a family to begin."

Two days earlier Margot had seen hurt and pain wash over Alexandre's eyes as they'd paused after fleeing the angry crowd at the Seine. Now, as he raised his head and nodded to his brother, she couldn't determine what lived in the dark eyes that had fixed to the ground before her feet. Anger? His jaw was clenched, his fist wrapped about his rapier hilt. But that glint, a glitter of light softened his gaze. *Kindness.*

Oh, Alexandre, that is not the way to win against Nicodème de Verzy!

"Certainly," Alexandre said. "We will be off as soon as the supplies are unloaded from the king's cart. His Highness will expect the borrowed mount back before the morn."

"You brought supplies?" Margot felt the baron's grip around her waist loosen. "What happened to Planchette?"

"We met him on the way," the brother said. "You owe me twenty pistoles for the man's wages."

"Twenty? I promised five!"

"Ten," Alexandre said. He approached now, his head down, his posture as stiff as the sword grazing the ground near his boot. "But two men hikes the price up to twenty." He raised his head and gifted Nicodème with his usual grim expression. "Until you pay, we shall stay. Eh, Armand?"

"I'm not going anywhere without the coin owed me," Armand agreed.

Armand. Margot searched her memory. This was the one who served in the king's guard. A much-needed ally to Alexandre's accidental kindness. Could they together wrest her away from the baron? How? She was legally the man's wife. Alexandre could take her away from Nicodème a thousand times over and that still would not change her title.

"Baroness." Alexandre tipped his hat to Margot, bowed, and backed away until his shoulder connected with his brother's shoulder. "I shall leave you for the moment. We've horses to tend. Is there any water in this damned desert of a land?"

"You will not stay any longer than to water your horses," Nicodème raged. He shoved Margot aside and approached both men.

Armand's sword sliced the air and met the baron's chin.

Alexandre still had not looked at Margot. She couldn't figure what he was up to. If he was up to anything. Had he plans to merely water his horse, then ride off, leaving her to rot in this dismal wasteland?

Where was the challenge to her husband for her heart? Where was the gauntlet smashed across Nicodème's cheek? The duel?

Oh, what did she expect? Alexandre Saint-Sylvestre, kind heart, was merely a gardener. He did not have the skills or the heart to treat another man so cruelly. To set a challenge for a married woman's hand. He'd failed once at Versailles in a challenge to the baron. He could not risk another failure, for he had daughters to consider. He could not orphan them.

"There is a well behind the stable," the baron finally said. "Ensure the rope is tied to the bucket before you drop it, for if you lose it, I'll send you both down to retrieve it."

With that, Nicodème jerked away from Armand's

threat, flipped his hair over his shoulders, and hooked his hands at his hips.

Armand acknowledged the baron's offer with a silent nod. Together the brothers stood, for a moment allowing the baron to consider their combined strength, the force they could enact, two men against one. Where Alexandre was tall and agile, Armand filled the air with a brute power and deadly presence.

Nicodème held a stiff pose, his chin tilted upward in defiance.

Alexandre was the first to turn, and with a nudge to Armand's arm, they crossed to the stables in a stir of spur-sifted dust.

Her heart slashed by Alexandre's cold leavetaking, Margot could not fight the heavy weight of defeat that bent her knees and plunged her to the ground at Nicodème's boots. The world went black, until her spine screamed in pain. She was being lifted, hoisted most indelicately up from the ground. With a heave Nicodème flopped her over his shoulder. Cruel fingers dug into her thighs, and he started inside the castle.

As her mind fought the dizzying blackness that threatened to recapture her senses, she heard a few detached mumbles coming from the baron's mouth. ". . . more trouble than you're worth . . . bastards will get no money from my dry purse . . . find my pistol and end this . . ."

He had to admit he hadn't known what to do after learning Margot was already married to the vainglorious Baron of Blunders. Married? That single word worked like an ax cleaved into his heart.

But Alexandre had also known he could not walk away from Margot. Not until he found a moment to talk with her alone. She was frightened as a shivering kitten standing next to the baron. He knew she did not want this marriage. He would not leave without her.

But how to do that was the question.

Cool, stale water splattered Alexandre's shoulder as his brother lifted the wooden bucket out of the crumbling stone well and hefted it over to their horses. The sun was beginning to set. There was no moon that he could spy up in the vast gray sky. Not a tree slashed the horizon for leagues around. They stood in a barren land, this *Champagne Sèche* of France. How Margot would ever survive without the grass, the trees, colorful insects, and rain . . .

The rain. That was her very nature, wasn't it? Margot deVerona had been born to this earth on a rainy afternoon, Alexandre would not doubt that. To be consigned to live her days in such arid land would surely bring her death.

Shaken from behind, Alexandre turned as Armand gripped his shoulder and toed the base of the well with a dusty boot. "Tell me your thoughts, brother. And please let it be that you've a brilliant plan to wrest that sweet lady away from the devil himself."

If only.

Tugging his gloves off and shoving them under his arm, Alexandre dipped his hands in the bucket, pulled up a handful of water, and splashed it over his face. He spit out the awful liquid and swiped his arm over his mouth.

"My thoughts are about as ordered as the damned gardens of Versailles. I don't know, Armand. It would be a simple enough task to run my blade through that bastard's heart and be done with it, but I cannot do that. The man has done no harm to Margot that would justify such an action."

"I'll kill him for you."

The wriggling brow above Armand's left eye told Alexandre his brother merely jested. Armand might have spent a decade of his life riding the high roads, stealing coin and jewels from innocent people, but he would no more bring harm upon a man than Alexandre could. Deserving or not.

"I foresee our request to get paid as allowing us some time to muddle this out. The man didn't appear eager to cough up one pistole, let alone twenty."

"I wonder where he hides his wealth?" Armand said, casting a discerning gaze over the flat, dry ground and up the stable wall to the crumbling roof tiles. "You say he has promised to send Margot to the Sorbonne in exchange for a child?"

"She just told me that was a lie. He no more intends to finance her education than he would prefer a female child. The man is twisted."

"Wouldn't that be grounds enough to contest the marriage? If this promise was written in the contract, then surely—"

"How can we prove he will not eventually allow Margot to attend school? No, that is not the way."

Alexandre kicked the ground, stirring up a cloud of dirt. He'd been away from his girls for twenty-four hours and wondered now how they were faring. Cook would certainly coddle them with sweet treats and hugs, but their little minds had to be frantic with worry over Margot and their papa. He had to return soon.

But not without Margot.

"Perhaps we could find him a replacement wife?" Armand offered. "If he is concerned only for a child, it shouldn't matter who his wife is."

"And condemn another innocent woman to a life here under the devil's wrath?"

High above, a raven's call pierced the darkening sky. This was the end of the earth and no excuses for it. How to rescue an innocent lamb from the devil's clutches before it was laid upon the sacrificial fire?

Roughly deposited upon the kitchen floor, Margot came to at the sound of Nicodème's heels pacing back and forth near her head. The stench of manure clung to his tattered leather boots. Margot managed a long perusal of the boots as they shuffled through the dust. Why had she not immediately noticed how old and torn the baron's boots were? Just as were his clothes.

Because you were too busy swooning over his kisses.

That she had succumbed to a mere kiss and now found herself this man's wife was truly the most idiotic of all blunders Margot had ever committed. And now she carried the title Baroness of Blunders. Most fitting.

Slapping a hand before the baron's slashing legs, Margot stopped him mid-pace. "Help me up."

Icy tingles shot through her muscles. He jerked her arm so wickedly, she had to rub her shoulder just to assure it had not dislocated.

"That damned gardener has become such a thorn!" Nicodème pounded the wall behind Margot, sending a shock of awareness down her neck.

"You can easily be rid of him by simply paying his brother the twenty pistoles." Margot bit her lip. Was it really that easy to make Alexandre walk out of her life forever?

"It was ten I promised Planchette, and until I see that idiot lackey, I'll not hand over coin to those two Gypsy thieves."

"You haven't a single pistole to your name, do you?" Pleased with her knowledge of the baron's devastation, Margot dusted off the dirt from her sleeves and blew at the renegade curl trailing down the center of her forehead. "If Alexandre and his brother truly intend to wait until you've their payment, we shall all grow old together."

"Enough of your lip." Nicodème bent in the corner of the room and slipped a pistol from his waist. He burrowed inside his vest for what Margot thought might be a pistol ball. "I'll rid myself of the thorns growing up around here myself." He nodded toward the door. "You might find yourself a bucket of water and wash up. We've a family to get started."

"Still you insist on getting me with child. And how do you expect to raise a child when you've not a pistole to your purse? You know it does require food and clothing and—"

"I've got six months to worry about that."

"Six—for your information, it takes nine months to grow a child, and sixteen long years after that, my idiot husband."

He moved with the speed of a striking cobra. Nicodème's blue eyes bore through her breast and singed her soul with malice. "You will cease from calling me names this instant. I am your husband. Husband, do you understand? You will find your place, beneath me on the bed and in this world, and remain there complacent and quiet."

"Never!" She struggled, but he gripped her sleeve tighter and the arm he'd pulled her up by screamed with pain. "Let go of me!"

With a smirk that revealed all the evils brewing within his heart, he did release her, and Margot plunged to the floor again. Nicodème resumed tending his pistol. Margot now saw he'd produced another. He packed a ball in the barrel and stuffed down a wad.

"As for the expense of raising a child," he said, his head down, attention on the pistol, "I won't have to worry about that for long after you've produced my son.

My father's wishes were merely that I *have* a son. What I do with that child thereafter is entirely my choice."

Immediately Margot could read the baron's evil desires in the glitter of his eyes. Greed had colored his soul blacker than the pistol ball he slipped inside the barrel of his weapon. "You will leave us, won't you?"

He chuckled and fit a pistol inside his waistband and lifted the other as he stood. "You're quite perceptive for a wench."

"You cannot abandon a mother and child—your own family—what will we do? Where will we go?"

"You'll have this castle," he said, stretching his arms to embrace the crumbling interior. "A fine estate—"

"It is desolate! We will not survive a fortnight. It is a shambles, Nicodème. How could you be so cruel?"

"For a couple million francs"—he kissed the barrel of his pistol and spun it on his forefinger—"a man will do most anything."

"Bastard."

"Yes, yes, but my son will have a name, rest assured."

"But not a father."

"Would you desist with such whining? You'll fare well enough. Why do you think I insisted on marrying you even after I saw you were less than desirable?"

Margot slammed her fists to her hips, her much too narrow hips.

"You've raised an entire brood. You'll survive, no difficulty."

"How thoughtful of you to consider such." She should have poked him in the eye when the notion had struck back at Versailles. At least with her opponent half blinded, Margot might have had a chance at escape.

But he was already blind. It was as though the promise of millions blocked all rationality from his sight. He would use her, and their child, to become rich, and damn his family thereafter.

Oh, if only Margot had had the opportunity to make love with Alexandre. Maybe now the baron might reconsider going through with his twisted plot if he knew she did not possess her maidenhead. If there were even a chance she might not be clean—

Although . . . A deliciously sneaky thought coursed through her brain. Oh, it was evil and wrong, but it was certainly worth a try.

"What makes you believe this son will be yours? What if it is a girl . . . or even—" Margot paused for a dramatic breath. She inhaled and exclaimed, *"Twin* girls?"

Nicodème eyed her, the pistol dangling from his finger, all color bleeding from his face. "Are you implying . . ."

"What if I am?"

"Have you—damn, that blasted gardener *has* had you!"

Margot shrugged, feeding on the baron's anger to fuel her own lies. She wasn't sure it would be a successful lie, but it was the only thing at hand at the moment. "He could have, he might not have. I'll never tell."

"I'll kill him." Nicodème charged out of the kitchen.

Margot slapped a palm over her mouth. What had she done? She had intended to—"Oh, dear! Alexandre!" She skittered out of the kitchen and gained the baron's long strides, but with a slash of his hand he knocked the wind from her lungs and she hit the foyer wall with a bone-crushing impact.

"Did you hear that?" Alexandre dropped the bucket down the well—*sans* rope—and looked to the dark facade of the castle. "It sounded like a woman's scream."

The realization that there was only one woman within hearing range, and that scream had been a deep crimson—a hideous shade of a more desirable pink wave—stirred him to a run toward the castle.

* * *

"Stop!" Margot screamed as she followed in Nicodème's dusty wake toward the stables. The click of a pistol cock connecting with the steel pan tangled her footsteps in her skirts, and she stumbled gracelessly.

"Damn!"

Difficult to see in the haze of twilight, but that oath had come from the baron's mouth. Margot saw Alexandre stand up from a contortion. He'd dodged the pistol ball.

Raging up behind Alexandre appeared Armand. As Nicodème pulled the second pistol out of his waistband, Armand plunged for Alexandre and landed the two flat on the ground as the second shot whizzed over their heads.

"That is enough!" Alexandre declared, and pushed away from his brother to stalk toward the baron.

Nicodème tossed both pistols to the ground and matched Alexandre's challenge to battle it out with fists, locking his hands against Alexandre's shoulders as they contacted.

"She is my wife!" A well-placed blow by Nicodème to Alexandre's side separated the two for a moment.

Engaging his fist against the baron's jaw, Alexandre called warning to stand off as Armand lingered too close. "This is between the two of us!"

Dust stirred as fists connected with flesh. Margot clutched her skirt in tight fingers. It was difficult to see in the growing darkness, but every moan, every oath, tightened the muscles in her neck. What was Alexandre doing? He was wounded; the baron surely had the upper hand.

"Alexandre, please!" She bent and squinted to judge which man was which in the tangle that wrestled on the ground. The glint of Nicodème's hair was the only telling signal. At the moment it was he who kneeled over Alexandre and delivered unmerciful punches to his opponent's gut. "Do not harm him, Nicodème!"

Gripped from behind, Margot fought against Armand's gentle direction to ease her away from the scene.

"This is Alexandre's fight," Armand said in a low voice next to her ear.

"The baron will kill him."

"I won't allow it."

She heard the slither of Armand's sword inside the steel sheath at his hip.

"Have faith in my brother. He loves you."

"This is no way to show love," she said quickly, her hands still twisting in her skirts. "I would much prefer him whole and uninjured. He cannot change what has happened. I agreed to the baron's terms. I was such a fool!"

Armand's clasp from behind to each of her arms stayed Margot as she watched the shadows of her husband and the only man she had ever loved beat their fists upon each other.

Now Alexandre held the upper hand, his knee stabbing into the baron's gut as the dirt-smeared peacock contorted on the ground. "You will give to Margot every single thing you promised her—"

"Impossible."

Nicodème choked out a guttural moan as Alexandre's fist connected with his stomach.

"If you do not," Alexandre said between gasps, "I will take her away from you."

"And I shall call the guard after you for kidnapping my wife. Leave!"

Margot took some glee in the baron's gasps to speak.

"My personal life is not your concern."

Alexandre's reply was abbreviated into a yelp as Nicodème brought up his fist and punched his jaw.

"No, stop this now, please!"

Armand's fingers closed around Margot's upper arms as she struggled. "My brother has more fire in his heart for you than the baron. We shall see who wins this battle for your love."

Margot swallowed a heavy breath. Her body tingled for release, to lunge forward and wrap her arms around Alexandre's bloodied face and protect him from the evil that plundered him. But Armand was right. It had been fire Margot had seen in Alexandre's eyes an hour earlier when he'd stood before the baron and calmly stated he would leave. The fire had been for her, and he could have no more released such hate upon her gaze then than he could walk away from this challenge now. He had to release the flames.

"He won't kill him, will he?"

"You speak of my brother or that bastard clutching his gut like a schoolgirl?" Armand questioned.

"Both."

A loud, final *crack* split the chilling darkness and suddenly there was quiet. Armand released Margot and pulled out his sword. She clambered forward and plunged to the ground by the two bodies. Alexandre! He pressed his hand over his face. Blood glistened black on his forehead and chin. To his side lay Nicodème, still.

"Tell me," Alexandre mumbled from behind his hand, "tell me . . . I did not kill him."

Margot did not want even to look at Nicodème, let alone judge whether or not he was alive. But Armand had already taken to checking over the man. "He still breathes."

A heavy release of a sigh, accompanied Alexandre's small, whispered "Good. I could have never forgiven myself."

"You are a fool," Margot said as she kissed his forehead and smoothed his long hair away from his neck. She slipped a hand over his chest, feeling for blood, injuries, anything . . . protruding. Thankfully she found nothing beyond the blood that dripped from Alexandre's nose and mouth. "But a wonderful fool."

He reached for her head, slipped a shaky hand through her hair, and pulled her to him for a kiss. Too eager, Margot pressed hard and Alexandre jerked. She pulled away, touched the blood that rimmed her lips. "I'm sorry. We must get you inside and find a candle so I can tend your wounds. Oh, Alexandre, are you hurt badly?"

"My heart fares better than it did an hour ago. But there's still the matter of what to do with him."

"He'll be out for a while," Armand said. "You've some fist, brother."

"It was the pistol. I picked it up while we were scuffling and managed to whack him with it."

"Scuffling?" She felt her blood rush from her face in a shiver at such a casual definition. "You men and your silly boy's games. I should die of fright if you ever do anything like that again, Alexandre."

"Believe me," he said with a groan as he pushed to sit up, "I will not. As long as you promise not to go traipsing off, marrying barons whenever your whim strikes."

She nuzzled her cheek aside his. "I'm so sorry, Alexandre. I had no choice."

"I know you did not." He lowered his head to her breast and kissed her there. A stunningly erotic touch that crackled through her being, setting tiny fires throughout.

"Now comes the hard part."

"Hard? What could be more difficult than taking a beating from that pompous peacock?"

"Now we must convince the man that an annulment is in order."

"He lied to me. Is that not enough?"

"It might not be. Armand?"

"Don't ask me. I've no knowledge of the damned law that deems to change daily. Can you help me lift this man, brother?"

"I'll run fetch some water from the well," Margot offered as Alexandre eased himself over to the baron's side.

"There is no rope to reach the bucket." She made to dash away, but Alexandre caught her hand and coaxed her to his side. Even in the darkness the power that had compelled her to him in the first place blazed brightly. She could see his grin as plainly as she felt her heart flood over with love.

"I love you, Margot."

"I love you."

Careful not to press too hard, she kissed him. A tender seal. A promise that her heart belonged only to him. He moaned as he opened her mouth with his tongue. A painful kiss but as unavoidable as the rain on a hazy summer afternoon.

"We'll make things right."

She kissed the one spot on his left cheek that wasn't bloodied, hoping it wouldn't cause him too much pain. "We will."

Twenty-eight

The king sacrifices his crown of oranges.

He winced every time Margot touched the torn length of her water-soaked skirt to the assorted bruises on his face and shoulders and chest. With every wince she planted a gentle kiss to Alexandre's lips, each time eliciting a true smile.

"You are too kind to me," he said, gliding a hand over her hip and coaxing her to sit in his lap.

"And you should not have been fighting." She kissed the tip of his nose, about the only spot on his face that did not ache. "But it made me feel so loved to see you stand up to the baron. You were very brave."

"Yes, well, brave deeds often lead to"—he touched his swollen lip—"pain. But your kisses are just the ointment needed. Could I have another? Right here." He pouted his lower lip, and Margot placed another restorative morsel there.

Margot's sigh put him in a place of calm and happiness, and for the moment he forgot she still held the title of baroness. "I wish it could be like this always. You and me, together, in each other's arms."

"Bruises and everything?"

"No bruises. But lots of kisses."

"Sweet pink kisses," he muttered into her ear. The motion sent a shiver of desire through Margot's system. "I could make love to you right now."

"I would not stop you."

His hand slid up her waist and cupped her breast through the plush that was doomed to forever remain dirty and stained. A fine pair they made, looking like earth sprites stirred up in a carriage's tail wind. Alexandre bent and brushed his lips across Margot's décolletage, the action so light, more visceral than direct contact, for certainly it pained him.

"You smell like the sweetest rose, deeply violet, and all curves and circles."

"Now, I would question your perception this time, considering the position of your mouth. Right on my, er . . . curves and circles."

She felt his smile upon the mound of her breast, followed by the glance of his tongue. Hot shivers traced her breast and peaked her nipple. The tips of his hair tickled beside the trail his tongue traced along the neckline of her gown. A sudden jerk, and a suppressed moan signaled his pain.

"When you return to Versailles, I expect you'll take it easy for a good week." She forced a brave front and spoke as if the world had not ended and she was going on with her life the way she wished. "I must send word to Cook that she sees you in bed with your feet up. The girls can wait on you for a few days, nothing wrong with that."

His nuzzles moved along her neck toward her bosom. Sweet surrender, how the man vied to break her determination with his own brand of persuasion.

"You speak as if you won't be returning to Versailles with me."

"Alexandre, you know—"

He pressed a finger to her mouth. "Hush."

"But the baron—"

"Did I say hush?"

She nodded, silence the most difficult surrender. Intent in his succulent mapping of her flesh, another kiss pulled a kittenlike mewl from her mouth. They sat in the kitchen alone. Armand was off guarding the baron. It would be so easy to unlace her stays right now and give herself completely to this man.

"I want you," she gasped as his tongue flicked over her pebbled nipple. "Oh, Alexandre, I need you."

"Soon, my love."

"You torment me so. Right now, please?"

"Then I had better stop." But he didn't. Another flick of his tongue sent Margot's soul racing toward flight. "Soon, very soon, we can finish what we've never had a chance to complete. There is still the baron to deal with," he whispered against her breast. "But I have a plan."

Quite certainly every single bone in his body ached. Every muscle screamed. Every organ had been pounded at least once or twice. But the walk up the stairs to the baron's chamber had been the easiest walk he'd ever taken. With Margot's hand in his, confidence brimmed in Alexandre's heart. Tonight he would win the woman he loved from the Baron of Blunders.

He was the King of Oranges, after all.

Alexandre paused five steps down from the gaping chamber entrance that he and Armand had created by breaking down the door upon their arrival. The glow of a single taper escaped the room and wavered just above their heads. He turned to kiss Margot's forehead and slid down to the tip of her nose. She tasted of dust and salt and the delicious flavor of woman. His woman. "To the Princess of Practically Everything," he said.

"And the King of Oranges."

He glanced up the stairs. The shrill bite of metal scraping against stone echoed out from the doorway. "Let me do the talking."

"But—"

He summoned the sternest expression possible, which finally produced an agreeable nod from his mop-topped lover.

The bare room glowed. Candles had been dug out of the supply basket after the fight out back. Armand stood near the window, his legs casually crossed at the ankle and a stern look to his visage, until he saw that his brother fared well enough to walk tall and straight, but with a limp, of course.

With a kiss to her forehead and a gentle nudge, Alexandre directed Margot to the opposite side of the room to stand by Armand. She crossed slowly, taking in the glowering figure seated on the floor at the base of the infested bed. The baron's wrists were secured to each bedpost, his ankles joined with another length of rope. Each twist of his boots in an attempt to loosen the rope scraped his spurs across the stone floor. He did not seethe so much as growl when Alexandre began to pace before the man.

"Take note, Margot," Alexandre said.

"Yes?"

Alexandre paused in his pacing and looked over the sorry man struggling with the ropes. Blond hair hung heavily clumped by dirt and sweat. Assorted bruises and a split lip had gussied up the pretty visage though. "Baron juice is not so much purple as it is red."

"Idiots!" Nicodème spouted in a spray of blood-tainted saliva. "I will have my satisfaction soon enough. I shall have the two of you arrested for assault."

"And what of Margot?" Alexandre maintained his calm even while his insides steamed and threatened to boil over at the audacity of the baron's convictions. "She has told me of your plans to abandon her after your son is born."

"You cannot prove what the future will bring."

"Are you speaking of the fates that will bring you a female child instead of a male, or the fates that will decide your fickle alliance to Margot?"

"I don't need to answer any of your questions."

"Indeed, you do not." Alexandre crossed his arms over his chest and resumed pacing. This bastard was beyond idiotic. How the hell he had succeeded thus far in his plan was beyond reason. Logic mightn't have a chance against the baron's nonsensical thinking.

Alexandre eyed Armand, who, with a wink, silently conveyed his confidence in whatever it was his brother had planned. Margot stood squeezing Armand's hand. Most likely she wasn't aware that grip was beginning to make his brother flinch.

Time to get on with things. There was only one way to see that Margot was given the life she was promised. One heart-wrenching sacrifice. He had worked all his life for such a position. But if Alexandre could not take her away from the baron, then he would do everything in his power to see she remained safe in his care. Even if that meant sacrificing his own livelihood. His very reason for living. For that reason had changed from tending the king's gardens to simply being with Margot de Verona. The king's crown of oranges must be removed.

"I cannot legally leave with your wife in my possession—"

"Smart man. You should have figured that one long before you decided to come here!"

"But I can ensure Margot receives the treatment she deserves from her husband, that she is not physically harmed or neglected."

Nicodème snorted. "How so?"

Alexandre stopped before the baron and looked down at him. "I will return to Versailles in the morning, pack up my things, and then take up residence here, where I can keep close watch over Margot's life."

"You can't—"

"I have no problem with abandoning a promising career at Le Nôtre's side when Margot's very safety is in question. My girls will certainly enjoy the open spaces."

"Girls? Oh, no, you will not bring those rodents into my home!"

"Surely they will take great delight in knowing they shall each have their own room. You can manage that, I'm sure, what with this large estate. Lisette and Janette will take great joy in helping Margot make this miserable excuse for a castle a home. Anything, as long as they are in Margot's care, for that is what matters most to them."

He glanced aside to find both Armand and Margot staring wide-eyed at him. He'd expected as much. He would get the same reaction from his daughters. But where he went they would follow, for indeed the lure of Margot was too great.

"Give me a year or two and I'll have that shambles of a garden out back blooming in all the colors of the rainbow. You know, boxwood does rather well in an arid climate like this—"

"You will not get away with this." Nicodème squirmed within his restraints and pounded the floor with a boot heel. "I will have you arrested for . . . for—"

"For what? Improving your property? Without pay?"

"For trespassing, that's what for."

"I needn't stay on your property when I am not gardening. But certainly I shall live so close as to hear Margot's every word, sense her every movement. Should you harm her—"

"You would not leave your position at court just to

hold watch over that ragamuffin of a woman. She is dirty and ill-mannered. She does not know her place. You think this will convince me to release her from our bargain?"

"I have no doubt that your stubborn pride will not allow such, and that I will suffer for my decision. As well, I risk imprisonment. But it is a choice I have made."

Now Alexandre knelt before the baron and studied the man's blood-smeared face. How could he have been so foolish to believe this man was better for Margot than himself? Just because a man was moneyed—well, he'd initially thought as much—did not make him a fine match.

But while Nicodème was certainly lacking in manners and morals, the fact remained, he was Margot's husband.

Imprisonment? Could he risk as much when he'd the girls to care for? He should not. But . . . he must play this bluff. It was Margot's only chance.

Serious conviction sharpened Alexandre's words as he spoke. "I will not suffer you to live should you harm one hair on Margot's head. And when your child comes into this world, I will be standing behind you at all times to ensure you do not flee his life. A child needs a father just as much as it needs a mother."

"There is nothing you can do to stop me. I will be rich. I will have the money to buy you out of my life."

"There is not enough money in the world to buy me out of Margot's life. If you force me to move in with you, my lord, I promise I will stand by my word. And I will make you stick to yours."

Alexandre stepped back and allowed the baron to think through his ultimatum. The room remained silent for a very long time. He did not look to Margot, could not for fear of exposing his true feelings to the baron. He would win this one. He must.

"You know," he decided to add, "Lisette is very good

with a man's hair. She'll have you braided every morning. And there's Janette, who's quite the rambunctious one. Of course, there's Ruby as well, who tends to find a man with long hair so romantic."

"R-Ruby?"

"My third daughter," Alexandre reassured the baron. "The silent one."

"Enough!" Nicodème gave one last heave at his ropes, then sank against the bed defeated, long, dirty hair hanging in clumps over half his face. "I concede. You may have the wench. Take her away from here and never again let me look upon her face. I'll find another woman. One who doesn't come with a damned gardener and rats."

Alexandre tipped the baron's chin up with the tip of his boot. "You'll sign annulment papers?"

"Bring them to me. Bring me the priest from Cherchez and I'll rip up the marriage contract before your very eyes. Just don't bring any rodents to my castle!"

Alexandre nodded to Armand. "Can you ride to Cherchez?"

"I'm off."

"Then it is done. My brother will find the priest who married you. Margot and I will unload the supplies from the cart and prepare to ride when Armand returns. Margot?"

Released from her state of frozen wonder, she scurried across the floor, her skirts lifted in her hands, and lunged into Alexandre's arms. Inertia spun them about as she planted a kiss to his mouth, bittersweet and painful against his bruised flesh, but very, very right.

She pulled back and fixed her tear-filled eyes to his. "Would you really have moved in to keep watch over me?"

"In a heartbeat."

"Enough of the droll sentiment!" Nicodème pounded his boots on the floor. "Release me!"

Alexandre slipped a possessive arm around Margot's waist and led her to the chamber entrance. He called back to the baron. "It should take no more than a day for my brother to return with the priest. Until then, you'll keep."

It was late the next day when they arrived at Versailles, weary, but at the same time giddy. Alexandre had explained his desire to send a stipend to Margot's family. She wouldn't have it. But he would not have it any other way. Together they would deliver it, and then Margot would have a chance to question her mother about her affair with Nicodème's father. Alexandre sensed that information was a new wound to Margot's soul, and he would do everything he could to ensure she found the answers she sought.

Saving funds for the Sorbonne would begin immediately. But Margot was quite content to begin her education by Alexandre's side as an apprentice. Things would work themselves out. He knew it as he knew the sun would rise every morning and the leaves would fall from the branches in but weeks as autumn tiptoed across the land.

Alexandre swung off his mount and Margot leapt from the cart to the ground and right into his arms. The horse would have to be stabled, but Alexandre could think of nothing more than finding his daughters.

"Go," Margot beckoned with a kiss to his cheek and a gentle touch to the corner of his bruised eye. She took the horse's reins from him. "The girls must be out of their heads for their father by now. I can find someone to brush down the horse."

He kissed her, his mouth not as sore as it had been a day ago. "And you they miss as well. Don't be long?"

"I'll be right behind you."

The palace was quiet. Lingering points of pork glittered along Alexandre's body as he neared the kitchen. Must have missed the evening meal. He hoped Cook had saved something. The swish of a rush broom signaled someone was still awake in the kitchen. He limped in under the glow of three or four tapers, quiet not to interrupt Cook's rhythm as her broom moved across the floor with exact precision.

He glanced around the room. It was good to return to order, peace. Every pot, every spoon, was in its place. A long braid of garlic hung on the far door. The hearth fire sizzled in glowing embers.

No girls. It was late; they must be sleeping.

"Oh!" The broom handle cracked on the floor as Cook's hands flew up to her cheeks in surprise. "You made it home! Oh, Monsieur Saint-Sylvestre."

Alexandre pressed a finger to his lips, for he assumed Cook had bedded the girls down in her room. But no sooner had Cook proclaimed his arrival than the patter of twin feet plunged into the room.

"Papa!"

Kneeling to catch the wave of eager excitement that headed his way, Alexandre winced at the impact as his gorgeous little girls plunged into his arms. He noticed Cook saw his reaction as well, but quickly nodded that it was of no concern.

"Papa, your face?" Janette pressed both hands to his cheeks and looked him over. "What happened?"

"It was the baron," Lisette said in a horrified voice. "That's why Papa's face has purple splotches on it. It's baron juice!"

"No, no, girls." Alexandre hugged them both and drew in the scent of innocence and beauty, sweet and soft. How good it felt to be home. "It's not baron juice, just a few bruises. They'll be gone in a few days."

"Did you kill the baron?"

"Lisette!" Cook admonished.

"I did no such thing."

"He's still got Margot!" Janette screamed. Ruby clonked Alexandre in the gut as Janette squiggled out of his embrace. "Didn't you bring Margot back with you, Papa?"

"You promised," Lisette chimed her sister's disappointment.

Alexandre stood and observed their quivering lips. Perfect angels, verging on tears. He mustn't keep them in suspense. "Indeed, I did promise. And I would never break a promise to my girls. Margot was right behind me. Ah . . ."

Margot's entrance charged up a new barrage of cheers and claps and squeals from the girls as well as from Cook.

"The King of Oranges has rescued the Princess of Practically Everything!" Cook declared as she bussed Alexandre on the cheek, then went to Margot to hug her.

With a twin attached to each leg, Margot shuffled over to Alexandre and slid her hand inside his. "We did it!" she announced grandly, and flung up an arm in triumph. "We defeated the Baron of Blunders!"

Janette poked her head up between Alexandre and Margot. "Now can we all live happily ever after?"

Alexandre looked to Margot, who blushed most exquisitely, even through four days' worth layer of dust and grime. "There is that possibility."

Compelled by the splatter of water on the stone walls and floor just down the hall, Alexandre walked onward, his heart pounding more fiercely than the force of the water against the hard stone. She was just ahead. Standing beneath the cool water. Naked.

An hour of cuddling with the girls had finally taken

its toll. Janette had been nodding to the sandman as Alexandre tucked her into bed, Lisette yawning furiously. As he lingered over their bed, Margot had squeezed his hand, kissed him on the forehead, and mentioned she was headed for a desperately needed shower. And then she'd winked.

It had been an invitation.

An invitation that had been presented many times since Margot deVerona had walked into his life. One that he feared more than facing down an idiot baron armed with twenty pistols.

Make love to me, Alexandre.

Yes, he wanted to answer the call of seduction, of desire, of want. And he must, for fear that to forever put off his desires would make him something he did not want to be. *Don't think of the past. Don't dowse your affections with the memory of what was wrong. Use only what is right to overcome.* The girls were right, so right.

And so was Margot.

The shower was just on the other side of the jutting stone wall. Alexandre fingered the strings at the neck of his shirt, untied the knot, then loosened the ribbons at his elbows and lifted his shirt over his head. The wound in his gut had lost the red squareness; now it merely ached like the bruises on his face. He'd taken a steel fist to the jaw, though Margot's gentle kisses did seem to possess some magical soothing elixir.

A heavy inhale drew in the crisp blue mint of the water. *Now or never. Do not resist this enchantress's powers for one moment more.*

"Margot?"

"Alexandre?"

A splat of cool droplets skittered across his brow as a wet hand slapped the stone wall aside his head and the still-dry ringlets on Margot's head appeared.

Alexandre's heartbeats tripled pace. *She loves you. You need not fear.* "I was . . ."

"Won't you join me?" she said. Her head disappeared, only to be followed by the splash of feet through the growing puddle. "I'm not shy!"

Indeed? She certainly knew how to appeal to his most tenacious fears, relaxing them with her easy charm and whimsical smile. Grinning to himself, Alexandre dropped his shirt by the wall and stepped around the corner.

Margot stood with her backside to him, her fingers pressed to the wall and the minty blue water raining over her head. Smooth pale flesh curved in all the right places and taunted with all the right tones. Somewhere, in the darkest recesses of Alexandre's mind, the fear atrophied and disintegrated.

Slowly she turned to reveal her body to him. Pert, small breasts offered up two ruby nipples. Her flat stomach served as a slick surface for the water to wash over. Pale blond hairs tufted at the apex of her thighs. Slender arms crossed, and she spread a hand over her garden of hidden delights, another trying to cover her breasts.

"I thought you said you weren't shy?" He was not embarrassed at his blatant study of her beautiful body. When had he ever the pleasure to simply look upon a woman without worry of recourse or demands? Besides, Margot was his now. And he was ready to become hers.

"Perhaps I *am* shy to have a man look at me in such a way." She backed against the stone wall, the water funneling over her and splashing the floor to soak Alexandre's boots.

"Think of it this way," he said as he carefully pulled her hand from her breasts and splayed her arm out to her side. "I am a botanist who has just discovered a beautiful flower and must now carefully study its petals to preserve it for posterity in my sketchbooks."

"You would draw me in your notes? Naked?"

He felt resistance in her arm as she thought to cover herself again.

"Did you not invite me here?" The thought to volunteer retreat briefly flickered through his mind. No. He would not allow himself any more excuses. He wanted Margot. The time was right.

Her fingers glanced out and hooked in the waistband of his breeches. "You have no fear of being here?"

"Not anymore. I don't want to live in fear anymore, Margot. Especially I don't wish to close myself away from you. I want to be yours completely, in every way possible."

Pink waves glimmered transparently over the silvery fall of water as Margot's whispered "I love you so much" found its mark in Alexandre's heart. "But you are getting wet."

"Isn't that the idea?"

"Take off your breeches and boots."

Arching a brow at that request, Alexandre slipped a finger behind the button that secured the left side of his breeches. Margot placed a hand upon his and facilitated the removal of the overly large cloth button from the overly small opening, then moved her hand to the right side. Drawing close, he immersed himself beneath the shower and gasped back a shudder as her tight, cool nipples skimmed his chest.

He slid his hands to cup her breasts. Two perfect peaches, each crowned with a luscious raspberry. Margot's moan told him he was not out of line. He could feel her fumbling with the final button on his breeches but could not concern himself with assisting her, for her body called desperately for attention. It had been a very long time since he had shared himself with a woman. And Alexandre knew beyond all measure this would be the first time he would share himself with a woman he loved.

If she had thought the clean, clear water slickening over her flesh brought about the most rapturous of sensations, the hot suctioning on her breast right now put that sensation to shame. Forgetting her intention to disrobe her lover—yes, her lover!—Margot dropped her hands to her sides and her back connected with the wet stones behind her. Mercy, but this was what a man's mouth was meant for!

"This is much better than kissing. Your tongue has remarkable skill," she said on a gasp. "Can we do this for a very long time?"

She felt him smile against the plump of her breast. Wet lashes flicked her flesh, tightening her nipple ever more.

"I love you, Alexandre," she whispered against the back of his shoulder as the soapsuds shimmied from his raven locks and tickled down his back. "You realize your breeches are getting a laundering?"

"Ah, yes."

With that, he shrugged the wet fabric down to reveal the telltale line of demarcation that betrayed his need to work *sans* shirt. Margot skimmed her palm over his buttocks. As firm and perfect as she'd imagined.

"You do not preach patience," he hissed in a voice that could only be tightened with the same desirous pounding she felt in her gut. Words ceased to register as he drew closer, and the long slick hardness of his manhood jutted up against her stomach.

"*Mon Dieu*, it is"—she wanted to touch, to caress, to finger the intriguing specimen—"quite magnificent. Can I . . . can I touch it?"

He slicked his fingers masterfully over both her nipples. But he wasn't about to change her mind with such devious distractions. Without invitation Margot eased the tip of her finger over the slick-capped weapon he wielded with intriguing charm and down around the staff.

Alexandre gasped in a breath; she felt his entire body tense against hers. His touch on her nipples pinched delightfully.

"It hurts?"

He gave her nipple another firm squeeze. "It feels as this feels to you."

"Oh . . . that good?"

A long, deep, slippery kiss answered her query.

"You might never take another midnight shower alone," she suggested slyly.

"Promise?"

"My promises have a tendency to get me in more trouble than I desire."

"You don't desire this kind of trouble?" He bent to nip her nipple. "Or this kind?" His fingers slipped between her thighs, awakening a whole new adventure of the flesh.

"Oh . . . I promise."

Epilogue

And they lived happily ever after.

"What is this called, Papa?"

Alexandre stroked his fingers over the delicate stalk of yellow flowers Lisette had picked. "Coltsfoot."

"I think I will pick a whole bunch for Mama," she said, and spun away to join her sister in the meadow of abundant flowers.

Smiling at the sweet giggles of his daughters, Alexandre bent before the patch of newly sprouted grass that topped Sophie's grave. He'd picked up the grave marker that he had ordered months before while in Paris, paying his respects to her family. They had treated him as if he had been the one to murder their child. He found he could forgive them that now, for he had not known her family well, and they considered class an important thing. Sophie's father had disowned her to survive among the country bourgeois with her bastard children.

Sophie Marie Saint-Sylvestre, loved by her family is what the marker read. At the time Alexandre had simply chosen an appropriate saying. Now he knew it was true.

He had, and did, love Sophie. As a mother to his children, as a woman, as a wife. Not as a lover. But he accepted that now. He only prayed that wherever Sophie was, she could accept that as well.

"They will always hold you in their hearts," he said as he touched the grass tips fringed around the stone marker. "Lisette will grow to be your double, Sophie. She is smart and brave and just a little demanding. As she should be. And Janette, she resembles you as well. I remember whenever I'd come upon you thinking, how the tip of your tongue would stick out from the corner of your mouth. Just like Janette. You gave me the greatest gift in the world, Sophie, and for that I will always love you.

"But I hope you can understand this new love I have found. The kind of love that feeds my soul, and the girls'. Margot loves them, you know. She will be good for them, as she will be good for me. Don't be angry."

"Why would Mama be angry?" Janette's voice startled Alexandre. He spun around to coddle her and seat her upon his knee. Lisette, her arms brimming with coltsfoot and a rogue butterfly fluttering above the colorful bouquet, joined them.

"I was just telling Mama about Margot," he said to the girls, beckoning Lisette to join him by sitting on his other knee. "I didn't want her to be angry that Margot has become a part of our lives."

"I think Mama is happy," Janette said, her eyes focused on the stone marker.

"Me too." Lisette stood and laid the flowers upon the ground, then she turned to Alexandre and pressed her palms to his cheeks. "Mama likes it when you are happy, Papa. She has to be, otherwise the sun wouldn't be shining on us right now."

"That's Mama's sunshine," Janette encouraged as she spread her arms around Alexandre's neck. Big brown eyes sparkled up at him. "Margot told us so. And when it rains, that's Mama's tears of joy at watching us."

"Margot seems to know very much about your mother," he said.

"That's why we like her. She always lets us remember her. It's good to cry for Mama too, Margot said." Lisette crawled back onto Alexandre's lap, and the threesome toppled over upon Sophie's grave.

His view of the sky between flutters of yellow coltsfoot petals and the bobbling aqua balls of Janette's giggles and Lisette's amber lines was very bright. Indeed, that might be Sophie's smile looking down upon them.

From this moment Alexandre knew everything was going to work itself out. The King of Oranges had done the right thing taking the Princess of Practically Everything away from the Baron of Blunders.

It was a surprisingly sunny day for the middle of September. The sun held high court in the sky, blanketing the Orangerie with a warm veil. Butterflies fluttered and gleamed in the warmth, and the stridulations of crickets beckoned Margot's interest down the side of the hundred steps. Below somewhere, hidden in the wood chips that lay scattered around Alexandre's wood-chopping site, sat a glossy black cricket calling to its mate.

A mating call. Margot thought about that one as she aimlessly descended the stairs. What is my mating call? she wondered. Surely it could only truly be heard when the rains fall from the sky. For that was her favorite kind of day, the rainy, sweet days of summer.

She smiled widely as she landed the final step and her slippers squished onto the plush grass. She'd been invited to attend a picnic this afternoon, just at the head of the Swiss pond. Dress special, the whispered invitation had said. Lisette had started giggling then, and had skittered away as quickly as she had appeared.

Special, eh? Margot smoothed her hands over the crimson plush gown she'd been saving for—well, that didn't matter anymore. She was a free woman. The baron had signed the annulment. He'd torn up the marriage contract and vowed to find a more fitting bride. One of the beau monde. Never again would he darken her life with his presence.

The best man had won her heart. And she in turn had won the best man.

The picnic was in view. Alexandre stood silhouetted by the bright sunlight. His tall figure was dressed in black breeches and a smart white shirt, his hair blowing loose in the breeze. Bracketing him were the twins, each in crisp white and ribbons. Lisette's smile widened as Margot approached, her little fingers twisting expectantly before her. Janette bounced on her heels; but both girls remained surprisingly quiet.

Alexandre was the first to step forward, bow, and kiss Margot's hand. "Mademoiselle, we are pleased you could attend our picnic."

Twin giggles prompted Alexandre to raise a brow in regard to his cohorts, but he shrugged and beckoned Margot to be seated on the blanket spread across the grass. The counterpane from Alexandre's bed, Margot noticed. Worn but warm. She folded her knees and tucked her legs under her skirts, a little unnerved at the twins' good behavior and Alexandre's formality.

What did they have in mind?

Alexandre knelt on one knee between his daughters and with a kiss to Lisette's cheek nudged her forward.

Lisette, prim and composed in her Sunday whites, with patiently crossed hands, stepped forward, curtsied, and recited, "We've prepared a delicious meal for our picnic this afternoon, Mademoiselle deVerona, but first . . ." She backed up a pace, as if rehearsed for hours, and Janette then took a step forward, bowed, and did the same with Ruby.

"We have a question to ask you," Janette recited sweetly. Then she cupped her hand to her mouth, giggled.

"A question?" Margot folded her hands in her lap, now thoroughly curious, and wondering up a storm. But this felt like a moment to let the wonders go and allow reality to take over. "Go ahead."

With that permission Alexandre embraced his daughters, one under each arm, and whispered a slow count, "One, two . . . three . . ."

They all spoke a perfectly rehearsed line, "Will you marry us?"

The spell of formality broken, Margot plunged forward and kissed Alexandre and Lisette and Janette, and, yes, even Ruby, and then declared, "Yes!"

And on the day Alexandre and Margot exchanged wedding vows, it rained. And for a few moments, as they stood in the center of the Orangerie beneath the gentle fall of spring raindrops, Margot was able to reach out to her side and feel dry air. The beginning. Of a whole new life.

Author's Note

In 1664 Louis XII's hunting lodge was undergoing remarkable changes. Construction was a constant for decades to come. Indeed, Louis XIV hired Le Nôtre straight from Vaux-le-Vicomte, along with Le Brun and Le Vau. The Orangerie wasn't quite the same as one might see today, though an Orangerie did exist. I did use this more current form of the Orangerie a few years before it actually became so.

I have also made the conditions surrounding the valley of Versailles a bit more "romantic" than they actually were. Versailles literally sat upon swampland, and these swamps were infested. Malaria killed thousands of workers. Every day cartloads of the dead were carried away. Many gave up their lives for the king's grand whim.

As for Alexandre's "affliction," synesthesia certainly is not an affliction. I do not have it myself, and to this day cannot truly imagine what it must be like to have such a confusion of the senses. But I think it is a gift. And those synesthetes that I've had the opportunity to meet online remark much the same. I have given Alexandre more instances of sensory crossing than most synesthetes experience. Most might only taste shapes, or see sounds, or perhaps have the colored letters. Though the combination and range of crossed senses might be infinite. You might wonder why I didn't use the term *synesthesia* in the story. It wasn't named until the mid-eighteenth century, so Alexandre could have had no idea what to call his gift.

If you have an interest in synesthesia, I would highly recommend Richard E. Cytowic's *The Man Who Tasted Shapes* for an introduction to this fascinating disorder. Also there is a chat room that serves the medical community, synesthetes, and those who are interested: http://clubs.yahoo.com/clubs/synesthesialistchatroom

Merlin's Legacy

A Series From
Quinn Taylor Evans

Call toll free **1-888-345-BOOK** to order by phone or use this coupon to order by mail.

Name _____

Address _____

City _____ State _____ Zip _____

Please send me the books I have checked above.

I am enclosing　　　　　　　　　　　$_____

Plus postage and handling*　　　　　　$_____

Sales tax (in New York and Tennessee)　$_____

Total amount enclosed　　　　　　　　$_____

*Add $2.50 for the first book and $.50 for each additional book.

Send check or money order (no cash or CODs) to:

Kensington Publishing Corp., 850 Third Avenue, New York, NY 10022

Prices and Numbers subject to change without notice.

All orders subject to availability.

Check out our website at **www.kensingtonbooks.com**

Put a Little Romance in Your Life With
Shannon Drake

Put a Little Romance in Your Life With
Constance O'Day-Flannery

__**Bewitched**   \$5.99US/\$7.50CAN
     0-8217-6126-9

__**The Gift**   \$5.99US/\$7.50CAN
     0-8217-5916-7

__**Once in a Lifetime**   \$5.99US/\$7.50CAN
     0-8217-5918-3

__**Second Chances**   \$5.99US/\$7.50CAN
     0-8217-5917-5

—**This Time Forever**   \$5.99US/\$7.50CAN
     0-8217-5964-7

__**Time-Kept Promises**   \$5.99US/\$7.50CAN
     0-8217-5963-9

__**Time-Kissed Destiny**   \$5.99US/\$7.50CAN
     0-8217-5962-0

__**Timeless Passion**   \$5.99US/\$7.50CAN
     0-8217-5959-0

Call toll free **1-888-345-BOOK** to order by phone, use this coupon to order by mail, or order online at **www.kensingtonbooks.com**.

Name _____

Address _____

City_____ State _____ Zip _____

Please send me the books I have checked above.

I am enclosing   \$_____

Plus postage and handling*   \$_____

Sales tax (in New York and Tennessee only)   \$_____

Total amount enclosed   \$_____

*Add \$2.50 for the first book and \$.50 for each additional book.

Send check or money order (no cash or CODs) to:

Kensington Publishing Corp., Dept C.O., 850 Third Avenue, 16th Floor, New York, NY 10022

Prices and numbers subject to change without notice.

All orders subject to availability.

Visit our website at **www.kensingtonbooks.com**.